# STORM OF BLOOD AND VENGEANCE

## BOOK 2

### STORM OF CHAOS AND SHADOWS

## C.L. BRIAR

First Edition published March 2022

Map Design © 2022 by C.L. Briar

Cover Design © 2023 Artscandare Book Cover Design

Edited by Second Pass Editing

Identifiers:

ISBN: 978-1-956829-03-7 (ebook)

ISBN: 978-1-956829-04-4 (paperback)

ISBN: 978-1-956829-05-1 (hardback)

*To finding someone who will dance in our darkness with us.*

# AUTHOR NOTE

# 1
# ELARA

Speckles of black, rotting blood misted the air as my blade burst from the graying flesh of the Fracture's throat. It smelled sweet, like wilted roses and burnt sugar, the dark spray coating my face in a splash of warmth. I inhaled deeply, letting the scent wash over me, fueling my ravenous need to slaughter the corrupt creatures before me —while I searched for him.

I combed through the swarm of bodies and clashing metal, needing to reach Zelos before it was too late. He was moving fast, nearly at the commander's side. Though he was a skilled fighter, one of the best, I knew he wouldn't win this fight. I needed to stop him.

My blade sliced through another and another and another. I was frantic in my hacking, uncaring of the mess of bodies left in my wake. My lungs heaved as my pulse raced. I paused only long enough to do another sweep of the field before me, my eyes darting among the men, peering through the mist of blood hanging thick in the air, as bodies fell.

His eyes found mine as the blade pierced his chest.

"Elara, the macarons!"

I blinked away the memory as a bun of tangled, silver curls pushed past me. Burnt sugar coated the air as she pulled a sheet of charred circles from the oven, the smell far too reminiscent of the horrors swirling in my mind.

Swallowing back the bile stinging my throat, I forced myself to meet her eyes. "I'm sorry, Greer. I was distracted."

Her hand took up residence on her rounded hip, thicker now that we had spent the better part of a year at the base. "Clearly. That was the third batch you've burnt this week."

I flinched. Burnt sugar. Burnt flesh. The flames rising higher as they consumed Zelos's burial shroud. A small, decimated mound of his ashes lingered, just outside the gates of the base. I'd checked yesterday, needing to remind myself why I needed to stay strong for a little longer. Why I couldn't let the darkness have me, just yet.

"Hey." Her voice dropped to a soothing tone as her fingers gripped mine. "Look at me, El. You're here. You're safe."

My guarded hazel eyes met her crystal blue ones filled with open concern. It was true. I was here. In the kitchen butchering baking recipes when I should have been scouring the seven kingdoms and enacting vengeance for Zelos's life, for the thousands-upon-thousands of human lives ripped away from this world because of the plague of Fractured left unchecked.

My jaw clenched but I managed to turn away before she could see, letting her fingers slip from mine. The red-eyed commander had called me the Dark Phoenix, the infamous source of destruction whispered of throughout the ages. The bringer of the end. The one to unleash a plague of death and shadows upon this world. I didn't want to believe it and was grateful no one else had heard the title—beside Zaeth. The dark fae seemed content with keeping my secret … for now.

Though I did my best to hide it, my thirst for battle never ceased. It simmered beneath my weakening will, waiting for me to succumb. But I couldn't. Not yet.

Lannie was working day and night to extract more information from the tarry black substance that pulsed through the Fractured. So far, she'd learned it could control the body but didn't harm it—at least not in the way a typical pathogen or poison did. The body continued to function, but was distorted. The quicker she could discover the inner workings of our enemy, the sooner we would hone in on their weaknesses and end this war. And if she was successful at crafting a cure for the Fractured? We could decimate their army in a single wave.

But until that fateful day, until I was sure I wasn't infected— that I wouldn't become one of them or transform into a far greater evil—I had to stay away from the temptation of war. My sisters didn't realize that was why I'd pulled back from training. Nobody did. They all thought I was broken after watching Zelos fall. Even Alarik assumed I was guilt-ridden at not stopping it—that I was nothing but a damaged soldier, like so many others—haunted and unable to be fixed.

Perhaps they were right, but not in the way they thought.

I was shattered and broken. I doubted any amount of time would mend what had been lost in my heart, but I'd been that way for a while, now. When I'd dug my brother's graves—when my raw, blistered hands had forced the shovel to carve out two more vacancies in the earth for my parents a week later—my soul had broken then.

And it had never fully healed.

A viciousness had grown among the cracks, sealing up the shredded, splintered pieces of my heart with an endless hunger. I'd spent the last seven years concealing that darkness, repressing my shadows, but they had grown tired of their cage.

I glanced over my shoulder as Greer dumped the ruined macarons into the trash. "Sorry about that."

The pan clattered loudly in the sink, holding Greer's focus a moment longer as she took in a deep breath. It took another five seconds before her gaze fixed on mine.

"El, you're my sister, and I love you, but this isn't working."

"I'll set a timer next time—"

She waved off my excuse. "This isn't about the baking supplies. The base has more than enough. What I mean, is this isn't working *for you*. Baking is a reprieve for me. It's ordered and structured, but still lends itself to a creative flare. It brings me happiness, but it's not the same for you."

A frown tugged at my lips. She chanced a step closer.

"It's okay to enjoy fighting." I flinched, the blow of her words causing me to stumble back. She stilled, voice softening. "I don't understand the allure, but you're in a base full of warriors who do."

*The allure?* Did Greer realize why I'd been holding back? Did she see through the mistaken façade of fear for what it really was—shame?

"I have to go."

"El, just talk to me—"

"Sorry for the cookies. I think you're right. Cooking isn't my thing."

"They're macarons and it's baking. But that's not the point. We should talk…"

I raced through the door before she could uncover more of my truth. If I spoke of it any further, if I acknowledged the lurking darkness pressing against the weakening confines of my mind, I wasn't sure I'd be able to contain it.

## 2
## GREER

I WATCHED HELPLESSLY AS EL MADE HER ESCAPE. DID SHE REALLY think I was as naïve as Alarik? She was my sister, for gods' sake. If she chose to let the others believe she was a scared novice then so be it, but I knew how ferocious she was. I'd seen the way she'd taken down wild beasts in the Western Woods. I'd watched as she refused to let me help with our parents' grave, even as blood stained the handle from her shredded hands as she drove the shovel into the earth again and again. She only let me help with the bodies because she wasn't strong enough to drag them from the house on her own. I was eleven—El only thirteen—when we realized there was nobody left in this harsh world to care for us. Nobody but ourselves.

No, one more death wouldn't destroy her. Any who thought differently didn't know her.

Turning from the now-cleaned dishes, I pulled out a cutting board and a batch of washed vegetables. The weight of the knife was familiar, the blade finding an innate rhythm as I diced the onions and carrots for tonight's stew. The kitchen staff was used to my presence by now, appreciated it even. It was refreshing feeling useful.

Gods, was it nice to indulge in this, in the peaceful flow of recipes and polished meals, in lavish spices, and decadent desserts. Only a few months ago, I had to ration even the simplest of seasonings. We had to allocate each morsel of food, stretching bits of dried meat for weeks.

But those days were gone. There was such an excess here. I'd even started packaging meals for the increasing number of families in the city below. More families were turning up every day since the battle at Neith, most were seeking refuge from the growing attacks. A hearty meal was the least I could do. It wasn't much, but I hoped it would provide some comfort.

Setting the prepared vegetables to the side, I cleaned my workspace, wiping my hands on the stained apron when I was done, before dropping it to the assigned hook. Everything had a place—a purpose. Another reason the kitchen was calming.

A sigh escaped me as I stepped into the mid-summer's sun, starting toward the healer's quarters. Lannie was expecting to see both El and me once we were done baking for a little bit of sister time. The two of us had been trying to get El to open up for the last week. We'd given her a few days to mourn in silence, but she was withdrawing and we were afraid to let her slip too far. From Lannie's rushed update this morning, it sounded like she discovered something that might help El, but I guessed she'd have to be content with updating only me.

Lannie would understand. She always did. We both knew El couldn't continue like this. It was killing her, this mask she forced herself to wear. A frown tugged at my lips as I pushed through the worn doors of Lannie's lab, the scent of simmering tonics and freshly set salves filling the air—clean but oddly relaxing.

"Hey, sis," I called, drawing Lannie's attention away from the specimen she was viewing beneath the microscope.

"Hey," she answered, eyes lifting to look beyond me.

"She's not coming."

Lannie raised a brow in question.

I shrugged. "Another flashback, I think. And she burnt *another* batch of macarons." I tsked loudly as Lannie rolled her eyes. "Vanilla with just a hint of cinnamon. They would have been delicious."

"She didn't say anything further?" Lannie asked, ignoring my attempt to lighten the mood as she led us past beakers and empty tin containers and into a large corner room she'd taken as her office. The lab was pristine in its cleanliness, but this space was a disaster. Old journals of Lannie's personal creation were stacked haphazardly along the wooden bookshelf home to plants, crystals, and other texts she found helpful. Bins of tea leaves, cups, candles, and oils were mixed with loose sheets of paper throughout the small space, the various herbs mingling into a surprisingly uplifting scent—eucalyptus perhaps. There was a narrow couch just before her desk, complete with a rumpled pillow and blanket bunched in the middle. She must have stayed the night. Again.

"No, she didn't say what was haunting her, but it's getting worse. She's... drifting. It's like the more I reach for her, the stronger the current is, dragging her down. I'm afraid one of these days she won't resurface."

Lannie's face grew dark as she rifled through the piles of loose paper strung about her desk with half a dozen colorful pens and three cups of stagnant tea amongst them. Most thought Lannie to be the structured one, and in some ways, she was, but it was me who kept inventory of the supplies growing up. I was the one who made sure we used the limited supplies sparingly.

Taking in the chaotic mess around me, I stepped nearer. "Do you need help finding—"

"Got it," she said, lifting an opened journal, the surface page slightly crumpled. She rushed past me, through the open door, and peered down in her microscope, a wave of sleek, dark locks spilling forward.

"Got what? Lannie, I appreciate that brilliant mind of yours, but we need to talk about El right now."

She waved a hand in my direction, eyes still glued to the microscope. "I know. This *is* about El. I'm getting closer to figuring out what this stuff is. Why do you think I've been sleeping here this past week?"

I blinked. *Week?*

She switched out a slide, the thin glass clicking into place as she twisted the small knobs. "There," she said, flipping her gaze to her journal as if to compare it to what she saw through the lens.

Stepping to her side, I peered in.

It was the same tarry substance I'd come to recognize. Lannie had been able to isolate the matter from the blood of those creatures—the Fractured—but the cells beside the black smudge appeared to be healthy. My brows knit together.

"Do you see?" Lannie asked, shoving her journal in front of me. I glanced at the drawing and then back to the slide.

I shook my head. "No, I don't understand. The drawing in your journal depicts dead cells. I thought you said it was impossible to isolate the two without compromising the host. But the cells below..."

"The ones below are still intact." She nodded.

My eyes widened as I noted the smile stretching across her face. "You found a cure?" If this was what haunted El, what plagued her mind with worry and fear, then maybe we could get our sister back.

Lannie's smile faltered, taking my hope along with it. "Not a cure, but a development. I was under the assumption this was an infectious organism, but it's not. This is not a human disease, but a fae one. A magical one."

"Meaning..."

Rolling her eyes, she pointed to the drawing depicting the dead cells. "These cells were blended with the black substance. I had to force the two apart and when I did, the cells couldn't sustain themselves. But, when the same black substance is presented with healthy cells, it can't enter. I've watched this slide for hours and a half-a-dozen others before this one. Each time the black substance swarms the cells, but is unable to corrupt them."

My jaw dropped as the pieces fell into place. "This isn't contagious?"

"No, at least not for humans. I've only tested it against my own cells, but at least we know humans are safe."

*El was safe.* I scooped Lannie into a hug, her willowy frame so much thinner than mine. "My brilliant sister! We can tell El she's not turning into a monster, and everything can go back to normal."

She stumbled as I released her. "Perhaps, but we aren't sure if that's what's been troubling her. Plenty of soldiers are affected by battle. It's normal to want a break from death."

"Maybe that's a normal reaction for most people, but our sister isn't normal." I shrugged. "El loves fighting."

"Training and actual war are two very different things," she countered evenly with a calm beyond her sixteen years.

I fought against the roll of my eyes. Lannie meant well, but I knew El. We'd kept the worst of it from Lannie, but El and I had seen plenty of killing when we were younger—when we were much more innocent to the gruesome realities of death. Now, we saw death as a normal evolution of life. I'd seen the way El looked at the corpses of Fractured being dragged into the base, the very ones Lannie and Healer Grant used to study. El had completely ignored the tall, dark, and wickedly handsome earth fae who'd dropped them off. She hadn't batted an eye at the large ram-horns wrapped back over his closely cropped hair. Her affections remained with Alarik, but still, I'd expected some type of acknowledgement from her; a side eye at my obvious mocking, a raised brow—something.

But El hadn't noticed anything except for the graying bodies. The color had leached from her face, her eyes tracking the twisted creatures as they were dragged toward a distant building. She'd stopped visiting the sparring rings that day, refusing to even sit on the sidelines and observe.

"Either way," I said, deciding there'd be no point arguing with Lannie. "I think we should tell her."

"Not yet. I need to run a few more tests. I've only tried this with my own samples. Healer Grant will be discussing our findings with General Holt and the Select Guard later tonight, but we'll need to test my working theory against multiple samples, including fae. I expect Evander will agree to donate, but I'd like a full-blooded fae, as well, just to be sure."

My nose scrunched as I glanced down at the slide containing my sister's cells. "What do you mean by 'donate'?"

Her musical laugh echoed around us. "It's just a swab from the inside of your mouth. What do you say? Want to be sample number two?"

# 3
# ELARA

Smooth fabric ran across my skin as I slipped into a white short sleeved dress with budding roses patterned along the bust. The soft material cinched at my waist with crisscrossing ties, before drifting out in a cascade of flowing fabric just below my knees. I twisted, inspecting the outfit in Alarik's long mirror. I'd brought a few spare outfits to keep in his room for mornings such as these. Better that than dashing downstairs in the same clothes as the night before.

A soft smile tugged at my lips as I recalled the first time I'd left in the early morning hours. I had been so focused on muffling my sounds while tip-toeing through his quarters, I hadn't noticed the maid coming up the stairs as I hurled myself down them. She nearly shouted, clutching the banister and her chest as I tumbled into her.

Since then, the cleaning of the third floor was completed mid-day. I wasn't sure if it was from Alarik's intervention or gossip among the staff, but I was grateful for it, nonetheless.

Summer sun shone through the windows, illuminating the disheveled white sheets of Alarik's bed, evidence of our time spent together the night before—and this morning. My lips twitched as I brushed out the knots gathered in my hair, leaving the wet chestnut curls down to dry on their own. Alarik and I weren't public about our relationship—if that was what this was —but everyone knew. With me no longer training, I was surprised to find no one seemed to care that I shared a bed with the esteemed General Alarik Holt.

There were a few circulating rumors in the city below, suggesting my desire to join the base was an elaborate ploy to gain Alarik's affections. Now that I'd secured them, the farce was over.

I'd first-handedly overheard the owner of a prominent dress shop speaking loudly and openly with her customers last week, just days after we returned from Neith, not knowing I was browsing through a stack of fabric in the corner. I'd managed to extract myself from the shop without replying—without so much as frowning. I made it all the way to the stables before my fury boiled over. Ember was saddled within minutes, my bow and quiver strapped to my back, a moment later, and then we were off, tearing through the vibrant forest.

The simple archery course laid out months before had been expanded by Evander and Vidarr in the days following our return from Neith. They'd insisted I have an outlet, one where I had no chance of hurting an opponent. They expected an explosion of rage—they all did. They expected the bright flames of revenge to spark and burn, but it wasn't fire that consumed me. No, it was a frigid detachment engulfing the flames within, strangling the need for action pulsing deep within myself—as if the coldest winter night had been plunged into an icy stillness.

All around me, the stars glittered and winked, frozen by the frost surrounding them. But people forget; stars are not composed of glittering diamonds or peaceful brilliance. They are raging centers of clashing volatile matter, burning with enough power to decimate worlds.

The frost was temporary. It would thaw, and when the ice

broke—when the fury and pent-up need for retaliation finally found the freedom they sought—I wasn't sure the world would survive. I knew I wouldn't.

I needed to eradicate this anger, to find some way to snuff out the smoldering stars within before it was too late... but what would I be without my darkness, without that consuming fire swirling in a sea of shadows? Would there be anything of me left or was this darkness all that I was?

I wasn't ready to confront that gut-wrenching truth.

So, I found Ember and rode. I didn't mind the way the wind tugged against my unbound hair, nor the way the cotton dress kicked up behind me. I flew through the forest, elated and alive, welcoming the sharp, fleeting stings of wayward branches against my exposed thighs and arms. I rode, my arrows finding their targets flawlessly, until my quiver was empty... until the frigid burning in my veins ebbed, and I could sense the warmth of the sun on my skin once again.

I'd ridden to the edge of the base, the towering walls stretching before me. I'd contemplated scaling them, hauling my battered soul over the bricks and mortar and into the wildness beyond. I could give into the darkness. If Greer, Lannie, and Will were safe, if I distanced myself from others, I'd be able to murder and maim as I pleased, tracking down the Fractured without mercy...

I hadn't allowed myself to hold a weapon since that day, choosing instead to remain at Alarik's residence, away from temptation.

Alarik and I had spent nearly every night together since the battle of Neith, since the fateful day we learned of the Fractured and their red-eyed commander. Since the day Zelos's body was set ablaze, taking what remained of his presence from this world into the next. Neither of us preferred to be alone when night swept this earth. And so, we'd fallen into a routine of sorts this last week. I would fill my time with mundane, uninspiring tasks, while Alarik fought to discover ways to keep humans alive in this harsh, fae-dominated world. But at the end of the day, we would find each other, choosing either his bed or mine to fall into.

I cherished those moments. The ones where Alarik's body warred with mine. When we battled each other for pleasure and peace, endless in our need to discover the blissful reprieve we offered one another. It was easier being together, easier pretending that everything was normal—at least for a few hours.

The sound of water cut off, followed closely by the subtle clang of the shower door and damp footsteps on marble floors. Alarik entered his room a moment later. My mind stilled as I tracked the fat water droplets coating his body. They linked together, joining into narrow streams that trailed down his chest, dipping along each defined muscle, until they slipped past the V of his hips, and were swallowed up by the towel covering him.

I forced my eyes up. He shot me a knowing smirk as he reached into his dresser, the look causing my cheeks to flush. They shouldn't. We'd done far more scandalous things just minutes before.

"The men are taking the day off. We'll be finalizing the transfer of a small force to Fort Dhara," Alarik spoke as he dressed.

It took every ounce of concentration I had to follow the conversation as his towel dropped to the floor.

"Fort Dhara? The place the dark fae are transforming into another base?"

"That's the one. I'll have to stay for the first few weeks, at least, but I'll have one of the Select monitor the base while I'm away."

"You didn't think to tell me this sooner?" I said, crossing my arms as the ever-present flame of anger grew.

He lifted a brow. "Training with fae is a rare opportunity, the dark fae even more so. Only those with the highest training will be invited to join. Though, we do hope to circulate training throughout the base once things are established." His eyes peered into mine, scouring them as if he could glimpse an unspoken truth lurking in their depths. "You haven't touched a blade since we've returned. If you would like the opportunity, lessons will start back tomorrow."

Memories of the battle of Neith came rushing back. Black blood pooling from lifeless corpses as my lips tilted into a wicked smile—as I delighted in the death around me. I turned away before he could see the gnawing hunger for battle reflected in my eyes. I hated how it festered—whatever had awoken that day—always teetering on the precipice of escape.

Forcing a steadying breath in through my nose, I kept my voice calm. "No, you're right. There's no need for me to go."

My voice was stiff, as it always was whenever he brought up the topic of me rejoining the base. And gods did I want it—did I yearn for it. But it wasn't safe. Not yet. I needed to make sure I wasn't turning into one of the Fractured, and, more importantly, to ensure the red-eyed commander's claim held no ground—that I wasn't the personification of the Dark Phoenix. Lannie needed a little more time investigating the Fractured's substance. She found cures for everything. Surely, she'd be able to answer this mystery, as well.

Not that Alarik realized any of this. He and the Select Guard were gone most of the time, riding to and from the nearby villages to stop riots sprung from Alderidges poisonous words or to help relocate those too worried to remain outside the protection of the base. He was doing everything he could to protect this realm... and I was just the simpering female, haunted by the gore of war. I'd done nothing to dissuade him from that assumption. Better he think me weak and broken than corrupted.

"I know Neith was a lot," Alarik said, his voice gentle. "The first battle is always the hardest."

Alarik's concern only served to deepen my guilt. I shifted my gaze, studying the map tacked against the wall before me. The red circle around the enchanted town shone like a beacon of destruction. The town itself had been saved, but so much had changed that day.

Neith was the only place to have survived an attack. News had spread, like wildfire in a drought, drawing endless troves of humans to their gates. The brothers Xaun and Skender had been forced to linger, ensuring the fae-human town remained safe. Likewise, Evander had been forced to return to the Light Kingdom's capital, Alora, immediately following the battle of Neith, but appeared back at base only days later. At least his cover and member status as being a member of the Legion of the Light remained unblemished. It worried me that I wasn't beside him, helping to keep our world safe.

Alarik's arms wrapped around my waist as his lips grazed my ear. "I wasn't sure if you had decided your break from training would be temporary. I wanted you to know you can change your mind."

A humorless laugh escaped me. Hadn't he been the one trying to keep me away from the battlefield?

His spine stiffened as his hands fell away. As if reading my mind, he answered. "Training and seeing battle are two different things. There's no harm in learning how to defend yourself."

"As long as I'm not expected to *need* any of my training," I muttered, unable to prevent the words spilling from my lips.

He pinned me with a glare.

"I'm sorry," I said with a sigh. "I'm still... adjusting. I've thought about rejoining but I'm not sure I'd be able to..." *Not sure I'd be able to stop.* Swallowing, I tried again. Alarik was a general, after all. Maybe he would understand. "It's too close to..." *Too close to battle, too reminiscent of the tip of my blade biting through skin and muscles as I forced it deeper with a smile licking my lips.*

The root of my worries was there, begging him to see it. But Alarik saw what he wanted in my face. And a part of me was grateful for it. I wanted his goodness, his strength. I wanted to bathe in the light of this world. Perhaps that was why I felt so at peace when our bodies were pressed together, when his arms were wrapped around me; I couldn't be changing into something monstrous—not if he chose me.

He nodded as words failed me, and as I watched his scowl soften into something more akin to sympathy, I knew he hadn't glimpsed the truth in my eyes. Gods, I hated pity. But I suppose it was better than fear.

"I just need a distraction. Maybe I'll try again in the kitchen with Greer."

An incredulous brow lifted. "You feel like burning more food, already?"

My eyes narrowed, but he had a point. "I was debating sitting in on one of her classes. With some instruction, I should be able to master it."

"Isn't that what recipes are? Instructions on how to not destroy food?"

"Ha. Ha." The exaggerated roll of my eyes had his lips twitching.

"If you're looking for a distraction, how about the celebration of Litha? With the increase of families seeking refuge, I could use the help."

"Litha, as in the summer solstice celebrations? I thought only fae took part in revels."

"It's not a revel. Gods, El, we're more civilized than that." He huffed out a laugh. "It's considered a formal affair. The men invite their partners and family up for the week. Celebrations are held throughout the day for the children, but the rest of us continue on with a ball starting at dusk. There's music and dancing. All very tasteful."

I'd heard stories of Litha, where faerie wine flowed, and pixies danced beneath the sun. Lutes and wood instruments played from dawn until dusk, enchanting the listeners, stripping them of their inhibitions. Nymphs were even said to appear at lively ones, with freshly cut flowers and herbs, letting the light of the day fill you with warmth. I had no doubt a part of Alarik would enjoy a good revel, but he was the general, and it was far too difficult to keep the base secure as it was.

"Does that mean fancy dresses and heels?" I asked, already mentally going through the dresses now a part of my wardrobe.

"The fanciest. We could coordinate outfits and everything." His emerald eyes glimmered.

"General Holt, are you asking me to be your date?"

He shot me a smile a little tight around the edges. "Not quite. There are a lot of things requiring my attention throughout the evening, but we could arrive together. It would be our first time in public as... as us," he finished lamely.

*Us.* Not as a couple, just *us.* But going to the ball together would be a statement of sorts, an admission that we were an *us,* at the very least. Something shifted in my stomach at the notion of 'us' growing to something stronger... it wasn't an unpleasant feeling but it wasn't exactly happy either.

"Is that a 'yes'?" Alarik asked.

I smiled as a shadow of uncertainty flickered across his face. "Yes. I'll warn my sisters. Greer will insist on planning our outfits immediately."

His brows furrowed. "But it's not for two weeks."

Stifling a snort, I pressed on to my toes, brushing my lips against his. "Exactly. Greer will be frantic with how little time we have left."

"Most of the larger things are done," he said, still not understanding.

With a smile, I silenced his words with another kiss, letting my hands drift up to link behind his neck. He answered with his own exploring hands, our conversation forgotten, as his fingers tightened around my waist. The other trailed down my thigh, gripping the soft fabric of my dress. His fingers bunched the ends, drawing it up at a tantalizingly slow pace.

"Don't you have plans to arrange?" I mumbled, lips barely breaking from his.

His eyes raised over my shoulder to the small clock situated on the nightstand, revealing how much of the morning had already passed. He grimaced. "I was supposed to meet Vidarr an hour ago."

Shaking my head in mock reprimand, I said, "Go, I'm starved anyway. If I leave now, I could probably make the end of Greer's lesson."

With a final kiss, he stepped back with a smirk. "That sounds nice. Who knows? Maybe one of these days you'll bake something edible."

4

# GREER

THE KITCHEN WAS POSITIONED IN THE OLDER PART OF THE building, the immaculate tile reverting to the raw, gray stone beneath, but the appliances were incredible. An entire wall was dedicated to three double ovens, one of which was filled with rising macarons. Black burners flared to life as the rest of the staff started on preparations for this evening. Spices and herbs scented the air as the bustle of activity picked up. Ideal chatter rumbled as butter sizzled, and I felt a piece of myself settle. This was the type of kitchen I'd always envisioned—a proper working space filled with others like me who found excitement and comfort in food.

I glanced toward the thick wooden doors swung wide to let light and fresh air in. I'd hoped El would've shown, but the morning was nearly over. With a heavy sigh, I focused on the rows of counters in front of me, currently occupied with men attempting to adhere to my instruction.

"As I was saying, it's important to not add all the sugar to the egg whites at once. The mixture should then be whisked until stiff peaks develop."

They heeded my instructions as I wandered among them,

helping where I could, until it was time to pipette the batter. Bending forward over my own baking sheet, I demonstrated, constructing perfectly round and identical pale green circles. I licked my lips, already anticipating how delicious the pistachio macarons would taste.

Low, muffled words followed by obnoxiously loud laughter sounded from the far corner of the room, pulling everyone's attention. Brushing back a few wayward curls that had escaped the bun atop my head, I stood to find the snickering pair.

"Do either of you gentlemen have a question?" I let a little of my irritation bleed through as my hands came to rest on my hips.

The smaller of the two elbowed the larger one, jerking his chin toward me as his hungry eyes took in the curves of my figure, as if I were a dessert on display. "I was just saying if that counter was a little lower, we would get to see the treats we're really after."

A few of the others in the class joined in, nodding their heads, but one of my youngest students, a boy no older than fourteen, looked murderous. He was all freckles and long limbs, but he shoved back from the table, whirling toward them in a blast of anger.

"Don't speak to her like that."

"It's all right, Brock," I said, purposely keeping my voice calm and sweet. "I can handle this."

The class stilled, curious how I would respond to such blatant disrespect, but I'd heard worse and dealt with far more threatening people than these fools. Savoring the building unease, I drew myself up to my full height, shoulders pulled back without a hint of shame. That was what they wanted, what they expected—embarrassment, guilt, concession—but I learned long ago their crude words and disgusting actions were reflections on their own faults, not mine. A sigh escaped me. It was exhausting knowing this world was filled with self-righteous, arrogant pricks.

"Okay, gentlemen. I know this," I gestured to my body, clad in a normal t-shirt and practical pants layered with a flour-stained apron, "can be a lot to handle. I get it. I'm the hottest thing you've seen in months, but I'm going to need you to remember how to use the head up here." I tapped the top of my hair. "Instead of the unimpressive one residing in your pants."

Their sneers faltered as a low rumble of laughter flitted through the room.

My saccharine smile stretched. "Women do not go about their day to impress you. Your opinion on how we look or what we wear never crosses our mind. It is not my responsibility to make you feel comfortable. You two are going to need to figure out how to exercise some self-restraint."

A crease formed between their brows, as if this was the first time they'd considered another's opinion. I let a glimpse of disgusted rage show in my eyes. "Be better, gentlemen. You're dismissed."

Not bothering to see if they listened, I resumed class. They muttered a few more instigating comments, trying to get others to join them, but it seemed my reality check had worked. After another minute, they headed toward the exit.

El stood in the doorway, fists balled and jaw clenched. My eyes widened as they approached her, knowing she must have heard what they'd said. El seemed to coil in on herself, like a viper preparing to strike, and those two fools were clueless. The tenuous grasp on her anger solidified, concealing the dark presence that would occasionally peak through her carefully crafted control.

Rather than gutting them, which she appeared to be seriously contemplating, El simply dipped her shoulder into the larger one as he pushed past her.

A slew of curses issued from him, his hand flying to his side.

My lips twitched, knowing El was sure to leave a mark. A laugh nearly escaped me as I watched him turn to confront her. The color drained from his face when he realized who was before him.

El's eyes darkened with a merciless hint of shadows. "Was there something you wanted to say?"

He opened his mouth and then promptly closed it, retreating a step toward the hall.

"No?" she asked, holding a hand to her ear. "I didn't think so. If I hear you speak to my sister like that again, or anyone for that matter, I will personally ensure you will be deployed to the darkest recesses of Pax *without* your most cherished body part." She dipped her head toward his pants before glowering at both of them like the vile insects they were. Her voice was barely above a whisper, but it carried with promised pain across the silent room. "Go."

They fled.

El stared after them a moment, looking as if she'd reconsider allowing them to continue breathing. Slowly, she unclenched her fists and exhaled. Turning to me with a satisfied grin, she said, "Hey, Sis. Good day?"

"I've had worse." I smiled, a warmth spreading through my chest at seeing her. "We're almost done, but you could help with my batch."

"Ehh. These look pretty good. Probably best I keep my distance."

"Nonsense," I said, rolling my eyes. "But let's stick to the filling, just in case."

The rest of the class returned to their own batches as El and I worked. She never quite seemed to find her place in the kitchen, but she took direction well and appeared distracted from her solemn mood well enough. Never happy or at peace—not like how she was with a blade in her hand and another half-a-dozen weapons strapped to her person—but she managed to acquire an adequate level of contentment.

Soon, the sweet smells of freshly-baked macarons filled the air. "All right everyone, good job. Next week, we'll focus on the proper breakdown of a hare. They gave their lives so we could be fed. It's only fitting to make sure we put as much to use as possible."

With that, the men filed out of the room, leaving my sister and me alone. I untied the strings of my apron, hanging it on a hook before taking a seat beside her.

"That was impressive, Greer."

"You've seen me make macarons dozens of times, though I admit it's nice using the top-of-the-line equipment. Did you know there's a whole oven dedicated to making fresh bread?"

El shook her head with a light smile. "That's great, but I meant the way you handled those guys."

"Oh, those jerks? I've dealt with worse." I waved her concerns away. "Why do you think I stopped taking Will to the market at Sonder after I turned fifteen?"

My face clouded with the memory. The men had been so much older. I hadn't realized what they were after, not until their filthy hands were on me, touching me as if they had the right—as if I'd *appreciate* the attention. Bile singed the back of my throat.

Thank the gods for Liam. And Will.

I still remembered the flood of light bleeding into the alley, followed quickly by the sound of Liam's voice and the swift flash of a wooden broom handle. They fled before we could identify them, but I'd never forget the look on Will's face as he peered around Liam's legs—confusion mingled with horror. It took me all night to calm him. Only once he was asleep did I allow myself to unravel, using the melodic patter of the scalding shower to drown out my cries.

Liam explained later that Will had started screaming inside

the bar. He was frantic, repeating something about a dragon being cornered and he wouldn't calm—not until I was with him. Liam only left to come find me for Will's sake.

It had been a terrible, wonderful coincidence. Will must have fallen asleep at the bar—must have had another one of his nightmares—and I'd never been more grateful for them.

My fate could have been worse. This world housed a plethora of cruel, corrupt beings. I knew many people had been in similar situations as mine and had not fared as well. I should be grateful—and I was... but sometimes I still felt it—the taint, the uncleanliness of their touch.

Fuck them. And others like them. I'd made the decision long ago to not let pathetic creatures like them steal another moment of happiness. Shaking my head, I forced the thoughts from my mind and met my sister with an unencumbered smile.

"They're trash," I said rolling out my shoulder and pushing past the memories, "But I loved watching you get all scary-El on them."

She laughed. "I haven't touched a blade in weeks. I doubt I was very intimidating, but everyone knows I'm close with Alarik. Might as well use that to our advantage, right?"

"Right," I said, studying her. El really didn't realize the impact she had. She was fierce and beautiful, but with a hint of confidence, or maybe power, shimmering beneath. It was true the base knew she and Alarik were dating—well, not dating, because both of them were too stubborn to admit any actual feelings were involved—but that wasn't why the men respected her. That wasn't why those jerks fled after her threat.

"Overall, I think the base is a great place, especially for Will," I said. "Most of the men are kind and respectful. There are a few rotten ones, but the entire batch never turns out perfect."

This was the first time Will had been around the same people for an extended period who weren't related to him. I'd had a few boyfriends over the years, but I'd kept things strictly friendly around Will. There were several reasons for that, but I mostly hadn't wanted him to get attached. He didn't need another person in his life leaving—or being killed. I'd been worried when Alarik started spending more time with Will, even more so when El and Alarik started sleeping together, but Alarik felt different. He seemed like the type of man who would visit Will, even if he and El fell apart.

"So," I drawled, wiggling my brows at El. "How have things been going with you and the general? I know you don't like to discuss things, but it's been long enough, and I'm dying to know what happened."

Her cheeks flushed. "I think you already know. You walked in on us the morning after."

"The whole base *knows*, but I'm your sister. I deserve all the inappropriate details."

She scoffed. "Like what?"

"Are you two an official item? What was it like? Did it hurt?"

El groaned. "We aren't an item—at least I don't think we are. We haven't talked about labels. His past is... complicated, and I'm not sure he's ready for anything real. I'm not sure I'm ready, to be honest."

There was more to it than that, but we'd save that conversation for another time.

"So, how was it?"

Her checks flamed scarlet. "It was nice. It hurt at first, but he was slow and sweet and—and then it felt good." *Slow and sweet.* Those were words El didn't often use.

"I'm glad it wasn't too painful. It gets better, or so I'm told, though it seems men have a far easier time enjoying themselves than women do. And I fully expect freely given details of monumental events in the future, like the first official date, fancy dinners, the first time you orgasm."

Her blush extended down her neck, but she was my sister and my best friend. We'd always been open about everything, which was another reason why I realized what the lingering silence implied.

"Oh my gods, El. You already climaxed? That's unheard of. I'm so jealous." Knowing she'd reached her limit of personal sharing, I launched into a story of my own, shifting the focus away from her.

Hours passed as we ate, helping ourselves to all that the kitchen had to offer while the staff was away. I smeared smooth butter across freshly baked bread, before setting down a plate of various fruit and cheeses between the two of us. We ate and chatted about nothing and everything, until the evening staff returned to prepare dinner and forced us to vacate.

Filling a box with macarons before we left, we walked at a leisurely pace, and decided to surprise Will, meeting him just as his classes let out. The three of us stopped by the healing quarters soon after, and Lannie shocked us all by leaving early to join us for dinner.

The night passed in a blur of full bellies and bedtime stories —reminiscent of life before coming to the base. Lannie fell asleep early, but informed me my sample hadn't been corrupted by the black substance of the Fractured. She insisted we wait to say anything until after she tested it against a fae sample.

I glanced at El, debating telling her myself, but noticed she kept looking toward the door, waiting for a certain someone to arrive. Will looked half way to sleep already. I might as well make this easier on her.

"Well, I've had a lovely day," I stood, walking nearer to Will. I couldn't believe he'd be turning nine this year. "But I think it's time for bed."

"No. I'm not even tired," Will protested, his eyes glassy.

"If you want to stay up a little longer, you can always read, but I'm going to sleep and El looks like she needs her rest, too. And remember, she may have important meetings with Alarik some days, so be sure to knock before entering her rooms."

Will's eyes shot to El's, checking to see if what I said was true. She nodded, fighting the blush threatening to show.

"Fine," he grumbled, stomping from the room. "I'll knock, but I don't understand why I couldn't be trusted to hear the meetings, too."

A smile tugged on my lips. He'd be asleep within minutes of his head hitting the pillow.

"You, sister, have a great night relaxing... or having impromptu meetings." I shot her a wink, making a show of checking the hall for Alarik.

She threw a pillow at me. I caught it and threw it back before stepping across the hall into my own rooms. I had just slipped into the crisp sheets of my bed when I heard a soft knock sound from across the hall. I smiled. At least she wouldn't have to worry about Will being an early morning visitor.

# 5

# ELARA

I STARED AT MY HORRIFIC ATTEMPT AT DRAWING, ALREADY HAVING failed at painting, ceramics, sewing, and baking. I'd seen Lannie draw since she was old enough to hold a stick of charcoal, but, despite my best efforts, I was only able to create random squiggles and harsh lines. Scowling, I threw the notebook across the room at the exact moment my sisters strolled through the doors. Odd. I hadn't seen much of Lannie outside her lab since returning from Neith, but when I did, it was only at dinner or for some vague update on healing tonics.

"I take it drawing is going about as well as baking?" Greer asked, her voice light.

I only glared.

"We thought we'd find you here," Lannie said, taking a seat across from me on the sapphire, buttoned sofa. Greer followed.

If I wasn't in the forest with Ember, or confining myself to Alarik's wing of the house, I was taking refuge in this small space. It was a meager room, tucked away from the others near the healing quarters, and had been covered in a thick, stubborn layer of dust when I'd first stumbled upon it, but I'd seen the intricate carvings framing the grand fireplace and knew I wanted to stay.

After tedious hours of cleaning, a sitting room with a fairly empty bookshelf spanning one wall, and two large windows along the other appeared. I'd removed the sheets covering the sofa, revealing rich sapphire blue cushions. It was lovely, but the fireplace was the focal point of the room. An ornately carved phoenix climbed the cherry wood on one side, its feathered wings furrowing out in great waves of swirling fire. A fierce dragon was poised on the other side, sharp talons and vast reptilian wings mirroring the phoenix as it ascended. Their tails trailed down the sides, hovering above damp earth sprinkled with beads of water, nourishing the blooming field of flowers beneath, but it was the great raven that drew my attention. It sat atop them all, with its wings stretched wide across the mantel, illuminated by a radiant sun circling from behind.

I pulled my eyes away from the carving once more, looking toward my sisters. Shrugging, I said, "I like it. It seems cozy and oddly familiar. What brings you two here?"

They shared a glance before Greer leaned forward with a smile. "We have good news about the black tarry stuff."

"Residue," Lannie clarified. "The residue from the Fractured. As you know, I've been able to isolate it from the corrupted cells, but haven't had success discovering other properties until recently." Her eyes bounced back to Greer.

"And?" I prompted.

"And you're not turning into one of them," Greer finished with an excited smile. "Isn't that great?"

My eyes widened as I looked between the two of them. Greer continued beaming at me while Lannie shifted on her feet, her face a careful mask of control as she silently waited for me to respond. But I couldn't speak. Had they known this whole time what worries plagued me? I swallowed, searching for an answer, but Lannie offered me a reprieve.

"We didn't mean to assume, but I've confirmed the black substance is not infectious, at least not for humans. I took the isolated Fractured particles and presented them with fresh cells, first my own and then Greer's, and then the rest of the Select Guard's. The cells remained pure. I've only observed Evander's half-fae cells for a few days now, but his, too, are clean. Alarik has granted my request to ask the fae for a sample when they arrive, but it appears anyone exposed to the substance will not be harmed."

My mind whirled. If what she said was correct, it meant... I wasn't becoming a monster. I was free—free to study war, to train, to wield a blade. I was free to fight, to avenge my family, my fallen friend, to destroy that repugnant red-eyed commander who'd had the nerve to smile while he plunged a blade into Zelos's chest. My smile faltered for a single moment, recalling the commander's claim: that I was the Dark Phoenix.

But that too, was now proven wrong. I couldn't be. Not as a human. The Dark Phoenix had immense power—the ability to destroy life and the world as we knew it. As long as I remained human, mortal and essentially powerless, I was safe from such a future. I felt a weight lift from my chest, only now realizing how much I'd been desperate for an unencumbered breath. "You're sure?"

Greer nodded as Lannie spoke. "Mostly. I don't believe it can enter cells on its own. Healer Grant and I think there was a binding spell used. His theory is that a powerful incantation is used to intertwine the substance and the body, possibly going further to tangle with a being's essence or soul, making it incurable once complete."

"Who could wield a spell that powerful?"

"That's the catch. Healer Grant was positive something of that magnitude, something powerful enough to splinter and warp the soul, would need permission from the host. I need to test it against a pure fae sample, but at least we know the creation of the creatures won't spread."

"Thank the gods for that," I said. "There are far too many of them as it is."

"Exactly," Greer exclaimed with a bright smile. "All we have to do is figure out who is working the magic, what the Fractured get in return for selling their souls, and put an end to it."

A huffed laugh escaped me. "Is that all?"

She waved a hand in the air. "We can figure out the specifics later, but for now you're safe and you're yourself. So, let's move on to the more important topic of this evening."

Lannie's brows furrowed, mimicking my own.

Greer rolled her eyes, mumbling under her breath. "The both of you, really. I don't know why I bother." She spun, pinning us with a glare as her hands came to rest on her hips. "The ball, sisters. We have three days—*days*—until the celebration of Litha. And a number of families will arrive before then. Have either of you decided what you'll be wearing?"

Her eyes bounced between Lannie and me, narrowing the longer the silence stretched. I shrugged in Lannie's direction before meeting Greer's hawk-like stare. "I figured I'd choose something from my closet. Maybe the one with the flower pattern…"

Greer's fair skin paled further. "You can't be serious, El. It's a *ball*—the first ball we've been to. Lannie, back me up."

Lannie sunk into the couch beside me. "Actually, I was thinking of skipping it. I've been working through the night, anyway and—"

"No. Don't you dare give me the 'I'm working' excuse, Lannie. And you," Greer said, rounding on me. "You have a boyfriend for the first time in forever and you're not going to dress up for the occasion?"

"He's not my boyfriend—"

"Love interest, flirtation, yummy eye candy—I don't care

what label you use, but he will be there, and the two of you, at the very least, are more than just friends." She inhaled a deep breath, pinching the bridge of her nose as she exhaled. "I will take care of the outfits. I'll need to speak to Ahmya—I'm pretty sure I have something for the both of you—but you two *will* be joining me for a night of unencumbered fun. Understood?"

We nodded, not daring to speak.

"Wonderful. Okay, sisters, I'm off. There is work to be done. El, would you mind meeting Will outside his class today? He hasn't been sleeping well and I think it would mean a lot to him to spend the afternoon with you."

"Sure," I said. "Nightmares?"

"As always." Greer sighed, the light in her eyes dimming.

"They've been getting worse," Lannie added. "The last few have included ravens. Something about protecting or a shield."

"Why didn't you tell me? I could have helped." When Will's nightmares worsened, we normally rotated sleeping in his room. It appeared the two of them had been doing so without my help.

Greer grimaced. "It seemed like you had a lot on your mind. We didn't want to add to it. Besides, it's only been a few days. I'm sure they will let up soon." She pulled each of us into a quick hug before heading out the door. "I'll catch up with you two tonight."

Will's smile stretched wide as he caught sight of me waiting under the cool shade of an oak tree across the dirt path. He looked as if he was contemplating dashing to my side like he used to when I'd returned from a long day of hunting, but instead he waved good-bye to his friends and set a perfectly normal pace in my direction. I supposed future generals didn't dash to their sister's sides.

There was a fresh sheen of freckles atop his cheeks, but his face had leaned further, the roundness of childhood waning with each passing day. We were losing the boy he had once been, to the man he would someday become.

"Hi, Ellie!" He closed the final step with a hug, and I couldn't help but squeeze him a little harder.

"Hey, there. How was your day?"

"It was great! General Holt stopped by and took us all down to the training pitch. We got to watch him spar with Vidarr. They're both so fast. And afterwards, he stayed to give me pointers on how to become the youngest general."

"He did?"

"Yeah. Well, sort of. I started asking him questions, but he answered every one! He even said he would try to stop by in the evening in case I thought of any others."

"Tonight?" Alarik and Evander had only just returned from Neith. Evander had let me know Mr. Sapo was safe, and just as stubborn as ever. He was refusing to open the gates, insisting the town was at capacity, despite the growing need for refuge. Evander and Alarik had been able to redirect the masses to the base, but it was only a matter of time before the confines of the city were filled.

"Yeah, but I have so much to study. I want to make sure I'm prepared. Can you help me?"

"Of course, Will. I'd love to."

Afternoon blended into evening. I had dinner sent up to my suite as Will and I read text after text. Everything excited him, each passage stirring a dozen additional questions he insisted be answered. When Alarik arrived late in the evening, Will started asking questions before he'd even closed the door behind him. A warmth spread through my chest as I watched to the two of them.

Will was comfortable with Alarik in a way that he wasn't with most people. It had been just the four of us for so long, and though we would occasionally take him into Sonder, Evander remained the only steady male presence in his life.

A pang shot through my chest as images of the twins flashed before my eyes. Will would have been everything to them. If things had been different, if we lived in a world that hadn't been decimated by death and plagued by war, Torin and Jem would have seen Will grow up. They would have taught him the skills of a warrior, but more importantly, they would have spent summers splashing in the river and climbing up trees. They would have carried him across their shoulders, and showed him how to sneak into the kitchen after Mother had gone to sleep to slip a few extra cookies back to his room.

My sisters and I did the best we could, but he would never know the feeling of having older brothers. Being at the base had offered Will a chance to glimpse what life might offer outside our family. He had friends now, a sense of purpose. He had a future.

"I hate to stop you from reading, but it's getting late."

"But I'm not even tired," Will grumbled, looking over the top of the book with heavy-lidded eyes.

I watched Alarik's lips twitch as he fought back the smile. "I actually need to discuss a few matters with your sister. How about you finish reading the chapter while we chat and then we can set up another day to meet?"

"Another day after class?"

"Yes. It may be a little while, but I'll see when I can clear an evening."

"Okay," Will said with a sleepy grin. "But next time, we'll meet in my room."

"Sounds good."

Alarik turned his emerald eyes to me, meeting my own twinkling stare as he approached. "Was there something you wanted to discuss, or was that just to get him to read on his own, and hopefully fall asleep?"

Following my line of sight, Alarik glanced over his shoulder to find Will settled deep within the cushions, the book already dipping low in his grasp. "He'll be asleep in minutes, but yes, I did want to catch up on a few things. Evander told me Greer took over planning for Litha."

"I thought you said we could help."

"You can. It's not a problem, but she's changed everything. I had it slotted to be a small celebration, a formal dinner followed by some light music, but the menu is now five courses with an hour of circulating hors d'oeuvres prior. She's changed all the decor. The staff are already rearranging the room, and we're still three days out. If the rumors are true, she even managed to procure a bottle or two of nevernectar."

My grin stretched wide. "I'm not surprised. She thrives at planning events. We never had anything like this growing up, but the mothers of Sonder would often ask her to weigh in on various parties or engagements."

He blinked. "I should have hired her sooner."

I nudged his shoulder playfully. "Something to keep in mind for the future."

Alarik's arms gathered around my waist. I inhaled the scent of him as he asked, "You're not feeling left out? I thought the ball was supposed to be a distraction for you."

*A distraction.* It had started out that way, but if what my sisters had discovered was true, there would be no need for further distractions.

"About that," I said, glancing over his shoulder to find Will fast asleep. "Greer and Lannie filled me in on the investigation into the black substance. It sounded like they'd already spoken to you."

"The residue from the Fractured?"

I nodded.

"Lannie came to me a few days ago with an update. She said the residue was not contagious, but she and Healer Grant are concerned it might be a fae spell. I've given her permission to discuss the matter with the dark fae when they arrive. I hadn't realized you were interested."

So, my sisters had not shared their suspicions about why I'd avoided training with Alarik. Good. That would mean less explaining. "I'd like to take you up on the offer to return—"

Will's screams erupted through the room. His body thrashed as his face contorted in pain, but his eyes remained closed.

"Will? Will, wake up. It's Ellie. I'm right here." Kneeling by the couch, I reached for his hand, but Will's cries intensified.

He threw himself from the cushions, rolling into a ball on the floor. Alarik cleared the small space, pushing the table away to prevent further harm, as Greer and Lannie rushed in.

"What happened?" Greer cried, hovering over Will's rocking form.

"Nothing. He was asleep, and then—"

"Nightmare," Lannie breathed. "I'll fetch the salts."

The hair along the back of my neck prickled as Will's cries shifted to incoherent muttering. I hadn't seen when Lannie returned, but she was beside Will now, with a small glass vial in her hands. Yanking off the top, she shoved the foul-smelling salts beneath Will's nose. Greer and I sprang forward as he fell back, catching his head before it hit the ground.

The three of us stared down as he blinked awake, eyes wide as confusion and terror flashed across his face.

"It happened again," Will's voice broke. "Didn't it?"

His eyes grew shiny with tears as Greer scooped him up, offering the same soothing words we always did when he awoke frightened. "Shh. It's okay. We're here."

"It was different this time," he said, limbs shaking. "It felt different." He threw his arms around her, falling into the comfort of her embrace.

Looking past his blond curls, Greer stared at us, brows

furrowed in unbridled fear. We both knew why. Will's nightmares had been bad before, but never like this.

Lannie pushed up and headed for the door. "I'll be back with his tea."

"Does that always happen?" I jumped at Alarik's voice, barely audible over my brother's cries. I'd nearly forgotten he was here.

"They've been getting worse," I said, Stroking my little brother's back. "And we've yet to find anything to stop them."

# 6
# GREER

I held Will for hours, even after he fell asleep. I held him until my legs were numb and I needed Alarik to help lift him off the floor, and tuck him into bed.

Alarik left in a rush, dashing up the stairs as soon as Will was secure. I couldn't blame him. Will's nightmare had been disturbing. Dragging my pillow, I settled in for the night beside him, being sure to keep the ensuite light on. He wouldn't wake to a dark room, and he wouldn't wake alone. I'd make sure of it; those were two things I could control.

It seemed my sisters had similar thoughts. El and Lannie slipped in minutes later with their own pillows, all four of us squishing into bed together. This was how we'd gotten through bitter winters and bleak days growing up. This was what we did best: protect each other. Protect Will, first and foremost.

Dawn took her time arriving, and when the first rays of sun finally shone through the window, we slipped across the hall and into El's room, cautious not to wake Will.

"Okay, what do we think? Just a really bad nightmare?" My voice was raised with forced bravado, but El wasn't having it.

"Maybe, but he's never thrashed about so violently."

"Not like that," Lannie confirmed with a reluctant nod, "but his nightmares *have* been getting worse."

"He's always had nightmares. I'm sure they'll calm down."

"You don't actually believe that, Greer," El said, her voice growing somber. "None of us do. It's been years and they've only gotten worse."

Silence filled the room. No, we each knew something was wrong. Whatever it was, Will's nightmares had been occurring nearly every night, despite Lannie's brewed chamomile tea. But they weren't quite nightmares... There were days when he woke and had difficulty distinguishing dream from reality.

"I'll search for some fresh herbs and see if I can figure out a tonic or, at the very least, improve on the tea. I've been looking into causes for nightmares since arriving. Healer Grant has the largest collection of medical texts I've seen, but there's nothing. Even the texts from the Light Kingdom haven't been helpful."

"If the Light Kingdom doesn't have anything, I'm not sure what else we can do," I said. "I'll stop by the library and see what I can find. El, Alarik has a personal library on his floor, right?"

"Yes," El said. "I'll see what's there. We'll tell each other if anything is found. Agreed?"

"Agreed."

Despite the three of us scouring the base's texts, nothing was found. Will hadn't slept for more than a few hours since his last nightmare. Whatever haunted his mind found him again and again, shattering the quiet of the night with his screams.

Truth be told, I was grateful for Litha and the distraction it provided. Ahmya confirmed the outfits I'd ordered for Lannie and El would be ready in time. Originally, I'd planned them as a surprise for Lannie's birthday, which fell only a few days after the Litha celebration. She'd made El and I promised to do nothing for the day, but I thought a small dinner would have been nice.

We'd long since forfeited celebrating our own birthdays to save what little funds were had for Will's, but I'd accumulated a nice sum working these last few months. It was easy to save when one had a steady job, and an endless supply of food and clothes, and I found myself wanting to celebrate.

I'd nearly forgotten what it meant to shop. Not just purchasing supplies but actually shopping—buying things purely for pleasure. It was exhilarating. I had already decided to surprise Lannie with her favorite cake on the morning of her actual birthday, but a night on the town was just what this family needed.

I had stumbled upon a small boutique on one of my trips to the city. The stone facade was chipped in places, but the swinging sign was freshly painted and the interior was clean. A young woman with midnight hair and matching eyes greeted me with a bright smile as I looked through the displays. The two of us fell into easy conversation and I learned that though Ahmya was officially a seamstress, catering to the larger businesses in the city, she wished to craft her own designs. After browsing through her sketchbook and describing my sibling's personalities, Ahmya and I had crafted the perfect outfits for a night out. She insisted on tweaking the outfits once we learned of the Litha ball, but assured me they would be ready in time.

Strolling through the cobblestoned streets, I wove my way among the early morning crowd and allowed the buzz of the city to banish the rustling of my mind. Cinnamon and sugar wafted through the air in front of storefront windows filled with fresh pastries. The clamor of business owners swirled around me, mingling with store bells jingling as doors opened and closed, the crinkling of package wrappings, and light-hearted morning conversations.

There was life and energy here. Happiness and hope. All of

humanity had suffered after the storm and continued to do so with the subsequent attacks, but the people of the base were determined to rebuild, to continue life and ignore the gruesome realities of the world surrounding them. I found it infuriating and fascinating all at the same time.

The familiar bell dinged as I pressed against the worn wooden door, the scent of fresh citrus and lemongrass greeting me as I entered Ahmya's shop.

"I thought I saw those silver curls of yours bouncing down the street. I'm finishing up the last stitch on the gown." Ahmya's head popped out from behind the brightly patterned curtains in the back. Her rich voice buzzed with excitement. "No peeking. I'm almost done."

My smile grew wide. "I still can't believe you were able to pull this off. But really, it was an emergency. You should have seen the dresses hanging in El's closet. There's nothing even remotely appropriate for a ball, and I'm fairly certain she would've paired one of them with flats—or worse, her running shoes."

Ahmya stepped from the curtains, eyes wide with horror. "She wouldn't."

I met her concerned gaze with sad resignation. "She would. But now, thanks to your brilliance, we won't have to suffer through witnessing it. Can I see them?"

Her smirk was filled with self-assured confidence. "They're perfect. See for yourself." She pulled back the curtains, beckoning me toward her studio.

A gasp stole from my lips as I gazed at her work. She hadn't been lying—they were perfect, rivaled only by... "Is that for me?"

"Of course, it is." Ahmya cut in, waving a hand as if the very question were insulting. "Your sisters will be stunning. I couldn't let you go to the ball in anything less. I hope you like the cut. I was originally thinking strapless, but figured that wouldn't be wise with your bust."

I gathered her into a hug, words failing me. "I love it. Thank you."

"It was nothing," she said, but hugged me back all the same. "Now, you really need to get these back to the base. It's half past nine and I have no doubt those sisters of yours will leave getting ready to the last minute. I already had the shoes sent up, but I wanted to see your face when I revealed the outfits."

Ahmya slipped the ensembles into traveling covers before turning to me with a frown. "Were you planning on carrying them back? The covers will keep them protected, but they shouldn't be dragged."

I snorted. "There's no way I'm dragging those masterpieces. I'll carry them."

She raised a skeptical brow.

Draping them across my arm, I smirked. "I'm stronger than I look. There's a lot of muscle beneath these beautiful curves, and you're right. My sisters will need help getting ready. If you're not too busy, you could stop by before the ball to get ready with us."

"I wish I could. I have a few other last minute pieces that need altering."

With promises of evening adventures, I backed through the door, outfits folded over my arms, and started up the hill toward the base. I made it only a few blocks when I heard the call of my name.

"Greer, is that you?"

Searching through the swelling crowd, I turned my head in search of the vaguely familiar voice. Her golden hair shone like a beacon in the bright summer sun as her blue eyes found mine.

"It is you. Gods, it's been nearly a year. Elara has been giving Liam updates, but it's different seeing you in person." She started toward me with a waddle in her step to compensate for her rounded belly.

"Lucy! What are you doing here? Oh gods, I hadn't realized how far along you were."

Her arms reached around me, pulling me into a shallow hug. "We arrived two nights ago. Liam is meeting with a few of the local tavern owners to see if there are jobs available. It was a tough decision to leave, but with the growing attacks..." Her hand dropped to the top of her swollen belly. "We thought moving to the base would be safest."

"I'd heard another wave of refugees had arrived. I'm sorry you had to leave your home. That must have been difficult. Resources have grown a bit tight lately, with the influx of people, but I'm sure Liam will find work. If not, tell him to stop by the base. We're staying at the general's residence, and can put in a good word."

She blinked. "The general's residence? As in General Holt?"

Nodding, I smiled despite myself. "He's actually a great guy. I was expecting an arrogant, self-obsessed narcissist, but he's pretty classy."

Lucy hunched forward, her hand coming to the lower part of her ribs as she grimaced from what appeared to be a rather strong kick. My eyes swept over her once more, noting just how low her stomach was, before swinging to the small wicker basket filled with meager herbs and poultices used for delivery.

"Just how far along are you?"

A soft smile graced her cheeks as she dipped her chin, staring lovingly at the life stirring within her womb. "Due any day now. Liam was racked with worry traveling. He was half convinced I'd go into labor on the road and he'd end up delivering her, himself."

"Her?"

She shrugged. "It's just a guess. As long as the baby is safe, we'll be happy." A shadow darkened her features, stealing that bright joy that had been there moments ago. Childbirth was already difficult, but now... very few infants lived to see their first birthday.

"You two should stay with us, at least until the baby is here. There are plenty of open rooms, and that way, you'll be right next door to the healer's quarters."

"As in, stay at the general's residence?" Her voice was wary, but I saw the hopeful gleam in her eyes.

"Yes. I told you, Alarik is great. It won't be an issue. I'll have a room prepared for you two by nightfall. Are you planning on attending the ball?"

"I can barely stay up past sunset these days." She shook her head. "Do you really mean we could stay at the base?"

"Understandable about the ball, and, yes. I don't want you worrying about a thing. I'll see you tonight."

7

ELARA

I TOOK A STEADYING BREATH AS I GAZED AT MY REFLECTION IN Greer's floor-length mirror. The person staring back was a stranger. It was perfect. I'd be accompanying Alarik this evening and wanted to live up to his reputation of being the well-adjusted, honorable general. To be seen with such a man meant I needed to be just as good—above reproach, as he was.

I studied my face, lifting my cheeks until a casual, yet kind smile was in place—one devoid of shadows and pain. If only I could keep up the facade indefinitely.

Letting the tension of my cheeks ease on an exhale, I twisted and turned, watching the fabric of my dress swish with the movement. I'd second-guessed my decision of leaving tonight's wardrobe up to Greer, but my fears were unfounded. The strap-less gown remained securely in place. The boned-lined top was snug across my waist, while the defined cups accented my breasts. The gown flared out below in gentle streams, the deep jade interwoven with panels of shimmering black. Dark spiked vines stretched up from the waist, winding across the bodice, as a few wandering tendrils drifted lower to mingle with the free-flowing fabric beneath.

Initially, I thought to leave my hair down, but Greer insisted it go up. She created several small braids, pulling up pieces of curled hair and pinning them together until only a few loose curls framed my face. The dark charcoal she painted along my lids accented my hazel-blue eyes, highlighting the subtle green tones complimented by my gown.

As much as I protested, it felt nice to look good. The rational part of my mind knew I shouldn't need an ornate gown to make me feel worthy or whole, and most days I knew my worth wasn't tied to my appearance, but gods did it feel nice to feel beautiful.

Once Greer had finished lacing me into the gown, she'd whisked Lannie into her closet. It was really more of an additional room than a closet, seeing as it was large enough to fit half a dozen people, multiple wardrobes, and even a small settee. I suppressed a grimace as I realized they'd been in there for nearly half an hour. Dressing up wasn't something Lannie enjoyed.

Just as I'd decided on saving Lannie from further torture, the door to the closet swung open. I turned, finding Greer bouncing on her toes with a proud smile gracing her cheeks. "May I present to you, Lady Melantha Tenebris!"

A giggle tore through my chest at the use of Lannie's full name, reminiscent of the times we would play at being lords and ladies of the realm when we were younger. Greer swept to the side, still clad in her dressing robe, to reveal our blushing, though smiling sister.

Lannie tilted her chin up as she strolled forward. In place of the gown I'd been expecting, she wore a pair of black fitted, ankle-length pants with a matching, loose jacket. It was similar to what I expected men to wear, but tailored to her body in a flattering way. A white lacy blouse lay beneath, hugging her willowy frame, and showing a sliver of her navel. High black heels with pointed toes lengthened her legs and her silky dark hair was tossed to the side in subtle disarray. Dark charcoal drew attention to her rich, brown eyes, but other than that, it looked like Greer decided on just a brush of gloss across her lips. Lannie looked powerful while retaining her feminine edge.

"What do you think?" Lannie asked, a hint of her newfound confidence slipping.

"You look incredible," I said, still stunned at the transformation. With a sisterly smirk, I gave a small curtsy, just as I had when we were younger, and said, "Lady Melantha, it is an honor to make your acquaintance."

Greer's laughter echoed my own. Lannie rolled her eyes at the both of us, but a soft smile lingered as she turned to the full-length mirror I'd occupied moments before.

"You don't think it's too much?" she chimed as she twisted, inspecting herself.

"Of course not! It's your seventeenth birthday celebration and the first ball we've attended. My work is perfect. Don't either of you touch a thing," Greer reprimanded as she vanished into the closet, returning a moment later with her own gown.

She draped the aquamarine silky material across the bed as she worked free of her clothes and stepped into the gown. It clung to her body like a second skin. The material pooled across her heavy bustline, surprisingly held in place with a concealed, interwoven bra and two thin straps stretching across her shoulders. A deep slit cut to her upper thigh, allowing the light material to flow as she walked toward Lannie's side.

"Wow," Greer said, inspecting herself in the mirror, hands curving along her bust. "Ahmya really knows what she's doing. This feels completely secure." She jumped, releasing a surprised laugh as her breasts remained fully contained within the dress.

"You said Ahmya did all of this?" Lannie asked.

"Yes. She owns the small shop across from the bakery. It's about three blocks up from the apothecary you like, Lannie. You two will love her. She's busy with clients today, but I'll introduce you at the ball." Stepping away from the mirror, she handed me a tube of color.

"What's this for? I thought I was done."

Greer rolled her eyes, snatching it from me and painting my lips herself. "Really, you two. What would you do without me?" She stepped away after a moment, grinning. "Perfection."

Turning, she finished up her own makeup before slipping into a pair of deep blue heels. They were barely there, with only a thin strap across her toes and one across her ankles, but she moved with the grace of someone born to wear such things.

Stepping closer to my reflection, I noted the way the deep red coating my lips contrasted nicely with the dark greens of my gown. It was enchanting—I was enchanting—all polish and shine.

I cocked my head to the side, inspecting my reflection. It was strange such a monster could look so pretty. Nobody would've ever guessed at the darker impulses simmering beneath my painted face.

"Are you sure that tarry substance from the Fractured is just the residue from a spell? There's no way turning into one of them is possible?" The questions were out before I could stop them.

Lannie met my gaze after a quick glance toward Greer. "I'm not sure if it's a residue or the actual agent responsible for their corruption, but it's unable to bind to human cells and Healer Grant is certain it requires a powerful spell with the host's consent. The problem is, the only way to test the theory is to know which spell was cast and to have a willing participant. Even if we had the spell, we wouldn't sacrifice someone's soul to test a theory, and we definitely don't want to make any more of these creatures."

Greer took a step toward me, her voice soft as if she knew my sanity depended on these answers. "You're safe, El. We are all safe, at least from that. Also, if you'd like to return to training instead of setting batches of cookies on fire, I know the entire kitchen staff would be grateful."

"It wasn't that bad," I said, a little chagrined as I recalled yesterday's attempt at dessert.

"There were literal flames."

Lannie snorted. I gave a sheepish grin. "I guess I'm not the best at baking."

"No, you're not," Greer said. "But I am happy to hear you call it 'baking,' instead of 'cooking.' Either way, you're happier with the soldiers."

Her words undid a knot in my chest. "I'd planned on bringing it up to Alarik before everything happened with Will, but I'll make a point of discussing it with him soon."

Greer smiled. "Good. Oh! I forgot to tell you. I ran into Lucy this morning in town. Her and Liam arrived with the latest influx of refugees, but don't worry. I've already spoken to the staff and am having a room prepared for them down the hall."

A shadow fell over the three of us. It was Lannie who broached the topic. "How is the pregnancy?"

"Lucy looks healthy, the baby too, based on the strength of the kicks she was experiencing." Greer's voice grew somber. "She's due any day now. I thought she and the babe would have the best chance being close to you and Healer Grant."

Lannie nodded.

"Liam mentioned something about Lucy's blood relations to light fae, however distant, being able to provide protection," I said, recalling a conversation months ago.

Lannie pondered this, her eyes getting the same far off look she got when working on a particularly complex problem. "It is a plausible explanation. Light fae have the strongest affinity for healing..."

"We can catch up with her tomorrow." Greer's voice sounded from the closet, returning a moment later with a box.

"El, let's get your heels on. I don't want to be late. I told the guys we would meet them in the foyer."

I snorted. "'The guys?' You mean the highly skilled military force with their accompanying general who is currently watching our little brother?"

She waved a hand in sisterly annoyance as she lifted the lid. "Yeah, the military guys. They're probably already down there."

Greer revealed a pair of pointed deep green heels, coated in ebony vines, nearly identical to the ones on my dress. My eyes widened as I took in their height.

"Gods, Greer. I can't walk in those."

She set them beside me, a brow raised as if I were being childish. "Nonsense. You'll have Alarik to hang on to."

I glared at her as I slipped them on, my toes already pinching. Greer shot back an innocent smile, moving to the mirror to secure a few of her wild curls with additional pins. Only half of her hair was pulled back, but judging by the number of pins now missing from the dresser, I wasn't sure how her head didn't ache with all the metal. Greer added a pair of aquamarine studs to her ears, turning this way and that, before smiling, satisfied with her appearance.

"Besides," she started, "There's no time to find alternative shoes. These will have to do."

"Will has been with them all day," Lannie added. "I'm sure they'll appreciate our return."

She did have a point. We'd dropped Will off early to spend the day with Alarik and Vidarr as the three of us got ready. It was remarkable how fast the day passed. I was grateful dinner would be served first.

Greer helped Lannie with a pair of black jeweled studs before swinging toward me to add a pair of earrings, the deep rubies and emeralds sculpted into the shape of a rose.

"There. The perfect rose. Now, let's go." Her excited squeals echoed down the hall as she dragged Lannie and I behind her.

8

ELARA

I was going to murder Greer for making me wear heels. I'd nearly twisted my ankle just getting down the stairs and had no idea how I was going to make it through an entire evening of walking in them, let alone dancing. Still, it would be nice to spend time with Alarik.

Unable to contain my relief at not becoming one of the Fractured, I'd been meeting with Vidarr for some unofficial training: running, archery, hand-to-hand sparring. It was nice to feel the familiar ache in my muscles after pushing my body to its limits, but I yearned to reclaim the weight of a blade in my hands. And that wouldn't happen until Alairk approved it. We'd only had a handful of moments together since Will's nightmare, nothing more than rushed pleasantries before he'd meet with Soter to discuss plans for training, or with Kavan and Evander for any updates on nearby attacks, but tonight was the perfect opportunity to let him know I was ready.

I thought it would have bothered me, our time apart, but it hadn't. We'd said from the start what our priorities would be. The base was his and my family was mine... and though Alarik had found a place in my life, I hadn't missed his presence as much as I probably should have—not when I could finally focus on training again without the fear of turning into one of the monsters destroying our world.

My footsteps halted as I spotted the men before us, my gaze snagging on Alairk and our matching outfits. His fitted dark green velvet dress coat was framed with silver cufflinks, the white shirt beneath tucked into black pants and the boots he wore were polished to the point of reflecting the sinking sun's rays.

"You look stunning," he said, extending an arm just as I stumbled.

"Thanks," I said, shooting Greer a glare. "Though I'm not sure how long I can survive in these things. Hopefully, it's easier inside on a smooth surface."

"Or you could spend the night hanging on my arm. You do make me look rather dashing." Alarik smirked.

I giggled, his gaze familiar and comforting. My eyes drifted over Evander, Vidarr, Kavan, and Cadoc before resting on Will. I doubted Greer approved the pain of worn boots he donned with the mahogany dress coat, but he looked like a little general, nonetheless.

A smile brightened his face as he spotted Alarik and me, rushing to our side moments later. "Most of the kids in my class aren't allowed to attend the ball tonight, but I told them my sisters said I could."

Alarik chuckled. "I'm not surprised they knew you could handle it. You're very mature for your age; a general in the making."

Will beamed.

"Okay, everyone. Let's go," Greer called from the front of the pack. "We are the most important people this evening and cannot be late. There are also delectable hors d'oeuvres that start circulating in a few minutes that nobody will want to miss."

Cadoc was the first to step forward after her, his eyes a little too hungry for my liking. Greer greeted him with a tight smile that softened when Will scrambled to their side, much to Cadoc's annoyance.

"How have you been doing?" Alarik asked, his arm tightening as I wobbled. "I feel like we haven't seen much of each other and I wanted to make sure you were processing everything."

"I am, actually," I said, doing my best to ignore the flutters of excitement in my stomach. "I'm ready to return to training."

He blinked.

"I know I haven't touched a blade since we've returned, but Vidarr's been helping me with sparring techniques and I never really stopped running. I don't think it will take me too long to be where I was before—"

The bright, open smile stretching across his face stilled my words. "Is that a 'yes'?"

"Of course. I didn't want to push you, not with what happened to..." His lips fell into a somber frown.

I gave a small nod. "I miss Zelos. I haven't forgotten the commander or the coward Alderidge for portaling his twisted army across Pax, but I'm done letting fear control me."

There was no need to explain the fear I spoke of was in regard to my own darkness. I mourned Zelos, but it was one more barb to add to my already punctured heart; the fresh wound was painful, but I'd long since been used to the brutal sting of loss. I contemplated telling Alarik the truth of who I was, but he was the general, the perfect savior of humanity who always made correct decisions, decisions that kept people safe. If I explained myself, my thirst for violence and bloodshed... I'd lose him. And I'd lost enough people. That didn't mean I couldn't still live up to the expectations set for me. I'd get a handle on these urges. I would craft myself into Alarik's perfect counterpart, and part of that was making sure I had a healthy outlet for my shadows.

Our steps slowed as other members of the base joined our general direction, funneling in toward the large building at the end of the road. It was smaller than Alarik's residence, tucked away in the older part of the base, but the polished stone walls and wide, diamond-set windows spoke of grandeur. Young couples passed under strings of twinkling lights, their faces warm with excitement, as they stepped through a set of large, open doors framed by bright flower arrangements. I had no doubt Greer ensured the beauty of the decor would continue once inside.

Alarik's thumb grazed my cheek before tugging me in for a quick kiss. "I'm proud of you for facing your fear. It's a process, one that needs continued work, but slowly, you will return to yourself. Vidarr will remain here for the time being, until we're able to fully establish Fort Dhara and rotate men through. I'll let him know you'll be joining the new recruits in basic exercises."

I blinked. "Wait, *basic exercises—*"

"Here we are!" Greer squealed, her heels clacking up the steps.

"This looks incredible, Greer," Alarik said, tipping his head toward her. "Thank you for making the celebration come together. The men need a morale boost."

She beamed, leading us into the space under a canopy of wildflowers, the bright pops of yellows and pinks mixed throughout softer shades of blues and purples. "Litha is a celebration of light and life. The decor needed to reflect that."

Alarik chuckled. "Consider yourself hired for all future celebrations."

"Agreed," she said, linking her arm through mine. "Now, let's get this party started."

I let Greer drag me away from Alarik and the half-finished conversation, and over to the bar. I definitely would *not* be starting all over again with basic exercises, but Greer had worked hard on the Litha celebrations. Sighing, I accepted a glass of honeyed wine she offered, surprised to find Lannie enjoying a glass of strong amber alcohol poured over thick blocks of ice. A warm flush tinted her cheeks before half the glass was gone.

Small tarts and bite-sized foods followed shortly as formal music played in the background. Everywhere I looked couples were beaming at each other, touching with soft caresses and whispered words, sharing the beauty of this evening together.

I glanced around, finding Alarik shaking hands and mingling with families of other prominent members of the base. The men he spoke to had wives along their arms with bright, unencumbered smiles on their faces. I never understood how people could be so at peace when the world was falling apart around them.

"You could join him, if you wanted to," Greer said, drawing my attention back to the present.

"Join Alarik? He warned me he had things to attend to tonight."

Lannie studied me, her refilled glass in her hands. "The others have their partners with them. You don't feel slighted?"

My gaze swung back to Alarik, to the dazzling smile plastered to his face. It would be an effort to keep such an expression in place. "No," I answered, surprised by the truth of the word. "I'd hoped we'd be able to spend time together tonight, but I don't care for these types of responsibilities."

Greer lifted a knowing brow. "Just the pointy objects and near-death experiences for you?"

I smiled. "Exactly."

~

Dinner came and went and only when we were full, nearly to the point of bursting, was dessert whisked away and coffee brought out, each dish more delicious than the last. Alarik excused himself once more, after Kavan approached, muttering something about 'guests arriving soon', but soon the musicians started playing lively notes, and Will insisted we join the various guests out on the dance floor.

After the third song, Greer dragged me along with her to the bar for another round of drinks, promising a rosy-cheeked Will we'd be right back.

"Gods, I'm having so much fun," she panted, her face flushed from dancing. A cool night breeze whirled through the open doors, causing a few of Greer's wayward curls to stir as she continued. "Everything really came together. I wasn't sure I'd be able to do it on such short notice but..."

Her eyes widened, snagging on something behind me. A general hush descended upon the room, my spine stiffening as I mentally prepared to face whatever lay behind me. Whatever it was, I'd confront it head on. Will was here. Cursing myself for not tucking a blade beneath all this fabric, I spun to face the creature responsible for ruining our night.

"Hello, love."

9

ELARA

"Zaeth, Soter, Jarek." Alarik called, strolling toward us. "I wasn't expecting you for another hour. Had I known you wished to join us for Litha, I would have invited you sooner." His presence immediately soothed the tension in the room, the final whispers of unease dissipating as the musicians started playing.

Though the base knew we'd formed an alliance with the dark fae, only Soter frequented the base. His visits were brief, typically contained to the training yard or Alarik's office. Seeing Zaeth, a dark fae, flanked by Soter and Jarek at a celebration was a different matter altogether. Most humans still feared the dark fae, despite our best efforts of explaining the Fractured had nothing to do with the northern kingdom.

The rest of the guests returned to their normal state of revelry, but anger and hurt pumped through my veins as I realized Alarik must have invited them and hadn't bothered to tell me. "I thought we were to meet in the Dark Kingdom tomorrow, at Fort Dhara." I meant to sound strong, if not a little upset, but my words dripped with jealousy.

Surprise flashed across Alarik's features at the use of the

word *we* before he leaned in. Zaeth tracked Alarik's hand as it pressed against the small of my back. "We will be leaving tomorrow. The Select thought it would be safer for the fae to guide us to Fort Dhara, rather than have us navigate the unfamiliar terrain on our own." Alarik pressed against me, his lips coming to the shell of my ear. "They were meant to arrive later and in my quarters. I hope they didn't frighten you."

*"Do I frighten you?"* Zaeth seemed to ask, raising a brow in challenge as a smile played across his lips.

He should frighten me. Zaeth was the only person who knew what the commander thought of me. Tensions were so high among humans; fear so thick it was nearly palpable on the very air we breathed. One whisper of me being the Dark Phoenix could jeopardize my place at the base. There would be too many questions in a time when uncertainty left room for doubt to fester. Alarik would defend me, but at what price?

Forcing a smile to my face, I said, "Not at all. It's nice to see you again, Zaeth."

His eyes dilated as her name rolled off my tongue. "The pleasure is all mine."

A small gasp sounded from Greer. I turned, catching her eyes fixed on the doorway, swirling with something dangerously close to wonder as the shadows shifted to reveal a fourth fae: Thick leather straps containing rows of weapons crisscrossed his defined chest, and a large broadsword was secured down his spine. The weapons were dwarfed by two great wings, the shade of freshly fallen snow with golden-brown feathers speckled throughout.

"Gods," she whispered, looking as if she'd run toward the warrior.

The air fae's wings bristled, his shoulders bunching as he cocked his head. His lungs expanded, inhaling the scent of the gentle night breeze stirring among us, as his predator eyes scoured the room—until they found Greer.

Dark eyes with mossy green flecks and vertical slits blazed as they held her gaze, dropping down the length of his body as his wings stretched wide. They eclipsed the open doors, the light of the room glinting across golden barbs peeking through soft feathers. It was a show of dominance, of strength, but Greer was not dismayed. If anything, she appeared enchanted with the fae. A few of the nearby guests turned to watch the scene unfold, but Greer didn't pay them any attention.

"Hi, I'm Greer," she said, stepping forward with a hopeful smile on her face. I'd never seen Greer look so captivated. Her eyes widened, the blacks of her pupils nearly eclipsing the light blue of her irises.

The air fae took in the length of her, his eyes dragging along every curve of her body as he stepped forward to meet her. A blush rose to Greer's cheeks as he leaned forward. "And I'm not interested."

The air fae's words rumbled through the air, finding their mark in the heart of my sister. Greer's face fell, her throat bobbing as she swallowed in a desperate attempt to conceal the devastation so clearly written upon her face. I spun toward the fae, intent on tearing him to shreds, but caught only a pair of snowy wings vanishing into the night.

My eyes narrowed on the remaining figures, but where I expected to see cocky arrogance, there was only an uncomfortable wariness. Zaeth tore his gaze from the now empty door frame, shooting Greer a questioning look. I could have sworn he flinched as I took a step forward, blocking her from his view. When his eyes met mine, I bared my teeth, pushing all the malice I could in a silent warning to keep his asshole friend away from my sister.

Alarik's hand tightened around my waist before letting go. "Allow me to lead the way."

Zaeth held my gaze, hand sweeping out before him. "After you, love."

I paused, looking from Zaeth's cinnamon gaze to Alarik hovering in the doorway. Just as I decided to step forward and join them, Alarik spoke. "Elara is not one of the soldiers selected to join us."

My cheeks heated as embarrassment flooded through me. Zaeth straightened, his gaze never leaving mine. "An oversight on your part, General. You forget we've seen her perform at Neith."

Alarik's fists clenched. "I allow you to govern your team, Zaeth. I'm owed the same respect when it comes to knowing what's best for mine."

My lips pressed thin but I held my tongue. Zaeth relented with a shrug and a smirk, his gaze finally breaking from mine as he followed the others into the night.

Fighting to reign in the staccato of my wild heart, I turned to Greer. "Are you okay?" I gave her hand a small squeeze, but her eyes stared longingly after the air fae. Stepping in front to block her view, I forced her hollowed eyes to meet mine. "Greer, is there something wrong?"

A myriad of emotions flickered across her face, each too quick to discern, but then she blinked and refocused. A fragile smile tugged at her lips—a mask, but if she wasn't ready to discuss what she was feeling, I wouldn't be the one to push.

"Doing great, Sis. I should be asking you that question." She made a vague gesture toward the door. "I take it your conversation with Alarik to rejoin the guys didn't go well?"

I deflated around an exhale, my shoulders hunching forward. "It went well enough. He's agreed I can return but at a basic level."

She shrugged. "That makes sense."

"What? how?"

"You told Alarik you didn't want anything to do with training, or war, or revenge." Her voice dropped as her eyes did a quick sweep, ensuring no one was listening in on our conversation. "I know the only reason you gave all of this up was because you were afraid."

"I'm not afraid—"

"Not of battle or blood. But of yourself—of what you thought you were becoming."

Her voice dropped to a whisper, but it tore through me all the same. She'd known my true fears and never once thought to abandon me. My heart clenched as I gave a nearly imperceptible nod.

"Alarik only sees what you've shown him. He probably thinks you're going to regress the moment you're in a stressful situation."

Grumbling, I conceded her point. I needed to explain to Alarik that I had no intention of shying away from conflict, no fear of the Fractured or of the possibility of death that accompanied them. I wasn't the person who feared darkness. I was the one who danced in it.

Releasing a deep breath, I sighed. "It would've been nice if he had, at least, told me the fae were arriving."

Greer nudged my shoulder. "I agree, but he probably didn't think of it. Just speak with him, El. I'm sure Vidarr would vouch for you. That guy is scary, in a killer, warrior kind of way."

I smiled broadly at that, knowing Greer was attempting to distract me from my worries.

"Though, I have to say," Greer continued, "he's got nothing on the fae. Did you see Soter? His eyes were like swirling pits of glowing honey. The light fae is, of course, gorgeous in an obvious sort of way—great fashion sense—but the dark fae—Zaeth." She made a rather loud, inappropriate sound that had a few guests turning in our direction.

"Shh, Greer! You can't make noises like that." But my own giggles joined hers.

"Come on, Sis. I think it's about time we opened that bottle of nevernectar."

We danced for hours, savoring the sweet taste of the fae drink. Nevernectar was incredibly strong, even the smallest sip imparting bursts of decadent flavors across my tongue. It tasted like the first rays of a summer sun peeking through morning clouds after a night of rain, of vibrant wildflowers swaying among flowing grasses beside a lazy brook of fresh water tripping over rounded stones. Everything was brighter. Everything tasted better. Felt better. Smelled better. For once, I let myself fall into an unencumbered state of relinquishing control and simply enjoyed the feel of the music as it pulsed through me.

Greer twirled me with a little too much strength, and I slipped, tumbling back into a familiar body.

"Lannie?" I glanced up, realizing she'd saved me from crashing to the floor. A soft, tired smile graced her cheeks, casting an air of delighted contentment that I'd rarely seen. Trailing sluggishly behind her was a very sleepy Will.

"I'm going to get this one up to bed," Lannie said, wrapping an arm around Will to let him lean against her.

"That sounds like a great idea," Greer said, join the two of them. "I'm exhausted. El, are you coming?"

I blinked. "You want to leave the ball? This is all you've talked about for the past two weeks."

Greer's smile tightened. She attempted a nonchalant shrug. "I know, but it's been such a busy night."

I wondered if this had anything to do with the air fae from earlier. Will swayed into Lannie, causing my heart to squeeze. Brushing back a few of his curls I said, "Get some sleep. I'll be up in a bit." With that, they started toward the doors.

Alarik and I had barely seen each other tonight... and I hadn't missed him. Maybe it was an oversight on my part, a romanticized idea I'd conjured up as I watched the couples engage throughout the evening, but I expected to dance. To flirt. To laugh. I expected to *want* to do those things with Alarik.

I looked after them—my family—watching as the doors

swung shut behind them. I knew they would love me regardless of which path my choices lead me down... but I *wasn't* turning into one of the Fractured. *They* were my priority. And it was time I started acting that way, with or without Alarik's permission.

# GREER

THANK THE GODS LANNIE CAME OVER WHEN SHE DID. WILL WAS practically asleep by the time we returned to our rooms. I'd stayed with him while she showered, preparing for bed, and now it was my turn for a little privacy. The three of us hadn't left him alone, not since that night, and most of the time I loved being with him, but after tonight, I really wanted a few moments to myself.

The Litha ball had gone flawlessly, exactly as I had intended —all except for the fae. I hadn't lied to El earlier. I was exhausted—exhausted with trying to conceal the anguish twisting in my gut. It didn't make sense, but I felt like my heart had been crushed, like there was a giant gaping wound where it once had beat, and I'd done my best to patch it up with a few thin strips of blood-soaked cloth, but the shredded organ just kept bleeding. I'd seen him for only a moment, seen the forest-green specks in his otherwise dark eyes shift to a fierce reptilian green overlying vertical slits—a glimpse of the hidden power beneath. It had been seconds, and yet, his presence had completely unraveled my perfectly happy existence.

A fresh wave of sorrow engulfed me. I didn't bother holding

back the tears as they swelled in my eyes. There was nobody here to see them. So, I let them fall. I didn't want to discuss this, to label the emotions filtering through me. I didn't want to analyze, and categorize, and understand. Right now, I just needed to feel. To let whatever this was wash over me until I was able to breathe again.

The gentle patter of hot water soothed my soul as much as my muscles as I savored the reprieve the shower offered. I focused on the calming scent of eucalyptus clinging to the steam, focused on the expansion of my lungs with each breath, the salty taste of tears mingling with warm droplets trickling over my lips. There would be time for logic and strength later, but for now, I concentrated on each moment, on the next beat of my heart, on the next breath, and let myself grieve for something that never was.

Once the tears stopped and the weight in my chest lessened, I returned to Will's room. "I'll stay with him tonight," I said to Lannie, mindful to keep my voice low.

Lannie glanced up from the desk in the corner, the small lamp illuminating the space just enough to allow her to comb through the stack of disheveled papers before her. "Are you sure? You stayed with him last night."

"I'm sure. Anything new?" I gestured to the papers, taking a seat on the sofa beside her.

"Nothing new for the Fractured, but Evander said Jarek and Soter agreed to give me a sample tomorrow before returning. I'm actually working on something new." Her voice trailed off as her eyes gravitated toward the sheet in her hands. "Our discussion earlier sparked my curiosity."

"Which conversation?"

"The one about Lucy and the babe. About if fae blood would provide protection to humans. I was thinking about what El first said when she returned from Neith." Lannie's eyes found mine. "Alarik admitted he believed the storm was an attack, one aimed at humans. I need to do more research, but based on the recent accounts, the towns targeted by the Fractured have been mostly human."

Her eyes glinted with a light that only blossomed when she was on to something. I shook my head. "I'm not following. Most fae are dicks. That's nothing new."

"Yes, but what if Lucy's theory is correct? What if the humans who survived the initial storm had some type of distant fae lineage? Something in their blood that acted as a shield against whatever magic conjured the storm—or not a storm at all but rather a curse?"

"I guess that's possible…"

"And if that were true, then these attacks from the Fractured could be targeting the remaining humans, or rather those with human blood, but based on the little research I've managed, I'm beginning to think fae and human genetics are more entangled than we were led to believe."

"That's a definite possibility. We've never ventured beyond the Borderlands. Our entire understanding of this world is based on information that has been passed down by other humans… most of whom have also not explored the world for themselves."

"True," Lannie said. "I wonder if I could ask the fae a few questions before they leave. I'll already be getting a genetic sample tomorrow morning. Might as well ask for a quick history lesson, too. Want to join me?"

My mouth ran dry at the thought of seeing a certain winged-fae again. "I already have plans to spend the entire day in bed."

Lannie shrugged, gathering sheets of paper as she stood to leave for the night. "I'll keep you updated on what I find." She started for the door.

"Lannie?"

She turned.

"If the storm was a curse and humans with fae blood were

protected, wouldn't that be a genetic thing? As in something that ran in families?"

"Yes, at least, that is my initial thought. Why?"

"If that was the case, then why did we survive when…" *When our brothers and our parents died.*

Her face pulled into a frown. "I'm not sure."

Will's screams tore through the room—through the house—through the night itself. They were wild and brutal, his body thrashing as if being bombarded by an unknown force.

Lannie and I were hovering over him in a flash, attempting to coax him out of it, to break this horrible spell, but he was trapped in his own mind, completely out of our reach.

Figures burst through the door, dashing across littered papers Lannie must have dropped in her haste to reach Will. Evander was beside us first, taking over my poor attempts to restrain Will's arms. Jarek was next to Lannie a moment later, mirroring us, in an attempt to protect Will from himself.

"What happened?" Alarik asked, stepping toward the foot of the bed to restrain Will's thrashing legs.

Lannie spoke. "Nothing. He was sleeping. This is another nightmare."

"A nightmare?" Jarek grunted skeptically, his light fae coloring so similar to Will's.

"Yes," I snapped, patience fleeing at the sight of my brother's jerking body, at the sounds of his pain-laced cries. "What else would you call this?"

Just as abruptly as it started, Will stilled. His body had gone limp, eyes remaining closed. The five of us stared at him, too afraid to release our grips. His head eased toward the center of his pillow in a slow, controlled motion, his blonde curls damp with sweat.

Tentatively, I released my hold as Will's chest rose and fell at a normal pace once again. The others followed my lead. "Will?"

His body jerked to a sitting position, eyes flying wide. They were the same crystal blue they'd always been, but unfocused and not quite his.

"A raven's wings protect the realm,

The final shield of the human's helm.

But creatures' crushing blows shall reign,

Shattering shelter, unleashing pain."

He fell against the bed, his hands gripping his ears as his voice pitched. "The raven will fall. The raven will fall. The raven will fall." Each syllable was broken and cracked, his voice protesting after such strain.

"Goddess save him," Jarek breathed.

Will's head snapped in his direction, his eyes latching on to the light fae with unnatural precision.

"Dark phoenix vengeance, harsh, unbending.

Torment abounds, unchecked, unending."

Jarek paled under his gaze, nodding as if he was frightened of upsetting Will. Will's eyes narrowed on him. "The raven must not fall."

Swallowing once, Jarek nodded. "I understand."

My brother's small form held his gaze a moment longer before collapsing.

## 11

## ELARA

I LEANED BACK AGAINST THE CUSHIONED CHAIR, WATCHING AS THE dancers whirled around me. Most of the families had retired, leaving the ballroom filled with enamored couples. The music had taken on a wild beat as the alcohol flowed freely. People were laughing. They were flirting and touching and filling this moment with everything wonderful life had to offer. The young owned the night. It was a time for delectable wickedness, of unexpected dalliances and intriguing romances—a time free of judgment.

I sighed, lifting the wine glass to my lips. The burst of sweet berries mingling with the tartness of tannins rolled over my tongue as I tilted my glass back, draining the remaining liquid.

Setting the empty glass down with a clang, I pushed from the table. No point in torturing myself further. Alarik clearly wouldn't be returning. I'd thought maybe once the meeting was over, he'd come find me, but of course, it wouldn't be a quick thing discussing Fort Dhara and their plans against the Fractured. I should have known—I *did* know. He was the general. He had responsibilities.

Just as I was turning for the door, the air shifted. Small

pulses of energy sizzled around me, accompanied by the earthy scent of cedar, and rain, and far off places. It enveloped me like a protective cloud, alluring and seductive. I allowed myself a single deep inhalation before turning, already knowing who I'd find.

"Hello, love." Cinnamon eyes peered down at me as his lips pulled to the side in a cocky smirk. "May I have this dance?" Zaeth extended a hand, dipping slightly forward.

"No," I snapped, tearing my gaze from his. Shaking my head, I attempted to dispel the haze surrounding me. I shouldn't have had that last glass of wine.

Zaeth's lips twitched, but otherwise he remained unfazed. "Come now, it would be a shame to waste the evening trailing after a man who is too busy to pay you the attention you deserve."

Those deep eyes seemed to glow a bit brighter as my fists clenched. "Don't presume to know anything about him. Or us."

"I know he's not thinking of you."

My stomach twisted, hurt by the truth of his words. Alarik occupied with plans to save countless lives was something to be admired, and yet, my selfish heart yearned to be his focus... to be the sole focus of someone's affections. But how dare Zaeth, a dark fae whose kingdom prized punishment, use Alarik's compassion—his honor—against him.

"Alarik is putting the good of his people before his own wants," I snapped, leveling him with a glare. "He makes sacrifices every day so the people of this base are safe, so that humans have a place to flee when the bloodshed of *your* world is too great. Someone like you wouldn't understand the weight of his burden."

I could have sworn hurt flashed in his eyes, but it was gone before I could be sure.

"Your dress is beautiful, fitting for one such as yourself, though the earrings do not match," Zaeth continued, as if we'd been having a pleasant conversation. His hand drifted toward my cheek, almost touching the gemmed roses dangling from my ears.

My eyes narrowed at his reach, causing his hand to still, hovering a moment longer, before dropping. My eyes widened, surprised he heeded my silent request. I was glad he had, relieved, and yet, I couldn't help but notice that my skin was a little colder for it.

"The vines of your dress are not roses. They do not flourish in the sun, but under the moon in the darkness. Stone's Lace is its name. It's able to petrify even the mightiest of creatures with a few pricks from its barbs. Truly powerful things do not bother concealing themselves with frail adornments."

His voice grew lower as he spoke and when his hand rose to my waist to admire the intricate pattern, I didn't stop him. My skin heated in the wake of his touch as he traced the ebony vines, his fingers following them across the boned corset to drift down along my navel. "It has no need for pretty petals or use for alluring scents. Its beauty stems from its strength, from its rarity."

I swallowed, hating the flush tinting my cheeks, ashamed of the heat that pulsed lower.

His nostrils flared, as if scenting my current state. Dark brown pools flecked with midnight skies met mine. He held me there a moment longer, trapped beneath his gaze, before his hand fell away. He was dark fae. They were ruthless beings whose main purpose in life wavered between fighting and fucking. The response he elicited from my body had to be a reaction to whatever magic lurked in his veins... but it felt nice to be wanted, even if it was disingenuous.

Shaking my head, I turned away, needing to get the thoughts whipping through my mind under control. I should find Alarik.

*But you still yearn for blood*, a voice whispered in my head. *You still crave the feeling of steel ripping through flesh, the copper tang of blood misting the air.* But I didn't want to think of those vicious truths, because that meant whatever was happening to me, whatever had been awakened at Neith... it was a corruption of my own making, of my own soul.

My eyes swept the room, already knowing I'd find it empty.

"He may not be thinking of you, love, but I am." I spun, a quick retort primed on my lips, but my tongue stilled when I found Zaeth mere inches from me, eyes beseeching.

Stepping back from the intensity in his gaze, I swallowed. "Why are you bothering me? There are plenty of other women here who would enjoy your company."

"They do not interest me," He said, waving a hand in annoyance before extending it toward me. "Dance with me, Elara."

The sound of my name from his lips rolled through me. He had a subtle accent, nothing distinct, but it twisted the syllables enough to hint at an ancient time, one long since forgotten.

Zaeth rolled his eyes, the effect humanizing his otherworldly appearance. "Just as friends, then. I know you're involved with the mortal, though I don't understand why."

"What does that mean?" I snapped, eyes narrowed.

His head cocked to the side, a playful smirk lurking beneath the surface. "Nothing. I'm sure the general is quite... entertaining."

I lifted a brow. "Zaeth."

"Yes, love?"

With a glare, I turned to leave.

A deep chuckle sounded behind me, its source blocking my path a moment later. His grin was pure predator, the tips of his fangs gleaming. "You can't expect me to behave all the time."

"This is you behaving?"

Another wicked laugh. I crossed my arms. "No antagonizing me."

His eyes lit with mirth. "For tonight only," he bargained.

"And, only if you dance with me. No fear or restraint. Allow yourself to have a bit of fun. After a few songs, we will part."

Emotions warred within me but I didn't want to retire just yet... and a few dances wouldn't hurt.

"Just as friends," I said, meaning for the words to be strong, but they tumbled out in a small squeak as he stole me away.

And then we were moving. Zaeth's steps were sure. When I fumbled, he simply held me up, unfazed with the additional weight. We twirled and dipped, spun and skipped and I allowed myself to get lost to the throws of the music, to have a moment when I wasn't consumed with rage... or the crushing raw, blistering feeling of thinking I wasn't enough. Not strong enough to protect Will. Not good or pure enough for Alarik. Not mentally capable of holding back the flood of darkness that spewed from my soul in endless waves. I was falling short in everything.

But tonight—tonight I forced those thoughts from my mind, and simply... lived.

A slower pace began, replacing the rapid tempo just as my feet started to ache. I made to step away from the dance floor, but Zaeth gathered me to him, his hand locking mine in place while his other dropped to my waist, leading us through the waltz before I could remember to protest.

"It's nice to see you smile. With all of the glares you level me, I wasn't sure you knew how."

A snort escaped me as he leaned in, the smell of cedar and earth and fresh rain washing over me. "Not all of us are as free with our smiles."

The mischievous glint in his eyes dimmed slightly, but his playful smirk remained, showing off the sharp tips of his pointed canines. "Now, what was all this nonsense of you not joining us at Fort Dhara?"

My eyes widened, surprised by the question. Recovering, I

forced an unencumbered shrug. "It's nothing. I sort of stopped training after Neith. Stopped everything, actually."

His gaze was steel, but his voice conveyed nonchalance. "Might I ask why?"

Meeting his unflinching glare with one of my own, I tiled my chin up. "Maybe that's what I wanted. Maybe I prefer a quiet life."

His laugh was a deep purr. "Come now, let's not bother with the ridiculous. Look around you. Dozens of pretty little families and doting wives, nearly all of them contented, docile creatures. But you... we both know you would eat them up."

"I don't know what you mean—"

"Oh, but I think you do. I know your darkness because it mirrors my own. I saw a glimpse of it on the battlefield, but when you finally give in to it, when you decide to fully relinquish the tethers binding the beautiful beast within..." A glimmer of silver flared to life around his irises. "How wonderfully she will play."

Words evaded me as my chest heaved. He'd seen me. Zaeth had seen me on the field surrounded by lifeless bodies *I'd* put there, and now, he'd confirmed what I'd feared for so long: I was a killer, just like him. And I hadn't been quick enough to save Zellos... I *still* may not be strong enough to stop the Fractured from decimating the rest of this world—the rest of my family.

My stomach turned as I stumbled out of his arms and across the dance floor, grateful for the cool night breeze that cut through the worst of my panic. Air—I needed air.

I rushed through the backdoors, not sure where I was going. Choosing the nearest path, I wrapped my arms around my stomach and walked, until the chatter of the hall quieted to be replaced by the soothing, subtle sounds of night. The scent of grass and night blossoms surrounded me as I slowed, and I inhaled deeply, letting the chilled air fill my lungs.

"There is nothing to fear." Zaeth's words were a whisper

from behind, but my spine straightened. "The drive to kill can be used for good."

My heart hammered in my ears. The darkness had always been there, even when we were young, ever since the storm took my parents and elder brothers from me. After facing the Fractured, I feared *that* was my destiny, a life of war and pain done at the bidding of another, but Zaeth—he spoke as if he understood what I was feeling. What I *was* and how I could use it to my advantage.

"Elara, look at me." It was a calm, steadying command and I latched onto it. "Has anything like what happened at Neith happened before? Have you had similar... impulses?"

I fidgeted with my fingers. "There was one time when Alarik and I were attacked by a few of the Fractured near my family home, but I didn't—change—the way I did in the clearing. At Neith, it was like everything went still—black but... clearer than I'd ever seen before. I knew where my enemies were before it was possible. I *felt* them—the icky filth of them." I swallowed, shaking my head. "Gods, I'm going crazy."

"Not today, love." His voice was light.

"If I'm not crazy, then what's going on? What am I? I can't be the..." I swallowed, glancing around nervously to ensure we were alone.

Understanding lit his eyes, his gaze softening, but I felt a part of him withdraw. "You need not fear the burden of being The Dark Phoenix, love."

The blood drained from my face as he spoke the title out loud. How often had that night haunted me? Forcing my breaths to remain steady, I whispered, "How can you be sure?"

Zaeth's lingering smile pulled tight. "The Phoenix is consumed with darkness and death. He is the reaper of immortals, and the creature other monsters fear. That burden does not rest on your shoulders." Zaeth stood, the fleeting vacancy in his eyes replaced by something far more mischievous. "You, love, I believe are something far more alluring."

Electric pulses kissed the air around me, my flesh peaking with the cool night air as Zaeth hovered a breath away. It felt like every nerve in my body had been lit, shimmering with warmth. The scent of him grew stronger, cedar and rain and power, coiling through me with an intensity that had me gasping for breath. It was gone in a flash, but the flush across my cheeks—the warmth between my hips—remained.

Zaeth's eyes simmered as he gazed upon me, noting my heaving chest, the rapid beating of my heart. "You are incredible, Elara. Extraordinary."

His lips quirked as if he would say more, but before he gave voice to his thoughts, his head cocked to the side.

I swallowed, willing my blood to cool as I followed his line of sight. My human eyes spotted nothing, but I knew our time together was growing short. "What am I?"

His eyes snapped back to mine. "Another time, love. It seems we are needed."

The patter of boots reached me a moment before Alarik rounded the corner, with Evander and Jarek following closely behind.

## 12
## GREER

WILL HADN'T WOKEN. LANNIE HAD LEFT ONLY LONG ENOUGH TO gather a few books, which she was currently scouring for any clues of how to control nightmares. We'd gone through dozens of books over the past few years, not once having found a remedy, but we had to try. I wanted to believe there was something out there to help our little brother... but the twisting of my gut warned we wouldn't find anything.

Jarek had been afraid—a light fae, an immortal being who had survived countless battles—he had been *afraid* of Will.

No, not of Will, but of what he'd said.

Worry knitted my brows as I brushed Will's blond curls back from his forehead. "Don't worry, little brother. We'll figure this out."

"Where is he?" El's high-pitched voice cut through the rustling of Lannie's papers. She was through the door in seconds.

"Shh," I cautioned. "He's sleeping."

Her eyes locked on Will as she sank into the bed beside him, pain and sorrow visible across her face, even in the dim light. "I should have been here. I'm so sorry—"

"Don't do that. We agreed a long time ago we wouldn't do that."

She bit her lip, but nodded. "Was it like last time?"

"Worse," I breathed, my eyes darting past El's shoulder, noting Zaeth had joined Alarik, Evander, and Jarek. No wings. No air fae. Good, there were far more important things to focus on. Sparing a glance toward our brother, I said, "Maybe we should have this discussion in your rooms?"

El's chin dipped. She pressed a kiss to his forehead before padding toward the door, her heels clutched in her hand. "Lannie, would you mind staying with him, just in case he wakes?"

Lannie hardly spared a glance up from the books before her. "I can't find anything. I don't understand it. We've done everything to treat nightmares, but they are getting worse. I just need to find the right passage—another tonic or potion—*something*."

El frowned as her eyes flicked between our brother and our younger sister. I stepped forward, my hand coming to rest on Lannie's shoulder. "Some things are out of our control. No one blames you, Lannie. I'll help you look through books tomorrow, but for now, I think it would be nice if one of us stayed beside Will. I can if you wanted to—"

"No." She sniffed, slamming the large volume shut. "I'm ready for bed, anyway."

El's frown deepened, but I stepped toward the door, linking my arm with hers before she could intervene.

"What happened?" El's voice was harsh as Jarek shut the door behind us, but I could hear the pain beneath her anger.

"A nightmare, I think, but there was no subtle build up or whimpering to let us know. He just started screaming—wailing —and then he was speaking. Or chanting. I don't know. It was Will, but not Will. And then he looked straight at Jarek..."

El's eyes snapped to the light fae. "He woke up?"

Jarek's troubled gaze held hers as he slowly shook his head. "No. He did not wake, though he did speak."

"What in gods' name does that mean?" El snapped. "Was he awake or not?"

"He was rambling. I'm sure it was nothing." The old excuse tumbled from my lips as if on reflex, but Jarek stopped me before I could continue.

"That was not *nothing*. It sounded like a vision."

Zaeth tore his gaze away from El to stare at Jarek. "A true vision?"

"I can't be sure. There hasn't been an oracle in centuries, but the words were far too specific to be a boy's dream."

"What do you mean by 'oracle?'" I asked, my stomach coiling with anticipated dread.

El turned toward the two fae, her face stoic and arms crossed. "Explain."

Alarik came to her side, brushing soothing strokes across her back, but the stiff set of her shoulder and the fierce glower she held for Zaeth didn't weaken.

He stared back at her, meeting her scowl with a cool detachment. "Oracles are thought to receive messages from the gods, mainly the goddess. They can manifest in the form of visions or sometimes dreams."

"You think Will is a conduit for the gods?" My voice rose with incredulity.

"It's one theory," Jarek said.

"The last oracle recorded walked the earth centuries ago," Zaeth added. "She delivered warnings from the goddess in an attempt to prevent the final fallout of the Merged and their fae descendants."

"The Merged have been gone for millennia," Alarik said, speaking for the first time.

Zaeth looked like he was trying hard not to roll his eyes. "The Merged no longer dominate Pax as they once did thousands of years ago, but they survived long past their society's downfall."

"What is of more concern, is the reason for an oracle." Evander's voice was low and laced with caution. "If the stories are true, oracles are blessed only in times of great need, when the goddess is desperate. What did Will say?"

"He kept saying, 'the raven will fall', over and over again." I met El's eyes. "He mentioned something about The Dark Phoenix. Lannie recorded it as soon as Will was calm."

I watched El swallow. She looked like she might faint. Zaeth didn't look much better.

Jarek stepped forward. "If you don't mind, I can repeat the words."

Giving him a small nod, I stepped back. "Thank you."

Jarek met Zaeth's eyes as he spoke, the dark fae's face devoid of emotion.

"'A raven's wings protect the realm,
 The final shield of the human's helm.
 But creatures' crushing blows shall reign,
 Shattering shelter, unleashing pain.
 Dark phoenix vengeance, harsh, unbending.
 Torment abounds, unchecked, unending.'

"He held my gaze when he warned, 'the raven must not fall.' I know it seems impossible. He's only a boy—a human boy, for that matter—but I believe him to be the voice of the goddess. Who knows what else he's seen under her guidance. I suggest we start with recorded prophecies. Track down as many as possible and see if a raven has been mentioned."

Zaeth nodded. "It will be done."

Jarek looked toward Zaeth. "Perhaps Ryuu can look into the boy? Watch him for anything suspicious—"

"Will *is* a boy," El snapped, pulling her arm away from

Alarik's soothing caresses. "He's not a subject to be studied."

"No one is saying he is," Evander soothed. "But if any of this is true, if Will has visions—"

"They're nightmares." El snarled. "Nothing more."

Silence stretched under her heated words. Zaeth was the only one brave enough to break it. "A part of you knows that is not true. If others hear Will, he could be in danger. We often fear what we do not understand. The people of this base are no different."

A piece of El's hard exterior crumbled at his words. All we wanted was for Will to be happy and safe, but how were we supposed to protect him from himself?

"What do we do?" I asked, my voice sounding small. "How do we stop this?"

Bright brown eyes met mine as Zaeth spoke. "I'm not sure. I'll speak with Ryuu tonight. He may have some answers."

"Ryuu?" El asked.

"The air fae," Zaeth said. "He isn't the most social, but if anyone has information about this, he will."

A shiver coursed through my veins at the image my mind conjured of Ryuu. Gritting my teeth, I ignored my body's response and reminded myself I knew nothing about the wretched air fae who was offended by a simple glance from me.

Clinging to the hurt and fury that burned through my veins at the recollection, I lifted my chin. "You'll share these answers before you run off to build your special army?"

Zaeth nodded. "You have my word."

"Wonderful. Now, if you please, my sisters and I have had a very long night." I stepped aside, gesturing toward the door. The men stared, unmoving. "We have no additional information at the moment, and speculating as to any number of horrible possibilities will not help anyone, least of all Will." With a pointed look and a rather large gesture toward the door, I ground out, "Goodnight, gentlemen."

## 13
## GREER

FLOUR CLOUDED THE AIR AS MY ARMS WORKED, BEATING THE thickening batter as I tossed in another handful of fresh blueberries. The staff had already prepared food for the day, leaving the entire kitchen to myself. Thank the gods. I needed this. Baking was easy. When the recipe was followed, the batch always turned out. Always.

The sweet scent of chocolate greeted me, clashing with spices and the fruity tang of my current batch of muffins. I'd planned on only one batch—chocolate chip—mostly for Will, but when they'd cooled and the dishes had been cleaned, I hadn't been ready to face the reality of what last night meant.

So, I'd started on a second batch, opting for El's favorite of apple cinnamon. The distraction hadn't lasted long enough and I'd now moved on to a third: blueberry, Lannie's first pick. She was still with Will. Gratefully, the base had taken the day off to recover from the festivities of last night, meaning there were no classes Will needed to attend or excuses that needed to be made. We had twenty-four hours to figure out our next step. Twenty-four hours to decide how to deal with this newest blow.

My arm pumped faster, the batter nearly spilling over the edge of the porcelain bowl.

Will had slept peacefully the rest of the night and had woken refreshed. He had no memory of what occurred, only a vague, blurry image of a black raven lingered, its wings stretching wide. I shook my head, adding more blueberries. He was just a boy—a long limbed, inquisitive boy that had yet to reach his ninth birthday. Why would an all-powerful goddess choose my little brother as her conduit? If it were up to me, I'd select one of those thick, well sculpted fae. One with glorious white wings flecked with brown and gilded with barbs of gold. One that had rich, dark eyes with just a hint of mossy flecks speckled throughout.

A wave of desire and longing swept through me, quickly replaced by the bitterness of rejection. Right. Ryuu had taken one look at me and snarled—*snarled*—as if he were some type of beast. My arm pumped as I mixed the batter, my speed drawing nearer to whisking than stirring. Well, Ryuu could fuck right off. I'd done nothing—nothing—to deserve that type of reception. I'd smiled at him. *Smiled* and maybe taken a step or two forward, but it wasn't like I'd draped an arm around him and insisted he join me for the evening. For him to think he's so far above me, such a powerful mighty fae, that he couldn't at least pretend to have some semblance of manners—

"Excuse me," a deep voice sounded from the doorway. "Are you Greer?"

"Who's asking?" I said, before looking up.

As if manifested from my thoughts, Ryuu stood before me.

The spoon stilled in my hand, my cheeks flushing pink as I quickly became aware of the state I was in. I was clad in a tank-top and shorts, hair thrown into a disheveled bun on the top of my head. I'd only gotten a few hours' sleep the night before— gods, I hadn't even put an apron on—and here he was just as beautiful as I remembered. His bronzed skin was a few shades darker than it'd appeared at night, and his long black hair had an almost indigo hue to it in the sunlight, but his eyes—those charmingly sinful eyes sprinkled with traces of a deep forest green—were the same. And they were just as judgmental as they had been last time—hard and cold, with a hint of defiance.

"My name is Ryuu."

Lifting my chin, I resumed mixing. "Can I help you?" There was no need for pretense and I didn't bother to hide the sourness of my voice.

His eyes narrowed, but he took a few strides forward, his wings tucked in close, until he stood before me. "That looks plenty mixed to me."

The wooden spoon I held clattered against the mixing bowl as my hands landed on the swell of my hips. The blueberries had, indeed, been pulverized. "I didn't ask for your opinion."

"Consider it an observation."

Brushing a few curls away from my face, I narrowed my eyes. "Is that why you're here? To offer useless *observations*?"

The flecks of green flared a little brighter as his lips pressed thin. "My—Zaeth sent me to inform you of your brother's condition."

All of the tension left me, replaced by a soul-deep, icy fear. I whipped around the counter to face him. "Will? Did something happen? Is he okay?"

Ryuu took a step back with a pained look on his face, as if he couldn't stand to be an inch closer to me. My stomach twisted.

"I don't have time for this. I need to see my brother." The words rushed from me in an angry mutter as I headed for the door.

"Wait. Your brother is fine."

Relief flitted through me, but my anger was back in seconds as I spun to face him. "You should have started with that! You can't just burst in here acting like a complete ass, telling me you have news of my brother with a twisted look of sickness and pain on your face, and then expect me to assume everything is fine."

Ryuu had the decency to look chagrined, his wings bristling. "I'm sorry. It's just you're..."

Exacerbated, I waved off his excuse. "As shocking as this may sound, your opinion of me is not something I care about." Not true, but he didn't need to know that. "What news do you have of my brother?"

He stiffened, but answered. "I spoke with him this morning. He has only vague memories of the vision occurring last night."

I gritted my teeth. "Yes, I made sure he was safe before I left. Have you discovered anything new?"

"Based on the description from Jarek and the recorded words from your younger sister, it appears to be consistent with what we know of oracles. He would be the youngest one and the first known human, but unless a different entity is filling his head with knowledge, we must assume these visions are coming from the goddess."

I felt the blood leave my face. "I'm going to deny the possibility of some unknown creature having access to my little brother's mind and go with the best, least terrifying option. These visions are not meant to harm him, right?"

Ryuu shook his head. "Not intentionally. They are only meant to impart information."

Narrowing my eyes, I recalled the sounds of Will's screams, so reminiscent of the day the storm hit—echoing my elder brothers' cries in the days before they died. Swallowing, I forced the question from my lips. "What exactly does being an oracle mean? Will the visions get worse?"

I must have truly been exhausted, because I could have sworn a flicker of sorrow flashed across Ryuu's stoic scowl a moment before smoothing out. "I'm not sure. My kingdom will have more information on the matter. The air fae still strongly believe in the ancient prophecies. I was raised hearing various versions of them, but I have to admit, even I have not heard of 'the raven' Will spoke of."

My chest fell. "So, we think he's an oracle, but have no idea what he's speaking of or how the visions will affect a human. Great."

"We know it's vital we keep this quiet. Some will view him as a direct link to the goddess while others will doubt his authenticity. He'd be seen as a false visionary, a threat to the royals' power. Even in the Air Kingdom, he will be met with skepticism."

Pinching the bridge of my nose, I inhaled deeply. "So, not only do we have no understanding of how this will progress, but we also have to keep it a secret because his life could be in danger from superstitious zealots?"

Ryuu gave a curt nod.

I exhaled. "Okay. Well, at least we won't have to worry about anyone finding out. It's happened twice and he's only had visions during the night. He should be able to continue life as normal."

Ryuu's head cocked to the side. "For now."

"Really?" I snapped, rolling my eyes. "Was the 'for now' necessary? I am already terrified for my little brother, knowing there's nothing I can do to prevent or change the situation, and you feel the need to add a foreboding comment like that?" Ryuu flinched, but I'd had enough of him. "Gods, it's like you can't help yourself. Do you have anything non-anxiety-provoking to add?"

"I won't be able to return to my kingdom for some time. I am required at Fort Dhara to oversee training. The Fractured are growing stronger and we have yet to stop an attack since Neith."

I narrowed my eyes. "The fate of the realm takes priority over my brother's life?" It wasn't quite a question, but he surprised me with an answering shake of his head.

"A life of an innocent is never the last priority. The life of a possible oracle even less so."

"I would think any innocent would be as cherished as the next."

"They are. That's not what I'm saying—"

"What, exactly, are you saying?"

The pupils of his eyes narrowed ever so slightly.. "I'm saying, though I am unable to make the trip myself, I will be sending a trusted messenger to retrieve documents that may be of use. Your brother will be protected."

He held my gaze as he spoke the vow, as if willing me to believe him. I wanted to, gods did I want to, but the weight which had settled in the pit of my stomach refused to lighten.

# 14
# ELARA

"I understand you have a lot going on, but It would've been nice having a warning before the fae showed up." I watched as Alarik added the last few items to his pack. They'd decided to leave at dusk, deeming it safer to move under the cover of night.

"It wasn't like I was keeping it a secret, but seeing as you're not going, you didn't need to know."

I grimaced. "About that. What did you mean when you said I'd have to start with basic training? I passed that mark ages ago."

Alarik didn't bother turning around as he slung the thick brown strap of the pack over his shoulder, before leaning it against the door. "You've been dealing with post-battle paranoia."

"Paranoia?"

He shrugged. "Lingering fear. Residual stress. It's very common. When it occurs, we start with the basics and slowly work our way up, making sure to look for triggers."

"I don't need that," I retorted, the words coming out harsher than I intended. He turned, meeting my frown with a lifted brow. Taking a deep breath, I forced my tone to soften. "Jumping back into battle will help me. I'm restless. I need to move and respond—without restraint."

"No." The word was quiet but it thundered through the room.

"What?" I asked, because surely I couldn't have heard him correctly.

"I said no, El. Trauma from battle is not something to take lightly. You could feel fine, but a certain swing of a blade, a specific smell, or even an unknown sound could send you right back to that dark place."

The air released from my chest, deflated by a single word— but I *wasn't* traumatized. He needed to understand that. Swallowing back a wave of nausea at what his response would be, I took his hand in my own. "It's not fear of fighting that's kept me away, Alarik. It's not even grief for Zelos. I thought I was turning into one of the Fractured, but I'm not. Lannie confirmed it's not possible"

His shoulders pulled back as the silence stretched. Finally, he spoke. "Why would you think that?"

"Because I was different at Neith... or more myself than I've ever been." I shook my head, willing the words to come. "War is a part of me. It was exhilarating, and terrifying, and being so close to death made me feel alive. I didn't realize that before, but know now. It's probably the same for you."

His head tilted to the side, weighing my words. "War *is* a part of who I am. I understand the necessity of it and respect its intricacies, but I've never enjoyed taking lives."

My stomach twisted under his piercing gaze. When I didn't speak, he added, "That trait belongs to the dark fae."

Flashes of conversation with Zaeth played through my mind from the Litha celebration, coiling my unease further. "I'm not a dark fae," I gritted out between clenched teeth.

Alarik's eyes narrowed slightly.

An incredulous huff escaped me. "You're seriously considering this?"

"Aren't you?"

"No," I snapped. "I would know if I were fae. My parents would've told me—they would've *been* fae. And incase you don't remember, they died in the storm alongside the rest of the humans. Not one pure-blooded fae died from its magic."

He frowned. "True. And bloodlust is a rare trait, beholden only to dark royals and very powerful bloodlines."

"I don't have an excuse for being drawn to the darkness. I'm exhausted with trying to find one, and to be honest, I don't need to explain myself." The words were out in a rush, and when I inhaled my next breath, the pressure that had been banding across my chest had eased. "Do you see now?"

*Do you see me?*

"You still need to integrate into the ranks slowly." I blink as Alarik pushed past me, reaching for his boots. "There are protocols in place for a reason—"

"You can't be serious."

"I assure you, I am." His voice was sharp, cutting. "I won't allow you to throw yourself into a situation you're not ready for. You decided to take a break for a reason—"

"Because I thought I was becoming a monster—"

"I'm happy you're ready to rejoin, but we need to do this safely. If not for your sake, then for the men. If I sent you into the field and something triggered you, you'd be..." He shook his head, biting down on his words.

"I'd be an asset," I said, fists clenching.

"You'd be a liability."

His words ripped through me, cutting off any further protests. To him, I already *was* a liability.

Alarik sighed, running a hand through his hair. "Vidarr will be staying behind to see to the base in my absence. He'll help you realclimate."

I forced my gaze to hold his, ignoring the urge to blink around the burn of tears.

"Maybe the distance between us is a good thing. I know you've been really worried about Will and there's a lot going on with the base..."

My eyes widened as his words registered, but the more I thought about it, the better it sounded. "Maybe it is. Maybe space is what we need."

He was right. We had never been each other's focus. My need for battle wasn't a hobby I'd develop to pass the time. It was something ingrained in me, a visceral urging that allowed me to protect my family. By ignoring it, by letting fear get the better of me, I'd only served to weaken myself, and the defense of those I strove to protect.

Alarik knew war well, but we understood it differently. He'd made it clear my attraction to death was not normal—not human.

*What am I?*

I'd once asked Zaeth that very question. He'd assured me I wasn't the Dark Phoenix.

*"You, love, I believe are something far more alluring."*

I'd sought Alarik's understanding, but perhaps he wasn't the one I should be speaking with.

"Space," Alarik said, holding my gaze a moment longer before pressing a kiss to the top of my head and walking out the door.

## 15
## GREER

HAVING JUST RETURNED FROM DELIVERING ANOTHER BATCH OF baked goods to the town below, I placed the empty wicker basket on the desk opposite my bed. Food continued to serve as a nice distraction from the cravings that plagued me night and day for a certain air fae. He'd been gone a week, and though we'd barely spoken, I found myself longing for the brute.

I glanced at the clock, contemplating meeting up with El, but she'd probably be training with Vidarr, as she was every moment she could secure with him. I'd barely seen her this past week. When Vidarr wasn't swinging blades at her, she was galloping through the forest, shooting targets from Ember's back, or running through the trees on her own.

Gratefully, Will hadn't had further nightmares—visions, I reminded myself—since the night of the ball. Lannie used it as an opportunity to immerse herself in research. The black substance from the Fractured hadn't bonded to any of the fae samples she'd received, which included dark, earth, and light fae. She was running a few more tests, but Jarek agreed all known spells of that magnitude required the host's consent.

Frantic pounding sounded against my door, snapping me from my thoughts. I opened it to find a pale-looking boy.

"Are you Greer?" His chest heaved as he fought to catch his breath.

"Yes. What's wrong?"

"Healer Lannie asked me to find you. There's a baby coming. The woman—I think her name is Lucy—she's screaming and, and *leaking*—"

I exhaled, relieved Will was safe. "Lucy went into labor?" The calmness of my voice surprised me and steadied the frantic boy.

He nodded.

"Did my sister say she needed anything? Any supplies?"

He shook his head. "She only told me to find you. She said she needs your help."

I followed after him as he dashed down the stairs and wove through the base. The healing quarters were close and I soon heard Lucy's wails echoing through the halls. I prayed to the gods she and the babe would be safe. Pulling my hair back into a chaotic curly bun, I pushed through the doors of the infirmary.

"You're doing great, Luce. Focus on your breathing." Liam was sitting beside a kneeling Lucy, her hands braced on the sheets in front of her. She shot him a glare between locks of damp blonde hair, as if to say, 'you do it then, if you're such an expert.'

"Or just do what you feel is best," Liam added, rubbing small circles across her back.

Lannie looked up, smock in place. "There's extra supplies over there." She pointed to the nearest wall. I dressed quickly before coming to her side.

"Hi, Lucy. I meant to stop in before now, but—" My lame explanation was cut short by another guttural cry.

"We'll catch up on the formalities later," Lannie cut in calmly. "Lucy is in active labor. She's fully dilated and ready to push."

As if on command, I could see a mat of dark hair cresting

between her thighs. "Gods," I breathed, taking a place beside Lannie.

"What?" Panic filled Liam's voice. "What is it?"

"Nothing is wrong," Lannie soothed in a professional tone, shooting me an annoyed look. "The baby is nearly here. The head is visible."

"Does everything look okay?" Lucy panted, her breaths coming in short bursts.

"Yes," I answered. "It looks like the baby has Liam's hair."

She whimpered an excited, tired laugh, meeting Liam's gaze with love in her eyes. She groaned a moment later. "Another one is coming."

"You can do this, Luce," Liam encouraged.

"When you feel the pressure increase, I want you to push for ten straight seconds," Lannie instructed.

Lucy's screams picked up moments later, delivering a small head. Lannie reached for a suction, clearing the nasal passages and mouth seconds before Lucy was pushing again, this time dislodging a pair of shoulders. It was quick after that, the baby sliding free with a trailing cord behind. Lucy rolled, gathering the baby against her chest as a small wail tore through the room.

Liam burst into tears with the sound, pressing kisses to his wife's forehead. "She's beautiful, Luce. Just like her mother."

Lucy shook with happy, relieved tears as she held her daughter, the infant kicking and crying a moment longer, before latching. Lannie tied the cord in two places as the infant nursed, ensuring the blood vessels at each end were secured, and then offered Liam a sharpened pair of scissors.

He uttered the blessings of the gods as he worked the blades through the thick tissue.

"Towels." Lannie's voice drew my attention. There was some blood, but it looked to be slowing. Lucy's stomach contracted again, triggering a groan of pain from her.

"What's happening," Lucy asked. "Is that normal?"

"Yes." Lannie's voice rang with reassurance. "Your body is preparing to deliver the placenta." A thick circle of vessels and tissue came into view, bringing with it a fresh wave of blood. Lannie gathered it, inspecting the placenta with the skilled eye of a healer.

"It's intact," she breathed, relief breaking through her calm control for the first time. I helped her with towels, replacing the saturated ones for fresh ones as the bleeding continued to slow and finally stopped.

Liam looked up. "Is that it?"

Lucy shot him a glare but Lannie's musical laugh cut through the tension. "Yes. The placenta has been delivered and the bleeding has stopped. It will take a few weeks to recover. Bleeding and even some clots are normal, but it shouldn't be continuous. I've blocked this side of the infirmary and would like you two to stay for at least a few nights to ensure your recovery goes well. We also need to make sure your daughter is eating and recovering herself, though based on how well she latched, it seems she will do just fine."

Lucy beamed at Lannie. "Thank you."

"You did all of the hard work. We'll give you three some privacy and check back in a few hours."

I followed Lannie, both of us removing the smocks and depositing them in a bin before leaving the room.

"That went well. Lucy and the baby are perfectly healthy."

"For now," Lannie said. "We need to make sure it stays that way. The first weeks of life are the roughest, at least in terms of long-term survival. From what I've been able to research, if the baby thrives in the first three months, meaning gains weight and develops normally, their lives are not claimed."

My smile wavered. "And if she doesn't?"

Lannie grimaced. "Let's just make sure she does. I've already settled on an alternative milk supply, and have sent word into town to see if there are any women with experience in infant care able to help should the need arise—all done with Lucy's permission, of course."

We turned down another passage, arriving at Lannie's office, the place as messy as ever. She took a seat at her desk, leaving me on the couch with the rumpled blanket.

"You were incredible," I breathed, sinking into the sofa cushions after tossing the knitted blanket over the armrest. "It was like you'd delivered hundreds of babies before."

She straightened up at that. "You really think so? I've assisted Healer Grant on two previous deliveries. One of the infants was stillborn, but the other is doing well. I sent word when I realized Lucy was so close to her date, but it seems he is still attempting to contact other healers in the Light Kingdom." A frown tugged on her lips. "He should be returning soon, or, at the very least, be sending word. I'm just glad we'll have happy news to report."

"I take it you'll be spending the next few weeks here to monitor the baby?"

Lannie nodded. "It's not ideal. I would like Liam, Lucy, and the babe to return to Alarik's residence as soon as possible to minimize exposure to others while the baby is most vulnerable to infection. And I need the infirmary to treat wounded soldiers. The attacks haven't slowed, despite the base remaining unscathed. I've moved most to the second floor, but if another riot breaks out at Neith, or an additional nearby town is attacked, I'll need all the beds we have."

I frowned. I'd heard of humans growing restless, masses of them spurred on by frustration and fear into attacking peaceful towns where fae and humans resided together, but I hadn't wanted to believe it. El told us about a rogue wild fae, Alderidge, posing as a human and instigating prejudices throughout the Borderlands. I'd hoped humans would see through the ploy, especially after he was exposed as an ally to the Fractured, but it seemed even the people of Sonder were lost in their anger.

"I can return tomorrow morning, if you'd like the extra help. I wouldn't mind staying the night, but figured with El diving into training again..."

"You'll need to stay with Will," Lannie finished. "She's been really intense since Alarik left. Vidarr even came to see me. He had bruises all along his ribs. I thought a horse had kicked him at first, but he assured me it was only Elara. *Only Elara*, as if the damage would somehow be less frightening." Lannie shook her head, the adrenaline from delivery giving way to worry for our sister.

"I'll check on her. She's probably trying to prove she can handle everything, but I am *not* getting up before she goes running, again. The sun hadn't even risen. I mean, really. There's a line that shouldn't be crossed."

Lannie laughed. "Agreed. You can try to catch her before bed. She's been arriving late, but without Alarik to distract her, she's mostly—"

"Reading. I browsed her collection yesterday, sure there'd be something with a bit of spice, but all the books pertained to war."

Lannie snorted. "You two and your romance novels."

I shrugged, letting my smile show. "I'll try to catch her before she starts another textbook tonight. I mean, it's just reading. I can interrupt that, right?"

Lannie leaned into her chair, a wary look on her face. "You can try."

Rolling my eyes, I started for the hall. "If you don't hear from me by dinner tomorrow, send someone to recover my body."

~

Summer was in full bloom and I let my hair down as I strolled through the base, enjoying the feel of my messy curls hanging loose to fan around me. It felt nice to feel the heat of the sun's rays across my cheeks, the subtle breeze keeping the worst of the humidity at bay as it swirled wayward silver stands around my shoulders.

The sounds of men training and the subtle prattle of apprentices having just ended their classes greeted me as I made my way through the base. Gentle rumblings from the town below reached up and, not for the first time, I marveled at it—at the simplicity of this base, this town. Beautiful moments of peace were captured here.

Rounding the corner, putting me on a direct path to Will's class, the subtle conversations mingling through the air turned sharper, concern cutting through the monotonous rhythm of the day. A coil of dread spooled in my stomach as my eyes fixed on a group of boys surrounding something thrashing on the ground. I just made out blond curls and a contorting, writhing body moments before his screams reached me.

"Will." His name was a dreaded confirmation of what was happening—and *where* it was happening. I dashed to his side, pushing through the swarm of scared boys. Turning toward the closest one, I forced my voice to remain calm. "Do you know who Lieutenant Vidarr is?"

The boy shook his head, eyes glued to Will's balled up form. My brother's hands were pressed tight to his ears, his head shaking as if trying to block out a thundering voice, but the only sounds were of his ragged, too-shallow breaths amid wails of pain.

"I do," another in the crowd answered. "I'll get him."

Will's screaming quieted, reverting to mumbled whispers as his body crumpled in on itself. I leaned down, tentatively reaching out. "Will? Can you hear me?"

His lips moved frantically with unintelligible words, his eyes yet to open. With my knees pressing into the packed dirt beside him, I brought my ear close, stroking back the wet, matted curls across his damp brow. The blood drained from my face as the whispers shifted into audible, haunted words—this was another vision.

"The three have returned.
   The raven will fall.
   They are coming."

"Will. Will, wake up." My voice was sharpened by panic. "Will, please, just open your eyes."

Vidarr pushed through the inner ring, scooping Will up, and sprinted toward Alarik's residence. My legs moved of their own accord, only a few steps behind them as we ascended the stairs and entered Will's room. Vidarr gently laid him in bed, the lines of Will's face already smooth. He was asleep once more.

"What happened?" Vidarr demanded. "The boy said Will grabbed his head, fell, and then started screaming and writhing on the ground."

The raw concern in Vidarr's voice sliced through me, but my gaze remained fixed on my brother. "I'm not sure. I was walking to meet him when I saw the group. It sounded like one of his nightmares. But that's impossible. There's no way he was sleeping."

"These are *not* nightmares, lass. He spoke of the raven again and The Dark Phoenix. It's not a coincidence."

My voice was little more than hushed breath as my mind reeled. "Gods, it's really true. He said they—the visions—could progress, that they weren't supposed to hurt the oracle, but Will is human and Ryuu said only fae have been oracles. He said the visions wouldn't hurt him, but this…"

Vidarr's voice was grim when he answered. "What young Will is experiencing, it can't be anything other than visions."

"What does this mean?" I breathed, barely finding the courage to voice the question.

A long sigh emitted from him before Vidarr turned to face me. "Did Ryuu explain what would happen if others discovered the truth about Will?"

The hairs on the back of my neck pricked and I drew my arms around myself to prevent the shiver from taking hold. "Some would praise him, consider him a speaker of the gods, while others…"

Vidarr gave a tight nod. "I'll send a messenger to Fort Dhara letting Alarik and the others know what happened. I know Will loves his classes, but it might be best if we kept him secluded for a few days, just until things die down."

"And if they don't? What's to stop him from having another vision? This time it was outside his class on a relatively quiet road, but what if it happens in the dining hall or in the forum?"

I took a seat on the bed beside my little brother. We'd spent so many nights like this, waiting along the edge of the bed for him to wake, for the currents of his mind to still. His ninth birthday was looming near, but he was still so young. Will should be running through the forest with other children, splashing through shallow streams, climbing trees, basking in the wild, reverent place between toddler and puberty. He shouldn't have to worry about visions—about the fate of the world. He shouldn't have to worry whether his friends would look upon him with fear.

"I'll send a messenger right away to tell the base that Will has had a terrible headache. I'm fairly certain the visions were spoken too low for others to hear, but I'll be on the watch for any talk."

I nodded. "Thank you."

"No need to thank me, lass." He frowned, stepping toward the door. "I'll send Lannie in to see him."

16

ELARA

I SPLASHED A HANDFUL OF COLD WATER OVER MY FACE, WASHING away the last vestiges of sleep before meeting my reflection in the mirror. It had been over a week since Will's last vision. Lannie had drafted half a dozen teas since then, most of which were ineffective, but the latest one seemed to be working. She'd listed various herbs in the tea, going as far as explaining how long it took for each element to stabilize possible causes for nightmares, but it all came down to Will not being able to resume lessons for at least another week. By then, we would know if the visions were controlled.

Tying my hair back, I moved toward my armoire, stepping over books and weapons as I went, to reach for the pair of worn running shoes tossed in the corner. They were covered with bits of dried mud, the flakes of which littered the surrounding floor. I was proud of how quickly I'd broken in the new pair, of the subtle visible proof of my regained independence.

We'd made the most of the situation by having Will join me each day for training. Vidarr used the first ten minutes to explain basic maneuvers, both for Will's benefit and to satisfy Alairk's condition for my return, but we'd spend the rest of the time testing my limits. I'd told Will he could watch until he grew weary of it. He'd yet to leave a session early.

It had been nearly two weeks since Alarik left. Two weeks of sleeping alone... and for the first time in a long time, that loneliness felt an awful lot like freedom.

I'd extended my morning runs, letting the fairy creatures guide me along harsher, more challenging trails. Playful flower sprites and summer pixies kept pace with me as I wove through lush summer trees and when I tired of running, I'd circle back toward the stables to unleash Ember, running through the archery course until I was skilled enough to complete it in my sleep. I'd even dared to explore past the outer walls of the base, enjoying the feel of wildflowers beneath my head, their petals warmed by streams of the summer sun.

It felt nice, not trying to deny the darker parts of myself. Training didn't nullify the urge to hunt down the red-eyed commander and every last Fractured under his control, but it did take the edge off. My body burned with the pain of overworked muscles every night, helping to drown out the restlessness of my mind. I was honing my skills, biding my time until I could strike, until I could exterminate the plague ravishing this world once and for all.

I jogged past the buildings of the base, inhaling deeply as I increased my pace along the swell of trees before me.

At least Lucy and the babe were safe. Cold relief washed through me at the happy news of her birth and the remainder of my fears had fled last night when I'd visited the new family. Lannie confirmed the babe was already gaining weight, a good indication her health would remain strong. Liam was beside himself, grinning despite the dark circles beneath his eyes, courtesy of the babe waking every few hours to feed. Lucy had told him he could sleep, but he insisted on being present for every second of their child's little life. They were safe. They were happy... but so many others had not been dealt the same fate.

I edged around a curve into the thickening forest, my jog turning into a run, as my mind drifted back to Will and the precarious position he was now in. Hopefully, this new tea Lannie created would last, but if it failed... I didn't want to consider what that meant for my little brother.

Will's visions may be granted from the goddess, but Pax wouldn't need saving if it weren't for the commander and his army of twisted souls—if it weren't for Alderidge and creatures like him. They were the reason Will was experiencing gut-wrenching headaches and immeasurable fear. I intended to see them pay for the suffering they'd brought upon him.

All of them.

Every last one of the Fractured, Alderidge, and above all, their red-eyed commander who thought himself conqueror of this world. I wanted to hunt him down, and like a hawk toying with a mouse, torture him slowly for the attacks orchestrated across the seven kingdoms, for my elder brothers, my parents, for the countless children who'd resided in the villages he'd destroyed—villages now drenched in blood and rendered to ash. I wanted the commander's suffering to be unrivaled. Infinite. Before I wrenched the last breath from his lungs.

My feet pounded the earth, rushing past gnarled roots and jutting stones, all of which seemed to want to drag me back to the base, back to the person who strove to stand alongside the hero. But not all of us get to walk a path bathed in light. I knew now that to defeat the monsters I needed to embrace the shadows; I needed to become something ruthless enough for the monsters to fear.

I lost myself to the burn building in my muscles as my legs pumped faster. Air scorched my heaving lungs, complying with my body's demand for oxygen as I tested its limits. I needed this. The numbness that came with pushing my boundaries. Pumping my arms, I neared the bend in the road that would bring me back to the stables. I must have set a new record.

The shimmer of iridescent wings caught my eye as I neared the bend. Summer sprites wove in and out of the forest parallel to the path, waiting to see what I would do. With a smile, I met their challenging smirks and veered left, pushing through the overgrown vegetation onto a path not regularly traveled.

~

A giant pair of snowy-white wings dotted with brown flecks and the glint of gold greeted me as I entered my room, Ryuu. Half of his long dark hair was pulled back with a leather strap, his arms crossed over his wide chest, the thin gray material of his shirt stretching over defined muscle. He was attractive, if not for the stoic glare of his dark eyes.

"Where have you been?" Ryuu rumbled in a low growl.

"Don't you speak to my sister that way," Greer snapped, her shrill voice cutting through my answering silence. Her smaller frame stepped out from the fae's shadow as she darted to my side, a vicious scowl firmly in place. "I told you El would return when she was ready. You had every opportunity to speak to me, but chose to stand there, instead."

"I was aware of the alternative..." His eyes traveled the length of her body, trailing up until he met her eyes, holding her gaze a moment longer before dismissing her with an indifferent turn of his head. "And chose to wait."

Greer's shorter, curvy form squared up to his larger, harder one, her voice laced with warning. "I am not your inferior and I damn well will not be made to feel like it. I don't know what your problem is, but I've done nothing to earn the attention of your asshole tendencies. Whatever happened to make you such a miserable person has nothing to do with me. Or my family. You will treat us like the living, breathing people we are, complete with the respect entitled to us—to any person. If you cannot muster at least a shred of decency in that poisoned, calloused heart of yours, then leave."

Judging by the intensity of his glare, Ryuu must have expected Greer to back down. She didn't. After a few more seconds of the two of them standing off, the air fae managed a tight nod before turning to me. "Zaeth sent me to collect you and your brother. You are to join us."

I blinked. "Why is Will involved in this?"

"It will be safer for him away from the others. Only a few dozen warriors are at the fort, all of whom have been approved by myself or Zaeth. If any were to overhear a prophecy, they will not fear him. He will be honored."

"He doesn't need to be honored. He needs to be a boy—to be safe," Greer said, the anger in her voice doing little to mask her concern.

"It makes sense," I said. her eyes snapped to mine. "Will is missing classes, and his friends have already started asking questions. The town is mere blocks from here. If word got out... there would be no stopping the rumors."

She flinched but conceded.

"We must go," Ryuu said, avoiding Greer's glare. "I wish to leave within the hour."

Greer snorted, muttering something about unrealistic fae expectations, but my heart was fluttering with hope, processing the information quicker than my brain could. I shook my head, willing it to move faster.

"Alarik approved this?"

Ryuu shifted his stance, wings twitching. "Zaeth insisted. Alarik is aware of the change in plans and has agreed to the new terms."

I stood there a moment, stunned, then Greer was there, steering me toward the bathroom.

"This does not concern you," Ryuu snapped.

Greer drew herself up, hands coming to her waist as venom

dripped from her words. "My sister requires a shower before gallivanting across the kingdoms. Will you let us pass or are you insinuating this Zaeth guy wanted you to throw her over your shoulder and deliver her immediately like the brute you're acting like? Or perhaps you mean to say he expected you to help her with even the most basic of needs, including bathing?"

I could have sworn the bronzed skin along Ryuu's cheeks deepened as he glared.

"Is that a 'no'? Good. Then, I expect you to get out of the way. Now."

Ryuu's nostrils flared as his jaw clenched, but he stepped back, retreating to the fireplace with a growl as Greer slammed the bathroom door shut behind us. She turned on the shower knobs, the rush of running water affording us as much privacy as we would get with fae ears lurking in the adjourning room.

"El, are you okay? I know things between you and Alarik have been strained."

Exhaling a long breath, I turned, leaning against the cool counter, slick from the moisture in the air. Alarik was right. We'd needed time apart, but I couldn't deny that I missed him. He'd been the first person I'd opened up to outside of my family, and I missed his companionship.

"I am okay," I said. "Alarik and I have different views on war, but our goals are the same. We both want to put an end to the Fractured. It will be nice to see him again."

She was quiet a long moment, seeing much more than I thought possible before answering. "I won't pretend to understand what you feel, but those creatures don't deserve your remorse. They've killed thousands of humans, including children and infants who were not yet old enough to stand. Maybe you don't regret your actions because they are not something to regret."

"You sound like Zaeth," I said.

"Maybe Zaeth is right." She shrugged.

"Maybe he is," I mused.

"Either way, you need to shower. That giant oaf out there won't wait forever. I'll pack your things before starting on my own. I assume you'll want all the gear and weapons you have?"

"Yes. Wait, did you just say, 'your things'?"

"Well, yes. Someone will need to stay with Will. Lannie won't be able to leave Lucy and the babe for some time, and the base needs her while Healer Grant is still in the Light Kingdom. You'll be training with the men, so that leaves me."

"Thanks, Greer." A ghost of a smile reached my lips. "I'll wash quickly. Try your best not to kill Ryuu while I shower."

"Ha. I make no promises."

# 17

# GREER

STEELING MYSELF TO FACE HIM, I RETURNED TO THE SITTING room. A pair of obsidian eyes spotted with flashes of forest-green stalked my every move with not-so-subtle loathing. Why did I have to be attracted to such an asshole?

I'd been denied before, like any other; mostly for my figure. My body seemed to be something coveted *and* scorned. The same curves which earned me attention at far too young of an age were the very thing men judged me for. The swell of my hips and my overly full bust were relished, but the accompanying softness of my stomach was not.

There was no winning this game, not if I allowed my happiness—my own self-satisfaction—to be determined by another's opinion. I had long since decided to love myself—to love each dimple and divot of my skin, to be proud of the roundness of my hips and know that I was every bit as worthy of love as the next person.

It had been liberating, realizing they couldn't take my self-worth from me. I'd vowed never to let another's opinion of me matter and I had kept that vow, never growing too attached, until now. But here I was, openly rejected by this arrogant air fae, and as much as I hated to admit it... it hurt. He'd been the first man I'd been drawn to in a while... and he completely despised me.

Rolling my eyes under his scrutiny, I stepped forward. "What could I have possibly done in the last five minutes to earn such a glare."

I pushed past him to gather El's belongings, the tips of feathers caressing me as I did. The subtle contact sent a wave of sensual warmth through my body. I shuddered.

His low growl sounded, cooling the heat swirling in my veins.

"And what is with the growling?" I snapped, not bothering to face him. "It's rude. If you have something to say, then by all means, say it." I prayed he didn't notice the blush rising to my cheeks as I sorted through bundles of clothing. Another tension-filled moment passed in silence. With a huff, I turned. "Well?"

His dark eyes peered back at me as he closed the distance between us. Swallowing, I fought the urge to take a step back, fought to keep the scowl on my face, and to conceal how my pulse raced as his massive wings unfurled, stirring the air with traces of earth and the subtle hints of mist hovering across great mountain peaks.

Gods, he smelled incredible. There was something wild about him. Something that promised adventure. I found the courage to hold my ground and resisted inhaling his scent further, but I couldn't stop the way my breathing hitched. He missed nothing, his pupils shifting as he tracked every move-ment of my body, every subtle shift.

I welcomed that attention. Desired it. Needed it.

If I leaned in, what would he do? Would he capture my lips with his? Would they taste as delicious as they looked?

I didn't think Ryuu was the type of man to be soft. Every-thing about him spoke of freedom, of doing what he wanted when he wanted. He'd sooner rip out my heart and take to the skies without a second thought than to return any feelings for me. I knew that, and yet... I chanced a look up, needing to see if he was struggling as much as I was. It wasn't lust I found, or even the angry gaze I'd been expecting, but something oddly close to fear flickering within his eyes.

The bathroom door squeaked, snapping our attention to a damp-haired El. Ryuu stepped back abruptly, nearly causing me to fall forward, before mumbling something about waiting in the hall. He was gone in a flash.

El paused, noting my flushed cheeks and Ryuu's swift absence. "Gods, Greer. What did you do to the poor guy?"

I stood there for a moment longer, too stunned to talk—that, in itself, was alarming. "I don't know. He just—" A strangled huff of air escaped my lungs as I fought for words. "He just drives me crazy. I swear I've never hated someone as much as I do that winged bastard," my eyes glanced toward the door as my voice lowered, "but seconds ago, I wanted to kiss him!"

"You kissed him?" El practically choked on the words.

I shot her a glare, jerking my head toward the door where Ryuu stood watch. "I said I *wanted* to kiss him," I whispered, "which is ridiculous because I hate him. It's a good thing too, because he'd sooner kill me than kiss me."

El's face softened with a knowing look. "I wouldn't think much of it. Besides, I thought you hated him."

"I do hate him!" I raked a hand through my mane of curls, causing them to spiral further out of control as I plopped across her bed. I sighed. "Do you really think this is what's best for Will?"

El finished getting dressed before meeting my gaze. "I do. We can't protect him here. There are too many people. Besides, he's enjoyed watching me train; can you imagine how excited he's going to be when he gets to observe the fae?"

That brought a smile to my face. "True. What about you?"

"I'm eager to learn. It would be nice testing myself against the fae."

"Maybe even a specific dark fae?" I asked, curious to see her response.

She bit her bottom lip as she nodded. It seemed I wasn't the only one vexed by a fae.

## 18
## GREER

"WHERE IS WILL?" RYUU ASKED, ARMS CROSSED OVER HIS BROAD chest as he stood against the far end of the hall, looking as if he couldn't wait to escape.

"He's with Lannie," I said, my voice unusually soft after our almost-kiss.

He started toward the door as we neared, making a sweeping gesture without turning. "Leave your things here. I will collect them before we go. First, we must secure your brother."

Pausing only long enough to ensure we complied, Ryuu turned toward the healing quarters. As much as I disliked him, Ryuu was determined to keep Will safe. Because of that, I'd put up with him for as long as necessary. That didn't mean I wouldn't have fun knocking him down a peg or two when his inflated ego required it.

We entered the building, weaving our way through halls until the subtle sounds of a baby cooing could be heard. A smile graced my lips as we entered the infirmary, now part nursery, which stretched into a wide grin as my eyes landed on Liam doting over his small daughter.

He was beaming when he looked up, every bit the proud

father, as the small bundle squirmed in his arms. "Lucy has just gone to shower. I'm afraid you've missed her."

"That's okay," I said, hovering over his shoulder to gaze at the new life.

"Lucy is doing well." Lannie's voice carried across the room as she entered with Will following close behind. "There's only the expected amount of bleeding and there have been no signs of infection. The babe is growing like a weed. She's been exceeding expectations."

Liam's smile grew. "She is rather remarkable. So like her mother."

"She's strong," El confirmed as the babe's hand closed around one of her fingers in a fierce hold. "With a grip like that, she'll be right at home among the soldiers." The baby cooed. "We'll have such fun training together, won't we?"

Liam snorted. "Don't you go planning my daughter's future when she's only weeks into this world. There will be plenty of time for Aunt Elara to corrupt her when she's older."

El's face softened, her lips parting slightly in wonder. "Aunt Elara?"

He shrugged, opening his mouth to speak, but Will bolted forward, eyes bright with excitement. "Does that mean I'm an uncle?"

A light laugh left Liam's lips as he met Will's eager gaze. "I suppose that does, if you're up for the task."

"I am," Will said, puffing up his chest. "I'll protect her with my life."

"That's a bit dramatic," Lannie pipped in, replenishing a stack of folded cloths and pins beside Liam. "The base is well protected and she is gaining strength. No need to worry about her life, just yet."

Will gave a single nod, his features composed in rare seriousness. "When the time comes for her to leave, I'll do my best to protect her, as any uncle would. I vow it."

A smile hovered along Liam's lips, mirroring my own, but he masked it before Will could see. "I appreciate your vow, William. We are honored to have your protection."

Will's face broke into a smile as he settled into the seat beside Liam, returning to the playful boy I knew well. Ryuu remained just inside the room, perched near the door with his eyes locked on Will with a protectiveness I rarely witnessed outside of me and my sisters, the sight causing my heart to flutter. His wings bristled, as if he could hear the traitorous beat a moment before his eyes locked on mine.

I forced a tentative smile to my face, only to be met with a look of disgust. Ignoring the pang of hurt and embarrassment, I turned, joining my sisters in the far corner so as not to be overheard by Will.

"I know, Lannie, but Ryuu's insisting we leave immediately." Ryuu's jaw ticked as El spoke, but other than that, he maintained his stoic composure.

Lannie's eyes flickered over him before shifting to me as I joined them. "You've agreed to this?"

"Yes. El pointed out that we can't predict when Will's visions will come."

Lannie frowned, directing her next question to El. "And you think a fort with a swarm of fae, including dark fae, is the safest place?"

"She's right, El. Are we sure Will will be safe among them?" I glanced toward Ryuu. "This one is an air fae and he is, by far, the most off-putting being I've had the misfortune of meeting. He's pigheaded and arrogant, self-righteous and—"

"This is ridiculous," Ryuu hissed under his breath, pushing away from the wall and sweeping toward us in a flash. "Humans are suspicious, fearful creatures who either seek to destroy or control all they do not understand. Fort Dhara will be safe. As I've said, only the most trusted fae are allowed to join us, all of whom view Will as an oracle—as someone to be revered. Only death awaits him here."

Lannie paled as El pulled in a breath, all of our eyes glancing toward where Will sat making goofy faces at the baby held between Liam and Lucy.

He drew back in a huff as I pinned him with a glare. "I do not mean to frighten you, but we are wasting time."

I didn't like the way he went about things, but Ryuu was right. "We won't be able to keep Will locked away forever. At least at Fort Dhara he won't be confined to his room."

"He will be free and safe," Ryuu confirmed, his voice still ringing with annoyance, but the tension across his shoulders had eased.

I locked eyes with him, stepping forward until they were little more than a breath apart. "Swear it."

Ryuu peered back at me, his scowl not quite softening but transforming into one tempered by understanding. "I swear on my life. I will do everything in my power to ensure no harm comes to him."

The rounded pupils shifted into vertical slits, but I didn't look away. The energy between us stretched, morphing into something else. Something dangerous. Ryuu's eyes dipped toward my lips. It was a fleeting glance, easily overlooked, but I saw it.

"I'll hold you to that."

Ryuu's chin jerked down once in a tight nod before he took a step back.

"I can't leave," Lannie said. "Not with Lucy and the babe. Maybe once Healer Grant returns, but until then, I'm needed here."

The reality of the situation hovered in the air. We would be separated. We'd been apart for only a week, maybe two, growing up while El ventured to the market, but beyond that we'd remained together.

"Perhaps we can send a letter to Healer Grant explaining you're needed at Fort Dhara. As soon as he's returned—"

"No," Lannie said, resigned. "He left to seek answers about the Fractured. Whatever is keeping him, it must be important. I won't jeopardize the safety of Pax because I don't wish to be separated from my family." Her gaze drifted to Will, a smile tugging at her lips as we watched his silly antics draw energetic gurgles and coos from the baby. "I'm sure Healer Grant will be back soon of his own accord. It won't be long till I join you."

19

ELARA

W‍ILL WAS ECSTATIC. O‍NCE HIS INITIAL REQUEST TO HAVE HIS OWN horse for the journey was denied, he insisted on riding with Ryuu. I expected a string of protests from the fae, but he gave Will a simple nod in answer as we arrived at the stables.

"It's about time." Cadoc's voice cut through the early afternoon air as a collection of saddled horses came into view. He was leaning against the fence with half a dozen men at his back.

"What are you doing here?" I asked. "I thought you were at Fort Dhara with Alarik and the others."

"I was, but I was sent to ensure everything went smoothly with your arrival." His eyes flashed to Ryuu. "The plan was to arrive together, but the fae took it upon himself to travel alone."

Ryuu looked down at Cadoc, meeting his blatant glare with indifference. He shrugged. "Flying allowed me to arrive early, and thus is allowing *us* to return as soon as possible. All parties have benefited from my foresight. Have your horses been properly rested?"

Cadoc bristled. "They have been exchanged for fresh ones. We've been ready to leave for some time."

Ryuu lifted an incredulous brow, suggesting he very much

doubted that, but held his tongue. "Wonderful. We are leaving now." He strolled forward, selecting the largest of the horses for himself.

"Tired yourself out already?" Cadoc sneered as Ryuu settled into the saddle after securing our luggage.

Ryuu ignored him, holding out a large hand to Will. Will took it immediately, allowing Ryuu to hoist him into the saddle with little more than a flick of his wrist.

"Ellie, look! A proper war horse!" Will's eyes sparkled with excitement as he grasped the horse's reins.

"It suits you," I said. "Exactly what a future general would be expected to ride."

Will beamed.

Cadoc neared with Ember and an additional mount in tow, his eyes fixed on Greer. "I hope this will do," he said, guiding the horse forward.

Greer gave Cadoc a tight smile as she swung up into the saddle. "Thank you."

Cadoc's eyes dilated as he watched her legs settle around the leather bindings, her cloak billowing out behind her. "My pleasure. Are you sure you wouldn't feel more comfortable riding with me? I wouldn't mind the company—"

"She's fine," I cut in with a sanguine smile. "Aren't we leaving?"

"We are," Ryuu answered, voice clipped. "Immediately."

The words had barely left his lips when Ryuu's hulking form rushed forward, sending an elated giggle from Will trailing in their wake. Needing no further prompting, Greer spurred her horse after them. Cadoc grumbled something under his breath as we followed, but remained silent soon after.

We rode for hours, picking our way through the Border-lands as we traveled northward. Will was given a dose of the tea Lannie had concocted. It continued to be effective, but it made him terribly drowsy. Even now, I could see Will's blond head lulling. He'd be out in minutes.

Greer trailed just behind Ryuu and Will near the head of the pack, but every few minutes Cadoc would attempt to ride beside her. Each time, she would increase her pace, closing the gap between her and Ryuu and each time Cadoc fell back.

I watched as Cadoc retreated once more to the middle of the pack with a scowl on his face. In an attempt to avoid unwanted attention, Greer lingered near Ryuu, drifting as close as his large wings would allow. The pair was held high so as not to hinder the horse, and I couldn't help but appreciate their beauty.

Greer leaned forward with a timid glance, so unlike the poised countenance I was used to seeing from her. "You said there would be other fae at the fort. Are they all from the Dark Kingdom?"

Ryuu stiffened under her attention but answered. "All were selected among those of Zaeth's army who fought at Neith. Most are dark fae, though there are a few others from the Air and Earth Kingdoms who've joined our ranks in recent years. We've attempted to sway the Earth Kingdom to cultivate their own army and join us, but our efforts have not yet been success-ful. Jarek is the only light fae among us. The Fire and Water Kingdoms keep to themselves, as you know, and even we aren't desperate enough to venture through the boughs of the Western Wood to seek out the wild fae." He cocked his head to the side, considering. "At least, not yet."

"What of the air fae?" I asked.

Ryuu's dragon-like eyes flashed over his shoulder, regarding me with shrewd calculation. "What of them?"

"The Earth Kingdom's loyalties have not been declared, but what of the Air Kingdom—your kingdom?"

A dark brow lifted at my question. "We will join the Dark Kingdom when the time comes."

Greer glanced at our brother, now fully slouched against Ryuu's broad chest. "There is no way to avoid war?"

Ryuu gave a single jerk of his head. "Villages are being destroyed. Humans and fae with human blood are killed daily, their bodies left to burn and rot while their murderers seek out their next victims. War is already here."

"Then why not strike?" I asked. "You may not have all the kingdoms on your side, but dark and the air fae are known for their skills in battle. Why not put a stop to this now?"

Ryuu's wings pulled in tighter, his voice a low growl as he answered. "We have only just learned the face of our enemy. We have no way to track or predict the portals Alderidge creates or the size of their army, only that it is vast. The red-eyed commander is their leader, but who is his and how was he able to create the creatures known as the Fractured? Believe me, I would like nothing more than to rid this world of the infestation, but it is not so simple."

Ember whinnied, pulling my attention to the forest around us. We'd crossed into the Dark Kingdom an hour ago, and the land had started to shift. The lush green trees grew leaner, the bark thicker, and the leaves more rigid and pointed. But we'd ventured further west than I'd previously traveled and the surrounding trees were unfamiliar.

This forest was older—wild and untamed—and an underlying pulse of power thrummed around us. Beneath us.

Warm rays of light streamed through the leaves of the canopy, highlighting the brilliant greens and browns, but the colors were offset by traces of purple. Rubbing my eyes, I looked again but found the bright purple hue only grew in frequency, deepening into maroon bands. Thick, gnarled roots were covered in torturous vines weaving around the base of the trees, snaking up along rough bark, stretching high into the canopy above.

Pops of deep red stains along the tips of branches could be

seen. I squinted as we neared. Tear-drop berries dangled in clumps, forming an umbrella of scarlet red above us as our horses passed beneath, their footsteps becoming more agitated the further we ventured. The branches were thick, but the rare beams of light managing to slip past their defenses reflected off clumps of berries, warping and brightening their ruby color, causing them to appear as drops of blood poised to fall.

A chill crept along my spine as Ember grumbled her unease. Even Greer and Ryuu had slowed, joining my side. Ryuu's eyes scoured the world around us, one of his arms closing protectively around a still slumbering Will tucked against his chest.

"What is this place?" I whispered. "It feels... cold. Like sorrow and rage... and hollowness."

Ryuu's moss-flecked eyes studied me, his frown replaced by cool calculation. "This is a place of death." His voice was low but carried, the men around us stiffening as a hushed silence enveloped the forest. "The vines devouring this part of the forest are bloodberries," Ryuu explained. "It is said to only grow in places where the blood of the fallen is insurmountable. Each berry represents a trapped soul, the essence of it captured by the blood spilled."

"Each berry is a life lost?" Greer gasped.

Ryuu nodded. "Legend has it, a great war occurred millennia ago. Battles and wars have been fought before, and will be fought again, but never to the degree of what was seen in this place.

On that day, Death was so ruthless, so gluttonous, the goddess herself thought to put an end to the battle. She was infuriated that her children had succumbed to their baser instincts of jealousy and greed. Furious that death was the route they'd chosen. She mourned the loss of her children but sought to make a lesson out of them.

"Embracing her rage, she snared the souls of those who fought, forcing them to remain on this earth for eternity—

forcing them to watch as their loved ones grew old and died, passing from this world to the next, until they knew the loss *she* felt as she was forced to watch her beloved children slaughter each other."

My eyes drifted up, taking in the clusters of scarlet berries stretching for miles in either direction. Each one a trapped soul. A life taken.

"They are trapped here? Forever?" I whispered, horrified by the thought.

"Perhaps. There is an obscured legend, some believed to be an ancient prophecy, which speaks of the day the goddess's descendant will unleash the souls to reap a final payment before finally allowing them to rest."

"Was there really no other way to reach the fort?" Greer said, her eyes darting to the canopy above. "You *had* to take us through the largest graveyard in all of Pax?"

Cadoc muttered his agreement along with several other humans. Ryuu's lips twitched as he looked at Greer. "The dead cannot harm you."

"That doesn't mean I want to be surrounded by them. Can we at least pick up the pace?"

"Of course, we can," I answered, sticking to the clearly marked path as I pressed Ember forward.

Greer shot me a thankful look as Ryuu shrugged his agreement. Our horses heeded our commands, launching into gallops, just as eager to leave this cursed land behind as we were.

## 20
## GREER

THE TWISTED TANGLE OF VINES AND DISTURBING CLUSTERS OF
bloodberries finally ended as the sun sank low along the horizon. Thank the gods. As if this entire venture wasn't bad
enough, Ryuu had to lead us through the forest of death.

*There is nothing to fear from the dead.*

I could still hear his arrogant response, only made worse by
the infuriating twitch of his lips. I'd wanted nothing more than
to dump him in the middle of those haunted woods and ride off.
We'd see then if there truly was nothing to fear in a grove full of
trapped souls.

I inhaled deeply, allowing the scent of pine and damp earth
to ease my nerves as El led us to a narrow, trickling stream. The
two of us let our horses drink their fill as we languidly dipped
our hands into the chilled waters. Seeing that the stream ran
clear, I lifted my cupped hands to my lips and drank. It was
crisp and cool as it trailed down my throat, mildly placating the
hunger in my empty belly. I licked my lips, curious as to the
subtle hints of sweetness lingering along my tongue.

"Does it taste sweet to you?"

El knelt beside me, head cocked to the side as she studied the water. "Yes, light and floral with hints of honey." She glanced at the horses, both of which had abandoned the stream in favor of clusters of thin green stalks adorned with yellow flowers, their petals forming small globes. Clusters of them lined the riverbank.

"Honeydew blossoms," I breathed, reaching toward the nearest batch and snatching a few for myself. "Do you remember when Evander brought us a bouquet of these?"

El smiled, plucking her own handful. "Yes. He thought he'd finally found the perfect bribe to get you to focus on training. He underestimated your stubbornness."

I shrugged, enjoying the taste of a sweet petal. "It worked for a little while."

"Only when he had fresh blossoms to give you."

"A girl can't be expected to work for nothing, El," I smiled, twirling the thin flower between my fingers. "If anything, Lannie would've been the one won over by a plant, though I know she was too young at the time." I sighed. "She would've loved this."

El nodded, taking in the beauty of our surroundings. The gentle sweet-tasting waters, the pine forest stretching before us and the cursed one behind. "Her diary would be filled with fresh drawings by now, complete with various tonics each plant could be used for. Knowing her, she would've enjoyed the blood-berries."

"We'll tell her about them when she joins us, but I refuse to return to that awful place. Surrounded by a bunch of angry souls trapped at their moment of death and forced to stay in a reclusive grove for millennia—no thank you."

My eyes drifted to the men a few paces up the stream. Ryuu had just pushed through the trees, having completed a sweep of the immediate area and deeming it safe to rest. Will had awoken. His eyes were bright, alive with the adventurous flourish our travels brought. Even when he was younger, Will had never been governed by fear. He viewed the world as something to explore, without a second thought as to the possible dangers lurking.

A part of me hoped he never lost that sense of wonder. His birthday was a little more than a month away. This year, we would give him a proper party, one with pastries and cake and all of his favorite foods. We already had a cluster of gifts hidden in my closet at the base, the three of us more excited for the day than Will was.

Ryuu helped Will from the saddle, looking after him as he dashed to the cluster of honey blossoms with an elated giggle. If I hadn't been watching, I'd have missed the softening of Ryuu's hard exterior. I would've missed the way his eyes brightened when Will launched into a story about the sweet petals of the flower and how there's a gaggle of dragons who will consume the nectar recreationally as humans do to nevernectar. Ryuu looked at Will as a father would his son. I would know. It was the same look my sisters and I gave him.

As if sensing my gaze, Ryuu's attention flashed to me. The openness vanished, replaced by a cold frown. My stomach twisted at the rebuke, and I desperately attempted to school my features into a mask of indifference.

Unable to stand his scrutiny, I turned toward El. "Is there something wrong with me?"

She shot me a puzzled look before glancing over my shoulder, understanding and anger flashing in her eyes a moment later. "There's nothing wrong with you. He's an arrogant air fae."

"I thought the same thing at first, but he cares for Will. So, it can't be a human thing. There has to be something about me."

El's lips pressed into a thin line. "He does turn into more of an asshole when you're around."

Risking a glance over my shoulder, I watched Ryuu hand a

bundle of bread and cheese to Will, insisting he keep his strength up while Ryuu got to preparing his tonic.

"He does, but he looks after Will with such tenderness."

Following my line of sight, El frowned. "There are other good men. Ones that won't scowl every time they see you. You shouldn't have to convince someone you're worth knowing. The ones who deserve to be in your life will already know."

"You're right," I said, pushing up from the soft ground with a sigh. Cadoc caught my eye as he started toward us, a pouch of food clutched in his hands. "Perhaps I should look elsewhere."

El followed my gaze and scoffed. "Cadoc? You can't be serious."

"Why not? He's clearly interested in me."

"He doesn't know anything about you. He's the same person he was a few months ago."

The same person who prattled on about himself for hours while simultaneously trying to get into my pants. I let my eyes take in the width of his shoulders and the thickness of his arms. He was strong, though smaller than Ryuu. Where Cadoc's dark hair was shortly cropped, Ryuu's was long and silky. His eyes were a bright blue, so different from Ryuu's dark smoldering gaze. El was right. Cadoc didn't care about me, not the real me, but I wasn't looking for a relationship. Only a distraction.

I shot El a smirk. "Then I won't feel bad for using him."

I wasn't sure if it was the dim light of day or exhaustion starting to get the better of me, but the shape of the trees grew more life-like with each passing moment. Trunks were shaped into graceful forms of dancing women, while others resembled gnarled torsos of forest giants or spindling fingers of ancient sorceresses. I'd been waiting for Ryuu to volunteer another horrific tale of curses at any moment, but he'd kept his distance from me.

Cadoc had performed as expected. A conversation had been too much to hope for. Instead, he offered a list of his *many* attributes, and after the second hour of describing in gruesome detail how his weightlifting journey had progressed, I escaped to ride beside El and Will... and Ryuu.

Though I would never admit it to him, I was glad Ryuu was here. I peeked over at the infuriating man, happy to see Will leaning sleepily against his chest. "Is Fort Dhara truly nestled among the foothills of the Jagged Mountains?"

Ryuu nodded.

Will perked up at that. "We're only a few days' ride from the Fire Kingdom?" he asked excitedly.

Ryuu's features brightened. "That is correct. I'm glad to hear you've been keeping up with your studies. We'll continue to expand on your knowledge of the fire fae once we reach Fort Dhara."

"I'll still have classes?" Will asked, his face brightening.

"Yes," Ryuu said. "Our focus will be learning Pax's history and the roles oracles have played in it, but we cover the same subjects you would have at the base."

"Can we start tonight?"

"No, we won't reach Fort Dhara tonight. Zaeth and General Holt have established camp a few miles further. We should reach it within the hour."

The tentative relief that washed through me vanished in an instant as Will's face went blank. His eyes rolled back, and his body slumped forward. Ryuu's thick arm wrapped around him, managing to keep him in the saddle, despite the quick pace of the horses, but my little brother's head bobbled with each jostle, the movements growing more chaotic as his body was plunged into another seizure.

A curse stole from Ryuu's lips as he pulled the horse to a stop, Elara and I mirrored him, pulling to a stop.

"How is this happening?" El cried. "The tea's been working."

Ryuu laid him on the ground, cradling his head with his palm as tremors raked Will's small form. "Dreams can be used as a conduit. It is easier for the mind to process what the goddess shares while in the state of limbo between waking and a true slumber, but visions may arise at any time. Especially if the goddess's warnings are not heeded."

"We'll heed them!" I shrieked. "If only she'd be clearer."

El leaned over him as his body stilled, watching the way his eyes flickered beneath closed lids. "Is it over? He's not thrashing anymore."

"No," Ryuu said. "But he's seeing something."

Will's brows furrowed as his lips started to move, muttering words too soft to hear. Another shudder twisted Will's body, his voice booming through the clearing for all to hear.

"The twins aren't getting better. An uprising. The prophecy. Preventing death." Will's body twisted, his face contorting in pain. "She's bound, as are the others. Adara, what have you done?"

*Adara*, as in our Mother? El's eyes flashed to mine as Will's voice dipped in an eerie imitation of her.

"I may have doomed us all. It will get worse. Many will die. A raven's wings protect the realm. The final shield. She's bound, as are the others."

Will stilled, his head lulling back as he drifted into the deep sleep that came after one of his visions. Ryuu brushed away the sweat beaded on Will's brow before gathering his small form in his arms. He held Will close to his chest in a protective embrace, eyeing each of the men surrounding us as his wings stretched wide, the golden barbs glinting in the rays of the setting sun.

"Not one word of this reaches anyone outside of Fort Dhara.

I will personally hunt down and delight in making an example of anyone who thinks to disobey me."

The men blanched, frantically nodding their agreements as his searing gaze swept through them. Even Cadoc's unwavering confidence was cowed by the threat. Ryuu was brutal and merciless—lethal—and he made sure everyone knew it.

He let the silence stretch a moment longer before swinging into his saddle. I caught El's eye, signaling to allow the others to slip ahead of us. Will would be safe with Ryuu, and we needed to discuss what transpired.

"He didn't miss a dose, Greer." The steadiness of El's voice wavered.

My eyes tracked the broad wings, now tucked in tight, his arms cradling our brother. I believed Ryuu would defend Will with his life. We couldn't prevent what was happening, but we could give Will the best chance at safety, starting with heeding the goddess's warning and figuring out these visions.

"He's not yet nine," El whispered, shaking her head. "We won't be able to keep it hidden forever. People will come after him. I'll start training Will right away. I'll speak to Alarik as soon as we get to camp and explain he needs to harness as many skills with a blade as possible—"

"El." It was a soft rebuke, but her words stilled, eyes swirling with the torment that came from knowing we were futile to prevent our little brother's suffering. I knew what she meant. She wanted Will to be able to defend himself when fear overtook those around him—when the world demanded his blood—but we both knew the truth: "A sword won't fix this."

Her face crumbled, head bowing forward. "I know, but we have to do something."

I glanced ahead at the others, slowing to put further distance between us and the rest of the group. "If what Ryuu said is correct," I said, dropping my voice to little above a whisper, "the visions will progress. It's best Will be surrounded by those we can trust."

"We can't trust anyone. You know that." El snapped under her breath, fear bleeding into anger.

We'd sworn long ago to only trust each other, but we couldn't weather this storm on our own. She read the resignation in my eyes before I breathed life into the words. "If Will is to survive this, we are going to have to trust the fae. We need to figure out what the visions mean."

The canter of a horse drew both our attention ahead. Cadoc was on his way back toward us. "You shouldn't be riding alone."

El met my eyes. *Not here.* I gave a small nod, agreeing to wait until we were alone.

21

# ELARA

STRANGE SOUNDS FILLED THE DIMMING SKY AS THE CREATURES OF the night awoke. The forest had thinned, allowing for more visibility and offering a false sense of ease to others traveling in our group. Cadoc was back to loudly boasting about himself, a stark contrast to the ever-quiet Ryuu. Will continued to sleep peacefully within his arms, as he would for the rest of the night. The visions had always drained him, and though we'd tried numerous times before, it was impossible to wake him until his body deemed it was ready.

My eyes raked over the air fae. Trust left us vulnerable. It was not something I was accustomed to giving freely, especially to a fae who looked like he was seconds away from growling at the slightest provocation. But Greer was right; we'd have to risk it.

My nose wrinkled at the thought of trusting anyone other than my sisters. Even when Alarik and I had been together, I'd still found it difficult to open up. I was vulnerable in a way I'd never been before, but a piece of me refused to yield.

Ember pulled up short, her ears pressing back as she stared at the road ahead. The other horses responded a second later.

Only Ryuu continued, urging his mount further into the looming shadows.

"Thank you for seeing to their safety, brother." The voice emanating from the darkness was honey smooth and wickedly enticing.

Ryuu slipped from the horse with Will safely tucked against his chest. "He had another vision. His body seems intact, but I'd like Jarek to ensure he's well."

There was a muttered agreement a moment before Ryuu's wings fluttered wide, back tensing with the weight of them.

"No," I breathed, urging Ember forward.

He turned, eyes glancing over my shoulder to where Greer no doubt was watching. "He'll be safe. I swear it."

Ryuu's powerful wings beat, launching him and my brother up through the trees and into the night sky beyond.

A curse left my lips as I pulled to a halt, sliding from Ember, my feet thundering against the packed dirt Ryuu had vacated moments before.

"Hello, love," the voice whispered softly from behind me.

I whirled around, searching for the fae I knew would be waiting.

Zaeth stepped forward, appearing to materialize from the darkness around him. His thick, branded arms were on full display, the ink extending up over defined muscles until it met the material of his black tunic. I narrowed my eyes along the script, realizing the ink was not looping designs as I'd first imagined, but ancient symbols linked together in an unfamiliar language. Judging by the tips visible along the skin just below his collarbone, they must span his entire chest. I wondered if they looped over his shoulders to stretch across his back.

"I assure you, Ryuu would rather end his own life than let a whisper of harm come to that boy. He's traveling ahead so Jarek can ensure Will is well."

My gaze lifted to meet his cinnamon eyes as I felt the

truth of his words. Will would be safe, for now. The sun had now fully sunk beneath the horizon and the first stars of the evening were winking to life. Will would be safer at the fort under Jarek's and Ryuu's protection. I gave a tight nod.

"Wonderful. Now that we have established that you trust me, I was hoping we could have a little chat before General Dearest joins us."

"Alarik is here?" I asked, peering over his shoulder and ignoring the rest.

"Not yet."

Crossing my arms over my chest, I lifted my chin in defiance, but it seemed Ember had no such qualms with the fae before us. She trotted toward Zaeth with a friendly whinny, pressing her nose into his hand. He chuckled, petting her behind the ears as she practically purred.

"Traitor," I grumbled at her, turning my attention to the glimmering stars, searching, but knowing Ryuu and my brother were long gone by now.

"The night is short, and I would prefer your attention to be focused on me."

Scowling, I met his eyes. "What?"

His lips twitched. "That's better. I've done what I could to secure you a position here, and not just for your brother's benefit. Alarik voiced concerns about you rejoining the men. Something about you not being able to handle it."

Anger flared, blazing through my veins. Denying me in his own base was one thing, but the idea of Alarik discussing my capabilities with anyone else was infuriating. "I'm perfectly capable of fighting."

He lifted a brow. "Good. I'll ensure you have access to everything the men do for as long as you wish.

"Why does it matter to you?"

His eyes flashed, but the emotion was gone before I could

name it. He shrugged, the perfect picture of nonchalance. "It doesn't."

I opened my mouth to call him on his lie, but the thunder of hooves pulled my attention toward the curve in the road beyond him. Alarik and Jarek appeared seconds later.

Alarik surged forward, eyes flashing as he noted who stood before me. I was forced to take a step back as his horse pushed between us, forming a barrier between Zaeth and myself.

He dismounted immediately, shoulders taut. He spun on Zaeth, placing his body before mine. "Why was she not brought directly to the camp? I agreed she could join *my* men. She shouldn't have been stranded in the forest with you."

"I was unaware Elara was your property. My apologies." Zaeth tilted his head in a mock salute. "I'll be sure to square away your belongings, General. Pray tell, would you like her bound and shackled or would a leash be preferable?"

"Zaeth," I warned, watching as Alarik's jaw clenched.

"Don't twist my words," Alarik said, voice dipping low. "Elara can as she wishes."

"If that was true, why did you tell Zaeth I couldn't handle training at Fort Dhara?"

The moonlight gleamed off the tips of Zaeth's fangs as smiled. Jarek took a step closer to us as Alarik stiffened, shooting Zaeth a look of pure venom.

"I never said you *couldn't handle* training," Alarik gritted out. "Only that I wanted to make sure you were ready. I planned to discuss the matter with you tonight."

My gaze snapped to Zaeth, betrayal flaring in my eyes. He shrugged. "That wasn't the impression I got."

"Alarik never said I couldn't handle training?"

"No," Alarik answered immediately.

Zaeth stared at me a moment longer, his features carefully crafted into a mask of indifference. "It was implied."

Alarik opened his mouth, but I held my hands up, stepping

around Alarik and between the both of them. "Enough. Alarik, I'm joining the others for training. If you have any reservations, you can send word to Vidarr and he'll back me up."

Zaeth's eyes sparkled, but Alarik gave a tight nod.

"And you," I said, whirling around to face Zaeth.

"Yes, love," he purred.

Alarik stiffened.

"You are not to take liberties with your personal interpretation of any conversation involving me. From now on, I'll be present when my future is the topic of discussion."

"As you wish, love."

"She's not your love," Alarik growled.

Zaeth's smirk grew, transforming into a taunting grin. "She's not yours, either."

"Seriously?" Greer asked, her disbelief cutting through the tension as she linked her arm with mine. "We get it. You two don't like each other, but there are more important things happening right now. How far away is camp? I'd like to reach Fort Dhara as soon as possible to make sure Will it okay."

The mention of Will snapped both men out of their staring contest.

"My apologies," Zaeth said, voice sincere. "Camp is just beyond the bend in the road."

"Thank the gods," Greer muttered as she started forward. "You'll gather the horses, won't you?" She asked as we pushed past Alarik and Zaeth, leaving them no choice but to comply.

## 22
## GREER

HALF A DOZEN TENTS WERE ERECTED IN A SMALL GRASS-COVERED clearing, nestled among towering pine trees. A man with dark skin and matching eyes greeted us, directing us to a pair of tents set aside from the others.

"Thanks, Kavan." El gave my hand a squeeze before dashing inside, making her escape just as Alarik and the others caught up.

"I'm staying here," Alarik said, gesturing to his tent, "in case El wanted to join—"

"Thanks, General, but I think El needs a night to herself. There will be time for the two of you to catch up tomorrow."

Alarik opened his mouth to argue, but decided against it after seeing the look on my face. He sighed. "I'm not trying to upset her, but there are protocols in place for a reason. I needed to make sure she was ready."

He turned beseeching eyes toward me. My gaze swept across his features, looking for hints of pride or insincerity. I found none. Alarik meant what he said, believing wholeheartedly he was doing what was best for my sister and the base.

"She's not like most people, General. El is fierce and determined. I know you have the weight of the world on your shoulders, but take a moment to watch her, to really *see* her. She doesn't fear, not in the way others do. Violence and bloodshed —they lost their impact years ago."

"I only wanted her to go through the normal integration process."

"The decision to keep her out of the worst of the fighting was not a personal one?"

Alarik's head snapped toward me. "I would never place my personal preferences above the safety of others. It's not just the base I'm responsible for. The base represents the last dregs of human strength in this world—a world where the fae grow more ruthless and hope is harder to grasp. If I send someone into the field who is not ready, it can jeopardize the entire mission."

"She's improved since you've seen her last. If she wasn't with Will she was training, but I understand you have to be sure. So, test her. Put her through the worst of it. She'll rise to the occasion. She always does."

~

"Will is going to be okay," El said for what felt like the hundredth time.

We'd changed and settled into our makeshift bed, consisting of two plump pillows and light sheets, perfect for the late summer weather.

"I know he'll be okay, because we are going to figure this out." I turned over to face her, twisting the blankets as I did.

She grumbled, tugging them back toward her. "You think it's safe to discuss this here?"

I sat up, letting the sheets pool on my lap as my ears strained. Sounds of men chatting around the cackling fire hovered in the night air, interrupted by subtle clanging of glasses and occasional laughter. "Most of the men seem to be enjoying themselves. If fae decide to listen they'll hear us, but based on how Ryuu and the others responded with Will..."

"Fae aren't the ones we need to be concerned with," El finished with a frown, pushing up as she did so. "At least, not the fae Ryuu has approved."

I nodded. It had been Cadoc and the humans who'd looked ready to flee. Or fight. I shuddered, hating the fear that was taking hold.

"Ryuu isn't my favorite person and I hate the way he looks at you," El said in a rush, as if afraid of what she was admitting. "But you were right earlier. I trust Ryuu over Cadoc, meaning I think we should heed his advice when it comes to the visions."

Nodding, I said, "If we can figure out what the visions mean and prevent whatever it is the goddess is warning us about, she wouldn't need Will."

I could tell El wasn't convinced, but we both wanted to believe Will wasn't condemned to this life.

"It wasn't a coincidence Mother's name was mentioned."

El nodded. "Will mentioned the twins, too. I'm sure of it. He said 'they aren't getting better'. That must have been right before they died."

Pushing away the pang of loss that always came with their memory, a nodded. "'An uprising' can refer to the war—an uprising of the Fractured, maybe?"

"Maybe. Or it could be us—humans—fighting back. Jarek mentioned he thought Will was referencing an ancient prophecy with his earlier visions."

"The ones involving the Dark Phoenix?" I asked, rubbing my temple in an attempt to banish the dull ache that had started.

"Yes, and 'the three' returning. The Dark Phoenix promises vengeance, death, torment—a rebirth of darkness. Maybe that's what we need to do," Elara said, looking oddly pale. "Kill the Dark Phoenix to stop the Fractured."

"Maybe, but I've seen no proof that the Dark Phoenix is a physical entity. Neither has Lannie or you, for that matter, and we've combed through every article of text at the base," I shrugged. "Maybe the Dark Phoenix is metaphorical."

El's lips pressed thin as her head dipped in a vacant nod. It was the look she had when she was hiding something—and feeling guilty over it.

"Anything you want to share, El?" She shook her head. I quirked a brow, letting her know I knew she was lying but was willing to give her space to work through it. Letting it go, I turned back to the task at hand. "The way Will spoke, it sounded like Mother was involved in a binding spell. 'She's bound, as are the others.' He's mentioned it multiple times. Same with the raven being a shield—the *final* shield."

"Jarek was most troubled by the part about the raven," El said with a frown. "When he mentioned the prophecy, the one with the Dark Phoenix..." She closed her eyes as she pressed her palms to her forehead. "He was more alarmed about the raven being the final shield."

"He thought the raven was a physical shield, but I'm not so sure. Ryuu denies any progress, though half a dozen ancient shields have been looked into."

El was bent over now, her head cradled in her hands. "Strange. I feel like we've discussed this before and not just at the base, but..."

A nagging restlessness stirred within my own mind igniting a sharp pain through my skull. "I know what you mean," I muttered, my hand pressing against my forehead.

"I think the raven is separate from the phoenix," El said. "I think the prophecy is referring to the war, the Dark Phoenix included. 'Dark phoenix vengeance, harsh, unbending. Torment abounds, unchecked, unending.' I heard something similar in the market on one of my missions. Most believe the Dark Phoenix's emergence will signal the downfall of the world. The raven sounds like our last chance to avoid it."

My brows knit together as I forced my mind to work despite the mounting headache. "'She's bound, as are the others.' Maybe the Dark Phoenix was bound? Or we *need* to bind it, and the shield is the key? But what would that have to do with Mother and the twins?"

El exhaled, the small sound revealed she was struggling just as much as I was. "I think you're right, Greer. I think Will's vision—or at least a part of it—was a memory." Her voice dropped lower, her fingers working over her temples in a futile attempt to nullify her headache. "It was right after the storm. The twins were sick and Will was just a babe, but I think it was real. I think we were listening over the stairs…"

My mind raced as her words tugged forth long forgotten memories. They were foggy at first, but it felt like years of dust were being cleared away the more she spoke.

"We crept to the edge of the stairs. Lannie was there, too." My face scrunched as El continued. "Papa was pacing. There was a fire…"

"And Mother was frightened." I gasped, that night flooding back in a wash of shadows and flame. "She knew the twins weren't going to survive. Gods, she knew Papa and her weren't going to either." My heart twisted as her voice rang clear in my head.

El's anguish bled into her words, just as raw as my own. "She said we would be okay, the four of us, and Papa made it sound like that was because she…"

"Because she healed us," I finished, the words tumbling from numbed lips. But that's impossible. Only light fae were capable of casting healing spells, and even then, it wasn't guaranteed to work. Mother was human, just as we were.

"Maybe she was skilled with teas and potions like Lannie," El suggested, both of us desperate for a logical explanation, but it rang hollow in my ears. If Mother *had* healed us, why would she not heal the twins, or Papa, or herself? If she had fae blood, she would've been able to. No, she was human, or at least mostly so.

"We should focus on the raven, on keeping the shield strong. I don't know why Will mentioned our family, but I can't see how it's connected."

El nodded. "Besides, Will is the first human oracle, right? Maybe it was just memories bleeding into his vision."

"Yeah, maybe," I said, fluffing up my pillow before lying down. But Will had been a babe, sleeping soundly at the time of that particular memory. I forced my eyes closed, listening as El's breaths evened out into a soothing rhythm.

We woke with the sun, the soft rays flooding the forest around us. Pleasant morning conversation bubbled around me as I dragged my exhausted body toward the fire, clutching a steaming cup of coffee in my hands. I preferred tea, but this would have to do. I stared into the flames, willing the caffeine to kick in as El and Evander helped pack up the camp.

"Good morning." Alarik came to my side, flashing a friendly smile.

"Why is everyone so awake?" I grumbled, taking another bitter sip of coffee. "The sun *just* came up."

He laughed. "You get used to early hours at the base. Once we get to Fort Dhara, I'm sure you'll be able to get back into your normal routine."

I mumbled a noncommittal noise, forcing the rest of the coffee down my throat before placing the empty cup in his outstretched hand. "That will be difficult seeing as how I doubt there will be a full kitchen to tend to."

He shrugged. "There's a small one, and the men need to eat.

A few of them can scrounge up a meal or two but nothing to your talents."

"I'll see what I can do," I answered distractedly, eyes snagging on my sister.

Alarik cleared his throat, his spine stiffening as El headed straight for Evander, avoiding all others. "Did she say anything last night?"

"About you not wanting her to train with the fae?"

"That's not what I said," he protested, running a hand through his golden hair.

"Regardless, it doesn't matter anymore. Everyone is aware El wants to train with the others. As long as you don't hinder her, it shouldn't be an issue."

"It wouldn't have been an issue in the first place if Zaeth hadn't implied I was being a controlling prick." Alarik's eyes narrowed, focusing on the dark fae in question, who just happened to join El and Evander in saddling the horses. El rolled her eyes at something Zaeth said as Evander fought off a smile.

"Or if you two spoke more often, it would've prevented the miscommunication. And not just about base stuff. I know you made a decision about giving each other space, you can still speak to each other, even if it is just as friends."

Alarik mumbled something beneath his breath, his eyes lingered on Zaeth a moment longer before he turned away.

The morning passed quickly, and within a few hours' time, Fort Dhara came into view. Evander pointed to a building in the distance, explaining where the healing quarters were—where Will was. El and I galloped ahead, willing our horses faster. Hooves beat the dried dirt path lined with bits of sprouting grass persistently pushing their way through the cracked earth.

I leapt from the saddle as I reached the building, El a few seconds behind me, as we followed Evander's directions down a staircase, and through chilled stone passages lit with torches, until our eyes fell on the flickering light emanating from an open door below a small sign that read: infirmary.

The energetic voice of our brother echoed into the frigid hall, allowing the tight band across my chest to release. He was safe. El and I shared a relieved smile as we neared.

"I've never met a dragon before," Will said.

A deep chuckle rumbled, the sound undoing something within myself, causing my steps to slow as I realized Will wasn't alone. "I'm no dragon, young Will. Though air fae once possessed traits related to earth dragons, most remaining dragon fae reside within the Fire Kingdom."

I peered through the door, hovering in the shadows.

"But you *are* a dragon." Will's voice held the boyish confidence that never failed him. "You aren't always one... but you were, long ago. And you will be again, when the time is right."

Ryuu sucked in a breath, eyes wide and face pale.

"It was an accident, what happened to her." Will's voice was soft, carrying maturity beyond his age.

I peaked inside, catching Ryuu nearly tripping over his chair as he rushed to put distance between the two of them.

"Please don't be afraid of me..." Will pleaded, his voice back to normal. The heartbreak—the sheer loneliness of the sound—forced me into the room.

Ryuu's eyes flashed with unshed tears as they swung to mine. I nearly stumbled from the torment raging within his gaze—within his soul—but he turned away before I uttered a word. When he faced me once more, he was the picture of control.

"It is not you I fear, young Will," he muttered before fleeing the room.

## 23

## ELARA

THE SUN FILTERED IN THROUGH THE SMALL WINDOWS FRAMING the door, the soft rays of morning brightening the small log cabin. The bed was pushed to the back of the narrow space, allowing for a single desk and dresser, holding clean linens and clothes. I'd left all my dresses behind. There'd be no need for them here.

I yawned, stretching out on the stiff mattress beneath me, the scratch of the white sheets reminding me I was far from the luxuries of the base. A smile stretched across my face. I was at Fort Dhara. With the fae. To learn not only battle tactics, but also be briefed on the movements of our enemies, all of which might help Greer and I uncover what Will's visions meant.

Will had been ecstatic to see Greer and I last night, the three of us staying up late discussing how life would work here. Jarek had met with us after, letting us know he'd placed additional wards on the healing quarters for Will's safety. Zaeth, Soter, Jarek, and Ryuu would rotate guard duty, each of them taking turns spending the night in the infirmary with him. Greer and I offered to stay with Will, as we always had, but Will insisted he didn't need his sisters doting on him.

So, we'd selected the nearest accommodations, two of the small cabins lining the main road. They were near enough where we'd be able to reach him in minutes should anything happen, but far enough away to provide him a semblance of privacy.

Alarik's rooms were across the way, but I hadn't run into him last night. I'd meant to talk to him, if only to clear the air, but I'd been enjoying myself with Will and Greer, too relieved with Will's good health to spoil the evening.

A sigh left my lips as I gathered a small bundle containing my morning essentials and a fresh uniform. Stuffing my feet into my untied boots, I headed off to find the washroom.

The scent of wild pine with hints of fresh mountain rivers greeted me as I neared the large building beside the healing quarters. Fort Dhara was different than I'd expected. The base had been full of grand structures and a bustling city beneath with all the luxuries one could ask for. But Fort Dhara was little more than a cluster of stables and small log cabins surrounding the centralized washrooms, a dining hall, and the quaint, though now reinforced healing quarters.

My eyes scanned the forest and I couldn't help but realize the fort would be difficult to defend. It was built at the base of a large mountain range, an outcropping of the Jagged Mountains, and while that offered some protection from the west, tall trees pressed in from the north and south. They were thinned, as if centuries ago the forest had been cleared, but they would offer a decent level of cover for an invading army. Stables encompassed the entire eastern wing with soft grasses stretching down toward the river. It was too shallow to offer protection, but it would be nice to have access to fresh water.

While most of the buildings looked neglected, I could see a few new roofs gleaming along the stables and several fresh logs of fencing. Improvement, to be sure, but there were no walls, no gates... no way to survive if the Fractured discovered us.

I spotted a few others coming and going from the washroom and sent a silent prayer to the goddess it wouldn't be too crowded, or at the very least, there were individual stalls for Greer and my sake. Nudity wasn't a big deal, but I'd be traumatized forever if I accidentally walked in on Evander showering.

Stepping through the washroom doors, I prepared myself for the onslaught of men, but was pleasantly surprised to find another set of doors facing me, indicating male and female sections. I bounded toward the left, relishing the thought of having my own shower and bathroom. A large open room lined with slick blue river rocks greeted me, complete with multiple shower knobs and small notches for soap. I placed my clothes in the cubbies lining the opposite wall, hanging my towel on the wooden hook near the showers' entrance.

The water took a few minutes to heat, but soon steam was flooding the space, highlighting the blues and greens of the rock surrounding me. I took my time washing, enjoying the quiet reprieve before the day started. But soon, hunger was gnawing at me, reminding me I hadn't eaten much yesterday.

After returning my belongings to the cabin, I made my way to the dining hall. The smell of sweet oats had my mouth watering as I passed through the doors. The expected clatter of silverware on plates and easy morning conversation was absent, replaced instead by a heavy silence. Fae sat along the far side of the room, with humans clustered among the near tables, distrust and unease hanging in the air.

"El, you're awake. I was just about to get you." Bright auburn eyes smiled down at me. Evander glanced around before guiding us toward an empty table in the back, setting a plate of food and a drink down before me.

"Is it always like this?" I asked, hunching forward.

Evander grimaced. "No. Well, yes, but it wasn't this bad previously."

I risked a glance around the room, catching a few glares aimed in our direction. "It's Will, isn't it?"

"They'll get used to it," he said. "The fae are comfortable with him. Most are honored to defend an oracle, but they're wary of the fear emanating from the humans."

"It's not like he has a choice in the matter," I grumbled as I took a sip of coffee.

"I know that. *They* know that. But it will take time."

Fighting the urge to shout at all of them, I took a rather large bite of the crisp apple Evander had brought.

"It's time to get you up to date, now that you're here. The Legion of the Light sent me to investigate possible attacks in the north."

"North? I thought their had been a new surge in attacks in the Earth Kingdom."

"The Fractured attacks are mostly in the south, but more and more human settlements are rioting. Don't get me wrong, the fae can be ruthless. Many of them deserve death, but the towns targeted by humans are ones where humans and fae live in peace. They aren't liberating humans, only increasing the death toll."

The richness of the apple soured in my mouth. "It's Alderidge, isn't it?"

Evander's jaw ticked. "We've spread the news of his involvement. Those who believe us have distanced themselves, most choosing to relocate to the base. But others..."

"They believe him."

He gave a grim nod. "Humans have suffered significant losses since the storm with many harboring a deep-seated hatred for fae long before that. Alderidge provides an outlet for their fear, for their frustrations in this life. He's giving them the semblance of power and using it to his advantage. All have been offered sanctuary, but if an attack is near and we hear word of it, we will be deployed to stop it, regardless if it's the Fractured or humans responsible."

I nodded.

"Hello, love. I'd hoped to find you here." I glanced up, finding a pair of cinnamon eyes staring down at me. "Are you ready for your official welcome to Fort Dhara?"

The blade felt heavy in my hands, my arms shaking with the effort it took to parry Zaeth's attacks. Sweat dripped down my neck in the heat of the midday sun as my lungs fought to pump much needed oxygen to the rest of my body. My muscles burned as I ducked and spun, slowing despite my best efforts.

Zaeth's lopsided smirk remained in place as he advanced. His blade lashed out, drawing blood along my arm. It was shallow, but I was still shocked to see the red stain. I hadn't thought he would actually spar with me, not to this degree.

"You can't improve if you aren't fighting your best, love. Again."

I gritted my teeth, angry at myself for being lulled into a false sense of security. I used that anger, letting it fuel me. My speed increased, matching his tempo—exceeding the standard he'd set for us.

Zaeth's blade lashed out repeatedly without slowing, forcing me to yield another step.

"Don't let yourself be backed into a corner. Anticipate. You won't be able to overpower many by strength."

I side stepped as he launched forward, the tip of his blade catching the top of my pants, not quite enough to slice through the skin of my thigh, but enough to slice the fibers up to my hip. He gave a guilty smirk before twisting into his next assault.

Dancing away, I desperately tried to regroup, but my energy was spent. His blade lifted, seeming to hover in the air for a moment before it came crashing down, angling toward my neck.

I brought my sword up just in time to avert the bite of steel, digging my heels into the earth with the force it took to stay his blade.

"Good work, but—" The pressure bearing down on me eased —just a bit—as Zaeth spoke. I didn't waste the narrowed opening, and slammed my knee in his groin with all the force I could muster. He doubled over, the blade falling from his grasp as his knees drew up. It wasn't the classiest move, but it was effective.

The tip of my blade held steady at the base of his throat, the sharp edge nearly pressing against his tanned skin covered with salt and sweat. Zaeth's chest shook with laughter as he peered up at me. "I thought you were out of shape."

Grinning, I helped him up. "Just wait till I'm *in* shape."

"I look forward to the day, love." He retrieved our water-skins, the thickness of his thighs shifting with each step, straining against the dark fabric of his black pants. I willed my eyes away, only to be captured by the veins along his forearms and the ancient script of brands swirling up.

"Eyes up here, love."

I glared at him, fighting to conceal the blush stealing across my cheeks. Handing me one of the waterskins, he stepped forward, bringing with him the scent of cedarwood and something else—something a little more... wild.

"Thank you for the welcome," I said as I lifted the water to my mouth, licking my lips as the cool liquid chilled my tongue, before settling in my stomach. The sun had climbed high in the clear summer sky, the day bright with the sounds of birds chirping over the gentle rumblings of the river in the distance.

"Anytime," he said, setting a slow pace through the field toward the dining hall. "I suggest we make this our routine. We'll meet for a light breakfast before spending the rest of the morning working on your stamina."

"My stamina?" I teased. "And here I thought I'd impressed you."

"That you have, love. It's rare to find another who enjoys that dance of death as much as I do."

My eyes flicked to his, expecting judgment, but they were pools of swirling cinnamon, pupils still dilated from the high we'd just created together. "Yes, I suppose that I do. I've actually been meaning to ask you about that."

"Ask me anything you wish."

I swallowed, ignoring the fluttering of nerves in my stomach. "At Litha, you said I was something alluring."

He grinned. "I find you quite captivating."

"No—I mean thank you—but that wasn't my question." Warmth burned across my cheeks. "What I mean to say is, it sounded like you were implying I wasn't human."

His eyes searched mine with a seriousness I was unaccustomed to. "Are you?"

"Yes," I answered. "I have to be. I'm flawed and a little disturbed, but me—just me."

*Just you?* As if you could ever be anything less than extraordinary."

Something in my chest squeezed under his words.

"We are all flawed, love." His hand lifted to tuck a stray curl behind my ear, his thumb lingering along the curve of my cheek. "It only serves to make you all the more captivating."

The tempo of my heart raced as Zaeth's wicked grin stretched, the tips of pointed fangs peeking out. I wondered what it would feel like to have his lips wrap around the soft flesh of my neck, to feel the gentle caress of his tongue mingled with the sting of his teeth.

"Until next time."

## 24
## GREER

I STROLLED DOWN THE STAIRS OF THE NOW FAMILIAR PATH THAT would take me to Will, grateful Evander had strengthened the additional wards placed by Jarek to make the lower levels the safest location at Fort Dhara. It had felt cold at first, but the men had cleared a storage room for Will to use. They had donated various trinkets, books, lamps, and maps until the room was buzzing with warmth. Will loved it.

We'd been here for a few weeks and had settled into a routine of sorts. Ryuu would meet with Will in the morning for lessons, leaving the afternoon free for him to practice physical combat. These were mostly done with El, but every now and again Zaeth would join them, the two of them cutting their morning workout short to spend more time with Will.

"Good, but keep your knees bent. Balance is key," El said as I entered the infirmary, wielding the wooden sword she'd procured last week. A grunt issued from Will as she knocked the back of the practice sword into his shoulders.

"Never turn your back on your opponent."

My stomach clenched, but Will righted himself with a smile and lifted the practice sword to try again.

"You're back!" Will called, spotting me from across the room. "Did you see me? Did you see how I nearly got her?"

My lips twitched. "Is that what was happening here?"

Will nodded, eyes bright.

"El better keep her guard up."

"Yeah, especially because Zaeth promised to get me a real sword, once I've had a little more practive. "

I blanched. "He did what?"

El rolled her eyes, muttering something below her breath that sounded like, "Of course he would."

"He did," Evander confirmed, stepping through the door with a grin. "And you will get your own sword, but first we have to master the basics with this one."

Our little brother studied the wooded blade for a moment longer before shrugging. "I'm sure it won't be too long, especially with all the training we've been doing. I'll be fighting next to you in no time."

El reached out to ruffle his curls, but he ducked beneath her hand before she could.

"Ellie, I'm not a kid anymore. What if Alarik walked in, or Zaeth?"

He shot her a glare worthy of the twins and I couldn't help but laugh. "I'm glad to see you're enjoying yourself. I thought we could head to dinner together."

Will turned his wide-eyed gaze on El. "One more round, first? Please?" He dragged out the last word in a boyish plea.

El gave him an affectionate smile, before lowering into her stance. "Very well."

"Have there been any other visions?" Evander asked, his question drawing my attention and causing my smile to falter.

"Nothing new since traveling here."

He gave a tight nod. "I haven't figured out the connection to your family, yet. We needed to rule out the possibility of fae ancestry for Will, seeing as how their hasn't been a human oracle. The twins were well past the age of a fae's first shift, and I would've known if Jem had fae affinities, but I looked into your genetics, just to be sure. I was able to trace your father's history to a small village in the Earth Kingdom, but I've found nothing on your mother's side."

*Fae affinities.* The thought had crossed my mind, but it wasn't something that could be hidden. You were either fae or you weren't. And, unfortunately, we weren't.

"Mother spoke about the Light Kingdom often enough," I said, humoring his request. My brows furrowed as I desperately tried to latch onto memories of the past. "I feel like there is more to it... like she told me more, but I can't recall."

I shot El a worried look, but she's too captivated with Will's sword technique to pay us much attention. "El and I had the same feeling when we discussed Will's latest vision on the way to the fort."

Evander frowned, his narrowed gaze bouncing between the two of us. "I'll keep looking, but for now, Ryuu and I agree that we need to focus on locating and protecting the raven."

"We thought the same. Protect the raven and maintain the 'final shield.' If only we knew what 'the raven' was." I said, watching Will parry a soft blow from El.

"Alarik, Ryuu, and I are working on it. Zaeth as well. He's left this morning to comb through the collection of archives in the Dark Kingdom."

My eyes snapped to his. "As in the *royal* collection? Gods, he's braver than I gave him credit for. Or incredibly stupid. I wouldn't want to risk irritating the royals—especially the dark royals."

Evander cleared his throat. "Ryuu sent a messenger requesting access to the Air Kingdom's records as well. They are known for their libraries and extensive historical recordings. Most follow the old ways and will ideally recall something of use."

"Ryuu *did* request a meeting with me this afternoon. Maybe he's heard something."

I forced a light tone but couldn't help the increased tempo of my heart. He'd approached me earlier this week after barely speaking to me since arriving at Fort Dhara. And I'd just stared at him—with my mouth open, the dull conversation of Cadoc forgotten. His dark eyes had glimmered as failed to speak and all the while Cadoc grew more irritated. After a few more seconds and extremely awkward silence, Ryuu mumbled something about assuming my lack of a denial was a 'yes'. He'd then shot Cadoc a bemused look before sauntering off.

Will lunged forward, his wooden sword slipping beneath El's arm in a fluid, graceful movement. She gave an exaggerated groan as Will lunged forward, his wooden sword tucking beneath El's arm in a pretend stabbing.

"Nice work, Will," Evander praised. "You'll have a real sword in no time."

"Once it's safe," I hastily added.

El rolled her eyes, pulling Will into a tight hug. "He's a natural, Greer. It's only a matter of time."

## 25
# GREER

EL BEGAN HUMMING A FAMILIAR TUNE AS WE FELL INTO STEP behind our Evander and Will. Even though Evander and Jem's wedding hadn't come to fruition, he would always be our brother. It had been seven long years since the storm killed my family—nearly eight—and Evander never once stopped being there for us.

A frown tugged on my lips as El's humming increased. A small headache blossomed as my eyes focused on the red-headed half-fae before us. It *had* been nearly eight years, and I'd never seen Evander with another. All this time, he'd been stuck in the past, mourning a love who would never return to him. I missed my brother desperately, but I couldn't prevent the sinking feeling in my stomach as I imagined a world where Evander never loved again.

My mind drifted, darkening my mood further as my headache grew, despite the rich pine scent of the forest and the clear, bright rays of the early morning sun. A memory surfaced as El continued humming. I was young, only eleven at the time, but I'd snuck into my brothers' room after the storm had hit, determined they wouldn't leave this world alone. I'd brought water and sung calming songs over and over again, slowly watching as their bodies deteriorated.

I'd known they were doomed as soon as they laid in those beds. It was as if a shadow had fallen across them—father too. Father had pleaded with me to go, but I'd sensed his fear, especially near the end. I wouldn't leave him. I couldn't.

Elara's pace slowed, my body unconsciously mirroring hers. We were still a few paces off from the mess hall, but I watched as Evander and Will disappeared within, the two of them without a care in the world at this moment.

The pressure between my eyes built as El's voice dropped an octave. Her humming transitioned into a song with hushed mumbles—not words exactly but the precursor to words. My eyes snapped to hers, seeing her brows furrowed in concentration—or was that confusion—as her mouth worked to form lyrics, though never quite got there.

A pang shot through my skull, causing me to squeeze my eyes shut against the throbbing. "Could you tone down the singing? My head is killing me."

El's voice abruptly cut off, but the pain in my head didn't lessen. "Sorry. There's something about that song. Do you know where it's from?"

I shook my head, hoping to clear it, but the pressure only grew. "It sounds familiar, though. Sing it again, with words this time. But keep the volume down."

"That's the thing. I can't remember the words. I *know* I've heard this song hundreds of times, but it's like my body remembers when my mind doesn't. My mouth wants to sing, but my brain isn't supplying enough information."

El started humming, her eyes searching mine for answers. I let the melody envelop me, let it flow through my veins, my soul, as her voice pitched and dipped. It was familiar but... lost, dancing along the periphery of my mind. I could almost grasp it, if I just pushed a little further...

On instinct, my hand reached for hers. A bolt of electricity shot through me at the contact, splitting something deep within the recesses of my mind. I gasped as light flooded my vision, the pressure in my head releasing immediately as a wash of memories rushed forward.

There were hundreds of them flashing before my eyes too quickly to understand. I latched onto one, forcing it to stay in focus.

*Mother was combing my hair before her ornate gilded mirror. My hair was lighter then, nearly white, and there was a darker splash of freckles across my cheeks, as if I'd been playing in the sun all summer long. I caught sight of El in the reflection, sitting across the foot of our parents' bed. Her eyes were wide, not yet shadowed by the harsh realities of life, and a soft carefree smile graced her lips. Lannie's small form was curled in a ball, already asleep on the pillows.*

*"The three of you will face a lot in your lives," Mother said, her words dripping with sorrow. "More than you should have to. If the worst comes to pass, look to each other for strength. I am not yet sure how this story will unfold."*

*My younger self looked to El in the mirror. She shrugged, not thinking much of Mother's speech. I'd forgotten how trusting she had been.*

*Mother set down the silver brush, her hand coming to rest on her still-flat belly as her eyes bounced between El's and mine. "I've made mistakes, but know that I've done everything possible to ensure they were corrected. Some of the decisions I've made may seem extreme, cruel even, but know always that I love you."*

*El sat up at that, coming to Mother's side as I turned to face them "We love you, too." El said, rushing into her arms in an embrace.*

*Mother pressed a kiss to her head. "One day, it will all make sense, my daughters. One day, you will remember. And I hope when that day*

*comes, you will not hate me for what I have done." She picked up the*
*brush again, singing as she did so.*


I blinked, the memory fading as the softer light of morning
returned.

"Greer? What is it?"

El was before me, her brows pinched.

"I remember, at least pieces."

"Remember what? The song?"

I started to shake my head, but stopped as the melody
returned. It had been the same song Mother was singing. The
one she'd sung to us every day.

"It's the lullaby," I breathed, my mind reeling. "The song you
were humming, it's the lullaby Mother sang us every night."

El's brows furrowed, looking as if she understood the truth
of my words but couldn't place it. A cold sweat broke over my
forehead as the lyrics rushed back, ones I'd known my whole
life but had somehow forgotten.

"I remember."

26

ELARA

G REER MUTTERED A NONCOMMITTAL NOISE BEFORE RUSHING OFF, leaving me to find Will and Evander on my own. I wasn't sure why she was acting so weird about a song. Mother sang us many lullabies growing up... at least I thought so. I tilted my head, rubbing away the last of the headache as I stepped through the doors of the mess hall.

"Where's Greer?" Evander's voice found me over the gentle clamor of the morning. The earlier animosity between humans and fae had waned. Parties still tended to separate during meal-times, but we'd found ways to work together. Baby steps.

"She had things to do," I answered, taking a seat beside him and Will after spotting the extra two plates they'd procured.

"More food for us, then," a smooth, playful voice said. Jarek appeared a moment later, sliding in between Evander and I as he reached for Greer's plate. His light blond hair was perfect, the shorter sides slicked back with the top styled in a messy swoop. There was a hint of kohl along his lids, and his lips seemed to give off the faintest of shimmers. "Good morning, all. It looks like the perfect day to get a little dirty."

Evander choked on his coffee, his sputtering causing the

mockingly innocent smile across Jarek's face to stretch. "On the training field, of course."

My gaze darted between the two of them, feeling like I was missing something, but Will spoke up before I could discern what it was.

"Can I come, too?"

"No—"

"Sure."

Evander shot Jarek a look. Jarek held his gaze a moment before shrugging. "Evander's right. Today will be mostly instructions. I'm sure you'll have more fun with what the general has planned for you."

Will looked to Evander.

"Don't worry. Alarik set you up for one-on-one training with Cadoc in the morning but he plans to stop by himself once the morning drills are underway. You two will mostly work on swordplay, but Alarik wants to introduce you to a bow."

I laughed around a mouth full of oats as Will's eyes lit with excitement, wondering if Cadoc knew what he was in for. Clearing my throat, I nodded encouragingly to Will. "That sounds like a great day."

"In fact," Evander said, glancing over Will's shoulder. "It appears he's ready for you."

Will whipped around, smiling like a child on Yule morning as Cadoc approached.

His broad frame and thick dark hair was as intimidating as ever. "Are you ready?"

Evander shot Cadoc a glare. "Cadoc is honored to assist you with your training today, Will. We'll meet up at dinner to review how the day went."

Cadoc's fists clenched but he pulled together a smile within seconds. "Wonderful."

Seeming not to notice the tension, Will bounded to Cadoc's

side, launching into a relentless stream of questions as he tugged Cadoc from the hall.

"So, what was all that talk of getting dirty?" I asked. Jarek didn't bother to hide his smirk.

"We start defense against fae attacks today with the pairings being one human and one fae. Most have been sparring regularly on their own, as you have. It's time to test their skills."

The amusement in Jarek's eyes had me blushing. Zaeth and I had been meeting every morning, only ever for training purposes, but I felt... lighter afterwards—happy even. He'd made no attempts to elaborate on whatever affinity for battle he saw in me and I didn't push. Spending my mornings surrounded by fae warriors and my afternoons teaching Will was a dream, a blissful reprieve as we prepared to face the horrors awaiting us once we were able to track Alderidge and the red-eyed commander.

The assaults continued, though Alarik was making great progress at relocating potential victims. He'd been able to isolate which villages were more likely targets, focusing on the number of humans and human-fae partners. With the help of the Select and Zaeth's men, the losses had been significantly reduced.

I glanced around the room looking for a pair of emerald eyes. We'd barely spoken about anything other than training since arriving at Fort Dhara—Will's training, even some light discussion on my progress with Zaeth—and while I was happier than I'd ever been, a dull ache throbbed in my chest when I thought of what we'd once shared. So, when he'd lingered after a session with Will and asked to meet with me this morning, I said yes.

"I wish I could join, but I'm meeting with Alarik this morning."

"How'd Zaeth take the news?" Jarek quipped.

"He was fine with it," I said, ignoring the flush of my cheeks.

Zaeth had been perfectly composed when I'd let him know I'd be missing our session, and his utter lack of a response had deflated something in me. I'm not sure what I'd been expecting, but there was not one raised brow or snarky comment. Zaeth simply nodded, holding my gaze for a few moments longer as if he were searching for something. Whatever it was, he must not have found it.

Jarek shrugged. "Either way, Alarik hasn't returned from the perimeter search."

"Perimeter search?" I asked.

Jarek nodded. "Soter is with him, searching for weaknesses to determine how best to strengthen our location. I've already placed protection wards, but it seems humans are more comfortable with a wall of some sort."

"Oh," I said, shoulders rounding forward. "I guess that means I'm free to join the others."

"Zaeth has been boasting about your skill. I'm intrigued to see it for myself."

A warmth bloomed in my chest. "He has?"

Jarek nodded. "Evander, too. Between the two of them, I'm expecting something incredible."

Evander looked at me with all the pride of a big brother. "Let's go show them what you can do."

I followed the men, fae and human alike, through the row of cabins and into the swaying green fields past the stables. The morning sun was high, the warm breeze swirling with the fresh scent of pine and mountain streams.

They had formed a semi-circle in the meadow, allowing for Jarek to step through into the center—to where Zaeth stood waiting.

Fluttering nerves stirred in my stomach as he met my eyes

with a smirk. He dipped his head in my direction, hands clasped behind his back, before turning his attention to the gathering crowd. Evander had settled along the side with the others, but the rest of the Select Guard were missing, along with Ryuu. I wondered if they too were working on the perimeter.

"Humans and fae are not so different." Jarek's voice was conversational with a hint of teasing, but every person straightened up to listen. "We've been divided for far too long with ancient prejudices poisoning our relations. It has left us weak and that weakness is being exploited. This world belongs to both of our people. It's time we start acting like it. Make no mistake, we are at war gentlemen. And lady." He gave me a quick wink as he stepped back, allowing Zaeth to step forward.

He was in a tight, short-sleeved shirt, black to match the ruins covering his arms. The thin fabric shifted as he moved, hinting at the expanse of muscle beneath. Zaeth towered over the others in the clearing, and when he spoke, they listened. "From what we can tell, the Fractured are supplemented by a group of rogue fae, half fae, and even a few misguided humans targeting villages home to humans or human-fae pairings. There is no distinction when it comes to age or health. No care for the thousands of lives taken, despite their innocence.

"Since the time of the blast, the land has undergone changes, becoming harsher and wilder. Clans which have been at peace for centuries have started squabbling. Creatures that previously content residing in dark forests or the deepest crevices of the sea are venturing forth. Ancient beings who have been slumbering for millennia are stirring once more.

"We are all creatures of Pax—all of us tied to this land. It would seem the ancient warnings of humans offering a balance to the ruthlessness of the fae may be true. As the breath of human life dwindles, the chaos of the world grows stronger. A balance must be found. These attacks must be stopped."

Mutterings lashed through the men as their fears were given

voice. Zaeth stood strong, waiting for silence to greet him once more before resuming.

"You have been selected as those most trustworthy and skilled to handle this mission. As fae, we will be revealing key weaknesses to help the humans in battle. For those of you who have any qualms, know this. Our only hope of saving our world —ourselves—is through saving them. We are in this together."

A few fae shifted uncomfortably, but most nodded.

"Right," Jarek said, clapping his hands. "Now that the pep-talk is out of the way, let's get to training, shall we? We need to work quickly and effectively. The humans will be rotating through their positions here at Fort Dhara in order to return to the base and distribute the techniques to the others. For now, we start with defense. Pair up, one human to one fae."

My eyes darted nervously around as my anxiety surged. Couldn't Jarek just assign us someone?

Evander stepped forward.

"Hey there, little sis. Would you mind being my partner?"

I blinked. "But shouldn't you be with..." The words died on my tongue. Evander was half fae... and half human. Which would he pair with? My cheeks tinted at my lack of tact.

He gave a light chuckle. "Don't worry about it. Most people aren't sure where I fit in. I've struggled with it my entire life, still do sometimes. But the numbers work out if I pair with a human. Do you mind sparring with a half-fae?" His voice was kind, but I was surprised to see genuine vulnerability beneath.

"As long as you don't mind being paired with a girl."

He laughed. "As if that's a disadvantage."

We mimicked the motions shown by Zaerth and Jarek in time with the others. Most of the defensive positions were familiar, courtesy of Zaeth's training, but Evander moved differently than he did. It was helpful training against someone new. We all knew humans wouldn't be able to survive a direct attack from a fae. Instead, we were shown ways to anticipate and, hopefully, deflect.

The humans and fae present had sparred together before, but it was abundantly clear the fae weren't holding back nearly as much today. It was exhausting and disheartening to realize how out matched we were. The Fractured weren't fae, but if the mounting rumors were true, if a large group of fae or dark creatures sided with the Fractured, it wasn't a matter of *if* we would fail, but *when*.

Despair hung heavy in the air, the rest of the men seeming to have the same worries as myself. Jarek looked around, noting the bruised and battered humans standing next to the fae who had yet to break a sweat.

"We do not expect you to fight this war alone." Zaeth searched the men's faces a moment longer, but only silence answered.

Jarek cleared his throat. "Let's switch to the fun stuff," he grinned, understanding the need for a morale booster. "Offense."

The atmosphere lightened as the clashing of metal resonated throughout the clearing. Evander and I dueled, reminding me of the early days outside my family home when small tree branches were our only weapons. I expected exhaustion to plague me, to strip me of this rare opportunity, but I didn't slow. Instead, my body listened to my unspoken commands, weaving through the movements with something akin to grace as the steps of battle became intimately familiar.

Evander was smiling with pride as he sliced overhead, causing me to duck before I struck up with my own blade. His weapon whipped around, generating a loud clang as it deflected mine.

"Is that all you've got?" I taunted, high on the adrenaline pumping through my veins. This was everything—this rush, this feeling of knowing how to anticipate, to move on a visceral level. There wasn't time to over think or worry. Only to act and react. I gave in a little more to my body, trusting my instincts to keep me safe as we danced.

Evander huffed a laugh before firing a series of attacks, pressing me back through the tall grass. A buzzing started in my ears, quieting the world around us as I fought to regain control of our waltz. I kicked out with my foot, connecting with his knee. It was a low blow, but it broke his repeated strikes and allowed me to regain balance.

I noted the flash of astonishment in Evander's eyes as I burst forward, peppering him with my own assault and earning back the ground I had lost. His smile was wide, gleaming as he took another step back, his sword easily deflecting my own. A laugh spilled from his lips as he side-stepped my latest thrust.

"Gods, El, you've really been training." His praise sounded genuine, but the ease with which he moved infuriated me. Why were humans forced to live in a world with the fae? How were we supposed to have a chance against beings who were able to level dozens of us in the span of a few moments?

I let the rage build, let the injustice of it all burst forth, fueling my muscles with renewed energy. The buzzing in my ears increased, drowning out everything except the hammering of my own heart. And the gentle rhythm of something else. I launched forward as a low growl erupted from my chest. I knew it was useless, knew I could never actually land a blow against Evander, or any fae for that matter. But while that fact alone spurred my fury, it also allowed for a release of all the pent-up rage I'd been holding back.

The steady, stable beat of my heart increased in tempo, pounding as I flew toward Evander, his form framed by an airy brightness. My mind drifted as I gave myself over to this tantalizing duel, twirling and thrusting, slicing and swinging.

I was the reason Alarik and I were over. He stood for everything beautiful and good in this world. I should have been grateful for being in his life; I should have done everything possible to make myself worthy of standing next to him. But maybe I wasn't meant to be by his side. Maybe we were meant as a balance for each other —his brightness to my dark, two sides of a coin constantly spinning around each other but never facing the same direction.

The bite of Evander's sword against mine sent painful vibrations down my arm, the stinging numbness beckoning me for more. He paused, checking to make sure I wasn't injured, but I smiled through the pain as I spun our blades, using the momentum to launch my next strike.

We had agreed to nothing. We'd made it clear neither of us knew how to use our caged hearts, both of them starved to nothing more than withered, dried-out husks. But somewhere over the last few months, mine had begun to beat. It pumped and bled and yearned for life. For love—or, at the very least, understanding.

Step. Strike. Advance.

Alarik had brought me back to life, and maybe that was enough. Maybe we ended there.

Evander's smile faded. He held my blade in place with his, meeting my eyes with a quizzical look before pressing forward. His speed increased, sending me back with each calculated move. A wave of fatigue leeched the last of my strength. I brought my blade up slower on his next strike, catching his sword but dropping to my knees with the effort. He disarmed me easily with one last swipe.

The faint halo of light weakened around him and the gentle rumble of the distant river and chirping birds returned. He offered me a hand with an astonished smile, pulling me to a stand.

I swallowed, eyes widening as I realized there were no sounds other than the forest creatures. No blades clashing or men panting. No grunts or taunts that usually accompanied training.

The rest of the men stood fixed in their positions throughout the field, all of them staring at us. My eyes found Zaeth, and he too looked at us with quiet reserve.

"What?" I asked through heaving breaths. "Did I do something wrong?"

"Good work today, everyone," Alarik called, walking toward us from across the field. "Hit the showers and regroup in the dining hall at dusk. I'll run through updates then."

"Yes," Zaeth added with an amused twitch of his lips, releasing the fae from their held positions. "Why not call it a day?"

Evander lingered near Jarek and Zaeth, the three of them waiting to see if we'd join them, but a small shake of Alarik's head let them know we'd be a bit. Zaeth's eyes shifted from Alarik to me as he gathered my discarded blade. I offered a small smile, which seemed to only tighten the press of his lips, but be left all the same.

Trying my best to ignore the jitter of nerves bubbling within me, I tilted my chin up to meet Alarik's gaze.

"I'm sorry I wasn't there this morning."

"It's okay," I shrugged, attempting nonchalance. "It was nice spending time with Evander."

"I was looking forward to spending time with you."

My stomach flipped under her intense gaze.

Alarik brought his hand up to my face, the pads of his thumb cool against my cheek, no doubt flushed with exertion. The movement was soft and tender and I felt something within my chest crack at his touch—at the memory of what it used to mean.

I leaned into his touch, heeding that small, questioning part of myself that wondered if we'd ever be what we once were.

"Will you walk with me?" My eyes fluttered open. "The fort

is the priority—the base, the men—but there are a few hours of sunlight left, and I would like to spend them with you."

"Okay."

His own smile met mine a moment before he pulled me in close, his arms wrapping around my waist. "I've missed you, El. I've missed talking to you, feeling you. Does any part of you feel the same?"

My heart clenched as his breath heated my ear, because I did miss him. A part of me *did* wonder what our future could hold, if there remained anything worth fighting for between us.

Tentatively, Alarik pressed his lips to mine, and when I didn't pull away, his hands drifted up against my back, pressing me closer. The stubble along his jaw scraped my lips as I moved against him, giving in to the familiarity of it all, searching for the people we once were.

He pulled back, well aware his breathing was just as ragged as my own.

"I heard there was an entire shower you get to use as your own"

A laugh fell from my lips as he tugged me toward camp.

We clashed and came apart together under the rhythm of the water, abandoning the soothing setting of the shower only so we could stumble to my cabin, falling into each other again, in a cloud of pillows and blankets.

Talking had always been the difficult part, the part where responsibilities and expectations chaffed—where our perceptions of each other never quite matched reality. But here, like this, we understood each other. It was a desperate plea from both of us—to find each other. To find ourselves. It was faulted and fleeting, but I couldn't find the strength to pull away.

Alarik rolled me under him, never breaking our connection

as he moved within me. His hands came down on either side of my face as his body continued to rock, spreading my legs wide as he worked. My body hummed, tightening with sweet longing. His mouth closed over the peaked tip of my breast, his teeth nipping and tongue soothing, tearing a moan from my lips.

Alarik tore his mouth from my breast, capturing the sounds tumbling from my lips with his own. "We'll figure this out, all of it."

My eyes fluttered open, not sure if we would—not truly believing either of us wanted to.

"No matter what comes," he said, eyes searching mine. There was sadness there, an answer we both needed. An acceptance.

I gave a small nod, and it felt a lot like saying 'goodbye'.

Alarik leaned down, lips devouring mine in a swift, brutal kiss, destroying the ability for rational thought. His hands gripped my wrists, pinning them above my head. Our breathing synced, as our bodies climbed and crested together, the both of us knowing this would be the last time we met like this.

## 27
## GREER

Ignoring the fluttering of my heart, I forced my steps not to falter as I ascended the last of the stairs. Ryuu was waiting for me in the library. Well, what this place called a library. It was tucked away on the third floor in the same building as the infirmary. There were a few stacks of half-filled bookshelves lining the walls, and half-a-dozen tables placed throughout the room containing only a quarter of the books held in Alarik's personal study. Most of the books had probably *been* his from the looks of it. And it was always empty, meaning Ryuu and I would be alone.

We'd kept our distance since coming to the fort. Without new information on how to manage or interrupt Will's visions, there was no need for me to see him. I only agreed to speak with him because he said he had an update. It was strictly for Will's sake, but after realizing El was singing Mother's lullaby, after the words of the song came crashing back along with the wash of memories, I knew my sisters and I were involved.

My mouth ran dry as my hand landed on the door knob. There was no need to be nervous. Ryuu was scowling less around me, but despite the glares he shot Cadoc or the bristling of his wings when others complimented my cooking, Ryuu hadn't expressed any hint of being interested in me. Meaning, I refused to show any interest in him. On principle. Taking a deep breath, I lifted my chin, hiding away any vulnerabilities, and stepped into the room.

A cheery giggle reached me first, followed by the long-limbed, blonde-haired air fae it emanated from. She was beautiful. Her majestic white wings preened as her deep red lips stretched into a wide smile. A perfectly manicured hand landed against Ryuu's chest as she leaned in, laughing playfully. My eyes narrowed as I watched it linger, the tick in my jaw increasing as she batted her large-doe eyes at him. I was caught between the impulse to smack her or flee. Being that I'd decided to *not* be interested in Ryuu, I chose the latter.

I'd made it all of a step before she spotted me, her green eyes still shining with mirth. Ryuu looked up from the book he was holding. The scowl I'd come to expect was absent, the hardness in his eyes softened, and his lips—his soft, pink lips—were tilted in a smile. *For her.*

A painful clenching twisted deep in my stomach. I fought against the irrational betrayal, the jealousy racking through me, and desperately worked to school my features into something halfway passing for nonchalance. The woman's hand dragged slowly across the muscles of Ryuu's chest. His spine straightened as my eyes narrowed, but he made no move to pull away.

"You must be Greer," she said, her eyes dragging down the length of my body. She flashed Ryuu another smile before sauntering toward me.

The knot in my stomach loosened marginally as her hand fell away, but the challenge in her eyes had me sizing her up in response. I wouldn't be made to feel small by her, or anyone else for that matter. Ryuu and I were nothing—certainly not friends. There was a time when I would've let myself feel lesser, let my insecurities and fears allow the woman before me to tear me down, to believe I was less than worthy. But I'd silenced that girl years ago. I refused to let her resurface for anyone.

Plastering my best dazzling smile on my face, I drew myself up as she stopped before me, internally groaning that I was a full head shorter than her. "That's me. Ryuu and I have matters to discuss, but you're more than welcome to wait in the dining hall."

Her lingering smirk sharpened with rage. I could have sworn I heard a snort from Ryuu, but his scowl was firmly in place when I dared a glance over her shoulder. I made to step past her toward Ryuu. She huffed at the rebuke, side-stepping to block my advance.

My nostrils flared as I inhaled deeply, fighting the urge to push her out of the way and out the window. "In case that was too difficult for you to understand, you're dismissed. I'm sure Ryuu will collect you once *we* are done."

"Greer," Ryuu snapped.

"What?" I said, not sure what had gotten into me. I was normally the cheery one, but it was taking everything in myself to not rip this girl's head off. "Is my brother's life no longer your priority, now that your girlfriend is here?"

"She's not my girlfriend," he said, causing the woman's jaw to clench as if it were a statement she planned on disproving.

"I'm the messenger," she gritted through clenched teeth. "I'm the one with information on the prophecies."

My eyes swung to him, pleading for him to deny it, but Ryuu nodded, his confirmation leeching the fight from me. I still wanted to tell her to get lost, but Will was more important.

Exhaling, I relented. "Fine. Let's get this over with, shall we?"

I stepped around her, heading directly for the table the two had been hovering around. It was stacked with scrolls and thick volumes, all of which looked to be in pristine condition. The air fae bristled at my rudeness and Ryuu shot me a glare, but neither of them prevented me from taking a seat. Much to my irritation, the two of them shared a silent conversation before deciding to join me.

"This is Cress," Ryuu said.

"Cressida, actually," she said with a sanguine smile. Ryuu raised a brow, the small movement causing her to roll her eyes and add, "Though since we will be working together for the foreseeable future, I suppose we can lose the formalities and stick with Cress."

*Working together?* My eyes narrowed on Ryuu. "I thought *you* were the expert on all things oracle related?"

"He is," Cress answered. "But seeing as how he's stuck in the middle of this dreadful forest, I'll be forced to play the go-between. It's unheard of to remove sacred texts from The Great Library, but his ma—"

Ryuu cleared his throat, shooting Cress a warning look.

She swallowed before starting again. "But Ryuu has allowed us to transport select items here, seeing as how your brother requires constant protection from himself and others."

"What do you mean by 'protection from himself'?" My voice grew strained.

Cress blinked, looking at me as if I were asking if the sun would rise tomorrow. "Of course. He's *human*." Her nose wrinkled as the last word was wrung from her lips.

I gritted my teeth. "What does that have to do with anything?"

Her chin lifted a fraction as she shrugged. "He's weak."

Ryuu released a low growl, the noise startling enough to prevent me from lunging at her.

"What?" she asked, looking down her nose at me from across the table. "It's true. Most fae oracles are trained at the first signs of being gifted. It takes years to master protection of the mind—"

"Cress," Ryuu said, glancing at me.

"No," I said. "I need to hear this." Because as much as I

wanted to slap that smug look off her face, I knew she was only stating the horrifying truth nobody else dared say.

"Your brother is still in his first decade of life. He has no fae traits from what I've been told, other than the goddess's blessing. We need to find a way to prevent his mind from shattering, to keep his visions separate from reality. His life is already significantly shorter than that of a fae, but if we can find a way to shield him from the bulk of her power, we might be able to ensure his survival for another decade. Maybe two." She finished with a shrug, as if she hadn't just sentenced my little brother to a short, painful life.

A chill settled in my bones; my body processed her words before my mind could. "You're saying he's doomed? Just like that?"

Her piercing green eyes met mine. They were cold, but not ruthless as I'd thought. She was calculating but held no malice or ulterior motives. She believed what she said. And that was so much worse.

"With the proper blessings and rituals, maybe a few protection spells, we can extend his life. Most oracles were reported having visions a half of dozen or so times a year, but your brother seems to be blessed beyond measure—"

"Cress," Ryuu's voice rang low, but she didn't stop.

"Based on how frequently he's gifted, if we can sustain him for even another year, it will be worth it."

My hand collided with her face, the slap echoing in the vacant room. She hissed, wings springing wide, as she shot out of her seat.

I blinked, almost uncertain if I'd really done it, but the stinging of my hand and the blooming red stain across her cheek confirmed that I had.

"How dare you—" she started, the sharp tips of barbs extending through the soft white feathers of her wings.

"My brother's life is not something to be used to record

trophies for your collection." I hardly recognized the deadly calm ringing through my words, the one that promised suffering. "You are here to help protect him for his own sake, to save the life of a child. If unraveling the goddess's riddles is the best way to do that, then fine. But *he* is the priority. Not his visions."

Cress turned her sights on Ryuu as if waiting for him to defend her. Anger smoldered in her eyes, igniting into offended rage as he stood. And then took a single step back. Toward me. Her nostrils flared and her gaze darted to the pile of texts stacked along the table, debating her options. After another moment, her wings folded neatly behind her back before she reclaimed her seat.

"Fine," Cress muttered through clenched teeth. "We may have alternative reasons, but our priorities are the same. Decipher the prophecies, extend the oracle—*Will's*—life. I have a few theories on the bits of information Ryuu has managed to pass to me, I'd like to know if there has been anything new?"

"No," Ryuu answered, taking a seat. "He's taking a tonic and I've been blessing Will at night and no further visions have emerged."

"Blessing?" I asked.

Ryuu's eyes swung to mine. "It's a prayer that offers peace. Nothing further."

I studied him a moment longer before nodding my thanks.

Cress frowned. "I'm glad even basic prayers are working, but I haven't found any recordings to be similar. Most prophecies overlap with previous recordings, effectively giving us a starting point on where to research. Without a complete vision, it's nearly impossible to know where to begin."

Seeing my furrowed brow, Ryuu explained. "Will speaks in short phrases. They are disjointed, mere fragments. Most are full sentences or poems. Some are paragraphs."

"It's probably another shortcoming of the oracle being human."

I narrowed my eyes at Cress and was rewarded with a flinch. She cleared her throat before dipping her head and pulling a scroll toward herself.

"Poems?" I asked, my mind gravitating toward Mother's lullaby. "Would it be possible for a prophecy to be the length of a song?"

Recently returned memories flitted through my mind. All of them were related to the lullaby in some way. I'd run away from El this morning, too startled to speak, but the longer I focused on the lullaby, the more sure I was that part of Will's visions were referencing it.

"Some are of that length," Ryuu said with a frown. "Did Will have another vision I was unaware of?"

I glanced between the two of them. "No, but I might be able to help."

## 28

## ELARA

THE DAY OF TRAINING FOLLOWED BY THE NIGHT WITH ALARIK left my body beyond tired. If it hadn't been for the growling of my stomach, I would have skipped breakfast all together. I tugged on a pair of worn pants and a loose top, ignoring the soreness between my thighs which reminded me I was in desperate need of a shower. It would have to wait until after I had a meal.

I entered the dining hall walking through the tables of men and fae enjoying their breakfast, until I joined the members of the Select Guard, knowing Evander would be there. Alarik glanced up, offering a gentle smile as I neared.

We'd spoken last night, before he left, verbalizing what had passed between us. Alarik had a piece of my heart, and I his. There had been no expectations when we had first come together, but through all of this, we had somehow managed to heal parts of one another. He showed me there's more to life than fighting, and I think I helped him realize that it's possible for him to love after Rhyson. Not with me, but perhaps someday he'd find another.

Kavan scooted over, allowing me a seat next to Evander, the latter handing me a plate already piled with my berries.

"Thanks," I said as I scarfed down the sweetened bowl of steaming oats, burning the tip of my tongue in the process, before biting into a handful of plump berries.

Alarik gave a small chuckle. "Try not to eat everything before I get back."

"I promise nothing," I said, content with the calmness that had settled between us.

He smiled before making his way to the front of the room.

I watched as he made his way to the front of the room, my eyes drifting over the group of others he joined. My mouth ran dry, causing the half chewed lump of pastry to lose all sweetness as I caught sight of Zaeth.

His nostrils flared, bright rings blazing to life around his irises as they swung from Alarik to me. Zaeth's gaze traveled down my body, noting the loose top and sweatpants before meeting my eyes. He knew. Shame and the desperate urge to explain myself roared to life.

I reached for water to clear my throat, willing the scarlet stain across my cheeks to fade and the sinking pit in my stomach to less. When I lowered the glass, Zaeth's features were smoothed into a mild look of disdain. Alarik had taken a spot beside him to address the room together, but Zaeth stepped forward, positioning himself in the place of power as he spoke without so much as a nod toward Alarik.

"We've been impressed with the level of dedication, skill, and teamwork observed between our people." His voice was clipped, tense despite the semblance of control. "Alarik and I have agreed to move forward with regular combined daily training sessions led by Jarek. He will be placing you in alternating pairs to assure both fae and humans learn from one another."

A low rumbling of energized murmurs rang through the room, but Zaeth continued before they could grow.

"Another village along the foothills of the Jagged Mountains was attacked last night." The room fell silent. "Two others in the Earth Kingdom were destroyed last week. We expect everyone here to take training seriously. Patrols along the surrounding area will be implemented starting tomorrow. Everyone will be required to participate in the rotation. It's time we stopped losing innocents."

Zaeth's eyes landed on me, the cinnamon depths simmering with rage. "Fort Dhara is not a retreat. If anyone here is not ready to take this seriously, not ready to fight and die for the innocents of this world, they should leave."

His voice slipped into a predatory growl on the last word before he turned from the hall, stalking out into the grounds beyond. With a quick cock of his head, Jarek signaled for Ryuu to follow him, the two of them chasing after Zaeth.

The blush which had finally cooled along my cheeks flared to life once more.

Alarik cleared his throat as all eyes turned to him. "Integrated training sessions will be held daily. We will be cycling out three men each week to return to the base and distribute knowledge of the new techniques. Ryuu has agreed to escort the men to and from the base. Traveling in small parties is risky, but it's the best option we have. A schedule will be distributed with your assigned roles and posted tomorrow."

The crowd dispersed with his dismissal as Alarik and Soter left for their perimeter sweep.

I took my time in the shower, savoring the way the gentle patter of the water drowned out this morning's conversation, well most of it. My stomach twisted as I recalled Zaeth's words, recalled the way he looked at me—disgust and disappointment.

He hadn't directly called me out, but it was clear he thought I was here for Alarik.

A curse left my lips as the clock chimed, signaling the start of lessons. By the time I made it to the field, training was well underway. Jarek casually wove between the men, offering adjustments as he went, but his eyes lit when he spotted me.

"Glad you decided to join us. I was beginning to think my partner wouldn't show."

"Your partner?" I asked, searching for Zaeth.

"Zaeth had some matters to attend to." My stomach clenched. "But I think it's good to rotate partners every now and then, as you did with Alarik yesterday. Zaeth is more of a one-partner sort of man, but I say why stick with just the one when there's so many to choose from?"

I narrowed my eyes at him, but found no hostility in his gaze. "I didn't realize Zaeth cared about my choice of sparring partners," I answered carefully. "But Alarik and I won't be meeting again. Last night was a farewell of sorts."

"Wonderful. I'll be sure to pass on the message."

"There's no message—"

"Of course not, kitten," Jarek winked, flitting over to a nearby tree before returning to my side in a flash. "I hope you don't mind a bit of swordplay with me. I've already taken the liberty of bringing you a blade."

I laughed despite myself, accepting the outstretched blade. "I'd be honored for the private lesson."

A wicked chuckle sounded from him as his eyes twinkled. "Ahh, well I'm afraid I would love to engage in *private lessons*, kitten, but I know of at least one hulking male who'd promise to remove some of my favorite pieces if I tried. It's best if we keep things strictly professional."

He ended with a wink, before dropping into a sparring stance. Before I had the chance to advance, the alarm sounded.

29

ELARA

OUR HEADS JERKED TOWARD THE NORTH SIDE OF THE FORT AS FAE rushed the tree line with swords drawn, leaving humans to position themselves further back with bows.

"Move." Jarek's voice boomed with authority before he was gone, rushing to the others with fae speed.

They broke through the trees in an explosion of branches and leaves, snarling muzzles red with smeared, dried blood from souls long since reaped. Their eyes blazed an otherworldly cobalt as the ridged hair along their back flickered with the heat of a searing blue fire. The cú sidhe.

"Gods," I breathed, willing my legs to carry me closer to the demons despite the fear coiling in my stomach. These were the beasts of the other realm, ones who killed for sport, who delighted in ripping bodies apart and devouring souls. They were supposed to be confined to the darkest niches of Pax, to the Shadowlands of the north and the misted pockets of the Western Woods, but somehow, they were here.

A familiar scream ripped through the air. My stomach dropped as I spotted Greer's tangled mess of blonde curls stumbling away from the forest just east of where the pack prowled, her basket of herbs forgotten behind her.

I cursed, changing direction to position myself between her and the advancing monsters. The first of the massive wolves launched forward, changing directions as it was drawn by her screams. Sharp, pointed teeth bared but a fae blade intercepted them. The silver glint of a sword whirled through the air, finding purchase in the flank of the beast. Green blood spilled from the gash as the shrieking creature crumpled to the ground.

There was a beat of silence before the pack raised their massive snouts to the sky and issued a blood chilling howl, the sound radiating into the trees at their backs. At least a dozen or so answered the call. The handful of fae present moved, darting through the trees at heightened speed as the cú sidhe launched into action.

Three of the hounds broke through the thin lines of defense. Our men wasted no time releasing the taut strings of their bows, arrows flying through the air. Two found purchase in the nearest wolf, slowing it enough for Jarek to decapitate it in one fell swoop. A mangled cry emanated from the woods. His eyes met mine, flicking to Greer's retreating form. He nodded once, leaving me to my fate, before hurling into the woods with the other fae, combating the brunt of the attack.

"Get inside!" I shouted, racing toward her.

"What does it look like I'm doing?" She shrieked, pumping her arms as she sped toward me.

A beast stalked through the trees, estranged from the pack at my back. Claw-tipped paws dug into the earth, each calculating step drawing it near as its fierce eyes locked on Greer's fleeing form with a predator's hunger. Its shoulders reached the level of my hips, rolling as it prowled toward her. I dared a glance over my shoulder, finding three humans nearly upon us.

"Greer, aim for the men. You won't make it to the infirmary."

She changed course, but the warning came at a cost. The

creature's attention snapped to me as it pushed off powerful hind legs, propelling it forward with its fangs bared. I side-stepped just in time, saving my neck from the fatal bite. It spun, the hair along its spine flaring into a cobalt blue, but before it could attack, two of the humans rushed forward.

"No!" I shouted, knowing their head-on attack was a sure way to end up dead. The cú sidhe were vicious, but intelligent. The first of the men swung wide. The cú sidhe didn't waste the opportunity. Its jaws clamped down on the thick part of the man's thigh. With a quick snap of its head, the beast tore a large chunk of flesh away, leaving the snow-white bone visible beneath ragged skin and frayed tendons, all instantly coated with a deep crimson stain as the artery began to pulse. The piercing cries of the wounded man rang through the air as the creature raised its head, gulping down the meat in a single swallow.

It turned gluttonous eyes on the next man, nostrils flaring as he backed away in distress, relishing the fear that rolled off him in waves.

"Th-there's more," the man sputtered, trembling as his friend's wails quieted.

I followed his line of sight, spotting two pairs of burning blue eyes peering out from the trees. The monstrous wolves appeared a moment later, flanking the one licking fresh blood from its jaws.

"Get behind me," I breathed, my voice somehow steady. He scurried to my side, whimpering as he passed. He was young, I realized. Around Greer's age. I saw from the corner of my eye she'd reached the other man, both of whom had snagged the attention of the beasts before us.

I side-stepped, positioning myself between Greer and the foul beasts before me. I'd die before they reached her. Swallowing past the dryness of my throat, I realized that was a very real possibility. Three cú sidhe against myself and a man who was more likely to faint than fight. Not great odds.

A shadow passed overhead a moment before Greer shrieked a futile warning, the jaws of the wolves snapping as they sprang forward.

## 30
## GREER

THE GROUND VIBRATED WITH THE IMPACT OF RYUU'S WINGED form dropping from the sky. He rose from his kneeled position, eyes trained on me as he drew the blade from his back. Those dark eyes flecked with green raked across my body, looking for injuries that weren't there to find.

"I'm fine," I whispered.

His eyes flicked up, holding mine. His pupils elongated, shifting into a reptilian slit a moment before he turned to the snarling pack awaiting him. Their bodies littered the ground in seconds, the green pool of blood expanding as their bodies cooled.

"Tourniquet his leg." He gestured to the felled man, blood still spurting with each weakening beat of his heart. "Leave the rest to us."

❧

It had finished in minutes. Ryuu swept the perimeter after he was done, ensuring there were no other packs lurking. Jarek was next, adjusting the wards to prevent creatures from crossing. The cú sidhe had walked the line of conscious evil and animal, but the oversight was rectified, now.

It had been days since that morning, and still I couldn't forget the way Ryuu's wings glinted as he fell from the sky. The power contained in his thighs to absorb the impact. The way the earth herself seemed to bow, dipping under his presence as he rose to his full height.

Blinking the enthralling images from my mind, I adjusted the pen in my hand and continued writing down every line of Mother's lullaby. Ryuu and I had spent the last few days together, comparing it to the various lines spoken by Will while he was under the goddess's influence and there was more than enough evidence to suggest the two were connected.

I shifted in the stiff wooden chair at the largest table in the library as I combed through Ryuu's collection of recordings. Apparently, he meant what he said about holding a deep respect for the goddess's oracles. He'd taken the time to list anything pertinent, including countless stories crafted by Will, even the ones shared in his waking hours.

The original batch of scrolls had taken me much longer than I'd intended and left me with a mild headache. At first glance, it appeared as if words or phrases were out of order or missing all together. I had to focus on each word, willing my mind to grasp the information contained within. My head pulsed from the concentration required and I felt utterly spent by the end of the day, but I'd compiled an impressive stack of notes to review the next day. A small headache was blooming across my skull as I worked through the next batch of scrolls, but it wasn't as debilitating as the first time around.

Cress insisted on leaving as soon as possible to return to The Great Library of the Air Kingdom. That idea sounded wonderful to me, but Ryuu insisted she stay until we brought El and the others up to date.

"Hey, Sis. Wards are secure," El's voice called from the

doorway as she strolled forward. Her hair hung in damp loose curls from a recent shower and she'd decided to forgo the training attire for a comfortable sweats-and-t-shirt combination.

"You don't have to tell me that every day," I said, though I knew the habit was more for her comfort than mine.

She shrugged. "It's always good to know."

"Is Alarik still beating himself up for not being present?"

It was a shock when El told me she'd spent the night with Alarik one last time and I'd been skeptical when she'd promised they'd agreed to be friends. Relationships hardly ever reverted. They progressed and then fell apart, but I was surprised to see that there was no awkwardness between the two. Just a calm understanding.

"Yep," she said, crossing the room and taking a seat opposite me at the table. "Where is everyone?"

"Ryuu and Cress should be here soon."

"Cress?" she asked, sitting opposite me while pulling one of Ryuu's open books to her side and flipping causally through the pages.

I couldn't help but scowl, recalling the way Ryuu had fallen right back into their easy conversation after I'd told them about Mother's lullaby, turning to each other with a familiarity that takes years to cultivate. Ryuu, the fae who barely spoke around me, was capable of holding civilized conversations with Cress. Worse—he was actually *nice* to her. It was infuriating.

"Whoa. What's that look for?"

My spine stiffened. "Cressida is the acclaimed air fae scholar who has been helping Ryuu track down everything there is to know about prophecies and oracles."

"I knew someone was here, but hadn't realized you met with her."

"Just the once," I said stiffly. *And that was enough.*

El's brows furrowed as she took in the tight set of my jaw. "And you hate her because…"

"Because she's terrible," I nearly screamed. "She flirts with Ryuu constantly, while I'm in the room. She basically acts like I don't exist and is always pawing at him. There is no reason for her to touch his chest every three seconds. This is a library for gods' sake."

El's eyebrows shot up in a look that suggested I was being completely unreasonable, but she would have my back no matter what because she was my sister.

A high-pitched giggle sounded from the hall, announcing Cress's return. My jaw ticked. I had no doubt she was hanging all over Ryuu, and my suspicions were confirmed seconds later as they entered the room. Her arm was linked with his and she leaned into him, nudging his shoulder. His lips quirked and her long fingers drifted up his arm, caressing the muscle through the soft material of his shirt.

I met El's eyes with a look that said, 'see?'

She nodded before plastering a look of disdain on her face. "If you two have had enough time acting like a pair of lovesick teenagers, I'd like to get started on finding ways to save my brother."

It was as if El had slapped Cress across the face. Her smile vanished in an instant, replaced by a seething glare. Ryuu's scowl was firmly in place again, but it hurt less to have him scowl at me than watch him smile at her.

He cleared his throat as he approached the table, all business once more. "We've just returned from speaking with Jarek and Soter. Neither have heard of the prophecy Greer shared with us."

"Prophecy?" El asked, her face swinging to mine in confusion. "You had a vision?"

"No," I said quickly, hating the worry in her eyes. "Ryuu's

referring to Mother's lullaby. He thinks it's actually an ancient prophecy."

El's brows furrowed. "I know Mother sang a lullaby, something about a dragon and phoenix but I can't recall the words."

"That's the other peculiar part, isn't it?" Cress added. "Greer said she felt the same way until the moment she was able to remember everything clearly."

El shook her head. Ignoring Cress, she turned to me for answers. "How were you able to remember it? And why can't I?"

My hand reached out to her, the two of us pulling strength from one another. "We don't have an answer yet, and there's no way to prove it, but Ryuu thinks Mother may have had a memory spell cast on us."

El looked at me as if she thought I was joking. I pushed forward.

"I know it sounds crazy, but I think it's true. When I remembered the song, I had a flashback, or I guess a resurfacing of a suppressed memory. You, Lannie, and I were in Mother's room. She said we would one day understand, and when that day came, she hoped we wouldn't hate her."

My sister yanked her hand away as if I'd burned her. She stood, fingers pressing to her temple as she paced the room. After a moment she turned to me, gaze hard. "You have the lullaby—prophecy written down?"

I nodded.

"Read it."

Swallowing, I sorted through the stack of papers on my right until I came to the crisp sheet with freshly penned letters, knowing the words contained on it could very well change our reality forever. My voice rang clear as I read:

"Driven by pride, brothers wandered deep,
Through splintered realms to the shadowed keep.

Severing bonds, they ventured too far,
Enduring pain and harrowing scars.


A raven's wings protect the realm,
The final shield of the humans' helm.
But creatures' crushing blows shall reign,
Shattering shelter, unleashing pain.


The three returned, vengeful, demanding.
Intent on war with clever planning.
Fierce dragon's tears, releasing, freeing,
Breaking constraints, finally seeing.


Silent lotus, sprouting redemption,
Flourishing without compensation.
A flicker of light preserving hope,
Gripping fiercely to the savior's rope.


Dark Phoenix's vengeance, harsh unbending,
Torment abounds, unchecked, unending.
Immense powers merge, blending, pooling.
Great storms of chaos twisting, spooling.


When wrongs are righted and wounds mend,
When fear is conquered at battle's end,
Darkness will spring, devouring all,
With malicious tendrils none can stall.

.   .   .

When wicked forces of old arrive,
Death will reign among the ancient hive."

My hand shook as I placed the sheet in the middle of the table. The silence stretched, the three of us watching El. Her brows drew together as her hands pressed on either side of her temples.

"My head is killing me," she breathed.

I shared a quick glance with Ryuu before coming to her side and guiding her onto the chair. "That happened to me right before I remembered. I think your mind is breaking through the spell."

She groaned, pressing the heels of her hands into her eyes. "Why would she do this? Why repeat the prophecy until we memorized it, only to force us to forget?"

"Fae have been known to do such things." Ryuu's voice was surprisingly calm. "Even the strongest memory spells do not last forever. Some are cast with specific expiration dates or meant to be undone with a triggering event. Something Greer did or said or heard must have unraveled the spell."

"Your memories are returning now because your mind was directly confronted by the true memory," Cress continued, speaking to El with a kindness she never used with me. "It weakens the bonds. Some strong spells can withstand it, especially when they have been strengthened, but the initial casting must have been completed years ago."

There was a small gasp from El as her hands fell away and then her eyes were searching mine. "It's true. The lullaby, the memories—there are dozens of them."

I nodded grimly. "All related to the prophecy."

El nodded, her face slightly pale, but she forced her back to straighten as she met Ryuu's stare. "Any ideas on what this means?"

Ryuu looked between my sister and I before releasing a long sigh. "I spoke with Zaeth this morning. He came to the same conclusion Cress and I did. It would seem your mother has a role to play in discovering answers. Whether that is a large or small role is still up for debate.

"We know she, at the very least, is responsible for the memory spell. In Will's latest vision, he mentions being 'bound' before using her name, 'Adara.'"

A look of unease passed between El and I as Ryuu laid out his recordings.

"We are assuming she was referring to binding your memories only."

I frowned. "You think there's more to it than keeping the prophecy a secret?"

"Perhaps." The forest-green flecks in Ryuu's eyes glowed a little brighter as he held my gaze. "For now, we need to focus on decoding the prophecy. Zaeth didn't discover anything useful in the Dark Kingdom, but he has others searching while he remains here."

"The point is," Cress cut in. "We need to be focusing on the prophecy. Your mother restricted your memories. Plenty of fae parents do that for the protection of their children and you said she had friends in the Light Kingdom?"

"Yes, but—"

"One of them probably helped her, thinking it safer to hide the prophecy among human children." Cress's gaze cut to Ryuu. "The prophecy she was concealing has to be linked with a previous oracle." She pressed her chair back, large owl-like wings unfolding as she came to Ryuu's side, clutching his hands with hers. "I must return to the Air Kingdom. I'm sorry to be cutting our time short, but you understand. The goddess comes first. I'll be back before you know it."

Cress pressed up on her toes, planting a kiss on each of Ryuu's cheeks, before vanishing through the door.

My jaw clenched. Thank gods she was gone.

Ryuu shifted uncomfortably as he noted my glare, choosing instead to ignore it. He turned toward El. "Zaeth and I agree the 'raven' is the key."

"We've concluded the same," she answered. "If the shield stays up, we're protected."

"Exactly."

"The rest of it won't matter. War, torment, the Dark Phoenix, as long as the shield remains, Pax is safe."

A spark of defiance simmered in El's eyes, the same one I could feel reflected in my own. We were going to stop this prophecy from unfolding, and in doing so, save our little brother.

"Let's find this raven."

31

# ELARA

I'D LET HOPE SIZZLE IN MY VEINS AFTER UNCOVERING THE TRUTH behind Mother's lullaby. I'd let myself believe we'd be able to save Will, but weeks passed and we were no closer to answers.

The Fractured continued to ravage smaller towns, their army no doubt portaling across Pax, aided by the traitor Alderidge. They had grown sloppy, though. A few survivors lingered, each reporting the same red-eyed, pale commander directing throngs of the Fractured in the attacks, the corrupted fae leaving only when bodies littered the earth and smoke and ash coated the sky.

The reprieve Ryuu's blessings and Lannie's tea had offered Will was over. Every few days, he succumbed to the visions, repeating the same shards of information—the raven, the three have returned, the dark phoenix. Pain. Blood. Death. I couldn't help the growing hatred for the goddess as I was forced to watch my little brother suffer again and again, each time taking longer to recover.

Greer threw herself into research alongside Ryuu. But I'd given up on books. I focused on training, needing the physical outlet to silence the worry, taking refuge in my sparring sessions with Jarek. Zaeth and I had barely spoken since the morning he stormed out at breakfast, but he would occasionally join training as a bystander, relishing pointing out each of my flaws. It was humiliating, but as much as I wanted to wish him away, a small part of me looked forward to seeing him.

Stepping into the crisp morning air with my sword in hand, I made my way to the training field. Gravel crunched under my boots as I crossed in front of the stables, my eyes doing the usual quick scan of the surrounding trees.

"I'm afraid it's just us today, kitten," Jarek said, stepping away from the sparring pairs of human and fae surrounding him.

A sigh escaped me as I did one last check. No Ryuu today, either. He was due back any day now with the new recruits from base. The lessons were said to be going well under Vidarr's instructions. Ryuu offered corrections when he cycled men out, but even he was impressed with the advancements. Each group brought to Fort Dhara was more aware of the fae fighting techniques, adapting quicker to our sparring sessions and stoking the flames of hope throughout the men. We were nearly ready, if only we could find a way to track the Fractured before they attacked.

"I promised to cover patrol for Evander this morning," Jarek explained.

My brows lifted in question. Favors weren't free.

Jarek shrugged. "I figured it would be nice to give you the day to recover since yesterday's session was a little rough."

A little? He had me run for hours, going straight into strength circuits, followed by sword fighting and then a final loop around the fort on Ember with a bow. I all but collapsed the second I was fed and showered.

"Thank the gods. Let's go." I looped my arm in his as we made for the tree line and Jarek whistled a melody as we scanned the lush forest, flourishing with life.

"Any update on the Fractured?"

Jarek sighed. "We'd need a wild fae of our own to be able to track Alderidge. Or an exceptionally powerful light fae who'd be able to feel the distortion of prisms, but without a portal of our own, our armies will be useless."

"Is anyone willing to travel to the Wild Kingdom? Maybe they're ready to help."

"Yes, Zaeth has already spoken to Naz and she's looking into it."Naz, as in Nazneen, the shadowwalker who helped save Neith.

"What are her plans—"

"Look, kitten. We have at least a few hours combing through this forest and I've already talked as much as I possibly can about war. Let's discuss something more... intriguing." A playful smirk lifted his lips and I couldn't help but be taken in by his joyful charisma. "When are you and Zaeth going to talk about an occurrence that happened with a certain general?"

My lips pressed into a thin line and I dropped my arm from his.

He quirked a brow, his smile stretching into a teasing grin. "Come now, kitten. I passed along the message that you and Alarik are no longer *sparring*. It's your turn to make a move."

I shot him a glare. "I have a better idea. Why don't you tell me why you are covering for Evander this morning."

His eyes narrowed. "Well played, kitten."

My lips parted in a small gasp, not expecting him to confirm it. Evander hadn't shown interest in another since Jem. "Is it serious?"

The question earned me an eye roll.

"I hope you're happy," Jarek said with an exaggerated pout. "Now we have nothing fun to talk about."

We wound through trees, being sure to find the blue markers indicating where the protection spells ended. They should be strong enough to hold back the Fractured, but we wouldn't know until it was tested. I hoped we'd never find out.

Our steps through the forest settled into a comforting rhythm, and I let my mind wander back to Alarik, and ultimately to Zaeth.

"Is it always this complicated?" I asked, surprising myself with the need to give voice to my tumultuous thoughts.

Jarek's light blue eyes shot me a questioning glance.

"I know I cared for Alarik, but it was like we grew in different directions. Still similar, bot not quite the same."

A rather obnoxious snort sounded from Jarek. "Of course, you're not the same. People change. Fae, humans, mages, pixies, nymphs, and flowers. We all change." He shrugged. "That's how we grow. It's a part of life, kitten. The trick to love is to find the one person or people you wish to change *with*."

"But can you be sure you'll grow together?" A pair of cinnamon eyes came unbidden to my mind. "Wait, did you just say people? As in, multiple?"

He wiggled his eyebrows at me. "I've already told you, you and I can't be together. We've gotten to know each other well these last few weeks, but I've come to see you as more of a sister."

I rolled my eyes.

"But to answer your question, yes, I was referring to relationships with more than one person."

I peered over at him. "I read something about that in a book on dark fae. Is is common among all fae?"

He gave a tight laugh which didn't reach his eyes. "Not particularly common, no. But in certain kingdoms, it's not considered unusual. The kingdoms of the north are far more inclusive and yet they're perceived as the villains of this earth. Though I must say, the Earth Kingdom has come a long way with reform. I believe their queen is facing current civil unrest because of her untraditional views."

"Do you prefer polyamorous relationships?" I asked hesitantly, unsure if it was something he felt comfortable discussing.

"It's okay to ask questions. Learning is never a bad thing. I'm open when it comes to relationships, though I must confess I gravitate toward monogamous relations if I'm choosing to be committed to another. But I don't judge others for their choices. I've never understood why others think they are qualified to condemn my soul for something which causes neither harm nor hatred."

He shook his head as we made it to the furthest stretches of the loop, nearly halfway around. I glanced at him, wondering why he looked so stricken. "Is Zaeth not accepting of your attraction to men?"

Jarek blinked. "Zaeth? He wouldn't care if I confessed I was in love with a tree nymph, long since solidified in her earth-bound form." He chuckled. "He'd simply ask if she consented to my attention and then congratulate us."

He looked pointedly at me, weighing whether to continue. I held his gaze and after a long moment, he spoke. "Has Evander spoken to you of my ancestry?" I shook my head, causing Jarek's lips to lift into a soft smile. "No, I didn't think he would. As you can guess from my appearance, I'm a light fae. A royal if we are being particular."

My eyes widened, mouth going slack. "A royal? As in the royal family of the Light Kingdom."

Jarek's shoulders stiffened, but he forced a light tone. "That's the one. And I can tell you that the light fae are not an embracing people. They're nice enough when you fit the mold, but they prefer things to remain as they are—tight, neat, and orderly. Anything other than a marriage with a pure fae woman from the nobility was unacceptable."

"And you prefer men?" I guessed, seeing where he was going with this.

"I prefer not to worry about labels. Why attempt to force ourselves in restrictive boxes, which others use to draw their own judgmental opinions? We are all beings with thoughts and emotions. Our actions, our beliefs, signify the truth of our souls.

"I desire witty banter and intelligent conversations. The vessel the person is contained within isn't a determining factor. Don't get me wrong, bodies are beautiful. So much so that I find it's hard to decide on just one. Soft sensual curves can be lovely in some, while sharp angles and firm planes are alluring in another. Currently, I'm obsessed with a certain pair of auburn eyes and matching hair." He wiggled his brows playfully at me.

Lifting a brow, I ignored his playfulness and pinned him with a glare. "Evander has been through a lot."

Jarek sobered. "He has shared his past. I'm sorry for the grief you must have felt losing your brothers and parents in a matter of days."

I swallowed the lump in my throat, not wanting to revisit those ghosts. "Did your family find out? Is that why you left?"

His eyes darkened with an unknown memory. "I left before they could. My family, my home—you have to understand. There are good people there, sheep hiding among the lions. But they are much too frightened for things to change. Me being honest about my preferences was not a simple matter of acceptance. Even when the goddess saw fit to bless my aunt with a mate, it wasn't enough to sway the royal family from their views. So, I left."

"What do you mean by 'mate'?"

His lips pressed thin. "One's match. The ultimate pairing. I watched my aunt suffer because of hers… I don't think I'd be strong enough to survive it."

"What happened?"

Jarek tensed, letting the silence stretch. Just as I had given up on an answer, he spoke. "She snuck out during Litha, intending to dance under the light of the moon with the locals and gorge herself on nevernectar until the sun rose. But she wandered further than intended, following a necklace urging, until she

happened upon a small camp of dark fae enjoying the celebrations.

"A beautiful fae with small soft curves and a large mane of
vibrant red hair reaching down her back in a tangle of braids
and knots twirled through the swaying grass, catching sight of
my aunt. It was instantaneous, but the two of them couldn't be
together in the Light Kingdom. Same sex couples are controver-
sial among the people, but unacceptable among the light royals.
So, they decided to retreat into the Wild Kingdom, my aunt
wishing to live in a small cottage together rather than in a
palace alone."

"When the other royals discovered she had run off to be with
a dark fae, and a female on top of that..." He fell silent, raking a
hand through his normally immaculate hair.

More questions flooded my tongue, but the sound of hurried
footfalls brought both of us to attention. Our blades were
drawn and ready in a flash. We held still, our ears straining.
Ragged breaths joined the sharp snapping branches.

It was headed straight for us.

## 32

# GREER

THE WARM, SOOTHING SMELL OF SUMMER-BLEND TEA SCENTED
the air as I sorted through the latest batch of scrolls Zaeth had
delivered this morning. His eyes had searched the small
confines of the library, his shoulders sagging slightly when he
found I was alone. I'd lifted a brow in question, but he gave a
tight, abrupt nod before excusing himself.

My lips twitched. We'd been told countless tales of the
wicked dark fae growing up, but I'd yet to see him murder for
sport or even eat a drop of blood. On the contrary, Zaeth
remained coolly reserved, similar to Alarik in a way, but with an
underlying darkness that spoke of centuries of battle. And,
oddly, I wanted to trust him.

It was clear Zaeth was a warrior, all the fae here were, but
while a buzz of nervousness hummed through most, he was
calm. This was a man who knew himself. He knew his evils and
accepted them, welcomed them even. I could see how that
might benefit El. At least she wasn't lying to herself here, and
had grown to accept who she was.

Swallowing a honey sweetened sip in an attempt to calm my
nerves, I placed the cup of tea on the wooden table as I reached

for another rolled up piece of parchment. Ryuu would be here any moment.

As if the images from the cú sidhe attack weren't enough to invade my dreams, I'd stumbled upon Ryuu sparring with Zaeth the other day. I'd been looking for El, and was happily surprised to find she'd finished training early, leaving the two of them to their own devices.

They moved with a fluidity that was enthralling. Zaeth was alluring, all bronzed skin coated in deep brands and short dark hair, but Ryuu mirrored one of the gods. His hair was pulled back, tied into a knot with a leather strap. A few sweat-soaked pieces had escaped, framing his strong jaw and the dark stubble lining it. Where Zaeth's skin held tattoos, Ryuu's was bare, leaving every bit of centuries' worth of thick, defined muscle on display.

His wings were everywhere, whirling around him to fend off blows. I nearly gasped the first time Zaeth's blade sliced into the brown-flecked white feathers, but a resounding clang rang through the clearing as the sun reflected against a glint of gold. The barbs hidden beneath had extended, acting as a temporary shield as Ryuu spun, diving in with his next attack. I watched, enchanted, as they clashed over and over again, until Ryuu shot into the air with a taunting grin. Zaeth had only given a quick shake of his head before retreating in the direction of the river with a beckoning gesture.

Before I turned to go, Ryuu's eyes found mine as he hovered in the sky. For once, his gaze stayed open. There was no hostility or anger, no scowl upon his face that he seemed to secure strictly for my benefit—it was just him, staring down at me with a hint of wonder as his magnificent wings pumped, holding his body afloat. His gaze slid lower, slowly savoring every inch of my body, until my face was flushed with his open gawking, but I wasn't going to pretend I hadn't enjoyed the attention.

*I'm not interested.*

His words had played over and over again in my mind, but it was clear these past few weeks there was at least something he found interesting about me—attractive, even. I lifted my chin, meeting his hooded gaze a moment before taking my own fill of his delicious body. I could have sworn his lips quirked with the hint of a smile before he shot into the trees after Zaeth.

It had been three days since that morning. Three days of my mind replaying the incident on repeat, questioning whether I'd misinterpreted the hunger in his eyes. I'd looked for him once, only to find he'd left to escort a group of men to the base. I was glad he was returning today..

I drained the remains of my tea in a large gulp, shifting to the next stack of texts, when I heard the echoing sounds of foot-steps coming from the hall—one larger and one significantly smaller than the other, both oddly familiar.

Her slick dark brown hair was cut shorter, barely grazing her petite shoulders, and there was a maturity to her features which hadn't been there before, but her smile was just as warm.

"I hope we're not interrupting."

"Lannie!" My chair scraped across the rough wooden floors as I bolted from the table and flung myself into her arms. "Will's been asking for you. He's going to be so excited you're here. Wait, why are you here? Is everything okay with Lucy and the babe?"

"See what I mean?" Ryuu muttered to Lannie as he hovered in the hall with the whisper of a smile along his lips. "Constantly talking. Doesn't let you get a word in."

I shot him a glare over Lannie's shoulder at the same time she let out a light giggle.

"Lucy and the babe are doing well. They've moved to our wing of Alarik's estate and Healer Grant returned a week ago and will be checking in regularly, just in case. We stopped by Will's rooms but found it empty."

"He's been training with Zaeth or Jarek most days. I think it was Zaeth who joined him this morning. They are normally back a little after mid-day."

"That works out because we need to talk about the prophecy." Lannie walked to the table I'd been sitting at with purpose, ruffling through loose papers until she found what she was looking for. "I'm sure Ryuu's been keeping you updated on Healer Grant's expeditions to the Light Kingdom?"

Crossing my arms, I shot him a withering glare. "No, he hasn't."

He only shrugged. "There was nothing important to discuss. Until now."

Lannie frowned but conceded a moment later. "I suppose that's an accurate assessment. You recall Healer Grant was inquiring about the Fractured before you left?"

I nodded.

"While he was in the Light Kingdom, he heard mention of a Dark Phoenix."

My skin prickled as she pulled free a small scrap of parchment, the edges brown with age. At least half of the page had been burned away. She placed the brittle scrap beside the paper she'd selected from the pile.

"He found this."

I leaned forward, clearly the only one out of the three of us who didn't know what it contained. My mouth ran dry as I read through the black smudges of soot to find an identical recording of the first two stanzas of Mother's lullaby:

"Driven by pride, brothers wandered deep,
 Through splintered realms to the shadowed keep.
 Severing bonds, they ventured too far,
 Enduring pain and harrowing scars.

. . .

A raven's wings protect the realm,
  The final shield of the human's helm.
  But creatures' crushing blows shall reign,
  Shattering shelter, unleashing pain.


"I've already ensured the document is authentic," Ryuu said. "This confirms Will is an oracle of the goddess." His tone had taken on an airy quality, bordering on pride.

"While I appreciate your confidence in my brother," I said, worry tainting my words. "It also confirms some other oracle was given the same message and wasn't able to change this future from occurring."

Ryuu grimaced, but Lannie didn't flinch under my glare as I turned to her. Ryuu had helped her shatter the memory spell shortly after El and I were freed, but the two of them took longer to recover than I had. "Any new memories?"

She shook her head. "I think I've recovered everything."

I slumped forward. "We're no closer to figuring this out."

"Actually, I think we may have found something," Lannie said. "Healer Grant found evidence of a well known tale in the Light Kingdom that dates back to the period following the banishment of The Merged. The Kingdoms were freshly forged and each distinct fae line was vying for dominance. As you know, the northern territories, particularly the dark fae, are known for their physical strength and skills on a battlefield. Naturally, they won most of the altercations, and assumed what they called, an over-seeing role across all of Pax.

"The three brothers of the Light Kingdom were born under this oppression. Though they knew their fae-gifted physical talents were no match for the northern kingdoms, the three brothers prided themselves on their intelligence. They spent centuries searching for a way to match the ruthlessness surrounding them. Their desperation grew until they struck a deal with darkness, finding a way to break through the confines of this realm and venture further to continue their search for power. Only once they've procured enough strength will they return to claim rulership of Pax and free the Light Fae."

My lips pressed thin. "You make it sound like they're liberators."

Lannie shook her head. "I don't think modern fae would agree, even most light fae wouldn't, but if they left in the time of northern territory rule, they probably believe they are saving Pax from a brutal existence."

"Never mind that the northern kingdoms ended their control shortly after their disappearance, and have essentially been living in peace since," Ryuu added. "At least since the last Dark King ruled."

"Peace?" I lifted a brow at him, happy to see Lannie doing the same.

He frowned. "*Relative* peace. Barring the Fractured, there hasn't been war for a few centuries. The kingdoms may hold different views and have squabbles from time to time, but it's nothing like what was seen in the time following The Merged, before fae came to be."

"Says the fae in league with a dark fae army," I said, rolling my eyes.

"Zaeth is an honorable man and has done more to keep this world safe than most."

I wasn't sure why I bothered provoking him, but found it difficult to stop, especially when his eyes blazed a bright forest green around his shifted vertical pupils. "Are you saying you've never seen him delight in killing?"

Ryuu's jaw ticked, his voice low. "Everything he's done is to protect this realm and its people."

"Regardless," Lannie said, stopping the argument from progressing. "Healer Grant believes the three brothers in the myth are the brothers referenced in the lullaby. If they truly did leave this realm, honing their skilled and cultivating plans for centuries, they could be the entity behind the attacks. They could be the source of the storm years ago. The ones who are controlling the Fractured."

"And other creatures," I added in a breathless tone, glancing at Ryuu as the memory of him battling the cú sidhe took root in my mind.

Ryuu gave a tight nod. "Some of the villages have evidence of tracks left in the rumble, indicating a non-human or fae presence. There may be many creatures not yet known to us that have joined the Fractured."

"Gods," I breathed, realizing the implications. "And if that is true..."

Ryuu nodded, his hard gaze meeting mine without blinking. "We are in far more trouble than we realized."

## 33
## ELARA

JAREK AND I FADED INTO THE SURROUNDING FOREST, ALLOWING our prey to come to us. I could only detect a single heartbeat, its ragged breaths drawing nearer with each crackling step it took. Jarek gave me a tight smile as the snapping of twigs sounded just before us, granting a glimpse of a pale figure between a net of green leaves.

With his sword poised to strike, he launched from the trees.

A girl with bright red hair and copper eyes stumbled in an attempt to avoid Jarek, a shriek tearing from her lips. He reacted quicker than I, sheathing his blade and reaching for her before she tumbled to the ground.

She stared up at him in dazed confusion, her shoulders braced between Jarek's steadying hands. Lifting a shaking freckled arm, she reached toward his cheek. "Are you real?"

Her voice was brittle, hoarse as if she'd been screaming. I gasped, the grime and fear warping her features made it nearly impossible to recognize her. But her voice rattled the memory loose. She'd been among the women and children of the shelter —the one I'd visited the night Neith was attacked. She'd been the one to warn us of the attack—the one gifted with a fae affinity for speed. My gaze roved over her wild sienna eyes, snagging on her bright red hair matted with debris and something that looked alarmingly close to blood. A thick layer of mud coated her face, only parted by streaks of tears. "Serephina?"

Her eyes swung toward me, relief filling them for a beat before her legs collapsed. Jarek lurched forward, scooping her up in his arms to cradle against his chest.

"What happened?" I asked.

"We have to keep moving. We have to go." Serephina's words sputtered forth in a wild frenzy. "I ran as long as I could, but they'll catch up. They'll find me. *Please*, we have to go."

Thick clumps of dirt, and dark red stains covered her clothes, riddled with tears that looked eerily like slash marks. Her hair had been brushed back, revealing an angry slice along the left side of her face from her upper lip to her brow. It was shallow with only a small amount of bleeding, but even I could see the skin was inflamed, the edges puckered with the early signs of infection.

Her eyes darted from Jarek to me, wild with fear, the scent seeping from her in thick waves.

"Gods," I whispered.

"What happened?" Jarek's tone was gentle but direct. She blanched as her eyes landed on his tipped ears.

I shot Jarek a look of alarm as we started toward base at a brisk pace.

"Shh, it's okay," I soothed, using the same tone I reserved for Will's nightmares. "We're here to protect you. Whatever happened, Jarek is a friend. We can help."

Serephina held my eyes a moment longer, before relinquishing her remaining strength and easing into Jarek's chest. Silent sobs shook her body, but her voice came out eerily calm. "You can't help. They're already dead. Everyone. There's nothing left."

"I'm sorry to ask this of you," I said, "But we need to know what happened."

She looked over Jarek's shoulder, staring into the forest beyond with a haunted expression. No words came from her lips. There were only the steady tears and the small trickle of blood dripping down her chin.

"They overpowered us—even the fae. Their arrows had an orange substance coating them." She lifted her fingers, the pads of them coated with an orange sheen. "Even touching it slowed me down..." Her eyes closed as her head lulled against Jarek's chest.

"Heal her."

Jarek gritted his teeth, brows pinched together. "I've been trying. Something is stopping me from reaching her. I can feel the wound, the blood leaking inside, but it's not responding to me." His eyes bored into mine as he gave a tight shake of his head. Not good.

The blood rushed from my face. "We need to get her back to the fort. Maybe with the other's help—"

Wasting no time, Jarek eased her head against his chest before breaking into a run. "Why don't we start with something a little easier? I'm Jarek and you are Serephina, yes?" Jarek's voice shook with the force of running, but she nodded her confirmation. He glanced down with a reassuring smile. "I promise you I won't let whatever torment you just left catch up with us, but I need as many details as possible."

She looked on the verge of fainting, but determination burned in her eyes. "I live in a small village, about half a day's ride from here. We'd heard the rumors of the attacks on human-fae villages, but the towns have been further out along the borders. We're a peaceful town with strong fae among us... we were. The thought of those creatures attacking didn't seem possible." Another tear carved a path through the soot and filth before blending into the fierce slash of red down her check. "We were wrong."

"I'm so sorry."

Her eyes swung to mine, ringed with pink from crying. "It wasn't just the Fractured this time."

"Was it the cú sidhe?"

She shook her head. "No, but there were monsters—goblins, I think. They laughed as they ripped us apart." Her lips trembled as her brows knitted together.

"You're safe, now"

She managed a small, grateful nod before her eyes rolled back, the remaining tension in her body draining as she fell forward against Jarek's chest.

"Serephina, can you hear me?" My voice took on a shrill note as our feet pounded against the earth.

Jarek cursed when she didn't move, his worry propelling him onward. He pulled ahead, thundering past the stables and toward the healing quarters. We were here. We'd made it to the fort. If only Serephina could hold on a little longer.

He sprinted into the building, barking orders to men and fae alike as they fell in around us. Zaeth, Evander, and Ryuu chased us as we flew into the infirmary, reaching for supplies as they did so. I helped Jarek position Serephina on one of the tables before locking eyes with Evander.

"Where's Alarik?" My breathing was ragged, coming in short bursts, but there was a force beneath my words.

He shook his head, eyes taking in Serephina's unconscious form. "He's out on patrol of the northern border with Xaun. I've already sent Skender to get them. Was it the cú sidhe again?"

I shook my head. "She said goblins, maybe. The Fractured attacked her village. Where's Will? Is he safe?"

"Cadoc is with him. I had them barricade the library when I spotted you two. They're instructed to remain there until we give them the okay."

"Thank you," I breathed, watching as Jarek attempted to pick out debris embedded in various scrapes and cuts throughout her body.

A tangled mess of silver curls shot forward, followed closely by the calmed controlled stride of only someone who had been in similar situations. Someone who was perfectly at ease with a patient in need. Lannie.

"Move out of the way," Lannie called, her voice possessing an authority beyond reproach. Surprise mingled with hope at seeing my sister. She'd be able to help.

She looked older than her almost seventeen years as she stepped to Serephina's side. Her face was set in a grim line as her fingers carefully removed the scraps of soiled clothes clinging to her lean frame.

"El, what happened?"

Greer and I stepped next to her, not wanting to risk slowing her down by trying to help. Even Evander and Jarek had stepped back, allowing Lannie's skilled hands to work.

"She was fleeing from something in the forest—the Fractured, possibly goblins. She said there was an attack on her village. By the sounds of it, she was probably running all morning, if not longer. She was shaken but talking and acting fine when we found her. She fainted just outside the fort."

Lannie gave a firm nod confirming she heard me as her delicate fingers worked through the cloth, pulling the last of it free to reveal a myriad of wounds beneath. Broad scrapes and thin lines of blood littered her skin. Painful, but they would heal. However, the dark purple splotch along the right side of her abdomen caught Lannie's eye.

"Jarek?"

"Internal bleeding. I'd guess she has another ten minutes before blood loss will claim her."

"You didn't heal her." Lannie said, pausing her assessment just long enough to glance up at Jarek. "Why?"

He grimaced. "I can't reach her. I can sense the wound, feel how to close it, but there's something blocking me from reaching her."

"She mentioned an orange substance that slowed her," I said, glancing at the stained pads of her fingers. "Speed is her fae affinity. It must be a type of poison preventing you from helping her."

"Greer. Evander," Lannie called. "I need you to bring me a pot of boiled water. There's normally at least one pot ready for tea or cooking in most kitchens." Lannie's words were clear commands as she held out her hands toward Ryuu. He deposited her healing kit without question. Lannie rolled out the bundle on the table, quickly removing a few instruments as Greer raced off to heed her instructions.

Lannie's hands never stilled as she worked, the same strong calm issuing through her words as she spoke to me. "We'll need to replenish fluids as quickly as possible and stop the bleeding."

She extracted a mess of tubes attached to a deflated bag full of dried medicine, the other end tapered to a sharp point.

Greer rushed into the room, hands in protective gloves, carrying a large pot of water, while Evander clasped a bucket of ice. Lannie immediately filled the bag, the dry remedy swirling and mixing into a uniformed fluid giving off a subtle glow. The liquid ran down the tubes until meeting a stopping point just above the needle. She thrust the bag into a bed of ice, letting the temperature cool before placing it in Ryuu's hands, instructing him to keep it elevated. With skill beyond her years, Lannie swiftly and effectively pierced the point through the crease of Serephina's arm.

Lannie released a switch, allowing the shimmering substance to enter Serephina's veins. I watched as the light expanded from the needlepoint entry, connecting in a brilliant glow as it wound through her vessels.

It was mesmerizing. The fluttering beat of her heart pushed

the liquid further, winding it through her body until it found the ravaged parts. The slick lines blurred, expanding out into a large cloud where the vessels had been torn, just beneath the large purple bruise. Serephina's thin body hid little, each beat of her heart pushing more of the healing serum through her veins. I could practically see the haze around the injury dimming, structuring into solid lines as the liquid rebuilt the walls of her ruptured vessels, reconnecting them to her battered organs.

Ryuu squeezed the bag, pushing the remaining bit into Serephina's body. There was still a purple haze along her skin, but the potion was illuminated in thick, whole cords; the tissue beneath all but healed. Lannie removed the needle, the small entry point sealing as soon as the metal was removed.

I let out a breath of relief as Serephina's breathing evened out. "Thank the gods."

"No, thank Lannie," Jarek quipped, eyeing my sister with narrowed eyes. "That was a light fae potion, was it not?"

Lannie blushed as all eyes turned to her. "The original was, yes. I've made some adjustments. She'll need time to heal. She's lost a lot of blood, and while the potion can mend the vessels and supply some extra fluid, her body will have to replenish the rest."

Serephina's eyes fluttered open, squinting from the light in the room. "Where am I?"

"You're safe. This is my sister, Lannie. She just saved your life." I took a steadying breath, making the decision to press for a bit more information. "Do you remember how many Fractured or goblins there were?"

Lannie shot me a disapproving glare. Serephina's skin paled further as she attempted to sit and for one terrifying moment, I feared she would lose consciousness again. Lannie rushed forward, pressing her back before meeting my eyes.

"She needs rest, not an interrogation." The authority of her tone pulled me up short.

Serephina looked over my shoulder at the towering fae warriors. Ryuu sat, his wings tucking in close, in an attempt to appear less imposing. Jarek and Zaeth simply stood, willing the answer from her.

Her eyes found mine. Fresh tears pricked the edges, but she swallowed them down. "Dozens. I'm not sure. But they're too strong, too fast. We didn't stand a chance. Everyone is dead."

I gasped. "But the sanctuary is secure."

Serephina's face crumpled. "They attacked in the day. We weren't prepared. The guards were overwhelmed before anything could be done, and with the poison..."

Lannie whispered soothing words as Serephina fell apart, urging her to rest as she draped a blanket around her.

Bile burned the back of my throat as faces flashed before my eyes. Serephina had an elder sister. "There were only women and children inside...infants."

Serephina's copper eyes found mine, holding nothing but bleak, unending grief. "You'll see soon," she breathed. "They're coming."

# 34

# GREER

EL LOOKED LIKE SHE WAS HAVING TROUBLE ACCEPTING LANNIE was really here. A dozen questions burned in her eyes darting from Lannie to myself, but they would have to wait. Evander fled the room with the promise to return immediately after the alarm had been sounded. The fort needed to be secured. Zaeth and Jarek were in deep conversation, debating whether to attack outright or plan a defense. El gravitated toward them, but my attention stayed focused on Ryuu as he lifted the girl's body off the table.

Lannie and I followed after him, her eyes scrutinizing every shift of Serephina's body positioned in Ryuu's large arms as we made our way from the main infirmary to a small room in the back.

The moment she was settled, Lannie shooed us away as she bustled around the girl. "She can't be left alone. I'll stay with her tonight."

"That's really not necessary—" Serephina started to say, but stopped short with a single glance at Lannie's face.

"I say it is necessary," Lannie said as she pinned her with a glare. "And seeing you have lost a good amount of blood, I believe I'll be making the decisions, at least until you are recovered."

Serephina gave a sheepish smile and allowed herself to sink into the pillows Lannie had just fluffed.

"Update me on what's going on out there." Lannie gestured to the main portion of the infirmary where the others could be heard debating strategy. "Greer," she whispered, her eyes meeting mine as her controlled professionalism cracked. "I haven't seen Will, yet."

My heart gave a small squeeze. She hadn't seen him in weeks. She'd finally managed to break away from the base, and then this happened.

"The library is just upstairs. I'm going there now. Once we know everything is safe, Will and I will slip down and be sure to spend some time together."

Her shoulders dropped as the tension in her chest released. "Thank you. Only if it's safe. If this does end in a battle, tell them to bring all the injured to the infirmary." She gestured to El, Jarek, and Zaeth. "I'll be prepared either way."

I opened my mouth to speak, but words evaded me. She sounded so calm, as if the idea of caring for a ward of injured men was just another night. I wasn't sure when she'd grown up, but somewhere amid the mounting Fractured attacks, she'd shed the remainder of her childhood innocence.

"Thank you for tending to the girl," Ryuu said, "I'll escort Greer to your brother. He will remain safe."

Lannie gave him a small smile of thanks as Ryuu led me back to the others. Evander had done well preparing the fort. Many more had joined us, each offering their own input on how best to proceed.

"Serephina said there's nobody left to save," El said, her voice cutting through the noise. "If we attack in haste, our movements will be sloppy."

"I don't like the idea of waiting to be attacked," Jarek said. "Though I do see your point." "What do you suggest?" Zaeth asked, further silencing the crowd as his eyes focused on my sister with an intensity I wasn't sure I liked. But if El felt the force of his gaze, she didn't let it show.

"This isn't the easiest place to defend, especially because we don't know exactly what we're up against. I say we form a small recon group. We need to be quick and quiet, gather as much information as possible and return to the fort. The others will remain here and prepare for an attack. That should give Alarik enough time to return. He'll be able to make the final preparations for defense."

The others nodded, mulling over her plan, but Zaeth was the one to speak first. "Done. Kavan, prepare the fort for an attack. The men should be strategically placed in case the wards fail. We now have three untrained humans to defend in the infirmary, meaning this is where our final line of defense will be."

El's shoulders pulled back with a hint of pride as she realized he hadn't included her in the tally of untrained humans. I don't know why she continued to be surprised by praise like that. Anyone could see how deadly she was.

"I'll stay." Ryuu shared a loaded look with Zaeth, but after a moment the dark fae nodded.

"Defend the fort," Zaeth said, holding Ryuu's gaze. "If we are overrun, get them out."

Ryuu nodded as the rest of the men heeded orders and began to prepare. El turned to join us, but Zaeth stepped in her path before she could reach my side.

"Not yet, love. You were past the half-way point along the southern trail when you found the girl, were you not?"

"Yes," El answered, suspicion in her tone.

Zaeth kept his eyes trained on her, but directed his next question over his shoulder. "Jarek, you carried the girl, leaving Elara to run on her own?"

"Yes."

"The three of you returned to the fort in less than an hour?" Zaeth asked the question as if he already knew the answer and was merely giving voice to it for my sister's sake.

"Yes." Jarek's voice was clear. El's eyes darted to Jarek in question as my own brows drew together in confusion. That couldn't have been right. Maybe for a fae, but that pace was impossible for a human.

"Good. Jarek, inform Soter that Elara will be joining us."

"What?" El and I gasped at the same time.

Zaeth continued speaking to Jarek, ignoring our outburst. "Be dressed and prepared to leave in five minutes."

Jarek nodded, before turning swiftly from the room.

"He can't be serious," I said.

"I assure you, he is," Ryuu answered, his eyes trained on Zaeth.

Zaeth's glimmering brown eyes met my sister's questioning gaze. "I suggest you bring a cloak if you have one. It will be nightfall before we reach the village."

"Wait," she called, her hand catching his arm. Her cheeks flushed as his eyes landed on the point of contact, his full lips tilting into a coy smirk revealing the hint of fangs.

"You want me to go with you?" she breathed.

"Of course. You found the girl and got her back safely. You were also first recruited for reconnaissance by the general, were you not?"

"Yes, but—"

"You are qualified for this task, Elara. And are stronger than you realize. If you wish to stay with your sisters and brother, I will not take you from them, but I believe you'd be an asset in the field. The decision is yours."

El bit her lip, the only tell of how indecisive she really was. Zaeth's eyes dilated as they noted the small movement and I wondered if she truly had no idea how others saw her: Strong. Brave. Beautiful.

"I want to go."

Zaeth's lips tilted into a confident smirk. "Wonderful. I'll see you at the stables."

~

"What's Zaeth's deal?" I asked as Ryuu and I made our way to gather supplies for the evening.

We'd decided to sleep in the library with Will tonight after Jarek had placed further protection wards on the third floor at Zaeth's request before they left. We'd used the time to escort Will down for a few minutes, allowing Lannie and him a quick reunion, before Jarek completed the wards. He assured us he'd be placing additional protection wards surrounding the entire building, but we wanted to keep Will away from the infirmary in case war found us..

"His deal?" Ryuu asked as if the words tasted foul on his tongue.

I rolled my eyes, stacking three pairs of blankets. "Yes. His *deal*. One minute, he's avoiding El, and the next, he's inviting her on impromptu recon missions."

Ryuu took his time leaning a cot against the door frame before answering. "I wouldn't worry about them. Zaeth knows he can't have lasting relationships."

"Oh?" I asked. "Is that like a vow you guys took? Only engage in frivolous relationships?"

Ryuu tilted his head, waiting for me to elaborate—knowing I couldn't help myself.

"It's just that I haven't seen your girlfriend in a while. Is she planning on hiding in the Air Kingdom forever or will she do what she promised and help us unravel the prophecy to protect my brother?"

Both eyebrows raised on Ryuu's face, but I could have sworn I saw a small twitch of his lips. He turned away to pull free a third cot as he answered. "She's not my girlfriend."

"Could have fooled me with the way you two hang all over each other."

Ryuu pinned me with a glare. "I do not *hang* on anyone."

I squared up to him, hands on my hips. "But you admit she hangs all over you?"

He held my gaze, but didn't deny it. "Cress is... affectionate."

A scoff scraped the back of my throat as I turned with a rather large roll of my eyes. "I suppose you're going to tell me it's nothing serious and the two of you aren't into labels?"

"I wasn't aware you cared."

"I don't," I snapped, cursing how clear the lie was. "If you want to spend your time with someone who is heartless enough to not care about the boy beneath the curse of an oracle, then be my guest."

The cots clattered against the wall as Ryuu spun to face me. "She didn't mean it like that."

My stomach twisted with his defense of her. "She did. We both know she'd sacrifice Will in a moment if it meant his *gifts* would pass to a fae with a longer life span. One who was able to reveal more prophecies."

"I would never let that happen." Ryuu's promise was little more than a growl.

The deep green flecks in his eyes flashed as I pressed closer, my anger feeding the warmth between us. "You'd protect my brother in the light of day but spend your nights with *her*."

The silence stretched. After another moment, Ryuu turned away with a heavy breath. "No. I told you, Cress is like this with every male in line for—Just, there is nothing going on between us anymore."

*Anymore.* The word was like a sharp blade to my gut.

"There never will be, again. She knows that."

I bent to gather pillows, swallowing the bile that had risen in the back of my throat. "Is that why she hasn't returned?"

"She's researching. It will take some time to track down the older prophecies. Your mother's lullaby is not new, but I have no recollection of it. It's a wonder your sister was able to track down a portion of it, in the Light Kingdom, of all places. If we can discover when it was first uttered, perhaps we will find more information on the raven."

"You sound surprised at not being familiar with it."

"I am. I've dedicated decades to our goddess, to her prophecies in particular. Even if I hadn't memorized the words, I should be familiar with the phrases or the time period, at the very least. Prophecies are often delivered in segments, sometimes over centuries. Pieces of it should be contained in other recordings, and yet, I do not know of it. It is either very old or very rare."

"Or others have been made to forget it like we were."

I started to place the last of the blankets on the top of the pile, but Ryuu was staring at me with a hint of wonder. "Perhaps you're right."

The forest green flecks in his dark eyes shimmered as they peered down at me. I'd become so used to the scowl, to only seeing hints of the kind fae beneath, it was intoxicating to see his shields down. For once, he was looking at me—*me*, as if I held the answers to all his questions. As if I was the only person who mattered in this world. Maybe he felt it, too, this fire between us.

I leaned forward, following the tendrils of heat burning between our bodies, willing them to grow.

Ryuu's hand reached out, brushing back a stray silver curl before tracing the curve of my cheek. His eyes tracked the slow movement of his hand across my jaw, until his thumb grazed my lip. Heat flared through my body, pooling low between my thighs. His pupils dilated as I pressed forward, capturing the pad of his thumb in a soft kiss.

His body stilled, and I hovered there, waiting to see if I'd gone too far. When he didn't pull away, I brought my hands up, letting them explore the broad span of his chest with featherlight touches. My heart thrummed in my ears as my fingers dipped across the thick bands of muscle, drifting up, until they brushed through the loose strands of his dark hair. It was as soft as I'd imagined. I wondered if his wings would be softer.

Ryuu's entire body was taut, but his palm shifted, cupping my cheek. I dared a glimpse into his eyes, surprised to find a tenderness peering down at me. Something shifted in my chest as I stared back at him, cracking the last bit of self-preservation I had left.

I reached up at the same time his fingers found the nape of my neck, curling in my hair and tugging my head back. His lips descended on mine in a fierce, possessive kiss. It was desire and fire and frustration. It was everything I'd dreamt of and still not enough. My need grew urgent as his tongue swept against mine.

A breathy moan escaped my lips as his other arm banded around my waist, pressing me flush against him. My body hummed, searing with need as he devoured me, claiming me with every sweep of his tongue, every touch of his hands.

When his fingers dropped to the hem of my cotton shirt, tugging it up in question, I lifted my arms, willing him to take more. To take everything.

Ryuu broke our kiss, staring down at me with desperation blazing in his eyes. His fingers slowed as he worked the fabric up, savoring every inch of skin he uncovered. This wouldn't be quick. I intended to erase every memory of Cress and any other person who'd dared touch him before me. I intended to watch as the dragon lurking beneath his flesh flared to life, until both the beast and man were mine.

A scream sounded from upstairs. We jerked away from one another, fear gripping my heart as I spotted Cadoc racing down the hall.

"It's Will. He started seizing."

## 35

# ELARA

WE DARTED THROUGH THE FOREST, EASILY FINDING WHERE Serephina had first emerged and followed her trail back into the thick surrounding trees. Our horses were nimble, maneuvering among the branches with ease.

"Earlier, you heard Serephina's approach?" Jarek's voice was low, though I was sure fae hearing allowed for the others to hear.

Not taking my eyes off the tortuous path in front of us, I nodded. "So did you."

"Did you hear her or did you notice I acted, and so you reacted?" His tone was purposely casual, but there was a tightness to it that reminded me of Zaeth's earlier line of questioning.

"I'm not sure. I think we heard her at the same time, but who cares? If you want the credit—"

A gasp left my lips as I finally understood what they were implying. Jarek should have heard Serephina much sooner than I did with his fae hearing. I tried to swallow, but my mouth was dry. I glanced up into Jarek's penetrating gaze.

"I was increasing our pace when we were sprinting back. I expected you to fall behind and when you did, I planned to slow. But you never did. You never fell behind."

I blanched, pressing my lips into a thin line. "I'm not sure what your point is, but my mother and father were both as human as I am. All of my siblings are human. If they had been fae, they wouldn't have died in the storm."

"But not all of them died. You didn't."

Being fae meant a long life free of illness. My mind raced as I thought back on my childhood, searching for any sign that would allow Jarek's theory to be true. Some fae children had tipped ears since birth, but most appeared human until the settling, when their fae abilities would emerge. But one or both of my parents would've had to have been fae, and in each of my memories, they were disappointingly human... though there were wisps of uncertainty. Flashes of conversations that hinted at something other—something more than our meager life in the woods.

Gods, to be fae. To have intrinsic fae abilities at my finger-tips—abilities that would lend me power. And freedom. The freedom to carve out my own destiny, to ensure the remainder of my family was protected and guarantee revenge for the ones who had been taken too soon.

"As much as I would love to believe I'm fae, I'm not, and no magic spell or pretty tool can change that."

Jarek eyed me a moment longer before galloping ahead.

We rode for hours, the previous tension between Zaeth and I smoothing out with the focus of our mission. It was easy to follow the snapped branches and disturbed grass Serephina had left in her wake, but soon the sun fell behind the horizon, dimming the world around us. It was harder for me to discern the exact path, but Zaeth and the others didn't seem to have the same qualms. Yet another sign I was just human. I fell back, riding beside Evander as Jarek trailed us, leaving Zaeth and Soter to ride ahead.

The earth fae had only now returned from his time away with Naz and the dark fae army. He'd provided a brief update as we rode, relaying the few villages that had been evacuated further east.

"Has Naz located Alderidge?" Zaeth asked.

Soter shook his head. "The portals remain untraceable without a wild fae."

Zaeth nodded. "Any whispers on the raven?"

I sat straighter, my heels clicking to draw Ember and I nearer. "You're looking for the raven?"

Zaeth lifted a brow as he shot a look over his shoulder at me. "Of course, love."

"Naz shadowwalked to a rural village just outside the Shadowlands," Soter continued. "There was a wise woman who dedicated her life to the goddess, one who claimed to have known the last oracle. She believes the raven we seek is not a weapon, but a person."

Zaeth tilted his head, weighing this piece of information as the full moon rose with her entourage of stars close behind. It felt so similar to before, when I'd been galloping toward a different town to face the Fractured—a night that had ended in death.

"It's possible—" Jarek started, but fell silent as Zaeth held up a hand.

He cocked his head to the side, listening. Zaeth dismounted, motioning for us to do the same, before slinking through the darkness of the trees, leaving the horses behind.

The light of the moon was bright overhead, but the forest remained still. The gentle rustling of nocturnal animals was absent, casting an eerie hush on the world around us. A foul stench coated the air as the forest thinned, mingling with the tangy scent of charred meat. It grew stronger as we combed through the trees, discovering small trails as we neared Serephina's village.

My eyes focused on the clearing ahead, a dozen or so buildings outlined by a faint, orange glow. I made to step closer, to step out of the safety of the tree line and the coverage it provided, but Evander was there, pulling me back before my foot could land.

I shot him a questioning look. His nose wrinkled against the growing stench as he lifted his hand to point to the spot of ground I'd almost stepped on. My eyes took a moment to adjust the darkness of the forest floor, but as the clouds shifted, releasing a bright beam of moonlight, I was able to make out a thick cord draped across a bed of leaves. I blinked, mouth running dry as I followed the cord back to the torn abdomen of a corpse a few paces away.

My stomach twisted as bile coated my tongue. Fighting the urge to vomit, I managed to swallow the acid singeing my throat. I stayed behind Evander after that, not allowing myself to process the horrific scene that must have taken place here as we stepped over pieces of entrails and deep pools of blood. The metallic tang seared my nostrils as we passed, merging with the growing smells of burning wood and smoke.

Zaeth held up a hand, drawing us into a tight huddle poised a few leagues away from the flickering light of the town. "Scout first. I would prefer information over a battle tonight. Elara, you are the only one with the scent of a human among us. They will not be able to discern your smell from any others left here."

"Even if there are no survivors?" I asked.

"The air is heavy with the lingering scent of human blood. Lakes of it coat the town. Yours will not stand out. The rest of us will need to stay downwind, but we need you to venture closer. See if there are any survivors. The rest of us will spread out but remain further back."

I paled at his words, but forced a steadiness to my tone. "I'll be running this mission alone?"

Zaeth studied me, the cinnamon of his eyes flaring bright as I lifted my chin under his scrutinizing gaze. I wouldn't have him thinking I was weak. Or afraid. There was no place for either of those in this world. Not if I intended to survive.

"I'll stay a few paces behind you in case you need rescuing," he taunted, the edge of his lips quirking up.

A flush of heat warmed my cheek but I gave a single, grateful nod. If the Fractured were indeed recruiting other forsaken creatures, there was no telling what we'd find. I was strong, brave even, but I wasn't stupid. With Zaeth nearby, I'd have a chance of escape if I was discovered, though I could only imagine the smug look he'd have. Better to remain hidden at all costs.

"Jarek and Evander assess the east. Soter, loop around from the west if you can. Minimal risks." The others nodded silently before heeding his orders, blending into the night as they went.

I swallowed as Zaeth's rich eyes found mine, alive with the glow of the stars overhead. The trees were thin here, the glow of the moon reflecting the bright ring surrounding his irises. It flared to life now, just as it had months ago when he'd rescued us from the Fractured. When we had faced Alderidge and the commander.

They could be here tonight, I realized. It was a long shot. The Fractured and their army rarely lingered, but they'd been growing sloppy.

"I'll be within hearing distance," Zaeth said, drawing me from my thoughts. "If you find anything of interest."

"Or if I need saving?" I raised a brow.

He smiled, my eyes snagging on the tips of fangs as he did so. "We both know neither of us are the type to need saving." He took a step nearer, eyes shimmering. "Try not to kill anything, love. Like I said, information is more valuable tonight."

I felt my own lips tug up into a smile before Zaeth faded into the trees. Squaring my shoulders toward the flickering flames in the distance, I crept forward, seeking out the fellow monsters of the night.

## 36
## GREER

THE WOODEN DOOR OF THE LIBRARY WAS FLUNG WIDE, LEAVING the path open for Ryuu and I as we shot to my brother's side. Cadoc was close behind, rambling about Will saying strange things about his family—warning Cadoc he needed to let go of his anger, but I couldn't be bothered with Cadoc's problems right now.

Will's small form was convulsing on the hard floor, his body jerking and twitching, as his eyes rolled back. I blinked and Ryuu was beside him, kneeling, as his hand pressed to Will's chest. He muttered the blessing of the goddess, but Will's body didn't calm. I crashed to my knees, my hands desperately attempting to shield his head from the hard, wooden floor beneath as Ryuu continued, repeating blessing after blessing, until it was nothing more than a ragged plea, his voice cracking as the words issued forth.

The tremors raking through Will's body finally calmed but somehow, the utter stillness left in their wake was more terrifying. My own chest quieted, terror gripping me as I bent, pressing my ear to his chest. A cry of relief washed through me —his heart beat steady and strong.

Ryuu's palm pressed flat against his chest once more.

"You don't need to do that. It's over now."

"This is to check for injuries. I won't be able to heal him, but we'll know if it is safe to move him."

My pulse shot up again as I realized what he was implying. Will had been thrashing for gods knew how long. There could be injuries not detectable by the human eye. Ryuu muttered an additional spell, focusing all his energy on my little brother's limp form. Ryuu's eyes shifted, the pupils growing thin and long, stretching into vertical slits while he worked. He blinked and they were normal, once more.

"Well?" Cadoc demanded. "Is the little fae alive?"

He said the word 'fae' as if it tasted foul in his mouth. If only Will were fae. He *should* be fae. And after what Jarek had mentioned about El earlier, it sounded as if she had fae affinities, too. The possibility had taken root in my mind after Ryuu confirmed Will was the first and only human oracle, but everything I found in my research claimed there was no way to conceal a fae's affinities.

Ryuu exhaled, giving me a brief, relieved nod.

"Thank the gods," I breathed. Will was safe.

Ryuu shot to his feet, snatching Cadoc by the throat, slamming him against the wall. "You were supposed to keep him safe."

Ryuu's words were little more than a snarl, the force of them radiating through the room. Cadoc clawed at the hand circling his throat, failing to loosen the grip of Ryuu's fingers.

"I don't see any intruders here," Cadoc spat. "Just a fae-bastard changeling, bringing more death to my people."

"Cadoc!" I gasped, shocked at the hatred etched across his face.

Dark eyes met mine, holding on to the anger bubbling within a moment longer. The tension from Cadoc's body lessened on an exhale. "I don't know how to prevent something like that from happening." He jerked his chin toward my brother's still unconscious form. "He was spouting nonsense about my family—things he had no right knowing about—and then he started rambling about a raven and some brothers—"

"What did he say? The exact wording is important," I demanded, still cradling Will's head on the floor.

Ryuu's jaw ticked but he released Cadoc, realizing we needed him to speak. He crumpled into a heap on the floor, hatred burning in his eyes.

"Nothing made sense," Cadoc said, his hand massaging his neck.

Ryuu's eyes narrowed as he crossed his arms over his chest.

"He kept repeating, 'the raven must hold', but then he would say, 'the raven will fall'. After a few rounds of that, his voice grew low and his head cocked to the side. I thought it was over, but then he said, 'the brothers have returned', and something about them being cursed or trapped but their 'confines are weakening'. Then he started shaking."

Cadoc looked at me as if I'd say something on his behalf. Something that would save him from Ryuu. I pressed my lips together.

"This isn't on me," he sneered.

"Leave," Ryuu commanded, raw power slithering through the word.

With one last glare and shake of his head in my direction, Cadoc left, slamming the door as he went.

Ryuu turned to face me with something akin to guilt swirling in his eyes. "He's not wrong. This wasn't his fault. It's mine"

"What?"

Ignoring my question, he knelt beside Will, brushing away the faint sheen of sweat across his brow. "He needed to rest."

Before I could agree, Ryuu fled the room. My mouth was

still hanging open when he appeared a moment later with the three cots and bedding stacked ontop one another as if they weighed nothing. In another moment, the cots were set up, grouped together in the middle of the room.

"May I?"

Ryuu reached down as I nodded, scooping Will into his large arms and lowering him gently onto the middle cot. I tucked him in, adjusting the pillow and arranging his blankets, before crawling onto my own cot beside him. Ryuu hadn't moved toward his cot, his great wings on display while he faced the door as if waiting for an attack.

"This wasn't your fault."

His wings bristled, but he remained silent.

"Will's visions have been getting worse. This isn't the first time he's seized."

"I could have helped—"

"No, you couldn't have."

"You don't know that," he growled, spinning toward me at last. "If I'd said the blessing sooner—"

"It may not have changed anything."

"But it could have." He searched my eyes for something, frantic to find whatever it was, but I wouldn't let him place this burden on his shoulders.

"The only way to save my brother is to figure out what the prophecies mean and stop them from coming to pass."

He gave a tight nod, but some of the tension in his shoulders eased. "Lannie should be informed. Perhaps her newest tonic for him is ready."

He left before I could utter a 'thank you'.

Lannie stormed into the library, her pouch of personal healing supplies clutched tightly in hand. Ryuu stepped through the door next with a resigned, slightly uncomfortable look on his face, his arms full of containers and vials.

"Describe what happened," Lannie demanded, flinging back the covers to get a good view of Will.

I glanced at Ryuu, but he only shrugged, the small movement nearly toppling the contents of his arms. "We weren't here. Cadoc said he mentioned the brothers and the raven again—"

"I don't care about the prophecy right now. What happened to Will? He had the vision and then what?"

Frowning, I answered as best as I could. "Cadoc said he started seizing. It sounded like it was right after the prophecy had been delivered. But the convulsions lasted at least a few minutes."

Lannie evaluated Will from head to toe, just as she had done when we were younger. "Any speaking while seizing?"

"No."

She finished her assessment before plopping down in a wooden chair opposite me. "From what I can tell, he's stable. We won't know how the seizure affected his mind until he wakes, but his reflexes are intact and he didn't lose control of his bowels."

My face paled. "So, he's okay this time, but..."

Lannie grimaced. "But if they continue to progress at this rate, he could suffer permanent damage. I've been working on tonics in an attempt to curb their influence, but it's vital we find a way to stop the visions."

"That's not possible." Ryuu's voice was little more than a whisper.

Lannie's spine stiffened, but I could see the quiet remorse beneath Ryuu's stoic countenance.

"We have to try."

He met my eyes, jaw clenching, but nodded. He wanted them to end—the visions. Despite them being a blessing from the goddess, Ryuu cared more about Will's life.

Lannie directed him to place the items on the table. She rifled through them, extracting key ingredients and combining them with freshly boiled water.

"Be sure he drinks the entire thing when he wakes. I've done what I can to sweeten it with honey, but it's bitter."

"You're not staying?"

She shook her head. "Serephina is very weak. She's putting on a brave show, but if any of her internal injuries were to reopen... I would need to be there to stabilize her. A few moments could be the difference between life and death."

Ryuu leaned against the table, crossing his ankles as he peered at my sister. "The liquid you used to heal the girl, you created it?"

Lannie took a seat beside me on the cot. "Not entirely. Healer Grant, the main healer at the base, has countless texts of light fae healing techniques. There are a few from other kingdoms, but the tonics or salves that work best come from the Light Kingdom. The one I used on Serephina was originally derived as a topical healing potion, meaning it needed an open wound to work. Great for deep lacerations or stab wounds from the battlefield, but not so great for injuries sustained from blunt force trauma.

"I started looking into the possibility of adapting it when Lucy delivered." Her eyes swung to mine. "I was worried for weeks she would start bleeding and I wouldn't have a way to save her. So, I adjusted the potion to fit my needs." Lannie shrugged as if adapting a revolutionary potion was standard.

Ryuu's eyes narrowed. "You've done this before?"

"Many times. They don't always work, but normally if I adjust only a few ingredients they've been doing well."

The silence stretched as the two of them looked at each other.

I cleared my throat. "Lannie's always been skilled with healing. She's the only reason we didn't all die from random illnesses growing up."

Ryuu's eyes zeroed in on mine. "The four of you were ill often?"

"No... not often." My brows furrowed as I looked at Lannie. "I really only remember Will being sick, and El being wounded from hunting..."

"It was mainly Will." Lannie confirmed, our eyes drifting to our sleeping brother. "I'd bind El's wounds as needed, but they'd never fester. Greer and I were just lucky, I guess."

Ryuu raised a brow. "Perhaps."

"The brothers Will keeps mentioning in the visions," Lannie said, tearing her eyes away from Ryuu to face me. "Do you think it's the same brothers mentioned in the story Healer Grant uncovered?"

"Yes," I answered. "The story has been the only piece of evidence we've found matching Will's visions. It's circulated for centuries in the Light Kingdom, meaning it could have first been told from a long-lost oracle. We have to assume the prophecy is foretelling the brothers' return and the impending fallout that would occur if they are successful with their conquest."

Lannie shook her head, unconvinced. "I know parts of it match, but it's a little far-fetched. The brothers haven't been seen in centuries if the story is accurate, longer even. Obviously, the part about them spanning realms is fantasied, but I suppose they could've been dwelling in the far recesses of Pax, biding their time until an opportune moment to strike presented itself."

"You don't believe the myths?" Ryuu asked with only the smallest inflection revealing he gave myths more credit than Lannie did.

Lannie blinked. "I prefer tangible evidence and logical explanations."

"Says the person who constructed a potion to mend vessels," I joked, trying to ease the odd tension spanning between them.

"The potions I derive have a specific set of ingredients and rules that need to be applied. It's true some of the products used contain fae blessings, but it's not *magic*. If I altered one small part of my technique, the potion would be just as likely to kill someone as to save them."

"And you?" Ryuu questioned, my heart jumping as his deep gaze fixed on me.

I allowed myself two seconds of being lost in the intensity of his gaze before I lifted my chin. "My name is Greer."

It looked like he was trying desperately not to roll his eyes. "Do you possess the same... skills?"

"No. Lannie was the one who kept us healthy, and Elara kept us safe. I was just along for the ride."

I'd meant it to be sarcastic, but the words rang with a truth I didn't want to face. I hadn't contributed to the family, not like they had. I was the one Mother intended to acquire suitors, the one who needed to appear beautiful and calm. To cultivate the perfect picture of gentry. I'd never wanted a stagnant life. A crafted still-life painting that was beautiful, but lacked depth. It was painful thinking I'd amounted to little more.

"That's not true." Lannie gripped my hand, forcing me to meet her eyes. "You took care of the food—"

"El did the hunting."

"Anything besides meat, you found," Lannie countered. "You took point on raising Will. *You* made sure he always knew he was loved."

"We all did that."

She shook her head gently, a well of sadness and love swirling in her eyes. "Not like you. You were the one who kept us together, especially during the dark times. When we hadn't had fresh food for weeks, or when the night grew cold and there wasn't enough wood to burn, you pulled us from the edge of bleakness. Don't ever doubt your importance."

A vast warmth spread through me. I was important, loved—

"So, no aptitude for healing?" Ryuu's matter-of-fact tone sliced through the moment.

"No. No healing powers for me."

I shot him a withering glare. He gave an unbothered nod, as if it had been the perfect moment to point out my lack of abilities. "And the scrolls?" he continued. "Are you nearly finished?"

Ryuu and his obsession with those damn scrolls. Fighting off the urge to roll my eyes, I answered, "Yes. I have only a few passages left from the last set you brought. You can check my progress, if you'd like."

"No need. I'll wait until they are complete. I'll look into the three brothers, but our focus needs to be on discovering who or what the raven is. If we've correctly understood Will's visions, it is our last defense."

"We?" The word tasted foul in my mouth as I drew the syllable out, my mind already imagining Ryuu spending late nights with Cress.

He lifted a dark brow at me, crossing his arms to match his legs. "Mostly Jarek, Zaeth, and I, though Evander and Soter have joined on occasion. I've spoken with Cress about the situation as well, though only through messages. As you know, she is currently in the Air Kingdom attempting to shed light on our current predicament."

Lannie looked at me with a bewildered expression as I gave Ryuu a tight nod.

"No further information on who the raven might be?" I asked.

Ryuu shook his head. "Naz is looking into it. The fae, the wise woman, who recalled mention of the raven, has no clarifying information on who the raven is, but the more Naz speaks with her, the worse it sounds. She refers to the raven as 'the shield' but also as 'the sacrifice.' When asked to clarify, she gave a cryptic answer about how it was a matter of perspective."

"As if that's not confusing," I muttered.

"What about the Dark Phoenix?" Lannie asked. "Mother's lullaby clearly mentioned—"

"The Dark Phoenix is not our priority." Ryuu cut in.

Lannie pursed her lips. "I suppose it can wait. If we discover who and where the raven is, and are able to protect them, it will buy us some time before the brothers arrive."

"And if we find a way to stop the brothers, we'll be able to stop the visions," I finished out my sister's train of thought, the both of us gazing down at Will's sleeping form.

"If the goddess is willing to release him," Ryuu added as he pushed up from the table and headed for the door. "I'll stay in the infirmary to allow the three of you some time alone. I will not be able to heal the girl if she needs it, but I'll be able to detect if her body is succumbing to any further damage and alert you to the change."

Lannie appraised him for a moment before exhaling. "Thank you. I'll be down shortly."

With that, he left. It took her all of a heartbeat before she whirled on me.

"Okay, what is going on between the two of you?"

"What do you mean?" I asked, tugging on a wild curl and letting it spring back as I shifted under her gaze.

"Really? You practically bit his head off when he spoke of working with another person. You didn't even know it was a woman."

I rolled my eyes. "Oh, I knew. Cress has been clinging to him every chance she gets. I've only managed a reprieve from her presence recently because more research was needed. But the moment she obtains it, I've no doubt she'll be right back here batting her lashes at Ryuu."

Lannie laughed. It was a small, surprised sound at first, but grew into a wild snort. "You're jealous. You like Ryuu, and it must be a lot, because I've never seen you think twice about a man who didn't want you, let alone pine after one."

"I'm not *pining*."

"Okay." She shrugged, clearly not believing me.

"Maybe a little." I groaned as her smile grew. "I don't understand why. He's terrible. He practically held up a large 'denied' sign in my face the night of Litha, then spent the subsequent months scowling and—and *growling* at me! Like some type of wild beast.

"But there are glimpses where I swear it's like he's afraid to allow himself to care... I know it sounds insane, but I think he does care for me. Or, at least, would if he allowed himself to."

"Nothing has happened between the two of you?" Lannie asked.

"We kissed." I shrugged as if it weren't the most earth-shattering kiss I'd ever experienced. Lannie saw through my defenses, but held her tongue.

We sat in silence for a while, clustered around Will. She stood, brushing his silver curls, so like my own, back from his forehead. He was growing his hair out. I'd caught him a few times attempting to tie half of it back with a leather strap, strangely similar to the way a certain air fae wore his hair. Will's skin was tanned from the last few weeks spent in the summer sun, the splash of freckles across his cheeks had darkened.

Lannie stood. "We'll find a way to save him."

I bit my cheek, not wanting her to see the frustrated, bitter tears swelling in my eyes as she headed for the door. Her hand lingered on the frame, hovering on the threshold, but she faced away from me as she spoke.

"If you see something worth fighting for with Ryuu, go after it. The best things in life will demand your effort, your time, and the most valuable thing of all, your heart. Anything worth having will test you. Do not be afraid to fight for what you want."

## 37

# ELARA

THE CRACKLING OF FLAMES AND MURMURINGS OF ROUGH, RAW voices grew louder as I picked my way through the remaining branches. My heartbeat thundered in my ears, but I was careful to keep my breathing steady. An intoxicating rush of energy coursed through me as I peered through the underbrush, ducking beneath a large oak tree and gazing upon the once quaint village, now soaked in blood.

A wild bonfire raged in what would have been the center of town. Flames licked the night sky over a wide field of smoldering embers with a large metal contraption setup over the glowing embers to look like a wide steel stage. The fire surged, illuminating the surrounding creatures and piles of flesh-tinged debris.

Three short, stocky beings with large, curved noses and pale molting skin lurked near a pile of bodies, the flickering of the fire twisting their grotesque features further. Goblins. They continued dousing the pile with a gleaming, slick substance, their wide frames turning with their work to reveal broad, though pointed, ears with small divots and bites removed along the edges. Their faces were pinched as they moved among the piles of flesh, grumbling about their task.

"I don't understand why we're confined to killing off only these pathetic little towns. It's unheard of for the followers of Veles to bow to the whims of the fae. I say enough with these scraps."

The largest of the three dumped the remaining slick contents of his jar across the closest mound of rubble. I blinked, my vision adjusting to the flickering firelight as I scanned the piles. The nearest held a pair of legs, the torso having been ripped away to leave ragged red stumps on the ends. The goblin reached out, rubbing in the liquid it poured moments earlier —oil.

My stomach roiled. They were basting the corpse... preparing it for the fire. Fighting desperately to keep the limited contents of my stomach in place, I focused on the mutterings of the goblins.

"I say we stop waiting. My belly yearns for the taste of fae flesh. Enough of these soiled humans."

"Silence!" A voice boomed through the square, a swarm of goblins at its back. The goblins surged forward, eager for a meal, but the shrouded figure clung to the treeline, its body a few inches taller than me and covered with a dark cloak. "You will listen to the orders of the light fae because that is what your master commands. Or have you forgotten your place?"

The light of the flames flashed against the towering figure's large black eyes, the pools of cruelty the only things visible in the shadows. The goblins cringed, shrinking back among severed limbs.

*Orders of the light fae.* They truly were behind the attacks, working with the red-eyed commander in their extermination of the human race. All this time, we'd believed they were working on a cure for the linger effects of the storm, working toward helping our people, our dying babes—when the whole time they were orchestrating their demise.

Praying they couldn't hear my thundering heart, I crept forward around the large oak tree and crouched among the tall brush, intent on hearing every bit of information I could.

"N-no, Your Excellency. I only thought to point out there's no further need for pretense. We have the numbers—"

The goblin's voice was cut off as a bony spindled hand lashed out from the darkness, its long, knobby fingers locking around the goblin's throat. A chilling rumble sounded as the hidden figure emerged. Swirling tendrils of shadows still clung to it but there was no mistaking the splintered soul housed within. There was a waxy sheen to its pale skin, mottled in shades of blue and gray, stretched thin across sharp cheekbones. Cavernous eye-sockets were hooded in darkness with bone-white pupils peering out, simmering with a cool rage. Black rags hung from its thin body, revealing bands of lean muscle clinging to spindle-like limbs.

The subtle late-night breeze changed directions as it moved forward with a large scythe clasped in a long-fingered grip, stirring a wave of putrid stench toward me. Death clung to this creature, causing the breath in my lungs to seize. My body heaved with revulsion, but I willed the contents of my stomach to stay down. If my position was revealed, these beings would rip me apart before Zaeth could reach me.

Needle-sharp teeth corrupted by years of decay snapped at the goblin, causing it to tremble. "You are not qualified to think, goblin. You have relinquished your soul to better this world, to prepare it for your master's return, and yet you think yourself worthy to question him?"

The arced blade lashed through the air, fully returning to an upright position before the goblin's head slouched off his body, thumping to the ground with pleading words still tumbling from its mouth.

"Veles has instructed us to play this game. In just a few decades, he has turned this world against the only kingdom that could pose a threat, the Dark Kingdom. The wretched fools trust us with their salvation, with finding a cure to the lingering effects of the storm that ravaged their people years ago." The gaunt creature's face pulled back into what might have been a smile, the vicious pointed teeth on full display.

Low rumblings from the crowd swept the square in support as my mouth ran dry. This was a lot bigger than we'd realized. I shifted slightly, fall back behind the tree, but the ears of the nearest goblin twitched, stilling my motions. I'd have to wait for an opening.

"Soon, we will reign, no longer confined to the shadows of this world or to the void of the last. Never forget our destiny has been foretold: darkness will spring, devouring all, with icy tendrils none can stall."

The thick bands of grayed rope-like muscle wrapping around the creature's torso shifted as it brandished the bloodied scythe while pacing before the crowd and the blazing bonfire. Crazed murmurings cackled among the goblins, the beginnings of a great wave of praise.

"The wicked forces of old arrive, a war of death, leaving none alive."

Shrieks and howls filled the square, answering the creature's words.

My heart beat wildly as the creature of death turned abruptly, stalking closer to the cluster of branches I was crouched beneath. I held my breath, willing my thundering pulse to quiet as it neared, worried the creature would be able to hear it. But its gliding strides carried it past me, toward a large mound of oiled body parts. It thrust a bony hand among the pile, tossing limbs to and for until it yanked its arm back. A thick thigh coated in a wash of congealed blood was gripped in its spider-like fingers, complete with a large slash exposing a shiny piece of tendon running down to the outside of the knee.

An evil smile spread across the creature's haunted face as it lifted the butchered slab of meat into the sky. "Enjoy the spoils of battle, tonight. In two weeks, this facade will end. Fae flesh will fill our bellies. We will no longer be confined to frightened whispers of the night, but we will rise, becoming the embodiment of fear itself as we take this world for our own."

It tossed the leg onto the metal grate overlying the fire, the contraption cantering under the added weight. The smell of burnt hair assaulted my nostrils as oiled flesh sizzled. The creature stalked away, unleashing the goblins from their held positions, and they surged forward, rushing toward the pile of flesh, adding meat to the burning metal with frenzied hunger—as if they were roasting hares rather than humans.

I used the rush of movements to cover my escape, fleeing the cursed feast behind me as quickly and quietly as I could. Zaeth found me, manifesting from the shadows a moment later.

His arms came around me, one supporting my shoulders as the other swept my knees out from under me before flitting us a safe distance away. I flung myself free of his grasp the moment we stopped moving, landing on my knees with a thud not a second too soon. Finally losing the battle of restraint, my stomach heaved, but the burning of my throat was a welcome distraction from the horror I'd just witnessed.

Gentle hands pulled back stray strands of my hair as my stomach clenched once more, purging its contents in a fierce wave. I took a few strangled gasps before peering up, surprised by the tenderness of Zaeth's touch.

"You did well, love. None of them heard you." He offered me a waterskin before stepping away.

I took my time gargling water and spitting it out before meeting his gaze. "I'm not going to fall apart," I said defiantly, wishing anyone other than Zaeth were here to witness my weakness.

"I know you won't. Not for a cluster of hungry goblins." His face twisted with foreboding. "But far worse things lie ahead of us."

"You saw?" I asked, letting a gulp of water sooth my raw throat.

He gave a tight nod. "I was able to perch high enough in the trees to catch glimpses. The shifting of the wind provided the rest."

"What was that thing?"

"It was a shadow wraith. I've long suspected the goblins' involvement, but if shadow wraiths have agreed to support the Fractured and their masters..." He shook his head. "It's worse than we thought."

Zaeth reached a hand toward me and I took it, allowing him to help me up into a standing position with little effort. He held on a heartbeat longer than needed and I forced my cheeks not to heat as I took a step back.

"Who is Veles?"

A quick shake of his head was my answer. "I'm not sure. I have theories, but they need to be tested."

I gnawed on my bottom lip. "It sounded like the Fractured, the goblins, and that shadow wraith creature were following his orders. The Light Kingdom, too. All are under his control."

"I feared as much. Who else would be bold enough to impersonate the dark fae? This confirms it."

"The shadow wraith said Veles had planned this for years."

"Decades," Zaeth amended.

My stomach twisted, but the breeze offered a cleansing wave of cool night air, having shifted to blow the stench of the wraith and the massacre away from me, back toward the devastated town beyond.

"We've been training to combat the Fractured since Neith. Everything we've done has been to thwart them and their red-eyed commander." My eyes snapped to him. "The commander. Do you think he could be Veles?"

Zaeth gave an unenthusiastic shrug. "It's a possibility."

"You don't seem convinced."

He exhaled, frustration written in every crease of his brow. "It would be easier if it were that simple, but if I'd planned an invasion—an annihilation— for decades, I'd send the pawns to test defenses before risking the king."

My chest fell. Zaeth was right. The commander must be receiving orders from someone. I'd prepared for war, for a bloodied uphill battle with half-alive fae, but I hadn't considered others would flock to their aid—that infamous creatures of cruelty would align with them. I hadn't considered an entire kingdom of royals would be at their disposal. There was no way we could win this. We were doomed to fail—my brother's life... cursed to the whims of an absent goddess—

"Don't do that," Zaeth's words were cutting, harsh even.

"Don't do what?" I snapped. "I didn't say anything."

"You didn't have to. Your thoughts are loud enough, and I'm not going to stand by while you drown in self-pity."

"I'm not."

He scoffed, rolling his eyes before fixing them on me. "Stop pretending. Stop trying to make yourself smaller than you are. You do not need to fit into *their* ideas of what is good. What is proper. You are stronger than them—greater. You were not meant to cower."

His eyes bored into mine, seeing through the layers of my hardened exterior, blasting through each wall until he found my center. I felt him there, like a gentle summer breeze caressing my frigid soul. Warmth settled within me, taking root, breathing life into an ancient slumbering part of myself.

Zaeth inhaled sharply, eyes darting to our surroundings. A

predatory growl rumbled from his chest as the rich cinnamon of his eyes flared to life, a surrounding silver ring erupting to focus on the patch of forest we'd come from. His fangs elongated into fierce points, the air charging with his dark fae blessing as he released an animalistic snarl.

## 38
## GREER

WILL WOKE, THRASHING AND SCREAMING IN THE MIDDLE OF THE night. I feared it was another vision—that he was succumbing to a second seizure so soon after the first, but it was only a nightmare. Gods, when had nightmares become something I was relieved about?

"Shh, it's okay, Will. I'm right here. You aren't alone."

He blinked, searching for my face in the lingering dark. Will found Ryuu's first, his face crumbling as tears welled in his eyes. "You didn't leave."

I blinked in surprise as Will fell into Ryuu's arms. Ryuu gathered him closer, holding him as the terror of the past few hours poured out in shudders of tears. Rubbing Will's back with gentle strokes, I offered calming words, just as I used to do when he was little, promising we'd always be here for him. The 'we', I realized, now included Ryuu. Whatever path our futures held, I'd forever be grateful for his kindness with Will.

"I remember," Will muttered, the words muffled against Ryuu's chest.

My hand stilled. He never remembered. Nightmares, sure,

but the visions had always passed straight through him. "You remember the nightmare?"

He nodded, pulling himself to a seated position. "Yes, but I remember the vision as well."

I shot Ryuu an anxious glance, asking the silent question: 'was this normal?'

He gave a small shake of his head before focusing solely on my brother. "Are you able to share what you saw?"

"She wanted me to tell you," he whispered, his gaze locked on his hands resting in his lap. "She said I *needed* to remember. That I was running out of time."

"Who said this?"

He looked up to meet Ryuu's gaze. "I'm not sure. She was glowing. It was hard to see, but I heard her and I think I've heard her before."

"The goddess," Ryuu whispered, eyes wide.

Will swallowed, finding the courage to continue. "It started out like one of my nightmares. There was the army of the forsaken—the Fractured as you call them. But then it shifted. She showed me a different place, a different town, but it was being destroyed by these short creatures with large black eyes and—and they were cutting apart humans and *eating* them."

Will's face turned a shade of green. "I'm so sorry," I stammered, hating that he was forced to witness such things. "Ryuu can look into the creatures."

Ryuu nodded. "It sounds like goblins."

I pulled Will into a hug, wishing I could take his pain and fear away. "We're working on finding a way to stop the visions."

But his body remained stiff in my arms. Tentatively, I pulled back.

His eyes locked with mine. "That was just the beginning."

Swallowing, I forced a neutral expression to my face and waited for him to continue. I would burden him with my fear, as well.

Will's chest expanded with a few ragged breaths. "The vision shifted to another place. There were monsters—"

"Can you describe the monsters," Ryuu asked. "Anything that could help us identify them?"

"This group looked like skeletons with strings of muscle clinging to their bones. They were covered in shadows and each had a long pole with a curved blade at the end."

"Shadow wraiths," Ryuu growled.

Will lifted his shoulders, unable to confirm. "I've never seen them before. But then the images started moving fast. There were groups of really large wolves but they had smoke surrounding them and glowing eyes. Other monsters appeared —dragons of fire, yellow-eyed serpents—things moving in the dark, surrounding slabs of pulsing silver-blue stones. It all tangled together with flashes of light and blood. And then you were there."

Will looked at Ryuu, brows furrowed. "It was you, but you were different. And you had a spear in your hands. The tip was a bright orange. It was stone, but almost looked like it was on fire. The creatures were afraid of it."

Ryuu paled. I lifted a brow at him. "Do you know what spear he's talking about?"

Slowly, he nodded. "Yes, but it's a myth. The spear is made from fire opal. Many shadow creatures fear it."

Will's voice cracked when he spoke again. "The last image was a fae with red eyes. He had black claws for fingers, but everything else about him was white, like the color of bone."

Ryuu and I shared a knowing glance. It sounded like the commander from Neith.

"Could you see where he was?" I asked softly.

Will shook his head. "But he wasn't alone. There was this— this ghost behind him in the darkness surrounded by ice and a king sitting before him."

"A king?" Ryuu asked, eyes searching Will's face.

Will's chin jerked down with a nod. "I know he was a king, but I don't know why. He wasn't wearing a crown... A large raven appeared before them, but the three closed in. It should have flown away, but it stayed, stretching its wings wide before them. They glowed a deep red color, stretching and growing until they blocked the three of them completely. But then everything started to crumble. I was scared. And then everything went black and I was trapped in the darkness. Alone."

Tears welled in his eyes, my own following suit. I pulled him into my arms, vowing to never leave him alone, to make sure he never had to face this or any other horrible vision by himself. "We will find a way to stop the visions from coming to fruition."

I spoke the vow with absolute certainty as my brother fell apart all over again. Ryuu lifted a brow at my impossible promise, but remained silent. Instead, he pushed back from the cots, retrieving the tonic Lannie left for Will.

"Your sister was here, but her services were required in the infirmary. She made you a tea to try to help."

Will sat up, but stayed close as he accepted the cup from Ryuu with a suspicious look. "It's going to taste bad, isn't it?"

My lips twitched despite the precarious situation. "A little."

He shot me a boyish glare, letting a whine creep into his voice. "That means a lot."

A real smile stretched across my face. "I promise to bake you extra chocolate éclairs when we have a proper kitchen and ingredients, again."

His mouth drew to the side as he contemplated my offer. "And I get to eat as many of them as I want," he bargained.

"Deal."

Will brought the cup close, nose wrinkling as he caught a whiff, but he drank it all the same. "I like it here. I like the base, too, but..." His eyes flicked up to Ryuu. "I fit better here."

Ryuu's dark eyes seemed to soften as he stared down at my brother. After another moment, Ryuu dipped his head, bringing their eyes level. "You have been chosen as the voice of the goddess. It is a blessing and a burden, one that is immense for anyone to weather, let alone someone as young as yourself."

Will's chin tipped up, a retort posed on his lips, but Ryuu continued before he could utter a word.

"I know you have a warrior's spirit. Only the strongest are selected by the goddess, but you are still young in age."

Will exhaled, looking down at his hands folded in his lap.

"The important thing to remember is that you are unique, in an incredible way. That power can be isolating, but you will always have a place here, among your family and among mine."

I swallowed as tears welled in Will's eyes, biting back my own. Ryuu glanced over at me as Will threw himself into his large arms, not sure how to respond.

With a smile, I mimed a hug. Ryuu copied the gesture, patting Will's back before settling into the maneuver. I nearly laughed. Ryuu was a predator, one who had no doubt seen dozens of bloody battles, defeated countless challengers, and traveled the world, but he was rendered speechless by a young boy's hug.

I thought back to our kiss, to the way his eyes held mine, swirling with attraction and something deeper. My tongue flicked out, drawing my bottom lip between my teeth, as if I could still taste him there.

Swallowing, I dragged my mind back to the present, taking a seat on the cot beside the pair. Ryuu held him as he cried, cradling him until Will's heaving breaths evened out as he drifted off to a peaceful sleep. Will looked so small at that moment. He'd grown at least three inches this summer, but here, with the terrors of his most recent vision leaving tears along his freckled cheeks, I couldn't help but think how unfair everything was.

Ryuu carefully laid him down on the center cot, the both of us tucking the blankets in around him. Our fingers brushed, sending a wave of warmth through me, more comforting than provoking. A simple graze of his fingers slowed the chaotic worries of my mind. Daring a glance up, I was rewarded with finding his deep eyes focused on me, an array of emotion flashing through them: desire, confusion, fear.

I made to reach for him, unwilling to let our earlier moment of passion be a one-time occurrence, but he flinched back, jerking away from the cots into a standing position.

"I need to ensure the fort is prepared for a possible attack."

"Aren't the others doing that?" I breathed, pushing up to join him.

His shoulders pulled back as he swallowed. "I'd feel more comfortable seeing for myself."

I chanced a step closer. "But you'll return?"

"Perhaps. Any progress with the most recent scrolls?"

I blinked, but gestured to the table in the corner. "I finished them earlier this evening after you left." Each time I finished decoding a batch of scrolls, he'd insist on comparing notes. Something about language translation being up for interpretation. Most of the scrolls had faded spots or missing segments, and the meaning of passages was often inferred based on the legible pieces. I thought it tedious at first, using several texts to help with translation, but it had grown easier the more I completed. I'd come to look forward to the process, secretly enjoying when my translations matched Ryuu's.

But I wouldn't be distracted from my question. "It would mean a lot to Will to have you here." His cutting gaze bored into me, causing my heart to flutter, and forcing the truth from my lips in a soft whisper. "It would mean a lot to *me*."

I took a step closer. Ryuu mumbled an excuse about securing the perimeter and fled, his fae speed leaving nothing but a whoosh of his masculine-scented air in his wake.

## 39

# ELARA

"I THOUGHT I SMELLED DESSERT." THE SHADOW WRAITH STEPPED forward with the pack of goblins slinking at its back. Their black soulless eyes zeroed in on us, glittering with hunger.

The clouds shifted, causing the light of the moon to filter through overhead branches and catch on the wraith's malicious grin. Its needle-like teeth glistened, the bits of gore and fat dripping down his chin in a slick oily mess.

Sunken hollowed eyes met mine as it grinned. "Enjoy."

The word was a shrouded command, releasing the goblins from the forest in a ravenous cheer.

I unsheathed my blade, knowing it wouldn't be enough, but determined to take down as many of these bastards as I could. Zaeth unleashed a thundering growl, the sound alone causing a few of the goblins to yelp and retreat but the majority surged forth.

Zaeth swept through the swarm in a burst of rage before they reached me. I watched, transfixed, as his fangs clamped down on the goblin's throat, ripping the soft flesh free in a spray of red. Its eyes widened in horror as it brought its hand up, cupping only spurting blood and empty space before collapsing.

Zaeth had already dismembered three more before I regrouped, the bodies left in pulsating heaps flooding the ground in deep crimson stains. Most of the goblins formed a ring around him, assessing. He unleashed his blade from the scabbard strapped to his spine, offering a malicious grin before diving into the crowd.

Two goblins rushed me from the left, the snap of branches affording me a lifesaving moment of warning in which I was able to dive to the side. I sprung up with my blade ready, absorbing the brunt of the first blow. Steel clashed and then screeched against each other as I dislodged the heavy blade, spinning my sword around in a quick arc to slice through the vulnerable flesh of the goblin's neck.

The other had thought to attack from behind, bringing his blade down with a loud cry. I dashed to the side as the rusted blade descended, letting the goblin's momentum force the edge of his sword into the body of his headless companion. That was all the opening I needed for my dagger to find purchase in its throat.

I listened as the gurgling of blood bubbled through the hole left by my blade, relishing the way my body pulsed with life as theirs ended.

The shadow wraith stalked Zaeth, its thin lip curling back in a snarl as it watched him flash through the goblins, Zaeth's own darkness seeming to swallow him up and spit him out as the bodies of the dying hit the ground.

I sliced through another goblin that rushed my way. Then another and another. A smile twisted my lips as agonized cries filled the air. My body hummed with adrenaline, the steady beat of my heart intensifying as the world around me slowed. Black smudges shrouded the goblins, extinguished by a blazing flame of light surrounding Zaeth, the glow matching the bright ring of his eyes. The brands along his arms glowed with the same strange power, extending over his chest and back. They pulsed faintly in time to the beating of his heart as he cut through the black-clouded haze all around him, the darkness evaporating as the goblins' bodies fell.

Zaeth was the embodiment of vengeance and the promise of death. A whisper of golden light splayed forth from his back in a wide span, giving the impression of wings. It propelled him onward in a burst of strength as he danced among the corpses. He was unstoppable, a ruthless avenging god, enacting justice for the murdered souls of the village. Demanding repayment for the blood spilled these past years.

I caught a glimpse of a smile, the pointed tips of his incisors gleaming, taunting the shadow wraith, as he flitted among its failing army. He disemboweled two others before the wraith shot forward.

Zaeth whirled, his blade catching the edge of the descending scythe and throwing it back before it could find its mark. A hiss of rage bellowed from the shadow wraith as Zaeth landed slice after slice across its torso, the shredded ribbons of cloth acting as proof his blade had pierced flesh—but there was no blood, only the gathering of shadows slithering along each of the wounds.

Goblins continued to swarm Zaeth from behind as he darted between the wraith's counterattacks, but he flitted among them, dropping bodies as he went.

My vision sharpened as I rushed forward to help, my sword making quick work of those too slow to see me coming. The goblins were nothing but splintered beings, corrupted beyond saving with the same gritty, rotting feel to them the Fractured had. There was more to them, something hinting at independence flickering beneath the ink stain surrounding them, but it was bound—pledged to the shadow wraith. And to their leader, Veles.

A goblin turned, its eyes widening a fraction of a second before my blade swept across its neck. Just enough time for it to issue a last cry, alerting the others to my presence. I smirked as they closed in around me, meeting their furious glares with a hunger of my own.

Zaeth spared a glance my way as he decapitated another, not quite checking on me, but I gave him a reassuring nod all the same. He smirked, recognizing the gleam in my eyes as I attacked. "Enjoying yourself?"

My lips twitched as I pierced the belly of another goblin, slicing up before pulling it back, watching as loops of entrails fell to the ground. "I couldn't let you have all the fun, now, could I?"

Another three rushed forward. Their movements were not as synchronized as the Fractured, making them more difficult to predict. But they moved with an anger, a hunger for flesh that left them eager and sloppy.

I impaled the first with my sword, pressing forward until I felt the final release of tissue as the blade erupted through its back. He dropped, taking my sword with him as another rushed forward. Unlatching my long dagger from a sheath along my forearm, I slashed, the slick blade cutting through its neck like a hot knife through butter. A grunt alerted me to another. I attacked before it realized I'd turned, thrusting my dagger upward through the base of its chin. A sickening crunch issued as the blade punctured its skull, the force of the blow resonating along the hilt.

Reattaching the blade along my forearm, I released my sword from its meaty sheath, my foot braced along the goblin's chest as I yanked it free from the cage of ribs and muscle. The goblins used the opening, rushing forward in a wave of snapping teeth and rusted blades.

With a crazed snarl of my own, I met their attack, pairing swords and blocking attacks. It was too much. There were too many, but somehow my body anticipated each strike, dividing out counter blows as I worked through them.

A dark whirl of horns and a flash of molten gold cut a line along the periphery, snaring my attention. Soter. He launched into battle, aiding Zaeth against the shadow wraith. The look cost me.

I cried out as talons swiped at my thigh. I was able to roll away before they found purchase, leaving only shallow, angry gashes, but blood welled in thick pools, flowing down my leg. Not fatal, but the cuts burned as I pushed to stand, my movements much too slow. Fear sprouted for the first time, causing my pulse to quicken, pounding through my veins as the goblins descended from every side.

Zaeth was there in a flash, the wisps of shimmering wings carrying him through the swarm, blotting out the darkness of the goblins. He swept through them, shredding bodies as he went until only one remained: the goblin responsible for the searing pain along my thigh.

I glanced toward Soter and the shadow wraith. A flash of blond hair had joined them. As if sensing my gaze, Jarek stilled long enough to shoot me a crooked grin before whipping around the wraith once more.

"No. No, please." The goblin was trembling as Zaeth stalked forward, a foul pool darkened the earth between its legs.

Zaeth's hand lashed out, lifting the goblin by its neck before slamming it against the wide trunk. The bark cracked beneath the force as Zaeth grabbed the goblin's hand, lifting it to scent the stain of red along its talons. My blood.

"You made a grave mistake."

He twisted, snapping the bones with a mere flick of his wrist before plunging a dagger into its stomach, slicing the blade up in a vertical slit. He paused, only long enough for the goblin's innards to spill forth as the creature issued a blood curdling cry.

Zaeth's lips twisted into a malicious smile as he plunged his hand into the bleeding cavity, yanking his arm back a moment later with the still-beating heart grasped between his fingers.

Blood spurted, coating Zaeth in a wash of scarlet as the goblin fell.

A metallic scent filled the air as Zaeth met my stare. His face was splattered with red, the color deepening where it clung to his hair, but his cinnamon eyes were as bright as ever, ringed in a dazzling light.

"You killed them all," I said, eyes wide as I realized the number of lives he'd claimed.

He lifted a brow. "I kill a lot of things."

"No remorse?" I asked around the fluttering in my stomach. It was a foreign feeling, watching someone like me, someone openly enjoy themselves while blood misted the air and bodies littered the earth.

"No, love. Some things are in need of killing. I am not ashamed to be this realm's reaper."

"If you're done playing around, we could use a little help," Jarek called as the shadow wraith snarled. Soter deflected another bow, his blade swinging around to sink deep into the creature's chest. It only enraged it further, causing the creature to twist, nearly dislodging his hold on his sword.

With a distraction from Jarek and a great tug, Soter retrieved his blade. The two of them fell back, joined by Evander a moment later.

"Fools, all of you." The shadow wraith sneered. "You cannot stop us. We are the forces of old melded with the bodies of the new. Your world will fall, regardless of what you do. But Veles can be merciful." Its piercing eyes found mine. "Join us."

Deep gashes and plunging cuts adorned its body, but shadows swarmed where blood should have been. It took a step toward me, its already pale skin blanching further. It may not bleed but it could die.

Zaeth tensed, but didn't attempt to shield me from its attention. I lifted my chin, feeling emboldened by his confidence despite the bite of pain in my leg. "What other creatures have aligned with you? Where is the rest of your army?"

A maddening cackle erupted from it; the sounds of a doomed creature aware its end was near. I allowed him the pleasure of his last laugh, bearing the weight of his gaze as the disquieting white irises peered down at me. "Why do you fight for them? They are nothing to us, a cluster of maggots eroding the foundation of this world. Their mere presence leeches our primal power. Without them, we would be unchecked. Our power would be unencumbered by the strains their mortal souls enforce on this world. We would be free from this slavery—"

"Enough. Tell me where to find the others. Who is Veles?"

It darted forward, scythe lashing out, as its body flickered with swarming shadows. But Soter was quicker. The crazed gleam in its eyes was still in place when its gaunt body fell backward, the deafening silence interrupted only by the sliding suction of its neck parting from its body. No blood came. Only the last shifting of shadows before the corpse stilled entirely.

Zaeth stood tall, his brands pulsing as fiercely as the bright ring surrounding his eyes. He tilted his head, glancing from Soter to the lifeless wraith.

"Beheading?" Zaeth asked.

Soter shrugged. "Seems to have worked. When in doubt, remove the head."

Zaeth's lips twitched. "Noted. We'll need to find fire opal."

"Agreed. A lot of it."

"Where's Jarek?" I asked, my eyes darting around the clearing.

"He's tracking a few of the goblins we let escape," Soter answered. "There was no portal this time, suggesting they have a base of some sort nearby. Jarek will find it."

Zaeth looked me over, his attention snagging on the crimson stain across my thigh. "How bad is it?"

"Not bad." I grimaced, more embarrassed than anything.

Shifted my weight, I tested it. The cuts burned, not nearly as bad as they had initially. Gingerly, I pulled away the shredded scraps of cloth, inspecting the wound. "Weird. It's shallower than I thought," I said, reaching into my pocket and pulling out the small tin Lannie insisted I bring. "Nothing a little salve won't fix."

Zaeth's eyes narrowed. "That's a lot of blood for such a small wound."

"I guess I'm a bleeder," I shrugged. "Unless you have another explanation?"

He shared a glance with Soter. The earth fae nodded, confirming Zaeth's unspoken question. "Did the goblins appear similar to how you view the Fractured?"

I lathered the salve across the three claw marks, praying Lannie's talents were enough to prevent it from festering. "They moved differently—"

"I'm not talking about fighting techniques or tactics," Zaeth cut in. "I mean for *you*. Did they appear the same?"

My hand stilled along the cuts. I took my time ripping away the soiled cloth, leaving a large hole in my pants. Evander stepped forward, offering a patch of clean cloth that appeared to have been shredded from his undershirt.

I hadn't spoken of the battle haze that consumed me, not since Neith. I glanced up, my eyes darting between Zaeth and Soter, but only awaiting curiosity greeted me. Inhaling deeply, I answered. "They had similar black clouds surrounding them. I could feel the same corruption in the goblins as I felt in the Fractured. But fae and humans appear different."

I looked beyond Zaeth. "Evander, your glow is the same as it was last time, warm and bright. Alarik had a similar, though slightly dimmer glow at Neith."

"What of Jarek and me?" Soter asked in a deep baritone.

"The two of you appeared brighter than Evander and Alarik, but with the same hints of gold." I contemplated a moment.

"Jarek's was closer to a silver like Evander's but you had richer tones of wheat mixed throughout."

Zaeth's inquisitive smile stretched wide without a hint of fear. "Go on, love. How do I look?"

Letting my eyes wander, I focused on the now dimming glow of brands scrolled across his body. "You're different."

His smile faltered for a moment, but he drew himself up with what I thought looked a lot like forced bravado. "How so?"

"You're clearer. The glow around you isn't as hazy. It's more of a reflection from your brands. They pulse, like a heartbeat. It's the same light that surrounds your eyes. Where the others have a golden hue, yours has flecks of silver and pure white mixed in." I tilted my head, assessing. "There were also shimmering stretches of light around you during the battle, clustered across your back and spanning out similar to..."

Similar to the shape of Ryuu's wings.

"It's true," Zaeth breathed, more to himself than to me. "It has to be."

"What is?" I realized then that Soter and Evander were staring as if I were a dangerous landmine they had just triggered. "What's wrong?"

Evander looked me over before shaking his head forcefully, but when he spoke his eyes swept past me, toward Zaeth. "There's no way. I've known her nearly her entire life. I would have seen or felt something."

Zaeth's eyes stayed fixed on mine, his head cocking to the side as a hawk would before snatching its prey. "Not necessarily."

I waited for him to explain, matching his curious look with my own frustrated glare.

"Soter," Zaeth continued, "with the information gleaned from the base, your own research, Ryuu's assessment, and what you know of Elara's... particular talents, what is your leading theory?"

Zaeth posed the question to the earth fae, but kept his eyes on me, the bright ring fading as the final rush of battle dissipated. A heaviness settled in my bones, Zaeth's lips pulling down as he noted the change.

In a clear, steady voice, Soter spoke. "I don't believe the Tenebris family to be human."

## 40
## GREER

Ryuu didn't return that night. An emptiness expanded in my chest, twisting with worry that he regretted our moment together... and that we'd never get another. My heart clenched as the thought swirled in my mind. I yearned for more of him. More of the fae who comforted Will when he was scared. The one who promised retribution to anyone who considered harming my little brother... the fae who had kissed me like I was the very air breathing life into his lungs.

But he hadn't returned.

I'd drifted off to sleep sometime before dawn, not waking until the sun was high in the sky. Will was still sleeping, which was not surprising. Normally, he was out for hours after the visions. It was a wonder he'd awoken as soon as he did, but judging by the shadows lingering under his eyes and the slight sheen of sweat along his brow, it had taken a toll on him.

Carefully extracting myself from Will's arms, I made my way to Lannie.

Whispered voices trickled through the ajar infirmary door as I neared the back room where Serephina was resting. Lannie's musical laugh rang out just as I pressed through. Both of them were beaming, bright smiles stretching across their faces. The shadows beneath Serephina's eyes had lessened and Lannie… Lannie looked the happiest I'd seen her in months.

"Sorry to interrupt, but I was hoping you'd stay with Will while I showered. He awoke in the middle of the night and drank the tonic you provided."

Lannie stood, eyes wide. "He woke so soon after a vision?"

I nodded with a wary frown, not wanting to sap the hope radiating from her. "And he remembered the vision. Added to it, actually." My eyes drifted toward her patient, unsure if I should continue.

Serephina looked away awkwardly, but was unable to move from bed. Lannie cleared her throat. "Right. We can catch up after you've had time to yourself. Ser's doing a lot better. I'll stay with Will till you return."

"Thanks, Sis."

"Ryuu stopped by earlier."

I'd made to leave, but my hand lingered on the doorframe as I turned to face her. "Oh?"

Lannie's lips twitched as my voice came out an octave too high. "He reassured Ser there's been no sign of an attack. The perimeter is constantly being monitored and the protection spells Jarek placed are reinforced."

I gave a tight nod, mentally chiding myself for thinking his visit had anything to do with me—with our kiss. Ryuu was a fae warrior tasked with defending this fort and the goddess's oracle. He'd traveled across Pax and had probably taken lovers as often as he cared to—lovers such as Cress. Ignoring the way thoughts of him with another woman twisted my stomach into knots, I plastered a light smile on my face.

"Good to know we're safe." He may be a devastatingly gorgeous fae with immense power pulsing through his veins, but I wasn't one to be overlooked. And I definitely wouldn't allow myself to pine for him.

Lannie raised a brow, but stayed silent.

"We're *not* safe. They're coming." Ser's voice was strong, despite her pale complexion. Her jaw was set in a firm line as she looked between us. "The only reason I survived was because of my speed."

Lannie's brows furrowed. "I thought you said the orange substance leeched your fae affinities?"

Serephina swallowed, her color blanching. "I ran when they came." Her bottom lip trembled as her gaze fell to her lap. "I made it to the edge of town, taking a small trail north when I tripped over a body. An arrow was protruding from his chest, coated with the orange substance. The burst of energy I fell when running started to wane shortly after. I left everyone there... my mother. My sister. They told me to flee, to get help, but I knew it was too late. I knew they would die, and I ran anyway."

Lannie sank onto the bed beside her, shooting me a glare as she did so.

I raised my hands up as if asking, 'what?'

She shook her head, wrapping Serephina in a tight embrace as the girl was overcome by guilt and tears. "If you're feeling up to it, you can join me while I visit Will."

Some of the sorrow surrounding Serephina faded as she looked up at Lannie. "Are you sure? I wouldn't want to intrude."

"Nonsense. It will be good to see how you move. When he wakes, we'll return here." Lannie turned toward me. "We've got it covered, Greer. See you in a bit."

A suppressed memory resurfaced as I squeezed water from my damp curls. So many had returned at once. Most were still hazy, offering only glimpses of the past, but when I focused on them they clarified, as this one was doing now.

The twins were racing through an obstacle course they'd constructed near the house. Torin had climbed *his* tree quicker, but Jem was gaining as they dashed across the field and neared the river. Both dove into the running waters headfirst, pumping their arms as they headed down stream to the next checkpoint. Torin was the stronger swimmer, a fact he exploited as he shot Jem a cocky smirk over his shoulder.

He didn't notice the increased depth of the river, nor the fierce swirl of chilly currents as he neared the half-submerged rock outcropping. His head smashed into the slick boulder with a sickening *thunk* before he could heed our warning. Jem surged forward, avoiding the rocks and snaring Torin's limp body before the river claimed him. I rushed to the shallow water's edge, helping Jem drag Torin across rounded stones and up onto the side of the riverbank, while El sprinted for Mother.

Mother appeared in a flash, terror clear in her crystal eyes as Torin lay unmoving on the muddy grass. Words were tumbling from her lips as she kneeled on the damp earth beside him. She pressed a hand to Torin's chest, a soft pale light flickering beneath. A moment later, Torin's body heaved as water spurted from his mouth. Ragged coughs raked his chest, but he was breathing. He was alive.

Mother laid him on the grass, fussing over him. When she stepped away, Torin was sleeping.

"He needs rest, but he will be all right."

"Thank the gods," El whimpered.

Mother smiled down at her, cupping her face in her palm. She placed her hand on El's forehead. It was brief, but a spark flashed. El's expression turned blank, her brows knitting together in confusion a moment later as she peered into Mother's eyes with a dazed look. Mother whispered something in her ear too soft for me to hear, before rushing to Jem and repeating the process.

I took a step back as Mother met my eyes, a chill running down my spine.

I wasn't as close as the others. She knew that. Knew I'd seen how she healed Torin and how she had done something else to Jem and El.

She stood slowly, hand outstretched, but a tightening in my gut warned me to flee. Mother's lips tilted in a sad smile as I took another step back, afraid of her—of Mother—for the first time in my life. But before my fear could grow, she'd flitted to my side with inhuman speed, her hand pressing against the silver curls of my head, before everything went dark.

My head was throbbing again, as it did every time a stolen memory resurfaced, but this memory felt different. The chanting and the way Mother placed her palm against Torin's chest mirrored Ryuu when he blessed Will. It was intrinsically fae.

Slipping into a loose-fitting pair of pants and a cotton tank top, I made my way down toward the dining hall. I needed to speak with El about the memories. She hadn't returned to the infirmary last night, but I knew she was safe. There was no way Zaeth or Jarek would let anything happen to her. What would she think about Mother?

All signs pointed to us being fae, with Mother as the likely source, but the ability to heal—to steal memories—that was powerful magic. More than a human with a distant fae relative should have. I had the sinking feelings that Mother may have taken more than just our memories.

I pushed through the doors of the dining hall, my eyes sweeping the place as the smell of fresh coffee and day-old biscuits surrounded me. If we were going to stay at Fort Dhara much longer, I needed to have a serious word with Alarik about upgrading the less-than-ideal kitchen facilities.

"—shouldn't have been forced to go. How could you let her

be pressured into that situation?" Alarik's voice carried through the near empty hall.

Most of the men were busy with patrols, but the few lingering fell silent. I followed their line of sight. Alarik stood glaring at Ryuu with Kavan, Skender, and Xaun at his back.

"Elara wasn't forced to do anything," Ryuu countered, his voice low, with only the faintest hint of anger bleeding through. "Zaeth presented her with options. She made a choice."

"She wouldn't have chosen to race into danger with only a half-dozen warriors at her side, leaving her sisters and brother behind."

Rolling my eyes, I let an exacerbated laugh escape me as I made my way to the food. The sound stilled their conversation, both of their attention now fixed on me. The nerve of them discussing my sister's actions, as she would do anything she didn't want to.

I took my time selecting two of the least stale biscuits, piling on butter and honey before meeting their flustered, though awaiting looks.

"El wouldn't view it as abandoning us. She probably thought it was the best way to protect us—heading off the attack before they even came close to the fort."

"She wouldn't be that reckless," Alarik countered.

Swallowing a particularly sticky bite, I tilted my head in his direction. "You really don't understand her, do you?"

His shoulders pulled back, spine stiffening. "I think I know her fairly well."

Taking a large sip of steaming tea, I shrugged. "She *is* reckless. She thrives on it—on the adrenaline and the danger of the unknown. El will never be a damsel in need of saving. She *is* the savior, the warrior. She would rush into a horde of the Fractured if she thought it would protect us."

Alarik looked like he wanted to disagree, but held his tongue. *Good boy*, I thought, licking honey from my fingers. I'd hoped he would come to understand El's dark side, hoped he would *see* her—all of the parts of her, but it was clear even their friendship would need work.

"The plan was to obtain information on our enemy," Ryuu said, snapping Alarik's gaze from me to him. "They should arrive—"

His eyes cut to the door, searching for something beyond their limits.

"What is it?" Alarik asked.

Ryuu flitted from the room, not bothering to answer. Alarik rushed after him, pushing through the open doors.

"He couldn't have just answered?" I grumbled, stuffing the last of the honey covered biscuit into my mouth, before following.

But it wasn't El who returned.

Three horses barreled toward us. Two of their riders were men I recognized from the fort, but the center figure, with silver-streaked hair interwoven with small braids pulled back in a knot at the base of his skull, complete with a pristine beard, could only be Vidarr. But he shouldn't be here. He should be overseeing the men at the base.

"What's happened?" Alarik demanded the moment Vidarr's feet touched the ground.

"We were attacked along the outskirts of the city. It was just like Neith. Witnesses reported a portal opening, allowing a flood of the Fractured through."

"Their commander?"

Vidarr gave a tight nod. "But he was only observing. They fanned out across the wall until the base was surrounded. Our archers never stopped shooting as they searched the perimeter, no doubt looking for a way in. They were unsuccessful. After an hour, they retreated."

"Did they attempt to breach the walls?"

"No, only searching for weaknesses. Our archers took down hundreds of them, but they never once fired back."

"You need to plan for an attack. A real one," Ryuu said.

Vidarr shot him a look that said 'I know' as Alarik ran a hand through his already disheveled hair.

"Where will find the men?" Alarik asked. "We're bracing for a breach here, and I've had to send dozens of men to secure villages.." His eyes landed on Ryuu. "Any chance Zaeth could spare a few soldiers? Even a handful could make a difference."

"I'll ask when he returns," Ryuu said.

"I thought you were his general?" I asked.

Ryuu shook his head. "I lend a hand when needed. Soter is the general of Zaeth's armies. Jarek oversees intel and reconnaissance missions, though both report to Naz. Her last briefing indicated their armies were stretched thin. The girl who Jarek and Elara saved came from a prominent stronghold, Selene. I was told even the sanctuary housing women and children was destroyed. Their forces have been sent to secure and fortify other such villages, relocating as many innocents as possible."

A curse flew from Alarik's lips as he turned to Vidarr. "Double the archers at each post and triple the guards at the gates and any known weak points. The walls are holding, but if they enter the city, the base is lost."

Vidarr nodded. "And you? Will you keep the fort open?"

Alarik's eyes found mine, indecision clear. "I'd like to discuss the matter with Zaeth when he returns. But we can't afford to lose the base."

My lips pressed thin but I nodded. We had left to keep Will safe, but if the base required the return of Alarik's men and Fort Dhara was no longer secure, then we'd have to risk taking Will back. And risk all the exposure that came with it.

Ryuu turned to meet my gaze, his dark eyes alight with the adrenaline of impending conflict. "Once Will is stable enough to travel, I suggest taking him to the Air Kingdom. It's a long journey by foot, but if Will and I flew, we'd arrive in days."

"The Air Kingdom?" I asked. "You think that's best?"

He shrugged. "The Air Kingdom is safer and most of my—its people honor the goddess and her oracles."

"He has a point," Alarik said.

"Especially with the pending attack," Vidarr added.

"You'd come back for my sisters and me?"

"Lannie would be needed at the base," Vidarr cut in. "Healer Grant has tried to reproduce her treatments, but none have been as strong. If there is to be an attack, we'll need her skills."

I nodded, but didn't like the idea of the four of us splitting up again. "I'll speak with my sisters when El returns, but I need to check in on Will. He should be up by now."

"I'll join you." Ryuu brushed past me, the tips of his soft feathers grazing my shoulder. The subtle caresses sent a shiver coursing through my body. I ignored it. Now was not the time to notice the span of Ryuu's shoulders, or the way his backside shifted with each powerful stride he took. Dragging my eyes up to a reasonable level, I followed after him.

41

ELARA

I AWOKE TO A GENTLE ROCKING RHYTHM, THE SCENT OF DAMP wood mingled with a freshness in the air that came only after a late summer rain. The smell filled my lungs, tinged with a hint of cedar and awakening me to the world. Blinking away the bright morning light, I became aware of leather beneath me and a warm chest pressed to my back. I was on a horse, cradled against a warm body.

"Hello, love." I felt the rumble of his words more than heard them. "Ember is ahead of us."

Rubbing the sleep from my eyes, I grasped at last night's memories. Vaguely, I recalled drifting to sleep and nearly tumbling from Ember's back, followed by Zaeth insisting I ride the rest of the way back to Fort Dhara with him.

Stretching as best as I could, I groaned as every inch of my body protested. I ached, the type of ache that came from pushing my muscles to the limit and then some.

Evander shot a nervous glance my way. My brows furrowed in confusion a moment before I remembered the topic of last night's conversation: my family wasn't human. But how was that possible? We hadn't had time to discuss the matter further, knowing we needed to return to the Fort in case other groups of goblins roamed the area.

"How can I be fae? Don't fae shift or go through the settling by now?"

"Some of the more powerful fae will shift young," Zaeth answered. "But most will transition between twenty and thirty years old. There's time."

"Or if fae blood is diluted enough, you may never shift," Soter added.

Zaeth shrugged like he didn't think that piece of information was pertinent.

"But neither of my parents displayed traits." I swallowed, needing to stamp out the grow tendrils of excitement before they consumed me. "And the last I checked, only humans died in the storm."

Soter nodded. "All cases documented have been human."

"Excluding humans with known fae ancestry?"

His molten gold eyes met mine and I felt Zaeth tense behind me. "Yes."

My shoulders slumped as a wash of disappointment swept through me. "See? There's no way I'm fae, despite my... *gifts*. My parents and two older brothers died in the storm."

"But you, your two sisters, and your brother survived." Zaeth said. The softness of his voice was disarming. Zaeth was blunt and flirtatious, savage and charming, but not soft.

"Perhaps, now is not the time?" Evander called, his words stiff.

"Not the time for what?" I asked, twisting in the saddle to catch Evander's eye. He was terrible at lying.

A low rumble rang through Zaeth's chest, dangerously close to a groan. "Careful, love. If you keep shifting like that, I might never let you go."

I stilled, my cheeks flushing.

Zaeth's laugh was low and silky, sending the heat of his

breath against my neck. Each point our bodies touched was alight, pulsing with electricity. A shiver ran along my spine as I fought against the temptation to lean further back into him.

"Tell me, love, does the idea of me keeping you close intrigue you?" My head tilted to the side, his lips brushed the ridge of my ear as warmth pool low in my belly.

"Zaeth." Evander's voice cut through the fog of my mind, the electricity pulsing through my veins dulling as his auburn eyes slicing into Zaeth with a protective glare.

"I didn't do anything," Zaeth insisted and I could hear the smile on his lips. "That was her own energy. It's stronger than most. I was simply... drawing attention to it"

Evander frowned at me.

"What energy? You mean Zaeth's poor attempt at flirting?"

My eyes bounced to each of them, but only Zaeth was willing to speak. "Both of us know how much you enjoy my attention. There's no use denying it."

"Zaeth was using his affinity for..." Evander cleared his throat, and my cheeks flushed as I realized what he meant.

"Oh my gods, Zaeth." I squirmed, attempting to glare behind me.

Zaeth groaned, his hands tightening on my waist."What did I tell you about shifting, love?"

I stopped moving, sitting up straight to put as much distance between us as possible. "Why would you do that?" I asked through gritted teeth.

"Maybe I wanted to."

"Zaeth," Evander call.

He sighed, one hand drifting up to twirl a piece of my hair. "To prove a point, love. I did use my fae affinities,"

I tensed.

"But only a little. A mere caress. Fae respond stronger than humans. And I think we can both agree your response to me was strong."

Ignoring the lingering ache between my thighs, I got back on topic. "You still haven't explained how I could be fae if my parents and elder brothers died in the storm."

"It's complicated," Evander said.

"Then it's a good thing I'm capable of understanding complicated situations."

"Your siblings may not have been your blood relatives," Zaeth answered.

"Only the twins," Evander clarified quickly. "The others are your blood."

"Though, it seems less likely your remaining family are your *full-blooded* siblings," Soter added in an offhanded tone.

My chest heaved, head spinning as I tried to process what they were saying. "My brothers..."

"They were human," Evander admitted. "Jem's father may not have been your father. We believe the twins were from a previous union, before he met your mother."

"As you most likely were from a previous union of your mother's making." Soter shrugged.

Evander glared at him as my eyes widened.

Soter blinked. "What?"

The frantic beat of my heart blared through my ears as Soter continued, clearly thinking the glares were due to *lack* of information. "We believe your mother birthed all of your younger siblings with her mortal companion, the man you called father. Based on the records of when she and her mortal partner arrived in the Borderlands, it's not possible for him to be your biological father. That would also explain why the twins perished in the storm."

My breathing came in short, staggered gasps as my pulse raced. A thin sheen of sweat broke out across my brow as my lungs fought for air, the atmosphere suddenly too heavy to process. I shook my head, not wanting to believe it. "Because they were human..."

"Yes. Your younger siblings survived because they share your mother's blood. She must be at least part fae. The dark-haired sibling—"

"Lannie."

Soter dipped his chin. "Lannie. She looks human, but she possesses immense skills with healing. She's able to create salves and tonics with far greater potency than any other mortal I've come in contact with."

"Light fae," Zaeth supplied more for my benefit as it seemed the three of them had already discussed this.

Soter confirmed with a nod before continuing. "Greer has the looks of a light fae, though her rounded figure would suggest human influence."

I narrowed my eyes at him, but he spoke in a detached, clinical sort of way. There was no judgment.

"She is good with plants, though not as skilled as her sister. Her talents appeared more subtle, though Ryuu has a theory. Now, the boy's talents are obvious."

"So, we have traces of fae blood, but remain too powerless to shift? Will continues to weaken from his visions. If our blood is diluted to the point where it can't be useful in the most basic ways—protecting his life—then why does it matter?"

"I don't believe your blood is diluted," Zaeth answered smoothly. He shared a look with Soter, the two of them seeming to have an entire conversation in the span of a few seconds. "I believe your fae essence is hidden."

"It's been done before, centuries ago. Not many would know how," Soter supplied.

"A binding spell?" Evander questioned. I shot him a grateful glance. I guess I wasn't the only one left out of late night conversations. "Not concealment or a suppressant to weaken fae abilities, but a *true* binding spell?"

Zaeth spoke to me as he answered. "It comes at a grave cost, but it would account for why your mother didn't survive.

Certain spells require more than blood or even a few years off your life. Powerful magic, like the type needed to bind a fae's powers, requires a sacrifice of the soul. For fae, our souls are linked to our immortality. Your mother could have offered up her immortality to complete the spell, interweaving her magic in a cocoon of sorts around you and your siblings. Her soul would have been fragile, too weak to survive on its own after being wrapped around the four of you."

"She would have required a mortal tether, binding her life to another's." Evander whispered to himself, his voice brokering on crazed disbelief. I met his eyes swirling with resignation and pain. "She must have chosen Jem's father—your father. He *was* your father, El. Even if he didn't share a drop of blood with you, he loved you and raised you as his."

Tears pricked my eyes. I swallowed them back, unable to offer him more than a nod of gratitude.

"She would have been bound to his life line, which would explain why she died shortly after he did."

"It may not have occurred all at once," Soter mused. "After constructing a binding for her first child, Elara, it would have been simple enough to extend the bond to her other children, essentially linking their seals together. Each child would further stabilize the magic, creating overlapping bonds that reinforced each other. There's normally a physical manifestation of such a spell. A marking of some sort." His golden gaze found me.

"None of us have anything like that, but why would she bind us? Why give up immortality to suppress who we are?"

They all finally stopped talking. Tears pricked my eyes as my heart accepted what my mind couldn't. I was fae, at least partially, and pieces of myself had been ripped away, restrained and shrouded until only a lingering ache of emptiness remained. Maybe that was why the shadows had found a home within my soul. If I'd been whole, untainted and complete, would I have been talented like Lannie? Could I have been happy like Greer? How great might their lives have been if they hadn't been hindered before they had begun.

Gods, and did that mean Will's suffering—his inability to weather the toll of the goddess's visions—was that because he was cut off from the piece of himself that would have provided protection?

"Can it be undone?" I asked.

"There have been recorded cases of binding spells being broken, but we don't know how." I focused on Zaeth's words licking my neck, on the way his breathing synced with mine. "I feel the pull this world has on you. You are tied to our fate, as are your siblings. We must discover what your mother meant to conceal by suppressing your memories and binding your affinities if we're to stand a chance at surviving this war."

"The war with the Fractured?" I asked, already knowing it had grown so much bigger than what we'd initially thought.

"The Fractured, goblins, shadow wraiths... even their red-eyed commander. They are pieces on a much larger game-board. We've been at war for years, and are only now realizing it."

I mulled everything over, my stomach twisting as I fought against the wave of nausea threatening to consume me. Something had scared my mother enough to bind us. I felt the truth of that revelation. My mind ached as I reached for the memories still shrouded in shadows. Maybe she bound us for our own protection but the gnawing in my chest told me there was more to it... more to do with me.

Mother fled her earlier life when she'd been pregnant with me. Something must have happened, scared her enough to cause her to turn her back on everything she'd known, on the Light Kingdom and the glory of the fae.

I swallowed against the dryness in my throat as the red-eyed commander's haunting words surfaced: *the Dark Phoenix.*

"Do you think this is linked to the Dark Phoenix?" I asked.

Zaeth's body instantly went rigid. "No."

"*No?*" I repeated incredulously. "The Dark Phoenix was mentioned in Mother's lullaby. You said yourself, you think she bound me, my fae abilities..." Swallowing, I forced the words out in little more than a whisper, knowing Zaeth would hear them. "You heard what he called me"

"No." The word was laced with power, his arm drawing my back flush against his chest in a protective squeeze. Zaeth brought his lips to my ear, his voice dropping low enough to not be overheard. "He was mistaken."

Jarek met Zaeth's eyes before lowering to mine as he crafted what was meant to be a comforting smile. "The Dark Phoenix isn't working with the Fractured."

"It's getting late," Zaeth cut in. "I'm sure your general will be worried about you. No doubt, he thinks we coerced you to join us."

My shoulders pulled back. "He's not *my* general. Not anymore. And I can make my own decisions."

"Yes, but does Alarik know that?"

"Yes," I snapped, answering both questions. "Alarik has only ever wanted the best for me—the best for everyone. He'd sacrifice himself without hesitation if it meant protecting others."

"True," Zaeth said, his voice lighter. "Though, not everyone is worth the sacrifice of my blood or my time."

My jaw dropped at his callousness. "How can you say that?"

"The innocent, the young, or the old who are not capable of defending themselves are exceptions, but why should I fight for someone who refuses to fight for themself?"

"Because it's the right thing to do."

"Is it?"

"Saving lives is always the right thing."

"It must be comforting to see the world so clearly, to divide decisions into black and white, but the world is a blend of gray. For example: if you were given the choice to save Will and your sisters or the lives of one hundred innocents, which would you choose?"

I frowned, realizing the response poised on my lips was probably not the right one. Alarik would choose the greatest number of lives, wouldn't he? Despite his personal connections, he'd choose the one hundred strangers because they would each have relationships of their own—brothers and sisters who would mourn them just as passionately as he would mourn his. But the thought of losing my family, of having the chance to save them and not doing it...

"Don't worry, love. I'm not expecting an answer. There are certain situations where you can't know how you would respond unless you've experienced them."

Zaeth nodded to Evander and Soter, spurring the horses into a gallop and saving me the need to respond.

He'd posed the question knowing it would have me second-guessing the world as I saw it. Because in my innermost heart, I knew I wouldn't abandon my family. There could be thousands of lives—hundreds of thousands—hanging in the balance and it wouldn't matter. I'd save Greer, Lannie, and Will, gladly sacrificing any unblemished part remaining of my battered soul if it meant they would live.

# GREER

Will and Lannie's cheerful voices echoed down the hallway of the infirmary as Ryuu and I approached, answered by the softer tones of Serephina's gentle laughter. I peeked my head in the doorway of the infirmary, glimpsing at the scene before us.

Serephina looked like a ghost each time I saw her. Her grief was apparent, but she appeared a little less devastated when Lannie was near. Will was acting out one of Lannie's favorite tales, his exaggerated movements and pitching tones causing a musical giggle to spill from my sister's lips. Serephina glanced at her, her warm brown eyes peering up beneath long lashes as her pale lips tugged into a timid smile.

"They seem happy," I whispered.

Ryuu stood at my back, the heat of his body bleeding into mine. I wondered if he stood that close on purpose. "They do."

"I haven't seen Will this carefree in weeks—not since before the visions worsened. Maybe we shouldn't disturb them. Alarik and Vidarr will ensure the fort is secure and we can discuss returning to the base as a family after El is back."

"Or traveling to the Air Kingdom."

My head bowed in a tight nod. "Or that."

Turning from the merry scene, we climbed the stairs, returning to our normal table at the heart of the library. I took a pillow from the pile of linens bunched in the corner along the stacked cots and adjusted it over the hard wooden seat.

"Have you discovered anything about the spear from Will's vision?"

"I'm looking into it, but nothing new. Did you finish with the latest set of scrolls?" Ryuu asked, taking a seat across the table from me.

Nodding, I extracted my notes from the pile and handed them over. His eyes flitted over the page and I could have sworn I saw a flash of pride.

"Did everything match what you interpreted?" I asked.

The goddess seemed incapable of delivering plain messages. Each prophecy I'd read had several possible meanings and the impression of the story changed with each reading. Ryuu and I agreed on most points, but this particular set of scrolls had been harder for me to get a feel for.

"Yes. Your inclinations are the same as mine."

"Really? It seemed more childish than the others. Each of these were related to a darkness, forced to hide in the shadows for fear of being rejected. It wandered alone for years before befriending a dragon, a ram, and a star—"

"The sun," Ryuu cut in. "Or light, if you stick to the more abstract description."

"Either way, it felt like the four of them were protected until the end. At first, I thought the catalyst for the change was inherent, but after a few read-throughs, it seemed like they may have had an encounter with something that left them vulnerable."

Ryuu's eyes bored into mine as he gave a stiff nod.

My brows narrowed as I tugged the scroll in question toward me. "But it's not quite a bird, is it? It feels bigger than that... more powerful."

"Perhaps. Did you suffer any ailments while working through this particular scroll?"

Startled by his change in topic, I glanced up. We typically debated possible meanings of the text for hours. It was unlike him to miss an opportunity to argue with me.

My eyes swept the length of him. There was a subtle tick in his jaw and his shoulders were pressed back. He was worried about something.

"Only a small headache," I answered. "It's the first one I've had in a while, but nothing a cup of tea from Lannie couldn't cure."

"Her affinity for healing remains impressive, as well as Elara's talents on the battlefield. She is a skilled warrior despite only starting her second decade of life. Then there is William. There remains no record of a human oracle."

My chest fell. "So, he is alone. Every day we fail, he grows weaker."

"Perhaps." The word was spoken low enough that I almost missed it.

"You heard Cress," I snapped. "Humans are not meant to be oracles. I'd thought she was just baiting me, but all of these prophecies have been from fae. All of them."

Ryuu stared at me for a long moment.

"Whatever it is you're debating telling me, out with it."

"I believe the particular talents of your family may be linked with fae ancestry."

I blinked. "You don't think we're human?"

He shook his head. "At least, not fully."

My mind spun as his words settled in my heart, igniting a blossom of hope. "Will. This could change everything."

"Perhaps."

I rolled my eyes. "Enough with the 'perhaps' comments. Tell me. If Will is fae or at least part fae, will he be able to withstand the visions?"

"There's no way of knowing, but I believe it will help shoulder the burden of their power. All previous oracles have completed the settling and embraced their fae affinities, but Will still has another decade until the average age of transition begins."

"Is there no way to speed it up? You said yourself he's blessed. Surely the goddess wouldn't set her oracle up for failure."

Ryuu shook his head. "I can't believe her desire would be for Will to suffer. There must be a reason he was chosen so young. The earliest settling occurred in the fae's sixteenth year and even then, it wasn't a typical settling."

"What do you mean?"

"The fae in question transitioned, his features transforming to embrace the classic fae traits of his kingdom, but his powers didn't fully awaken until nearly a decade later.

"Shifting links a fae to their immortal blood. The aging process slows significantly when they shift for the first time, but some of the most powerful fae will shift early without fully linking to their affinity. This allows access to their powers while their body continues to age and mature. Most settle within one to three years of their first transition. Those of more power will start the process sooner and finish later, but their aging is significantly slowed during that period."

I shook my head, stomach twisting as I read between the lines. "But if Will is only part fae, he may never undergo the settling."

Ryuu gave a small, tight nod in response. "But his affinity for prophecy is unrivaled, suggesting he may already be tapping into his fae affinity. We'll have to wait to see his fate."

My jaw clenched. "Fuck that. I'm not leaving my brother's life in the hands of fate."

"It is not only *his* future that is waiting to unfold." His dark eyes were trained on mine.

My brows furrowed, clarity rising to the surface of my mind past the cloud of frustration and fear. "Wait, you don't think my sisters and I are human either?"

"No."

With a snort, I turned away from him and focused back on the scrolls. "Lannie I could see. She's more talented than even Healer Grant when it comes to managing wounds and El has always felt more at home with a sword in her hands.But there's nothing fae-like about me."

My voice was light, but it felt like an ounce of lead had dropped into the pit of my stomach. My sisters were talented. Will was the chosen one. And the only talents I possessed revolved around cooking ingredients. I mean, I was fantastic in the kitchen, but that didn't stand up against healing, defending the realm, and being a voice for the goddess.

With an air of nonchalance, I focused on the last lines of the scroll before me, the one describing the darkness. It still felt like there was something more to it.

"You are special, Greer."

The sound of my name from his lips sent a shiver down my spine. His voice was deep and warm, the hints of a long-forgotten accent bleeding through to extend the final 'r' sound into a tantalizing caress.

I swallowed, my eyes lingering on his mouth. "You think I'm special?" I'd planned for sarcasm, but the words were little more than a whisper.

"You are a prized jewel hidden beneath a veil of ordinary."

My brows furrowed as I pinned him with a glare. "Did you just call me ordinary?"

His wings bristled, a sign I'd come to know meant he was flustered. "No. I called you a jewel—"

"So, I only look ordinary?"

"No," he rumbled, his jaw ticking. "What I'm trying to say is that you have fae abilities which are coveted and exceedingly rare."

"For a moment there, I thought you were trying to give me a compliment." The fluttering in my chest quieted, replaced with another sliver of disappointment.

"I was—"

"No. You weren't. You were praising some hidden talents you think I have, not the person I am." I waved off the protest I could see poised on his lips and desperately grasped at the threads of my pride to muster a casual tone. "It's fine. What are these 'abilities' you're so sure I have?"

The feathers of Ryuu's wings rustled again, but he answered. "You are able to break spells."

I blinked, waiting for him to continue, but Ryuu let the silence stretch, his dragon-like eyes tracking each and every shift of my features.

After another moment, I spoke. "I've never broken a spell in my life."

"You've broken many. Each of the scrolls you've reviewed were spelled to withhold information from anyone other than myself or my family. Being that this is the first time I've allowed the scrolls to venture beyond the Air Kingdom's borders, I wanted to ensure the encryption still worked." His full lips twitched, lighting up his face with the hints of a smile. "Suffice it to say, it was a shock when you were unaffected by the spell beyond a minor headache."

"A minor headache? I was in bed for hours after the first day," I snapped, recalling the extreme sensitivity to light and waves of nausea that had plagued me.

Ryuu shrugged. "Most would have lost their vision completely after attempting to glean the secrets of the scrolls."

My jaw dropped. "You knowingly asked me to look at a scroll that could blind me?"

"Only temporarily." He gave a sheepish grin. "Your vision would have returned in a fortnight."

"Unbelievable," I muttered.

"But your vision was *not* forfeited. You deciphered the scroll's contents nearly identical to my own reading. I had another attempt at it, to ensure it wasn't defective, but the protection spells were as strong as ever."

My eyes widened. "You had another 'attempt'—as in, you forced another person to lose their sight?"

"Temporarily." He sighed. "You're missing the point. You cracked the spell, not only for the first scroll but every scroll thereafter."

Straightening my spine, I crossed my arms and shot him a glare. "Were each of the scrolls spelled with some equally terrible punishment?"

He had the decency to look chagrined. "The protection wards have escalated in intricacy, as have their repercussions. But the last scroll was the only one with any potentially permanent effects. Had you failed." His eyes glanced down to the scroll lying open before me.

I pushed away from the table with a small shriek, launching to my feet. "What is wrong with you? How could you gamble with my life without even letting me know?"

"Your life was never at risk. The odds were in your favor."

"Really?" I snapped, hand poised on my hips.

"Yes. No harm came to you—"

"You didn't know that."

"I needed to know," he bit, his face breaking with a rare flash of pain.

"Why?" I held his gaze, refusing to let him hide. "The truth of it. Why does it matter to you if I can read scrolls?"

His eyes searched mine, swimming with unspoken words, but his lips pressed into a thin line, refusing to give life to them.

I sighed. "Did you ever stop to consider that I may have said 'no' to your tests?"

He frowned. "That thought had not occurred to me."

"Goddess save me." Inhaling deeply, I paced the length of the room, massaging the tension in my temples. Ryuu was infuriatingly self-assured, but if what he suggested were true, my entire family could possess fae abilities. "You make it sound like reading the scrolls is a big deal."

He nodded. "There are not many who are able to break or elude spells, even among pure fae. If I am correct, you have been blessed by the goddess."

My pacing came to a halt as I spun to face him. "Great! Another *blessing*. I think my brother being condemned to a short miserable life is enough of a 'blessing'. No need to add another."

Ryuu clenched his jaw, but his eyes flashed with pain. "I don't understand why this is happening to Will, but there is no cost to your gift. Most cursebreakers grow to be exceedingly powerful."

"After the settling," I added.

"Yes."

"Which I may or may not do, depending on how much fae blood I have."

After another calculating look, he answered. "Yes. As is common in the modern world, most who settle have at least one full fae-blooded parent. Those without may shift temporarily, but are unable to hold fae form."

*At least one full fae-blooded parent.* My head ached as I thought back to everything I'd learned these last few weeks. "And you think my mother was fae?"

"We're working on the specifics of your parentage, but there is a way to know if you are indeed a cursebreaker."

My eyes shot to his. "How?"

Keeping his gaze locked with mine, his hand slipped into his pocket to produce a small dark blue crystal box. Cobalt swirls surrounded a pair of intertwined dragons, their bodies glimmering as light caught on the raised surface.

"Open it." Ryuu placed the box before me. It should have made a sound as its legs met the table, but only silence greeted us.

"It's spelled?" I asked, knowing the answer.

"Yes."

My stomach twisted, already sensing an intensity radiating from the beautiful box. "What will happen if I can't?"

"Nothing. This is a different type of spell. This box is warded, similar to how the fort is warded. If you are unable to evade or undo the ward, it will simply remain sealed."

Ryuu's tone was even, but his spine straightened as I leaned forward to grasp it. I paused, my hand hovering just above the lid. His breathing hitched as I pushed past the fluttering in my stomach and grasped it.

It was cold at first, colder than should've been possible, like a block of ice in the middle of the desert. I held it closer, not wanting to let it go, knowing it needed me, my warmth, my soul. Releasing a nervous breath, I opened myself up, allowing the strange force to caress my mind. After another beat of my frantic heart, the icy barrier cracked and then dissipated. Warmth flooded my body, enveloping me in a calm embrace.

Ryuu cursed, but I was enraptured with the treasure before me. I made to open it, but couldn't locate a lock—or even a seam.

Shooting Ryuu a questioning look, I said, "It can't be opened. It's a solid block."

"I assure you, it can." He looked pale, but the dip of his head encouraged me to focus.

Turning it over in my hands, I studied the brilliant blue box. It was seamless, but he was right. I could feel something hidden beneath—something protected. Whatever it was, I was drawn to it, seeking it as much as it sought me.

Closing my eyes, I followed that feeling. This couldn't be forced. It had to be understood—understood, accepted, and then released. Pulses of power linked together in a chasm of dazzling light. They were bound in a web, twisted, and secured —blazing with the power of the sun. But this power felt familiar, welcoming me.

I brushed my thumb over where the seam should be, dragging it across the entirety of the box. A rush of heat and power and euphoria washed through me as an audible click sounded through the room.

My eyes fluttered open, peering down at a silver necklace. It was a swirl of loops, much like the box, twisting and curving into the bodies of two dragons wrapped around a precious sapphire.

"It's true," Ryuu breathed, sounding both awed and unnerved. "You're a cursebreaker."

43

ELARA

"How are you feeling?" Evander asked as we made our way from the stables.

"How am I feeling?" He flinched from the shrill tone of my voice. "I'm feeling like my world is crumbling around me, only to look up and realize the world is fine. It's carrying on, as always, and it's me. I'm the one that's falling apart. Papa isn't the father that gave me life, my little brother and sisters are my half siblings, and Jem and Torin weren't even my brothers. Then there's the whole part about our own mother binding our fae abilities, essentially condemning Will. Alderidge has somehow recruited wraiths and goblins and we are no closer to stopping anyone from dying."

I took a few steadying breaths, calming the raging storm inside. My eyes were beseeching, peering up at Evander. "Do you think it's true?" My words tumbled out in a whisper of betrayal and hurt. "Do you think Mother really cursed us—that we're really fae?"

His eyes darted between mine, saying everything he didn't want to. He pulled me into a fierce hug and I let him, needing this familiarity.

"It's okay, Sis. We'll get through this. It's not so bad being part fae. It can sometimes feel like you don't fit in, but I will always be your family. Same for Lannie, Greer, and Will."

"Gods, what am I going to tell Alarik?" The fabric of Evander's tunic muffled my question, but I felt him stiffen all the same. "Things have just started to smooth out with our friendship... You've known him the longest. Do you think it's going to freak him out?"

He shook his head with a huff. "Alarik is a complex person. I knew him before everything fell apart—before he lost *her*."

'Her' being Rhyson, his late fae fiancée—who had been murdered by her own parents because Alarik was human.

"Alarik knew me. Because of that, I think it made things easier. The fact that I dislike the royals also helps, but there was a period when his grief and hatred twisted him into a man I barely recognized." Evander ran a hand through his hair. "This will be something he needs to work through. There's lingering resentment for the fae, light fae in particular, since he blames them for not helping his sister when they had the ability to save her life, all because his family couldn't afford the tonic. Years later, when his heart had started to mend, his lover was brutally murdered before his eyes by her own fae parents. He knows the actions of a few cannot stain the image of the whole... but knowing and applying that knowledge is different. He loved Rhyson more than life—more than being the general. They'd discussed him stepping back from the role when they started a family together... but everything—his entire future—was ripped away. He's a good man, Elara. He works to correct any taint his past has on his current views, but he will need time to adjust."

I gave a tight nod, knowing there was nothing to be done.

"Elara?" Vidarr's voice cut through the disaster of my thoughts, snapping my eyes to his. The tightness of my chest released as I dashed to his side and threw myself in his arms.

"Vidarr," I breathed, letting him pull me into a deep huge.

"It's good to see you in one piece, lass. Though, you've always been able to take care of yourself."

Pulling back, I looked up at the familiar smile. His blond locks were streaked with a few more strands of silver than the last time I'd seen him, but the glimmer in his storm-gray eyes hadn't dulled. His beard was trimmed and the braids woven throughout his hair looked freshly done, completed with bits of metallic charms and something that looked close to bone. He looked crisp—groomed even.

"You're looking good," I said, giving him a long look.

His cheeks tinted with a hint of a blush as he cleared his throat. "That would be Ahmya's doing."

"Greer's friend? The one who owns the tailor shop in the city below the base?"

He nodded, shifting on his feet as if he were waiting for me to let him have it.

My lips twitched. "Are you two happy together?"

Vidarr nodded. "There was no persuading her. I told her there's an entire base full of more... appropriate men, but she just waved off my protests."

"She's a smart woman who knows what she wants."

He gave a sheepish shrug. "That she does. She's done a complete overhaul of my closet. Says she's starting on my linens and room decor next."

Vidarr gave an exacerbated shake of his head, but there was a warmth to his eyes and a softness to his smile. He was—happy. Truly happy.

I smiled. "Sounds like all good changes."

"That they are. Ahmya is—" Vidarr cleared his throat, looking down at his boots while he spoke. "Well, she's special. As long as she wishes to spend her time fussing over me, I intend to let her."

He dared a hesitant glance up, and I met him with a genuine smile. "I'm happy for the two of you. Goddess knows there's plenty of pain in this world. We should celebrate joy when we're fortunate enough to have it."

"Thanks, lass." His shoulder relaxed before his attention shifted to my appearance, no doubt noticing the sprays of blood and layers of grime clinging to me.

"Can't say you're looking too good yourself. What happened?"

"We encountered goblins near the village of Selene. A girl escaped earlier—"

"I don't mean the battle, lass. There will be time to discuss that later."

I shifted on my feet, grateful to find Evander lingering nearby.

Evander tilted his head. "He'll find out soon, anyway."

He had a point. Taking a steadying breath, I confessed. "I may not be entirely human."

Vidarr's eyes widened, bouncing between Evander and myself. "Fae?"

The tension broke as Evander snorted. "No, she's part goblin. Of course, she's fae."

Vidarr chuckled, a wide grin spreading across his face as his eyes found mine. "That would explain how you nearly knocked Evander on his ass when the two of you were sparring."

My brows shot up in question.

Vidarr shrugged. "Ryuu has been keeping me updated."

"I was going easy on her," Evander grumbled, a playful hint to his voice. "Though I won't have to worry anymore. Once we get your fae heritage to awaken, we'll have actual sparring matches. What do you say, Sis? Up for the challenge?"

I looked between the two of them, my eyes landing on Vidarr. "That's it? You're just okay with this?"

"Of course," Vidarr said softly. "You're the same person, lass. Now, let's find the others. We have much to discuss."

~

Vidarr filled me in on Will's latest vision, complete with the extra task of trying to located a fire opal spear that Ryuu believed to be myth. Once I was assured my family was safe, I joined Zaeth and the others, all of whom insisted on food before anything else. The fae and I loaded our plates with steamed summer vegetables and a thick slab of roasted hare as we waited for Alarik and the others to join us. Kavan stopped by the dinning hall, assuring us Alarik was on his way before ushering any lingering men from the hall. The gnawing ache deep in my belly had just started to ebb when Alarik entered.

Pausing mid bite, I abandoned my plate, switching to a glass of water as his eyes met mine across the room.

"El," he breathed in relief, but I watched the kindness leech from his eyes as he realized who was sitting opposite me.

"Hello, General." Zaeth gave a lazy, mocking smile around a bite of purple-hued carrot. "Everything well?"

Alarik's jaw clenched as he walked over. Unfazed, Zaeth chewed his bite slowly, washing it down with a languid sip of water, before finally acknowledging him.

"Was there something you wished to say?"

"I'm glad to see Elara is fine," Alarik said, reaching for a plate.

"She's better than fine," Zaeth said, selecting a slice of bright summer squash. His eyes roved my face, a spark of pride flashing in them. "She uncovered vital information."

A creeping flush bloomed across my cheeks. Zaeth drank it in, licking his lips.

Shaking my head, I swallowed. "They found us."

Zaeth shrugged. "The winds changed. You're unable to conceal your scent, through no fault of your own."

"They found you?" Alarik voice pitching as he took inventory of my body, searching for wounds. His eyes snagged on my thigh and the bloody fabric coating it.

"Yes," I said. "But nothing happened."

"Nothing happened? Elara, your leg is coated in blood. And not just your enemy's."

I shifted under his infuriated gaze. "It's shallow and mostly healed already. I let my excitement get the better of me, but we killed nearly all the goblins and Soter was able to dispatch the shadow wraith—"

"'Excitement'?" Alarik asked, but his frown seemed to say so much more. *You were excited to risk your life? To take life?*

My mouth ran dry. It was an effort to form words under his cutting gaze. "I…it's not like that—We had to try. There could have been survivors." Because if there was anything Alarik would understand, it was saving lives.

"Selene?" Alarik asked, bracing for the only answer he knew would come.

My gut twisted with the memory of gleaming oiled human legs licked by hungry flames as the scent of roasting flesh filled the air. Pushing back my plate, I willed the contents of my stomach to remain in place. "It's gone."

"There was nothing to be done," Zaeth said. "The town was lost long before we arrived."

I looked at him, surprised by the tenderness swirling in his cinnamon eyes.

"She could have been killed," Alarik said, voice low.

Zaeth lifted a brow, enjoying a sip of water, before deigning to answer. "She *could have* been, but she wasn't."

I reached for Alarik, grasping his hand with mine. Zaeth's eyes narrowed on the small gesture. "I wanted to go."

Pain lashed through Alarik's emerald eyes. "Isn't protecting your family your top priority?"

Fighting the urge to scream at him for not understanding, I

lifted my chin. "I *was* keeping them safe. I'm more useful in the field than sitting in a room waiting for an attack."

Alarik ran a hand through his hair. "I wouldn't have kept you from battle, El, but the fae should've investigated first. Once we knew who our enemies were, we'd have prepared, and then joined. Alderidge could have been there, the Fractured, the commander—an entire army of fae now pledged to their cause."

"Elara seems quite comfortable around fae." Zaeth stated, resuming his meal as if this were a perfectly acceptable dinner conversation.

"What is that supposed to mean?" Alarik rounded on him.

I shot Zaeth an exacerbated 'thanks for that' look. He shrugged, seeming to suggest the truth needed to be shared anyway.

"What Zaeth is trying to say, is I may not be entirely human."

Alarik's face went from burning frustration, to disbelief, to the carefully constructed mask I'd come to hate. He stared at me a moment longer before glancing over my shoulder with a silent question.

Evander spoke. "We're still figuring out the details, but it seems likely Elara and her family may have fae blood."

Alarik's shoulders slumped as he dragged his gaze back to mine. "It will be okay. We'll figure this out."

"There's nothing to figure out," Zaeth said, the words all the more dangerous for how calm they were delivered. "Or are you suggesting there is something wrong with being fae?"

"Zaeth," I snapped as Alarik's spine straightened.

"Yes, love?" he cooed.

"Stop," Evander said, hurrying to the door. "Someone is coming."

I only just noticed a blur racing through the fort before Jarek appeared before Evander. His hair was windblown and his normally immaculate posture was bowed with exhaustion, but his eyes glimmered.

"Thanks for the warm reception, Evander." Jarek winked as he stepped past him, dragging his hand across Evander's chest as he did so.

Evander flushed scarlet, muttering something beneath his breath before stepping back. Zaeth and the others pushed back from their plates, all of us coming to meet him.

"Were you successful?" Soter asked.

Jarek lifted a sculpted brow in his direction. "Would you expect anything less?"

"What are we dealing with?" Zaeth asked, cutting through the pleasantries.

The ever-present smile on Jarek's face faltered as he looked to each of us. "We need to prepare for war."

## 44
## GREER

THE TITLE 'CURSEBREAKER' ECHOED IN MY EARS AS I STARED AT the sapphire necklace. The pads of my fingers glided across the dragons, confirming I wasn't only human. I draped it over my head, letting the stone settle between my breast, drawing strength from it as I entered the dinning hall with Lannie and Ryuu.

Conversation halted. Lannie reached for me, uncomfortable with the attention, as Ryuu strolled forward. He gave Jarek and Soter a curt nod before settling in beside Zaeth.

"What happened to you?" Lannie rushed to El's side, pulling out the travel kit she insisted on bringing.

"I'm okay," El insisted, attempting to wave Lannie away from the wound along her thigh. Even I could see it was sure to be deep by the amount of blood on her pants and the makeshift bandages that seemed to have been hastily retied. "But there is a lot we need to talk about."

"Likewise," I muttered, glancing at Ryuu. I must have spoken louder than I intended because El and Lannie shot me questioning looks. "Later," I said, gesturing to El's makeshift bandages. "It looks like you were in the middle of something important."

"As a matter of fact, we were." Zaeth leaned against the table, his eyes cutting to my sister as he crossed his ankles.

My eyes narrowed, picking up on the weird tension between them—not quite friendship, but an understanding of sorts. I spared a glance for Alarik, curious to see how he would take this. His shoulders were stiff and his jaw ticked—not good then.

"Why are we here?" Lannie asked, finishing up with a fresh salve for El. "If this was the worst of it, we're in good shape. The skin has already knitted together."

I watched El shift uncomfortably under Zaeth's gaze. My eyes widened as I realized he was deferring to her.

El's gaze darted from Zaeth to Lannie and me. "We don't need to discuss this now."

"I think it's best that the truth be shared," Jarek said. "Mostly because we'll need your sister's talents before this war is over." His eyes landed on me, then drifted to Lannie. "Both of their talents."

My brow lifted as I caught Ryuu's eye. Could Jarek be talking about me being a cursebreaker? About Lannie's skills with healing? As if hearing my thoughts, Ryuu gave a small nod. They'd been discussing us more than I realized.

"Will everyone stop looking around and explain what is going on?" Lannie demanded. Her lips tugged down as she wrung her hands.

"It's true, isn't it?" I asked. "We're fae."

El's mouth dropped open in surprised confirmation, but Lannie stared at me like I'd said we should take a vacation to the Shadowlands.

"At least partly, right?"

El closed her mouth and then opened it again, as if she would elaborate, but Lannie spoke first. "How?"

Evander's lean frame stepped forward. He looked nearly as

awful as El did, hair matted with an accumulation of dirt and blood, but there was a kind, albeit wary tilt to his lips. With a relieved nod from El, he spoke.

"Your mother may have been a light fae, though your father does appear to have been human."

"Not only did she bind your memories," Jarek added, "but we think she also bound your fae affinities. As the death toll of humans climbs, Pax has grown wilder, reverting to a time of chaos. We believe this could be weakening the binding spell. You two, and even Will's fae affinities can be linked with light fae heritage, but El's are not. We haven't confirmed her heritage."

"That's not entirely true," Ryuu said. "Elara's physical abilities mimic that of dark fae or perhaps wild fae."

"So, we're dark fae?" I asked, looking to Ryuu for clarification. "I thought we were light fae. Or are we both?"

I expected one of the others to answer, but El met my gaze. "You, Lannie, and Will are light fae, like Mother was. But I might be different." El inhaled deeply, before speaking the words on a forced exhale. "Papa wasn't my father, at least not biologically. We don't know who my father was. Or what."

My stomach knotted as pain twisted El's features. My eyes met Jarek's, wishing I could wash away the turmoil surrounding my older sister. "Are you sure?"

"Yes. Your human father lived in a small town along the border of the Wild and Dark Kingdoms, acting as a trader for dark fae royalty."

I narrowed my eyes at him, not liking where this conversation was headed. Papa told tales of his traveling adventures, but he never mentioned going north to the Dark Kingdom, let alone interacting with fae royalty.

"He was living in the house you grew up in, with twin boys born to him from a mortal wife."

"Jem and Torin," I whispered, realizing this meant they

weren't my full-blooded brothers—just as Elara wasn't my full-blooded sister.

"He left for the Dark Kingdom a month before returning with your mother, who must have been already pregnant with you." Jarek looked to Elara. "That was twenty years ago. A hasty wedding was completed and five months later you were born."

El swayed, his words seeming to leach the remainder of her strength.

"El, I'm so sorry," I said. "I know how close you were with Father—"

"Don't be ridiculous," Lannie cut in. "He may not have gotten Mother pregnant, but Father loved you—you, most out of all of us. He raised and crafted you into the person you are today. Not some unknown fae. We are your sisters. Will is your brother, so were Jem and Torin. Even if we didn't have a drop of blood in common, that wouldn't change."

El's eyes shone with tears. She wiped them away before they could fall, and gave a tight nod.

"Agreed," I said, fighting to swallow the lump in my throat.

"Wonderful," Jarek clapped. "So happy that worked out, but we really do need to prepare."

"Explain," was all Zaeth said. His casual stance was maintained, but every muscle was honed, ready to launch into an attack at a moment's notice.

"It's worse than we realized. The goblins led me to Fort Carnifex. It's teeming with creatures and fully operational."

"Fort Carnifex," asked Vidarr. "The old human fortress only a day's ride from here?"

Jarek nodded grimly.

"Creatures?" prompted Alarik, the annoyances of the past few minutes temporarily forgotten.

"Yes. There were swarms of goblins, a half-a-dozen shadow wraiths, a few packs of cú sidhe. The Fractured were everywhere. No sign of the commander or Alderidge, but wasn't able to get as close as I would have liked."

The room had gone still, but Zaeth crossed his arms. "What kept you from infiltrating?"

"Wards," Jarek admitted.

Zaeth remained silent, staring at him as if this wasn't a problem.

Jarek closed his eyes with a long exhale before looking up once more. "Wards I am not able to break."

Zaeth stood from his reclined position, the table groaning as his weight lifted. "Similar to the wards around Neith?"

"No. Those were ancient, their roots sinking into the earth itself. These felt... cold. They were intricate—as strong as one made by a light royal—but there was an icy shield coating the entire thing, one that would trigger an alarm even if I were able to shatter it."

"If we had a force waiting," El asked. "If we were ready for the alarm, could you do it?"

A sad half-smile played across Jarek's lips. "It's not that easy, kitten. The wards are like a woven web—one meant to lure you in, but not allow you to leave. I'd have to find the core of the spell by projecting my fae essence into it, unknot it, and then backtrack from there, choosing each path delicately. If I made a mistake, the wards would be triggered, sending a wave of power through the spell work, trapping the intruder inside."

"Turning the fae into a vacant shell of a person." Zaeth added in.

My eyes flew to Ryuu, hand clenching around the sapphire around my neck. He lifted a brow, eyes darting from the necklace to the seething look on my face. Was this the type of ward placed on the necklace?

His eyebrows rose, seeming to understand my silent question before he gave a swift shake of his head. *Not the same.*

My hand relaxed, releases the jewel as I gave Ryuu a small nod in understanding, but he didn't seem to relax.

"Not to mention, some spells are powerful enough to harness the energy from the intruder's death and strengthen the wards," Jarek said, worry and a hint of shame flitting across his features. "I haven't felt a spell this powerful before."

El's eyes flashed. "You think a royal set them?"

Because who else could construct such a ward? Jarek was a powerful light fae—the fae most skilled in protection spells. If he couldn't break it, there were little who could... except for maybe a cursebreaker. My stomach turned.

"No. I'd recognize and be able to nullify wards placed by a royal, even a light royal.

"There has to be some way to get through," El huffed.

Jarek's eyes flashed to Ryuu. He gave a nearly imperceptible nod before their eyes found me. My stomach twisted. Gods, they really were thinking about me.

"What?" El asked, her eyes narrowing on the three of us. "With a force that large, they could kill hundreds. Thousands, even. What are you not saying?"

The silence stretched and I swear I felt my stomach twist further, bile stinging the back of my throat.

*Cursebreaker.* The word hummed in my mind, whispered over and over again from Ryuu's lips. I turned to him, only to find his fierce gaze already trained on me—noting my pale skin, taking in the way I was desperately trying to conceal the trembling of my hands.

His jaw clenched a moment before he met Zaeth's waiting stare. Ryuu gave a firm shake of his head. *No.*

Zaeth stepped forward. "Let's focus on what we can control. If we are unable to get in, we will need to draw them out."

I forced my rigid lungs to loosen, releasing the air caught within on a long exhale as relief flooded me. There would be no need to test the truth of my new title. Cursebreaker. I'd only just discovered my abilities, let alone figured out how to use them. Reading scrolls and undoing a trinket box, fine. But breaking through some fae-level security fort with hundreds of creatures poised to attack? No, thank you.

"We'll need a distraction," Soter continued.

"Agreed," Zaeth said. "I'll draw out—"

"Wait," El cut in. "If there's a way to break the ward, we *need* to discuss it. You can try this cat-and-mouse game if you want, but we already know it'll fail. They have no reason to leave the safety of the wards—especially if Alderidge can portal from within."

Ryuu grimaced. His dragon-like eyes found me again, but the fear coursing through my veins must have been clear because he didn't press.

My heart clenched. He wouldn't force me to do this. He wouldn't even let the others ask me to because he knew how much it frightened me. I stared into his eyes, memorizing the tenderness peering back at me. The protectiveness.

"Wait." Evander's tone was harsh, his eyes darting between Ryuu and myself. "She's managed a few scrolls. You can't seriously be considering her for the wards."

"Is someone going to tell me what is going on?" Alarik snapped, but I ignored him, keeping my gaze locked on Ryuu, realizing that I didn't have a choice in the matter, not when so many lives were at stake.

"Nothing about these wards are guaranteed," Ryuu said, his tone warning.

"But you're sure I'm a cursebreaker."

El's brow furrowed, but Lannie's narrowed, as they so often did when she was presented with a particularly eluding equation.

"Yes," He admitted. "But these are not typical wards."

"Cursebreaker?" asked Lannie, skepticism dripping from the word.

"Cursebreakers are fae who've been blessed from the goddess, similar to an oracle, though not as rare," Ryuu answered. "Light fae generally have a talent for healing and spell work, but a cursebreaker has the ability to unravel every spell, ward, protection, concealment, or even illusion."

"Meaning," Jarek continued, "Greer should be able to disarm any and all wards. Including these."

"No," El whispered, shaking her head in disbelief. Zaeth stepped forward, looking as if he meant to comfort her. "You've had no training."

"That's not exactly true," I said.

El's eyes hardened. "You have no idea how to fight. Even if the wards didn't kill you, one of their monsters would."

"Don't you think I know that?" I snapped. Ryuu came to stand behind me, the heat of his body bleeding into mine and lending me strength. I let myself reach for him, my fingers brushing the tips of his.

"This is why you wanted us here?" asked Lannie, her gaze sharp. "Because of our supposed fae affinities?"

"Yes," answered Jarek.

"If Greer is what you think she is, then breaking the wards would be safe for her?"

Zaeth gave a tight nod, but I felt Ryuu tense. "She's unlocked everything thus far, but the only way to prove she is a curse-breaker would be if she attempted to unlock something that would kill everyone else. I'd prefer not to find out."

I blanched, knees going weak.

"We've been tracking them for months," Jarek said, voice soft but firm, and directed at me. "This is the first time we've found a base. If Alderidge portals them away, if we waste this opportunity..."

"Then a lot of people will die." I finished.

Ryuu's fingers curled around mine. "There are other ways," he growled.

With a deep breath, I turned to face him. The dark depths of his eyes blazed, the deep flecks of green simmering around his dragon-like pupils. Gods, they were captivating. I wanted to stare into them forever, to banish the worry and anger swirling in their depths, but I couldn't live with myself if another village fell because I didn't try.

I attempted a lighthearted smile, more for his benefit than mine. "You said so yourself, I'm a cursebreaker. How hard could it be?"

45

# ELARA

WE'D RELOCATED TO ALARIK'S OFFICE, MAKING USE OF THE MAP strewn across a large table in the center of the room. Fort Dhara and the base were clearly drawn, our troops denoted with small, metal figurines, with a tiny yellow flag positioned over Fort Carnifex. Red 'X's stretched in every direction, revealing the extensive damage already caused by the Fractured.

"That won't work," Jarek countered, responding to something Soter had said. "If they know to prepare for an attack, Greer won't have enough time to unravel the wards. We need a distraction." He stepped forward, adjusting the figurines until they were heavily weighted on the west side. "We attack here, drawing their attention away to allow Greer and a small group of warriors to approach from the east."

"Who's joining Greer and me?"

Alarik frowned. His mouth opened as if he were going to ask me to stay, but he only sighed, eyes snagging on my rounded ears, before turning toward the map. "The two of you will be accompanied by a small contingent of skilled warriors. Fae would be best, leaving The Select Guard and myself free to attack from the west.

Zaeth nodded. "Ryuu should be included. He'd be able to flee with Elara and Greer, were they detected."

My gaze swung to Ryuu. His jaw was set in a familiar stoic line, but the tension around his eyes gave way to his troublesome thoughts. "You will protect my sister at all costs."

It was not a question, but he answered regardless. "Until death."

"That better mean your death and not hers."

His wings bristled. "No harm will come to her."

"The four of them should suffice," Soter said. "Though our enemy has the numbers, the Fractured and goblins are not particularly skilled in combat."

"No, but the shadow wraiths will prove difficult," Zaeth added, turning his attention to Alarik. "I don't suppose you have any fire opal available, or shadow crystal?"

"I have a few blades of shadow crystal, but they were ineffective on the Fractured." He glanced at me, no doubt recalling our encounter months ago near my childhood home.

Zaeth considered this. "It should be effective enough against the wraiths, but fire opal is deadly to any creature of the Shadowlands. Had we the time, I'd suggest a trip to the Fire Kingdom."

"Beheading worked just as well," Soter said.

Zaeth smiled. "True. See that the information is distributed among the men."

"Likewise," Alarik said to Vidarr. "See that every weapon with shadow crystal is brought as well.

"Yes, General," Vidarr said.

"Wait, you're bringing troops here? Wouldn't it be smarter for us to return to the base? We have less men here, and the base is better secured."

"All good points, love," Zaeth answered, "But we are in a much better position to mobilize forces against Fort Carnifex from here."

"But why risk the base?" My mind flashed with images of Will's young schoolmates, of the city below full of people relying on us to protect them. It clashed violently with the horrific memory of the red-eyed commander's hand wrapping around Zelos's throat, the scarlet blood dripping down as the black claws pierced his flesh. Swallowing back a wave of bile, I looked to Zaeth. "Can't you call in Naz and the other dark fae?"

"I cannot," he admitted begrudgingly. "Attacks have been growing closer to Caligo. Naz has drawn most of our forces back in defense of the capital."

I narrowed my eyes. "I thought you weren't in league with the royals. Let them defend the capital."

"El," Alarik chided. "There are three times the number of civilians in Caligo than there are at the base. We'll have to rely on the troops we have."

My cheeks heated with the reproach, but before I could respond, Zaeth spoke. "The fae present coupled with the volume of human warriors should be sufficient. Especially with the element of surprise."

*The element of surprise.* "Meaning, Greer must neutralize the wards."

Zaeth nodded.

"And if she can't?"

Zaeth opened his mouth, but Ryuu spoke first. "Greer will be able to sense the wards' power. If it's overwhelming, I won't allow her to attempt it. Our strategy would simply change. We should win, regardless."

Zaeth's lips pressed thin as Jarek scoffed. "There's nothing simple about it. The battle would be long and bloody. Let's hope it doesn't come to that."

# 46

#  GREER

I TOSSED AND TURNED ON THE STIFF COT, NOT READY TO START the day, regardless of the hour. The sterile scent of the infirmary surrounded me, but only the faint clamor of glasses and silverware could be heard. Will must be training with one of the fae.

My mind swam with all I'd learned yesterday. It'd been too much. I'd chosen to remain here for the night, surrounded by Lannie, Will, and Serephina, the three of us listening to Will's enthralling tales. He'd preferred the happy ones, recounting the same stories we'd read to him when he was a child.

It was strange thinking of that phase in his life being over—childhood. He would be nine next week, my own birthday following days later. Will exhibited a maturity beyond his age. I wanted to be proud of that, but the harsh stab of guilt was overpowering. He should have been allowed more of a childhood. Father and Mother would have protected him—had they lived. Had mother not wasted her life on restricting ours.

Pushing back the blanket, I gave up on chasing sleep and padded to the large room housing most of the infirmary's supplies. As I suspected, Lannie was already up, busy grinding a concoction of herbs into finely crushed flakes.

"Morning," she called, not bothering to glance up. "I took the liberty of making tea." She jerked her chin to the adjoining table, complete with three spare glasses surrounding a steaming pot in the center. "I know you prefer a ridiculous amount of sugar, but I couldn't find any of those cubes."

Taking the nearest cup, I filled it, before adding a heaping spoonful of coarse sugar. Inhaling the floral scent, I sipped cautiously, finding the tea had cooled perfectly. "Thanks, Lannie."

Her shoulder lifted in a lopsided shrug as she continued grinding the mixture. "Figured you could use it after last night. We have a lot to discuss."

I tilted the white cup back, savoring the granules of sugar as they poured across my tongue before answering. "I think it's true—us being fae."

She set the pestle down along the smooth wooden table, transferring the finely ground power into a chipped stone bowl of golden liquid. Wiping her hands on her smock, she looked up in a sigh. "It would make sense. Half the time when I'm working, I'm following an inclination. There's no reason for my choices, but I *know* when certain mixtures will work and when they won't… I can feel it."

"Ryuu says Will is powerful, more so than any other oracle."

Lannie nodded, her eyes focusing on me. "And you? Is it true what they said?"

"I think so. I've only tried breaking protection spells on scrolls. At first, I thought there was something wrong with my eyesight, but it got easier." My lips tugged down as I recalled each of the scrolls I'd transcribed for Ryuu. "I'd chalked it up to a strong wave of intuition but…"

"But now, it seems likely our fae affinities were driving us," Lannie finished. She pulled out a stool from the counter, urging me to do the same, as she refilled her own cup. "Healing, wards and spells, even visions are all tied to light fae. But the allure to battle—that's most closely aligned with the northern kingdom."

"El," I said, my lips tugging into a frown.

Lannie nodded. "Though it may not be such a bad thing, descending from the harsher territories." Lannie tilted her head, as she often did in thought. "The stories appear to be exaggerated, particularly when it comes to the dark fae."

"True," I agreed. "Zaeth is certainly dedicated to protecting this realm. Ryuu too. I haven't met a fire fae, but I won't turn my back on El, no matter how ruthless or scary she becomes. She's our sister."

"Agreed. We'll be here to pull her back. No matter what."

After breakfast, I returned to the library, seeking the comfort of solitude, only to find a mound of scrolls waiting for me. A single word was written upon a half-torn sheet of parchment beside them. The scrawl was jagged as if the writer had been upset at having to write a note at all: *Practice.*

My nostrils flared as I crumbled the sheet and hurled it across the room. Was it too much to ask for one day away from all of this? I knew I needed to *practice.* I already knew the consequences if I didn't. I'd attempt to undo the wards. Failure would mean death.

"You should take my advice seriously." Ryuu's low voice drifted across the room.

My eyes snapped to the door, glaring at the winged fae. His arms were crossed, the position highlighting the thickness of his chest, the width of his shoulders.

"I'm either strong enough to withstand the power of the wards or I'm not," I shrugged. "A few scrolls won't be the difference."

His wings bristled as he pushed off the doorframe, stalking

toward me. "Every bit of preparation is vital. You need to be ready—"

"Why do you care?" I said, standing to meet his seething glare. "Pick a side."

Ryuu blinked. "What?"

"Pick a side," I repeated. "You either care about me or you don't. And if you don't, it will be painful, but I at least I'll know where I stand. I can't handle you flipping all the time. You practically spat in my face at Litha, but then, last night, it sounded like you were defending me."

"Why?" The word was low, the heat of his breath washing over my lips as his piercing eyes held mine.

I swallowed, my gaze dipping to the fullness of his lips. "Why what?"

"Why would it be painful, if I didn't care for you?"

My eyes snapped to his. The dark pools simmered, churning with a concealed fire that drove me mad. There was hunger there. Desire. "Gods, you're really going to make me say it, aren't you, even after you were so cruel on Litha."

His lips twitched, but the smile didn't reach his eyes. His hand found a few of my wayward curls, brushing the locks with reverence. "I do care for you, Greer," he said, the long-forgotten accent dragging out the last 'r' of my name. The sound washed through me like a tender caress.

"Thank the gods," I breathed, pressing up to claim his lips with my own.

Ryuu's hand threaded through my hair, holding me to him. Electricity sizzled where our lips met, spurring me on in a wild frenzy. He tasted of fresh rain, and green meadows, and a wildness that was entirely his own.

I drew his bottom lip between my teeth, nipping it before soothing the bite. Ryuu let out a guttural growl that had my thighs clenching before he launched away from me.

"We shouldn't," he panted, his pupils shifted to vertical slits.

My chest heaved, my own breaths labored. My skin flushed. "Do you not want me?"

A tortured expression raked through him. "Yes. Gods, I want you more than I've ever wanted another, but you don't know me. I've done things—"

"I don't care," I said, closing the distance between us.

"You should."

I held his gaze a moment longer, giving him the chance to leave, to pull back. He didn't. Slowly, I leaned forward, tilting my head to the side as I pressed a kiss along his cheek, moving lower to the slope of his jaw. Relishing the slightly salty taste of his skin, I worked down his neck, nipping and licking as I went.

His wings twitched as a groan rumbled in his chest. I smiled, pulling back to hover my lips over his, but not quite touching them. My hand roved over his back, tentatively reaching up to brush the soft underside of feathers.

"Greer." It was nearly a growl.

"Tell me to stop and I will," I whispered against his lips.

For a moment, I thought he would. I made to pull away, but then his hands were on my hips, pulling me flush against him. My breathing hitched as I felt the hard length of him against me, my thighs clenching in response.

I held his gaze as my hand drifted down, exploring the hard planes of his chest, trailing down until I found the spot our bodies met. His wings bristled as I pressed lower, my fingers dipping below the deep vee of his stomach until I brushed against him.

"Maybe I should stop now?" I taunted, pulling back to shoot him an innocent grin.

A hissed escaped as I gripped him, his hooded eyes staring down at me. "You have no idea what you're getting into."

"Then show me."

He lifted me, moving us with fae speed until my back was pressed against the wall. Books tumbled from the worn shelves as his hand tangled in my curls, tugging firmly so that my mouth was open and waiting. His kiss was claiming, branding my lips with a ravenous fire that was all consuming. My breasts ached, growing heavy with desire as his fingers found my chin, tugging my head to the side. His mouth worked down my neck, leaving sparks in its wake.

I reached for him, but he pinned my hand to the wall. A gasp tore from my lips as his knee pressed between my thighs, parting them as he jerked up. There was just enough pressure, enough strength, to keep me helpless to do anything, but feel him exploring me.

Ryuu nipped the top of my breast. "You will be the death of me."

Before I could speak, Ryuu dropped to the floor before me. His wings fanned out, stretching wide to accommodate his position and when he looked up at me, with his eyes hooded and a wicked smirk on his lips, I nearly came from the sight alone.

His hands rode up the back of my calves, bunching the hem of my dress as he went. His lips pressed against my abdomen, dipping lower until the heat of his breath had me undoing the ties down the front of my dress myself.

A deep laugh vibrated through his chest as Ryuu's fingers gripped my thighs, the fabric of the dress pinned near my waist. "So eager."

"Less talking."

The last of the ties released as his smile stretched, and I allowed the flowing fabric to fall. Only the thin scraps of black lace separated us. Separated him from where I needed him the most.

I bit back a whimper as his fingers dipped beneath the fabric, pulling it aside. A low growl rumbled from his chest as he felt how ready I was for him. He yanked the cloth from my body in a quick tug, before his hands came around my ass, sliding me up against the wall.

"You may have noticed I'm not the smallest girl—"

All words flew from my mind as he hurried his face between my thighs, his tongue sweeping through me in slow languid strokes. I was panting when he placed my thigh over his shoulder, spreading me further as he feasted. Release found me quickly, but he didn't stop until my legs went numb and my body was tingling in a euphoric haze.

I stumbled with the first step, still trying to ground myself from the pleasure he wrought. Ryuu shot me a wicked smirk, licking his lips as he spun us to the table, brushing the scrolls aside before sitting me on top.

My stomach fluttered at his fae speed and a giggle escaped me as I linked my hands behind his neck. Wrapping my legs around him, I drew him closer, not wanting a breath of distance between us.

A sensual smile stretched across his face as he gazed down at me, the blazing fire transforming into a low burn. His fingers brushed along my arm, drifting up to graze the bare skin of my shoulder. It was nothing—a mere caress—but it tugged at something deep within myself.

Ryuu stiffened a moment before the door flew open. He spun, releasing a low growl. With a shriek, I realized my dress was in a pile across the room, but Ryuu's massive wings snapped out, shielding me from the intruder.

Ryuu didn't reach for a weapon, but the tension from his shoulders didn't lessen. I peeked between the bridge of his wings, praying to the gods Will wasn't in the door.

My cheeks flushed more from rage than embarrassment as my eyes landed on Cress.

# 47

# ELARA

THE SOFT CHIRPING OF BIRDS AND SUBTLE SWAYING OF BRANCHES in the wind awoke me. The soreness in my muscles had lessened into a dull ache, but I still felt tired despite hours of sleep. I rolled into a sitting position, letting the blanket pool in my lap. Discovering I wasn't a full-blooded sibling had hurt. I was grateful for Lannie and Greer's complete acceptance, but the idea of having to tell Will I wasn't his full-blooded sister had the knot in my stomach coiling.

The idea of Greer on a battlefield was even worse. She'd be easy to pick off, despite the distraction they had planned, and there was nothing I could do about it. I'd ensure I was with her, cut down any who attempted to reach her, but I was useless to prevent the wards from claiming her mind if she were unsuccessful.

Noting the time, I got dressed quickly, forgoing breakfast in an attempt to reach the western perimeter on time for my required rounds. I jogged all the way there, only to find Jarek missing and a smirking Zaeth waiting in his place.

"Good morning, love."

"Not today, Zaeth." I pushed past him, slowing into a brisk walk as I started on the worn path.

He kept up with me easily. "Do I detect a hint of irritation?"

"Spare me the lecture on controlling my anger. I'm not in the mood."

"On the contrary, love. I find it rather intoxicating when you dip into the darkness."

I skidded to a halt, whirling on him. "Do you think this is funny? That my life falling apart is somehow amusing?"

His smirk vanished. "A butterfly is not free until it sheds its chrysalis. This is all necessary growth."

"I'm not some useless insect."

"No." Zaeth's voice was low, his eyes smoldering. "You are something far more dangerous."

My heart stuttered, my gaze involuntarily dipping to his lips. "Not everyone thinks me being fae is a good thing."

"Not everyone's opinion matters. Never ask for approval to be yourself."

I narrowed my eyes, but resumed walking. "That almost sounded like advice."

Zaeth's lips tilted in a lopsided smirk. "I've been known to have a clever thought once in a while."

"'Once in a while' being the key phrase," I taunted.

He grinned. "And here I thought it would take much more convincing to get you to flirt with me."

I snorted. "I am not flirting."

"There's no need to be embarrassed. I am quite irresistible."

"And oh, so modest."

"Modesty is overrated. I prefer confidence."

"Clearly."

He lifted a brow. "Is there something wrong with that?"

"No. It's just easy to be confident when you've had a lot of experience, that's all. It must be easy for all dark fae." I could feel the beginnings of a blush surface.

"I see," Zaeth said, amusement lacing his words. "And that *confidence* is something you're lacking?"

"I'm not *lacking* anything," I snapped, only to be met with a bemused smirk.

But maybe I was. Supposedly, I was part dark fae. I had the brutality down, but seemed to be missing a very large part of a dark fae's affinity. I swallowed, pinning my gaze and the road before me.

"Everyone thinks I'm part dark fae, but I can't be. I've only been with..." Zaeth's lips pressed thin as I faltered.

Zaeth let the silence stretch. When he finally spoke, he kept his eyes on the surrounding forest, his words short and precise. "Dark fae are not hyper-focused on physical intimacy."

I quirked a brow in his direction.

"Okay, *some* of us are, but most of us actually care about sex and about the people we chose to engage in it with."

"Really?" I uttered the word, thick with skepticism.

"Yes, love, *really*. We are linked closely to our bodies, but also to the connection between physical and spiritual centers. We're skilled lovers because we understand for most, release isn't only about touch, but the primitive need to be seen, to be understood by another."

I pondered this for a moment before asking, "How does it work?"

His lips twitched. "Well, you see when consenting adults decided to engage—"

"I know how sex works."

My words wiped the smirk from his face, his eyes turning to narrowed slits. "Yes, I believe you do."

My cheeks heated. "Nevermind."

"I'm sorry. That wasn't fair. Plenty of people have sex, especially when there's an emotional connection." He looked like he was going to be sick as he forced out the last sentence, but his voice evened out into an informative drawl as he turned back to the topic at hand.

"Our sexuality is similar to bloodlust. What is love but another war? One fought with kisses and tantalizing touches, but a war nonetheless. When we shift, we enter a state of awareness involving ourselves, and, with practice, those around us.

"Those of us who have the ability to fully shift as dark fae hear the melody of pulses, feel the rush of blood and know where it pools during times of war—but also during times of arousal. We're aware when a touch sends our partner's heart fluttering. When a lick causes a rush of warmth. The connection helps with achieving climax, as I'm sure you can imagine."

My cheeks blared to a bright scarlet.

"A dark fae's affinity not only increases our perception, but also holds certain...influences."

I narrowed my gaze on him. "I knew it. You can force people to feel things."

"Yes." He shrugged. "And no. We can heighten a body's response but cannot activate sensors that are not triggered. In other words, we increase desire but do not create it." His playfulness waned. "There can be pleasure with the gift, but for those more powerful, it spills over into battle. It's true that all dark fae possess a semblance of it, but only a select few will be able to hone the trait. We call it bloodlust or battle craze. There are stories of early dark fae who yielded fully to bloodlust. Some were able to harness it, allowing them to decimate their enemies, while others were overcome by it... massacring enemies and innocents alike until they were stopped."

Zaeth glanced down at me, careful to keep a neutral pace as we walked. "The ability has become exceedingly rare, and is practically unheard of in other kingdoms. Most will view you as something to be feared. And you are, but only to those deserving of your wrath."

I glanced up then, daring to meet his eyes. "You do not fear me."

His lips twitched. "Creatures of the night do not fear the dark, love. In truth, having enough raw power to be able to shift fully and engage in bloodlust is exceptionally rare. I thought myself and Ryuu to be the only ones. Your biological father must be extremely powerful."

*My father.*

"You think I'm tapping into bloodlust?"

Zaeth gave a firm nod. "The black haze is similar to what I see, though each person's experience is different. But you *are* dark fae, Elara. Of that I'm certain."

A whirlwind of emotions swept through me. There was fear and guilt, yes, but no remorse. On the contrary, it felt like another small hidden piece of myself had resurfaced and clicked into place.

"Relationships are complex matters for fae. I'm sure you're aware, fae live very long lives. Most choose to get married at some point, but nearly all of the ceremonies have a clause—something to the effect of 'until we stop enjoying each other's presence'. When you live as long as we do, you don't want to be committed to an eternity of quarreling, or worse, boredom.

"Most have a set time limit, normally a one-hundred-year contract. The couple can then discuss renewing or going their separate ways once the century has passed."

"That doesn't sound too complex," I said.

"That's the basic level of fae relationships, and more traditionally upheld in the southern kingdoms. The north is less structured, as it is in nearly every aspect of life. Open relationships are common, as are committed ones involving monogamous couples or multiple partners. As long as all parties are consenting and aware of the parameters of the relationship, it's accepted.

"Dark fae strive to connect. We have a need to feel, to be

seen, to be understood and accepted for everything we are. To not be alone."

*To not be alone.* I swallowed. Something so basic, and yet, wasn't it one of the most difficult things to accomplish?

"Above all else, the bond of a mated soul is prized." Zaeth's voice took on a guarded edge as we made our way through the forest. Strange. He'd been so open about everything.

"Do you have a mate?" His eyebrows lifted. "Sorry. That was inappropriate. It just seemed like more of a personal topic for you."

A playful grin tilted his lips. "It's okay to be inquisitive, love. No, I don't have a mate. Nor do I expect to find one. The last match was over three centuries ago."

My jaw fell open. "Three centuries? Are you sure it's real and not some fabled idea told to children?" The idea of another being knowing you to the very depths of your core, of seeing every cringe-worthy part of you and loving you despite it—because of it—seemed like a fanciful dream, one that wouldn't survive the harsh light of reality.

As if reading my mind, Zaeth answered. "When the last pair was matched and mated, they didn't leave their home for over a year, too consumed with pleasuring each other to care about the worries of the world."

I blushed, though if he noticed, he didn't let it deter him.

"And the last time a dark fae mated..." He let out a low whistle as he gave a small shake of his head. "Mated dark fae are said to be the most primal of all."

The pink tint across my cheeks deepened to a fierce scarlet. Amusement shimmered in his eyes as he noted the color, but his features fell as his mind drifted. "Not all matings have a happy ending."

Pieces of an earlier conversation with Jarek flashed through my mind. "Jarek told me about his aunt—about how her mate wasn't accepted by the light royals."

A tightness had returned to Zaeth's shoulders, but he nodded. "The last mated pair. Sometimes I think the goddess is punishing us, refusing to bestow a mating blessing because of what horrors her last chosen pair endured."

"Jarek said she snuck away on Litha, that the two of them found refuge in the Wild Kingdom until..."

Zaeth's eyes hardened with the injustices of the past. "Until the royals were able to hunt them down. Jarek's aunt was spelled. It would have taken immense power to charm her, power that can only be achieved when strong fae combine their affinities, but they somehow managed to control her, to drive her mad."

"The light royals?" I gasped.

He nodded. "She killed her mate, ripping her apart with her own hands like a savage beast. And then they dragged her back to the palace, leaving her mate to the wilds of the forest. Only once she was secured within their walls did they lift the spell.

"She was refused fresh clothes for a month, forced to live in the ones slick with her lover's blood. They told her it was her own fault for choosing this—for embarrassing the family."

"Gods." The word was nothing more than a turn of the wind.

"Jarek said she soon pretended to agree with them, pretended to repent—to ask for *forgiveness.*" Zaeth looked like he was ready to slaughter an entire horde of light royals. "He helped her escape the first night they released her from the dungeon. We helped her travel to the forest, locating the shredded, decaying pieces..."

Zaeth swallowed but forced the words out. "She created a pyre in the clearing where they first met. Once the flames were high, she climbed the pyre herself, flames licking her skin in waves of searing heat, leaving angry charred lashes snaking across her flesh. But she climbed, numb to the pain, until she lay down beside her love, holding what was left in one last embrace, before she passed from this world and into the next to find her."

"You couldn't stop her?"

His stare was clouded, detached from the present. "There are worse things than death, love. It would be a terrible thing to be bound to another so fully."

"The mating bound wasn't the problem. It was everyone else." I mulled through the story as we walked. "It would be beautiful to know a love that pure, if even for a moment."

He gave a tight smile. "A moment of beauty to be left with a lifetime of ugliness?"

"Not all love ends in heartbreak. Isn't that the whole point? To find love, whether that be through friendship, or family, or a partner—to find just one other soul who sees all of you and doesn't run. It would be worth it then—for a love like that."

Zaeth's cinnamon eyes focused on me, searching for something. "If such a love existed."

"GET OUT." RYUU'S VOICE VIBRATED THROUGH THE SMALL ROOM with lethal calm.

Cress's wide-eyed gaze bounced from my crouched form concealed behind Ryuu's expanded wings, the golden barbs beneath the feathers glinting in warning, to the discarded lump of clothes in the corner, complete with a scrap of black lace on top.

Cress nostrils flared as her eyes blazed.

"Out," Ryuu repeated.

"Get dressed," she ordered, lifting her chin at me despite Ryuu's protection. "We have important things to discuss."

My heart fluttered. "Will?"

She gave a small dip of her head before fleeing from the room.

A curse left my lips as I launched myself from the table to retrieve my crumpled dress. "This could be it," I said, tugging the dress over my head. "This could change Will's life."

"Cress didn't say she found anything to help Will." Ryuu's voice was low, tinted with wariness. "This could very well have to do with the prophecy."

"Which would help Will," I said around a smile as I finished lacing up my bodice.

"Greer—"

"We'll finish this later," I said, pressing onto my toes and planting a quick kiss on his lips.

"Maybe we shouldn't."

Ryuu's voice chased me as I headed for the door. I paused, hovering on the threshold. Slowly, I turned to face him. "We shouldn't do what, exactly?"

His face crumpled, wings bowing in. "This was a mistake."

"You better not be referring to what we just did as a *mistake*."

His jaw ticked, but he didn't apologize.

I couldn't help but glance to the hall where Cress disappeared. "You said there was nothing between the two of you."

"There isn't."

I rolled my eyes. "What other reason could there be? I knew this was too good to be true. You've been pushing me away from the beginning."

"Greer, please."

"How could I have been so foolish?" Anger had sustained me this far, but I felt the fire dimming, leaving embarrassment and hurt in its place. And I couldn't let Ryuu see that. I couldn't give anymore of myself to him.

"I'm not with Cress," he growled. "I'm not with anyone. There are things at play here. Things you don't understand. It's not safe for you—"

"Just stop. I don't have time for your excuses. And I don't want them. Cress is waiting."


Cress was in the infirmary, clustered around pieces of worn, discolored scrolls with Lannie. I peered into the backroom, happy to see Will must still be out with Alarik and the others.

"Exactly. This matches with the story of the three brothers,"

Lannie said, pointing to one of the longer scraps with faded text.

"That's what I'm afraid of. Look here."

"Look where?" I cut in, striding to the table. Cress stiffened, her eyes flashing behind me to where I knew Ryuu was trailing.

"Here," Lannie answered, pulling forward what Cress had referenced, oblivious to the tension surrounding her.

Steeling myself, I moved next to Cress, refusing to let on how upset I was. The long scrawl was a near replica of mother's lullaby, but side notes adorned the margins.

"'Through splinters realms to the shadowed keep'," I read.

"But 'Phthartic' is written beside it," Lannie added.

"It's the realm of death," Cress added. "A dark, frigid tundra. It would seem this oracle thought it the realm the three brothers ventured to. To survive such a place is unheard of. To return —unfathomable."

"Fae cannot survive Phthartic," Ryuu said.

"But they weren't fae when they left," I breathed, mind spinning. "At least not if the stories are true. They were the ancient fae—what are they called?"

"The Merged," Cress and Ryuu answered in unison. I shot Ryuu a glare.

"There's more." Lannie shuffled the pages, until she pulled three sketches free. The ink was faded and stained with age, but Ryuu's fists clenched when he looked upon them.

He reached a steady hand out, sliding the one on the left that read 'Draven' forward. "The red-eyed commander."

"You know who this is?" Cress asked, eyes going wide.

Ryuu nodded. "He was at the battle of Neith, leading the Fractured."

"These were drawn over twenty centuries ago." Cress shook her head, brows knitting together in fear. "This is bad."

I peered forward, reading the scroll at the bottom. "Draven." Ryuu's spine stiffened. "Do you recognize him?"

"The hunter," Ryuu muttered.

"Tales of a mysterious hunter have been whispered among the oracles for millennia," Cress added. "He's a metaphorical representation for death or the ending of things. At least, we assumed he was metaphorical."

"It looks like you assumed wrong," I said, voice clipped. "What about these two?"

I gestured to the two other sketches.

Ryuu pointed to the one labeled 'Veles'. It depicted a compilation of faces, the rough, overlapping outlines blending together to create a monstrous fae. "Veles was spoken as a leader among the goblins. I've not heard of Olysseus."

The last image was nothing more than a smear of ink.

Lannie set the images beside each other. "Draven, Veles, and Olysseus: the three brothers."

Ryuu's gaze cut to her. "You believe the word of the goddess, now?"

"I believe what I can see," Lannie said, tapping the image of Draven. "This is tangible. We'd be fools to not prepare. You said you fought him at Neith?"

"He was present, though fled before we engaged."

"So, we have no idea how powerful he is or what his weaknesses are?"

"He's powerful," I answered solemnly. "El said he lifted Zelos by his throat."

"We should anticipate immense physical strength from all three if the story of the brothers is indeed true," Cress said, shuffling through the remaining scrolls. "They were born of this world before humans. Pax was a savage place where even the gentlest of fae saw bloodshed before their first century of life was over."

She set a picture of three viciously handsome fae above the sketches. The image was painted on a well-preserved canvas in bright colors. Draven had similar features, but the reds of his eyes were a bright blue, his skin flushed with life. Veles was in the center, shorter than the others, but with a cunning glint in his turquoise eyes. With his shoulders slumped and a step behind the others, Olysseus looked like an afterthought—still one of the three, but with a sentiment of sadness hanging about.

"If what I've read is true, the brothers may have the ability to cross into our world, but no other creature will be able to unless the shield is broken—the shield in this case being the raven." Cress pointed to a scroll with burnt edges and spotted in soot. "This is all I've found on the raven. It's hard to make out, but it sounds like 'silver winged raven, stained red'. There's something else written below, but I haven't been able to translate it yet due to the level of deterioration."

"I might be able to help with that," I said, dragging a finger along the dark stain.

The edges of Cress's lips tightened. "Great."

Lannie dipped her head, searching the table before her. "Anything on the Dark Phoenix?"

Cress shared a loaded look with Ryuu, the latter giving a nearly imperceptible shake of his head.

My fists clenched. I hated that they knew each other well enough to do that. "Well?"

"Not yet," Cress said, tearing her eyes away from Ryuu. "Though I doubt he will have anything to do with the brothers."

"He?" Lannie asked, eyes narrowing. "You think the Dark Phoenix is a person?"

Cress fidgeted with the scraps of paper and canvas before her. She shrugged. "Maybe but I really should start on these."

"Greer should join you," Ryuu said, eyes landing on me. "In case there are spells that would prevent you from deciphering."

Cress tensed, but I gave a small nod. I didn't want to be around her any longer than necessary, but learning of the prophecy could be the difference between Will living a long life or a short one.

Ryuu gave a curt nod. "The others will need to be informed. If Draven is present, we are ill equipped to engage in battle."

Cress looked at Ryuu. "Fire opal is your best chance. I'm not sure how potent it will be against the brothers since they are originally from Pax, but it will be effective against the lesser creatures of Phthartic."

Ryuu nodded. "Jarek has been sent to collect what's available, though Zaeth plans on venturing to the Fire Kingdom to acquire more, especially after Will's latest vision with the spear."

Cress paled, but nodded.

The thundering of hooves sounded. I tensed, but Ryuu only cocked his head. "The men have arrived."

# 49

## ELARA

THE SUMMER HEAT WAS SUFFOCATING. THERE WAS A SHEEN OF sweat coating my body, despite the long shower I'd taken that morning. My discomfort only increased as Alarik gave me a pacifying look before climbing into his saddle.

"This is the right move to make. The scouts confirm there's been no sign of the brothers."

I nodded. "We've been playing defense in this war for far too long. It's time to show there are repercussions, but I wish there was another way, one not involving Greer."

"You'll be with her the entire time. It should be quick, without either of you being in danger."

I narrowed my eyes. "Once Greer has undone the wards and is safely returned, I *will* be joining you in battle."

His grip on the reins tightened. "I'd rather you not tempt your dark fae affinities until we've had more time to discuss them."

"There is nothing to discuss." The words echoed between us... but that was the truth of it. This dark creature *was* the real me. I'd found comfort in accepting her.

Alarik's lips pulled into a tight, unamused smile. "I suppose you're right. Seeing as how you're fae, maybe Zaeth should be making the decisions as to your place in this war. Think about it."

He spurred his horse on, leaving me staring after him as the rest of our forces fell in line behind him. It took a minute, maybe two, before everyone had gone, leaving a handful of warriors left to look after Will, Lannie, and Ser.

With a frustrated huff, I turned, finding Zaeth behind me stepping out from the forest.

"He's not worth your anger, love."

"Were you listening?" I asked, my eyes narrowing.

Zaeth rolled his eyes. "Please, spare me the dramatics. This is hardly a private location. And really, love, I've told you before, you shouldn't concern yourself with the opinions of mortals." He shot a glare into the patch of forest Alarik had ridden into.

The retort posted on my tongue was that I *was* mortal, but that wasn't exactly true.

Zaeth continued, unencumbered by my silence. "The general will never understand you or others like you because you do not fit his perception of the world. To him, death is always a last resort. We know differently."

My heart stuttered as his use of the word 'we'. I peered into his cinnamon-colored eyes, pulling my bottom lip between my teeth and nodded.

His lips twitched. "Once Greer nullifies the wards, Ryuu will deposit her back here. And you, my little monster, you and I will ensure no creatures leave that place alive."

I passed through the doors of the infirmary, half my mind still occupied with Zaeth. He'd promised me a day of killing, and despite my fears for Will and my mounting worry for Greer, I couldn't help the small flutter of excitement. Maybe Alarik was right. Maybe everything would work out.

"Thank the gods," Serephina said, striding toward me with a hand clasped over her abdomen. She grasped my arm and pulled, practically dragging me to the back. "It's Lannie. She's not herself. I think she's been drugged."

Lannie was sitting forward on the edge of a cot, her head in her hands. Serephina dashed to her side, grabbing her free hand.

"What's going on?"

Lannie peered up at me with a dazed look in her eyes. "Nothing to worry about, but I'm pretty sure I was slipped a sleeping tonic. I think it was in the tea." She glanced at a cup on her workplace table, nestled beside beakers and loose papers. "I need you to brew an antidote."

I nodded, listening to her instructions as I combined various powders. Once the tainted cup had been disposed of and a fresh cup of the new mixture was half emptied in her hands, Lannie looked much better, though still a bit groggy.

"Ninety percent of the base is gone. Who would think to sedate you?"

The sounds of unhurried footfalls padded down the hall. "Hello?" Greer's voice called from the other room, her voice growing nearer. "Lannie, have you seen El? Zaeth and Ryuu are waiting—Whoa. What is going on here?"

"A sedative found its way in Lannie's tea," I answered. "But we can't understand who could have done it or why."

Greer frowned. "That does seem odd. Perhaps, you switched Will's tea with your own?"

Lannie shot her a glare, but Greer didn't seem to notice.

"Either way, we need to get going, El. Alarik and the others have been gone for nearly half an hour."

"Right," I said, pushing to stand. "Are you sure you're okay?"

Lannie nodded. "Besides, I have Ser here to keep me company." She nudged Serephina with her shoulder and the girl's face flared nearly as red as her hair.

"Where's Will?" Greer asked, peering at the empty cots. "I wanted to say goodbye before we left. You know, just in case." She fidgeted with her hands.

Lannie's glass clamored to the floor as she bolted upright. "Will," she breathed, one hand on her head. "It was Will. He gave me the tea."

"What—" Greer started, though stopped as we heard the clashing of a door thrown open. With a gasp, we stole from the back room. Ryuu was standing in the doorway, chest heaving, as his eyes darted around the room.

"Tell me he is here," he begged, eyes wide. "Tell me Will is with you."

Cress peeked around the doorframe, face falling when she took in the vacant room.

I shook my head, dread pooling in my belly. "He's not with you?"

"No." A curse left his lips as his hand crushed a discolored scroll clasped within.

Cress stepped forward, snatching the parchment from Ryuu. She smoothed out the edges before meeting our gaze. "I've deciphered the last line. The silver raven, the final shield separating this realm from the next..." She swallowed, the pads of her fingers resting over a symbol I couldn't read. "The prophecy calls him the 'mortal oracle.' Every oracle in existence has settled, fully coming into their fae affinities before the visions started. Every oracle except—"

"Will."

"Oh gods," Lannie breathed, one hand still wrapped around her temples. "The tea. He must have given me the sleeping tonic so he'd be able to leave."

I started pacing, my heart thundering. "Gods, he's done nothing but beg to join Alarik in battle."

"He's gone after them." Greer's voice came out as a hollow whisper, but Ryuu's attention snapped to her, his face contorted with worry.

"We must leave. Now," Ryuu thundered, glaring at us as if we'd argue. "He's the protector of the realm, the shield against the darkness. If he falls, we are all doomed."

"Not to mention he's our baby brother," I added tersely, checking my weapons as Lannie snagged a collection of small sacks.

"I've compiled a few healing sacks," Lannie said, handing them out. "There are extra salves to fight off infection. The powder will instantly stop bleeding of shallow wounds, and there are supplies for binding larger ones."

I nodded, securing mine to one of the straps across my chest before we rushed from the room, only pausing to meet up with Zaeth and Soter at the edge of the forest.

Soter turned toward Ryuu, shaking his head. "I did another sweep. Will's not here. Jarek reinforced the wards before he left, but we didn't think to place one to keep someone in. I'll stay with Lannie and Serephina and await your return."

Ryuu and Zaeth nodded once before reaching for us.

I blinked. "What are you doing? Where are the horses?"

Zaeth held his palm up with a wicked, lopsided smirk. "It will be quicker if we run."

I glanced over at Greer, seeing my questioning look mirrored on her face. She gave a small shrug.

"Okay..."

The word unleashed Zaeth. He scooped me into his arms, sweeping one under my knees, and cradling me against his chest. "Hold on, love."

The wind whipped against my face, pulling strands of my loose chestnut curls free from my braid.

He leaned down, his voice warm against the shell of my ear. "We'll catch up to the others. We'll find him."

I felt the force of his words—the promise—I just hoped Zaeth would be able to uphold them. Swallowing past the dryness in my throat, I looked up. "Cress said Will is the raven. *The* raven. The visions have been warning us to keep him safe this entire time and..."

*And we failed him.*

The words caught in my throat. Zaeth's firm hands tightened around me, drawing me closer to his chest, but he offered no further words of comfort.

We caught up to the others in half the time. The thundering of horses slowed to a crawl as they moved stealthily through thick bushes, just outside Fort Carnifex. We wove through them until the Select Guard came into view, with Alarik at the head.

Alarik cut us an alarmed look, scouring my body for signs of harm, but coming up empty. "You four are supposed to be on the southeastern side, away from most of the fighting—"

"Have you seen Will?" I asked, not bothering to hide the tension in my voice as I launched from Zaeth's arms to Alarik's side.

His horse took a skittish step back, but Alarik's gaze flashed to Ryuu. "He's not at the fort?"

"No," I snapped. "Why in the gods would we be here if he were?"

Ryuu gently set Greer down beside us, his hand supporting her lower back. "We think he followed you. Are you sure you haven't seen him?"

Alarik frowned, looking between us before dismounting and taking my hand in his. "I haven't seen him. I doubt Will could have kept up with us without a horse. He's most likely lost in the forest, but I promise I'll help look for him after we've secured Fort Carnifex."

Greer blinked, her brows furrowing, but anger ignited in my veins. "My brother is missing because he decided to follow *you* into battle. You can't be thinking about moving forward with the attack? It's too risky. I don't think you understand. Will has been listening to everything you've said. He knows where you'll be."

Alarik gave a small, sad shake of his head. "We have to see this through—"

I yanked my hands from his. "Did you not hear what I said? Will could be in danger."

"*Thousands* of people are in danger," Alarik snapped. "There could be hundreds dying at this very moment. We finally have a chance to wipe out one of their strongholds. This could save dozens of villages, hundreds of lives." He shook his head, pity clear. "I can't sacrifice all of that for one life."

The slap of my hand across his cheek was deafening. Alarik's head whipped to the side with the force, causing him to take a step back.

Ryuu stepped in. "Will is the raven, the last shield protecting this realm from the harsh creatures beyond it."

Alarik blanched and then cleared his throat. "Even if that proves true, you've said yourself, you don't know where he is. We have a chance at gaining the upper hand in this war. We will find him after this threat has been neutralized."

I shook my head, retreating subconsciously closer to Zaeth.

Alarik looked as if he might go after me, his eyes bouncing from Zaeth to me, but decided to stand his ground. "Kavan. Vidarr. Choose a dozen men and comb the forest for Will—"

"Don't bother," I seethed. "I'll find him myself."

"Greer is needed to nullify the wards." Alarik's voice rang clear.

I spun, glaring daggers at him. "Are you serious—"

"I'll do it, El." The words left Greer's lips a little louder than a whisper, but I heard them, regardless.

I whirled around, pinning her with a glare. "Will is in danger—"

"You think I don't know that?" Greer snapped. "He's moving forward with the plan anyway."

Alarik shifted under the collective glare, but swung up into his saddle.

Ryuu stepped forward. "I'll accompany Greer to the discussed location and *if* she feels comfortable unraveling the wards, she'll proceed. We will join Zaeth and Elara in the search for Will once it is done."

I frowned, but Alarik gave a curt nod toward Kavan. "The Select Guard will remain with me, but we will leave a dozen men behind to help. The rest of us will be waiting."

My initial response was to decline his help, but Zaeth nodded.

Alarik's eyes focused on mine. "I'll join you as soon as possible."

I lifted my chin, my eyes steel.

Alarik paused, a wash of pity flitting across his face before he gave a small nudge to his horse's flank, disappearing into the trees.

"IT'S BEST TO BE PREPARED," ZAETH SAID, SPEAKING TO THE remaining soldiers after Alarik and the others rode on. "We don't know what we'll encounter while searching for young Will. The priority is to locate and return him to Fort Dhara, but don't let your guard down. Once our enemy knows we're here, they may flood the surrounding area. Take a moment. Pray if it is something that brings you comfort, because we never know when our time is spent, when the oil of the candle has burnt through and the flame collapses."

A few of the younger men blanched at Zaeth's bluntness. It looked like it took every ounce of restraint Ryuu possessed not to roll his eyes as Zaeth's fangs peeked out beneath a diabolical smile.

Zaeth sent them on their way before scooping El into his arms and disappearing in the opposite direction.

Ryuu gave me a tight nod, awaiting my decision—if I could call it that. My brother was out there, alone and vulnerable, and the entire military operation depended on my ability to undo the wards. So, I would go. The memory of Ryuu's arms holding me close, his mouth ravaging my lips—my body—clawed at me every time I caught a hint of his scent lingering on my skin. All of it tainted by Cress.

I doubted her and I would've been friends regardless, but the fact that she'd been with Ryuu, that he decided we needed distance immediately after seeing her—well, needless to say, I didn't particularly like her. And liked Ryuu even less.

"This changes nothing between us."

Ryuu stiffened, but nodded. "I wish things were different—"

"Don't," I snapped, holding up a hand to silence him. "We're done talking about this. I need to focus."

He nodded, face a mask of control. Clutching me to his chest, we followed after Zaeth and my sister.

My heart thundered. I was going to cast my mind, my very essence into a misunderstood ward. Jarek had described it as a web and myself as the spider. I'd have to discover the smooth strands, and stay away from the sticky ones, treading carefully to avoid being trapped. The dragon box had been a lesson, one I intended to implement immediately.

The four of us slowed, dropping to a human pace as we crept through the tree line.

"How far back are the others?" El questioned, her eyes searching the surrounding forest.

Zaeth's eyes scanned the earth around us, prepared for the slightest intrusion. "Only a few miles. You better start. Alarik will be in place soon, and this may take a while."

Apprehension creased my brow..

"It will be a difficult process," Ryuu confirmed. "I'll do my best to aid you, but you will have to pace yourself."

El reached over, giving my hand a quick squeeze. "You can do this."

I worried my lip, but gave a firm nod. The last of the branches parted, revealing a graying stone wall with a wide-set tower, like an enlarged rook from a chess board, daring us to enter.

My eyes roved over the worn, cracked stone, pieces of it crumbling low enough for Zaeth and Ryuu to peer over. A few displaced boulders lay in the overgrown grass surrounding the fort, tumbling free from their original positions. A quick scan confirmed there were no Fractured visible—no guards at all, actually.

"They must have been spotted." Ryuu's voice rumbled low. "The attack has already started."

Zaeth cursed. "This is an outer section of the wall," he explained, seeing El's and my confused faces. "The closest tower isn't connected to the main fort and therefore acts as an additional barrier. The inner wall will have a patrol circling. Hopefully we won't be seen."

Taking a step nearer, I moved closer, drawn to a subtle humming pulsing through the air. "I better get to it, then."

I should have been afraid—a part of me was. But it was hushed, my apprehension pushed to the edges of my mind as curiosity took the forefront.

"Caution," Ryuu warned. "The enemy is aware of Alarik's presence. The wards may be strengthened. If you do not feel confident after your initial evaluation, do not proceed."

Taking another step forward, I held my hand out, searching. There was a feeling of familiarity, a soft buzzing drawing me nearer, like the fluttering of the hushed butterfly wings, barely perceptible but rippling the air nonetheless.

"There," I murmured.

"Yes." Ryuu nodded, encouragingly.

As I focused further the disturbance grew, transforming from a transient touch to an electric charge. Tentatively, I reached a finger out, stretching until it graced an unforeseen barrier. Great power sparked and jumped beneath my touch, flickering like lightning in an expanding arch over the fort. A gasp tore from my lips as I realized the intricacy—the impossibility—of this task.

Ryuu stepped nearer, as if to shield me. I met his worried frown, glancing from him to the stones. "How am I supposed to break through that?"

"Did you see that?" El asked, her voice coming into focus as I withdrew my hand. "The stones flashed, just like the ones at Neith during the attack."

Zaeth shared a loaded look with El, his lips pressed thin. "The wards could be similar, despite what Jarek felt. They may have been strengthened once the attack started."

"I don't think I can do this," I breathed.

"Yes, you can," El said.

The quivering of my knees threatened to steal my balance, but I met her hazel gaze with my own ice-blue stare. Swallowing the knot in my throat, I said, "If I don't make my way back to you, promise you'll find Will."

"Greer—"

"No, El," I snapped, needing her to hear me. To understand. "The others will search for him because of what he is. Because he is 'the shield', whatever that might mean. But we are the only ones who'd protect *him*."

El's eyes darted between mine, worry crossing their depths.

"I will do my best, but if I can't..." My words faltered, fear and grief strangling me at the thought of not seeing Will again.

"I understand," El said, the resigned calm to her voice ensuring me she was serious. "You *will* break through the wards and then we will find our brother."

With a final nod, I turned to Ryuu. There were so many words vying to be uttered. Words and anger and frustration. Of pain and longing and the foolish words of hope. Too much lingered between us. Too much, and yet, not enough.

Unable to breathe life into all that I felt, I lifted up onto my toes, and pressed a kiss to his cheek. Something changed in his eyes, the apprehension and pain stalling long enough to reveal a vast depth of longing, like burning embers trapped within a smoldering volcano.

It was gone in a blink.

Despite a nagging urge willing me to stay near him, I pulled away and turned to face the wards.

I raised my hands, palms stretching until they contacted the wards. A spark ignited, pulling a shriek from my lips with its intensity. It felt like the raw, blistering warmth of fire after hours in the snow. Prickling and burning, nearly to the point of forcing me to pull away, but an entire troop of men were counting on me. Will was counting on me.

Spreading my fingers wider, I pressed further, letting the power of the wards spread, until it encased my body in a searing, electrified light. I felt a few escaped curls lifted off the back of my neck, fanning out around me in a charged halo. My eyes pressed together in a tight grimace, chest heaving with the force of the current as I searched.

Words arose in my mind, tumbling from my lips as if spoken by someone else from a different time. The spell unleashed a golden shine under my skin. Following my intuition, I pressed into the barrier, directing the gilded power beneath my flesh forward. The web of intricately woven spells glowed, the light revealing a vicious network of sharp angles and crossing patterns stretching across the fort in a vast dome.

Focusing on the surface level protections, I gently moved among the web, allowing my mind to tap into the ancient words needed to undo each tangle. It was slow at first, but as I delved deeper, the spells needed grew more natural, my tongue becoming fluent as I slashed through each string.

Another lay beneath. And another. And another. I gave chase, venturing deeper until I was nothing more than another charged particle of air pulsing with power. I was connected to everything and nothing all at once, sensing the vastness of the sky and the reach of the ancient roots stretching deep in the soil beneath.

There was something else. Something nestled deep within the earth. Forsaking the glittering network around me, I drifted closer, wading through the darkness, peering through the shadows.

There *was* something. Something cocooned in stones pulsing with a foreboding silver-blue light. Vines swarmed the structure —a temple—as if trying to obscure it from sight, attempting to erase it from the memory of the earth itself.

The silver-blue light flared into talons, sensing my presence. It shot out, reaching for me with a deadly desperation. I whirled, snapping back into a gilded, crumbling cage.

The wards. Will.

I snapped back into my body as I pushed through the last of the spells. Fibers frayed and split beneath my touch. The remaining spells grew taut, strained with the mounting pressure of upholding the wards.

My neck was slick with sweat, my body ablaze with the pick of a thousand knives. I gritted my teeth, a guttural scream building as I severed the final string.

An echoing snap sliced through the air. The wards broke, rippling out in all directions in a wave of light, before giving way beneath my hands.

I lurched forward, but Ryuu was there before I met the ground. The scent of misty earth and embers washed over me, tempered with an underlying wildness of the winds, as he whispered words of praise and reassurance.

Inhaling deeply, I pressed my face into his chest, aware of the way Ryuu's wings shuddered. There were reasons why I was supposed to be mad at him, but I couldn't remember them. And I didn't care to try.

"It's done," Zaeth said from beside me.

"You did well," El uttered as Ryuu brushed a kiss to the top of my head.

My eyes threatened to shut as exhaustion raked through my body, but one look at Zaeth's stiff frame had me tensing.

"What is it?" I asked, eyes bouncing from Zaeth to Ryuu's scrutinizing gaze scanning the forest around us.

"There was no secondary alert," Ryuu answered. "When wards are breached as thoroughly as you just did, it should trigger a secondary form of protection, normally hidden spells or an illusion of some kind. A trapped beast, poison, even a small battalion of warriors. Something."

El's lips pressed thin as she reached for her blade.

"Maybe it was released with Alarik's attack?" I offered.

"Unlikely. It would be tied to the wards."

With one last sweep of the forest, Zaeth held his hand out for El. "Let's not wait around to find out."

## 51
## ELARA

WE SEARCHED FOR WILL, THE FOUR OF US KEEPING A STEADY RUN, as we picked our way through thick branches in the direction of the soldiers who'd hopefully located my brother. Keenly aware of each snap echoing from our movements, I glanced at Greer, surprised she was able to keep up with us. A pale sheen still clung to her skin, but she'd recovered significantly quicker than a human would have. At least Mother's binding spell hadn't hindered her from breaking the wards. I could only imagine how powerful she would be once we were free of it.

A hostile hush fell across the forest, the cracking of twigs beneath our rapidly moving feet proving to be the loudest sounds. Ryuu and Zaeth exchanged a look, aware something was off. They beckoned us to slow, the three of us both drawing their blades in a silent, fluid motion.

There. Distant cries.

"Stay here," Ryuu demanded before dashing into the trees after Zaeth.

I paused long enough to share a glance with Greer. She nodded, slipping free a small dagger from her ankle before heading after them.

Agonizing screams and clashing metal filled the air, urging us to move faster until we found the remainder of our men battling for their lives against an army of Fractured and goblins —outnumbered and outmatched.

It was a slaughter. Mangled limbs and splayed chest cavities littered the forest floor, dark pools of blood staining the earth with the extinguished life. Standing atop the mutilated corpses were the Fractured, their sickly gray skin so at odds with the black depths of their cold eyes. Hungry goblins crawled among them, reaching only to their waists, but reveling just as viciously in the gore they had created.

The nearest goblin turned to us, its dark hair half tied back to reveal pocked, molted skin, its ears lined with half-a-dozen rings. Its sneer widened, its bottom lip twisting into a hungry smile as it spotted Greer, highlighting the gruesome underbite coated in a wash of red.

I crossed in front of her as the creature took a step forward, but a flash of wings rushed forward before it came any closer.

Ryuu's wings beat, propelling him through the clearing in a flash. He dispatched the goblin with a flick of his wrist, but more were at his back. A dozen goblins pounced, attacking him from all sides. Ryuu whirled, his wings wrapping around his body, absorbing the brunt of the blows. With a great thrust, his wings expanded, the force knocking the nearest goblins back in a wide arc. His blade sliced through the air, adding fresh corpses to the piles growing around him.

My pulse quickened as the metallic scent of blood misted the air. The blades along my forearms were free before I thought better of it.

"Gods," Greer breathed. "We have to find Will."

Bright rings flared to life around Zaeth's eyes as the tips of his fangs elongated. He spared a single fleeting moment to meet my gaze before launching into the throws of battle. The spray of blood and the melody of metal brought elation to his features as he danced to the tune of death, daring me to follow.

My hand tightened on my blade, the weight of its slim hilt comforting against my palm. The quicker we dispatched this force, the quicker we could find Will. Sparse pockets of silver-gold light blazed to life, surrounded by dark, inky clouds. Our men were dying, quickly overwhelmed by the sheer volume of creatures against them.

Before I could join Zaeth, the goblins descended. One locked eyes with Greer, its gaze flitting to mine a moment before it called to the others. I tensed as the focus of the battle shifted, prepared to defend my sister until death.

"Stay behind me." The words were steady as I beckoned Greer back, but I could feel anticipation mounting as adrenaline pumped through my veins. My blade sliced through the first of the goblins, its dark cloud evaporating as its contorted semblance of a life ended.

I made quick work of the others, twisting and twirling around their slow movements. Goblins were predictable, always going for the easy kill. Sparing a glance over my shoulder to ensure Greer was safe, I yanked on the hilt of my blade currently lodged in the chest cavity of a particularly thick goblin. The metal scraped against the ribs where it was wedged deep, notched in the spine.

Another came, its dagger slashing down with vicious intent. A curse left my lips as I rolled, barely avoiding the blow. Unsheathing a dagger along my ankle, I thrust the blade up as the creature descended, entering the soft flesh of its belly before jerking up. A gurgle of blood trickled from its mouth as it collapsed.

Pushing to my feet, I dashed to the fallen body still gripping my sword. Placing a boot on its mangled chest, I gave one last, brutal tug and freed it.

"Have you spotted him?" I called over my shoulder.

"No," Greer answered, her back pressed against a large oak tree. "I don't think he's here."

The first tendrils of relief spread through me, my gaze cutting to the dwindling battle. "It won't be long, now."

Zaeth withdrew his hand from the stomach of a goblin, blood and bits of entrails dripping down his fingers, as he turned to the remaining foes. A wicked grin stretched across his face, the whites of his teeth stained red by the blood of his victims.

Ryuu joined him, the two of them descending like wolves on a flock of lambs. His wings spun, the late afternoon light glinting off the golden barbs extended through his feathers, now stained with the black, oily sheen and red spatter from the fallen. They offered protection as his blade lashed out, slicing through the air with deadly precision. Zaeth tore through the rest.

It was done in a matter of moments.

We'd lost the soldiers with us, but Greer was safe and Will wasn't among the fallen. We just needed to find him before—

I felt the light shift before my mind understood what was happening. Time slowed as my fae senses fought for purchase, but I was too slow. Figures materialized from the shade of the forest.

A scream wrenched itself from my chest as figures materialized behind Greer, taloned hands clasping her shoulders, and yanking her back under a cover of branches.

## 52

## GREER

A SHRILL SCREAM RIPPED FROM MY LUNGS AS THE SCENT OF BURNT sugar and wilted roses engulfed me, ripping me away from El.

My eyes flashed to Ryuu, finding him between the branches separating us, a moment before I was whisked away. His thunderous roar reached me, the vibrations echoing through the earth—a warning to the vile creatures stealing me away. A promise.

He would come for me.

I bucked and thrashed while the trees blurred, digging my nails into the pale flesh of the arms wrapped around my waist.

"You have her?" one of them asked, its voice light—almost musical.

Thrusting my head back, I dug my nails in further, drawing blood from my captor. I just needed them to slow enough for Ryuu to reach me.

He unleashed a curse, shifting me over his shoulder like a sack of potatoes. "She's prickly, but nothing to worry about. We need to reach the fortress before the others find us."

Pausing my assault, I realized which creatures had abducted

me. But they weren't creatures. I was surrounded by a dozen light fae, with alabaster skin, and hair ranging from platinum to a golden blonde. This was so much worse than the goblins.

Doubling my efforts to break free, I pounded my fists against the fae's back, my feet catching him in the groin. He flinched forward, tossing me to the ground with a snarl.

The impact was jarring, sending a wave of sharp pain across my shoulder. Gritting my teeth through the pain, I pushed up, sprinting for the patch of trees we'd come from. I managed only a few steps before another fae was before me.

"Enough of this," he said, his fist crashing into my gut.

I doubled over with the blow, desperately gasping for air as my stunned lungs figured out how to work again. I couldn't breathe. I couldn't think. All I could do was watch as the fae before me withdrew a bundle of cloth-covered arrows. He selected one, bending down to wipe the tip of it across the thick grasses, leaving behind a toxic orange smear.

"Are you sure that's a good idea?" the one I'd kicked asked, getting to his feet. "Veles wants them alive."

"There's barely any somnus left on the arrow." He shrugged, cold blue eyes holding my gaze as air finally worked its way into my lungs. "I've cast a few illusions, but the others are right behind us."

*They were coming for me.*

"I thought we wanted them to follow," another said.

The fae before me rolled his eyes. "We do, but we can't be caught. At least not yet."

"Just a little slice." A malicious sneer twisted his face a moment before searing pain blazed across my cheek. My pulse raced through my ears, but my body slowed. I willed my eyes to stay open, my limbs to move, but it took ages for my fingers to trace the wound. The cut was shallow, hardly anything to worry about, but there was a sticky orange substance smeared across the pads of my fingers.

"No!" Elara's voice cut through the fog of my mind. This was a trap.

I blinked, trying to find her. To warn her this was a trap.

The fae looked down at me in disgust, backhanding me with a quick flick of his wrist. My head snapped to the side, darkness overtaking my sight, as my body crumpled.

The sounds of metal meeting flesh woke me, my sluggish mind feebly attempting to orientation myself. I flexed my fingers and toes, gripping the hilt of my dagger as I found my body was mine again to control. My eyes fluttered open just as a spray of warm, crimson liquid slashed across my chest.

The earth thudded as the fae's body crumpled to the ground, and his head a moment later. Blood gushed from the exposed tissue—the same blood that now coating my hair. My face.

My stomach churned.

"We have to move." El heaved, lifting me to my feet and I nearly collapsed as she started to pull away. Reenforcing her hold on me, she frowned. "What did they do to you?"

"Poison," I said, my eyes focusing long enough to witness the mayhem before us. "Same as the girl."

Light fae whirled around Ryuu and Zaeth, the two of them fighting in a close circle, as they parried blow after blow. Another light fae dropped, ribbons of entrails falling free from the gash in his abdomen as El gave my arm a firm tug.

"We need to put distance between us. Focus on my voice. One foot in front of the other—"

An arrow shot from the trees, finding purchase in Zaeth's

thigh. He snarled, ripping it free before tearing the throat out of the nearest light fae with his hands. Blood sprayed, but another arrow flew through the air. And another.

"They have reinforcements," she cursed as a secondary group of light fae and Fractured rushed from the trees. "We need back up."

Arrows rained down, targeting Ryuu and Zaeth. They flitted between the attacks, blurring at a speed nearly too fast to see, but even with Zaeth's quick reflexes and Ryuu's barbed wings acting as a shield, I could see growing patches of orange poison speckling their forms.

"There is no back up," Zaeth gritted out, his fangs ripping through another.

El glanced over her shoulder, finding I was groggy, but still conscious. Still alive. "Hang on," she said, intercepting the Fractured racing toward us.

I was too tired to nod. Too tired to do anything but stand with a dagger clasped in my hand, willing my body to purge the worst of the poison from my system before it was too late.

Cold, depthless eyes peered down at me over my sister's shoulder, the black pools stark against the pale gray of his rotting skin. He yelled something to the others, alerting them to our presence before lunging forward.

His movements were sloppy and overconfident. Even I could see that. El stepped to the side, easily avoiding his blade. He lunged again, his smile faltering as her sword slashed clean through his arm. The limb fell to the ground with a dull thud a moment before she freed his head from his body.

She dispatched the group nearest to us in minutes, the stench nearly unbearable as the bloated, decaying bodies of the Fractured piled up.

"Greer, look at me." El's voice was a stern command, her hand settling on my shoulder. "Are you hurt?"

"No, but I...I want to sleep."

"No, Greer. Listen to me. You keep your eyes open. Okay? We need to get back. I'm sure Lannie can fix this."

She fought for balance, supporting nearly all my weight as I stumbled in an encumbered retreat.

"Ryuu is here," El said. "He's here for you. He's fighting for *you.*"

Somewhere between her last breath and this one, my eyes had drifted shut. I forced them open again, the image of Ryuu drawing me back to the present.

"Ryuu," I breathed. My gaze found him, surrounded by light fae with only Zaeth at his side. The cool countenance I expected from him was absent. His long dark hair was matted with sweat, his clothes riddled with puncture wounds oozing the awful orange color, and his wings—his beautiful, gilded white wings— were coated in blood.

"You need to shift again," Ryuu panted, his blade sinking through the belly of a fae even as his movements slowed. "We can explain later, but we need to get out of here."

"I know. I've been trying. I can't," Zaeth gritted out kicking the body of another away, the blade sliding out of the corpse's rib cage. "It must be the poison—somnus."

Shift *again?* I blinked through the haze of my altered mind, doing my best to keep up with El as she dragged us away from the others. I could see the golden barbs extended through Ryuu's feathers, his pupils stretched into vertical slits as the deep green of his eyes blazed with power. He was shifted. So was Zaeth, the bright rings around his irises and extended fangs clear.

Another arrow flew through the air, deflected by Ryuu's blade.

"Go," Ryuu grunted, fending off the remaining light fae.

Zaeth nodded before turning to the trees, seeking his prey. A swarm of the Fractured greeted him, preventing him from finding the archer. He sprang forward, ripping them apart with his hands and teeth. Sprays of blood rained down around him in rapid succession as he dug deeper into the group of screaming creatures, leaving nothing behind but heaps of carrion in his wake.

"Fire!" The cry rang from the clump of evergreens behind Zaeth and Ryuu, followed by a dozen arrows, the tips coated with a sickening orange slime.

A helpless sob tore from my lips as Ryuu's wings flared a second too late. I watched in horror as the sharp tips sank into the flesh of his back. He dropped to his knees, wincing with each expansion of his lungs.

My breath caught as a light fae materialized behind him, sword poised over the gap between his arrow-filled wings. It was a vulnerability, one seized upon as the fae launched forward, driving his blade down until the tip it pierced his abdomen.

Ryuu's head dropped, his hand coming up to inspect his stomach, trying to understand why there was a dark, crimson stain growing around a protruding point.

He dragged his dragon eyes up, searching until he found me. Confusion pooled beneath reptilian slits—and regret.

The fae ripped the sword free, jerking Ryuu's body, before he collapsed.

A blood curdling scream ripped from my lungs, and it felt as if the forest, the earth, the world itself shuddered with the force of my agony.

Time slowed, the seconds of life suspending, as something inside of me snapped. A searing glow rippled along my thigh, burning a pattern through the thick fabric of my pants until it expanded, coating my whole body in a thin layer of light.

It was warmth and fire. Comfort and agony. Every nerve in my body blazed as I watched Ryuu lying on the ground, the feathers of his glorious wings bent and splayed at odd angles.

I vaguely recognized Zaeth changing his trajectory. Watching him snarl and claw and slice through the throng of the Fractured and fae before him in an effort to get to Ryuu's side. But another round of arrows took to the sky. Another round piercing stumbling Zaeth's body—and Ryuu's still one.

El gave my arm a strong tug, but I wrenched free, stumbling forward. The poison still coursed through my veins, leaching my strength, but I kept my eyes locked on Ryuu. Something twisted in my chest, pulling me forward with an urgency I didn't understand.

A pair of cold firm hands yanked me back, slicing my neck just above the collarbone before I had a chance to scream. A dense heaviness fell over me. I tried to shake it, tried to blink it back. I needed to go, there was something I needed to do.

My eyes flickered open to see El battling a small group of Fractured. Her hazel eyes burned, and I swore the shadows around her deepened, stretched. I swore they seemed almost to bend to her will, quickening her moves, deepening the thrusts of her blade.

She ducked and slashed and the immediate group of foes around her fell. But there was more. Always more.

One of the Fractured tackled El, slamming her body to the ground, but her legs curled in against her chest, kicking up and sending him flying off her. She pushed up, sprinting toward me —a blurred, bloody Zaeth not far behind.

"Enough!"

My sluggish eyes rounded toward the light fae beside me. My stomach lurched as he drew the arrow back, aiming it at El.

I lunged forward, clumsily knocking it out of his hands.

"Foolish girl!" he seethed as the back of his hand connected with my cheek, sending me reeling to the earth.

He towered over me, peering down in disgust with cold blue eyes against a too-straight nose, the tips of his pointed ears showing through slick silver hair. He drew back the arrow, bringing the tip level with my face.

"You are nothing to us. I don't know what he wants with you, but when Veles grows bored I will be waiting."

He turned, fixing his sights on my sister. A mangled scream stalled in my chest as he let the arrow fly.

# 53

# ELARA

A SHARP PANG SLICED MY THIGH, THE PAIN QUICKLY FADING AS THE slow calm of the poisoned arrow washed through me. My knees crashed to the ground, snapping the shaft of the arrow, and sending a fresh blot of pain through me as I rolled. I barely had the strength to turn my head, but my eyes found Zaeth despite the mayhem around us. He fought through a swarm of darkness. Everywhere around him bodies fell, but his body was riddled with arrows, and his progression slowed.

I was helpless—trapped in this sluggish body—as the Fractured surrounded me. An image of a gnarled face with graying skin appeared in my line of sight. Its twisted sneer widened, revealing discolored, rotting teeth as the point of its blade pierced the thin fabric across my chest.

"Stop!" a light fae commanded, flitting before me. With a quick snap of his wrist, he backhanded the Fractured as if it were nothing more than a troublesome fly. "You know your orders."

The remaining Fractured stumbled away, doubling their efforts against Zaeth. He fought against the toxins pulsing in his veins, barely managing to avoid fatal blows as he maintained a protective bubble around Ryuu. .

"Gather the girls," the fae said. "Leave the rest. Veles awaits."

My eyes drifted shut, my body forced into a maddening state of immobility, as I was hoisted over the shoulder of someone. I fought to remain conscious, to hold on to reason, but the blood in my veins had turned to lead. It was too much. Too heavy. Everything was slipping away.

Zaeth called my name, drawing me back to reality, but another slash along my neck brought with it a wave of numbness.

I was weightless, and then the darkness consumed me.

Cold metal bit into the tender flesh of my wrists before we started moving again. Panic gripped me, forcing the toxin-induced sleep from my mind. Ryuu and Zaeth riddled with arrows. Oh gods. Greer had been taken by the light fae. And all the while Will was still out there. Still vulnerable.

I pried my eyelids open, just a sliver, as I drank in my surroundings. My bound wrists were indeed encased in metal, the short chain linking them dangling before my eyes. Looking past them, I noted the thick stone walls and crumbling steps as we descended, entering into a wide antechamber moments later. The air was cool despite the heat of summer and tainted with the scent of mold and rot. We were underground.

"I've never seen anything like it." The chest of the light fae carrying me hummed as he spoke.

A harsh laugh answered. "There must have been two dozen arrows sticking through the dark fae, and he was still fighting."

My gut twisted—Zaeth.

"The somnus barely slowed them down," the fae carrying me mused as we turned.

The shift in position allowed me a glimpse of the one behind. Greer hung limply from his arms, her neck stained in a smear of orange. My captor slowed as Greer was carried across the room, passing the opening of a dimly lit hallway. The light fae heaved her slumbering form up, securing the chain between her wrists over a hook hanging from the stained ceiling. The toes of her boots scraped the stone floor as her head slumped forward.

I was positioned in a similar manner, my shoulders straining as they were forced in odd angles behind my head. Willing my body to remain limp, I quickly took inventory. My fingers twitched, just enough to reassure me the poison was receding. Feeling was returning to my limbs, creeping up along my arms and legs in shots of electric pins. The need to fight, to rescue my sister and find my brother burned in my veins, but my body wasn't ready yet.

So, I allowed my head to drop forward, my disheveled braid providing enough coverage for me to crack open an eye.

"At least this one reacted normally," the fae before me said, the stench of his breath causing my stomach to clench. "Well, almost. Still had to slice her after the stick, didn't we?"

He chuckled as his fingers pressed into my thigh, reopening the wound and nearly pulling a scream from my chest. A wave of nausea rolled through me with the effort it took to keep my breathing steady—my shriek contained.

The other grunted in response, lifting Greer's chin toward his face. "What do you think got into this one. She's pretty to be sure, but I don't see anything remotely powerful in her."

My guard turned away from me, smirking as he did so. "Powerful or not, she resisted the somnus and kicked you clear across the forest when the air fae was wounded."

The other's eyes flared with rage. He lashed out, his hand connecting with Greer's cheek. Her neck jerked to the side, the smack sending her suspended body in an off-kiltered spin.

My body twitched in response, rattling the chains, but the sound was drowned out by the clanking of Greer's swaying body.

"The little bitch." The light fae grabbed her, pulling her unconscious form back to him. He leaned in, inhaling a deep breath.

"I'll show her what power is." He brought his twisted sneer close to her ear, licking the flesh along neck. "When I'm through with you, you'll be nothing more than a flayed sack of bones."

My fist clenched and my strength slowly returned. A few more minutes and I'd be free to gut that pathetic excuse of life.

"That's enough," the fae before me said, disgust evident even in his voice. "You know the orders. We're not to harm them, well not beyond repair. I've seen what you do to your women. I doubt you'll be allowed to play with her."

Greer's assailant sneered, before turning to the dark passage. "Come. We should let Veles know the informant was correct in their location and the sisters are secure. The boy is next."

*Informant. The boy.*

Someone had betrayed us. Adrenaline and the sharp tang of panic burned through me as the fae's footsteps retreated. I'd worry about the snake in our midst later. Right now, I needed to focus on getting out of here. My legs were sluggish, but I was able to bend them. Almost there.

Greer's head was still drooped forward, a red blot visible along her split bottom lip from the fae's brutal blow. The slice along her neck was stained with a smear of orange, but otherwise appeared healed. But it was the burned pieces of cloth along her thigh that drew my attention.

The exposed skin beneath was scorched, the burns snaring together in the shape of a dragon stretching toward her hip. The dark ink pulsed with a deep green hue, beating in time with her heart.

A gasp stole from my lips. It was her brand—probably the

one placed by Mother to bind our fae affinities, and if it was visible…

My eyes snapped to the cut along her neck, to her now healed lip, and finally landed on her ears. The once rounded curve was now tipped, the point jutting out between her disheveled curls. The spell was broken.

I tilted my head to the side, allowing the crest of my own ear to brush against the inside of my arm. Still round. No wonder it was taking so long for me to heal. But Greer—she should be better by now.

My ears strained for any sound of a return as I glanced to the shadowed hallway. Nothing.

"Greer?" I hissed under my breath. "Greer, you need to wake up."

Her breathing remained even and undisturbed. I was about to try again when the sounds of muffled footsteps descending along the stairs reached me. Willing my body to relax, I kept an eye cracked, my hidden gaze fixed on the steps.

A small form crept down, timid in its movements. Silver blond curls stepped into the light, jerking me to life.

Will.

No. No. No. No.

"What are you doing here?" I gasped, panic racing through me. My eyes darted to the hallway. Still quiet. "Will, you have to get out of here."

He stalled, foot hovering on the last step as he took in the room. His eyes lingering on Greer a moment before rushing to my side in a blur.

"It's okay, Ellie. I've been spying for weeks. Nobody can hear me when I want to be quiet. I think it has something to do with the fae blood in me."

His words sent another wave of shock rolling through me. "You know?"

He shrugged his shoulders. "I heard the soldiers talking one night and everything made sense. I was always the best at spying and I wanted to show that I can be included on missions. I *am* turning nine next week."

"I need you to use those spy skills and make it back to Fort Dhara. *Please*, Will."

Ignoring my pleas, will stretched a shaking hand up, searching for a way to help, but the manacles were just out of reach. "I followed the men when they scouted this place. But I've never seen so many of the creatures in the forest. I—I never needed a weapon before. They were everywhere. I tried to run back to Fort Dhara, but every time I started, another monster would come. And I'd—I would hide again." His eyes glazed over with tears and poorly controlled shame.

Guilt pierced through me. Will never should have seen this; seen war all around him with his older sisters bloody and chained. Choking back tears, I forced a steadiness to my voice. "It's okay to be afraid, but we can't let fear control us. Greer and I are going to get out of this, but I need you to leave—"

His gaze hardened. "I won't fail you, Ellie. Or Greer. I'm going to save you."

His small shoulders braced against my stomach, gallantly attempting to hoist my body high enough to allow slack against the chains so that I might work myself free. The beat of my heart was loud against my ears as I attempted to pull myself up once more.

There was no use arguing with him. Once he made his mind up there was no changing it. He needed to get out of here, and the quickest way to achieve that would be to free myself.

We changed tactics, and I managed a small push off Will's interwoven fingers. They trembled with the effort but held—it was the weakness lingering in my limbs that delayed us. The chain rattled as I failed to swing the links over the hook, and my body jerked down once more.

"Will, look at me. The poison is nearly out of my system. I'll be able to free myself when it is and I'll be able to help Greer, but right now I need you to complete a very important mission: you have to make it back to Fort Dhara as quickly and as silently as possible and tell Soter everything that happened."

Will glanced at Greer's dangling form and back to the chains keeping me captive. "But I can help—"

"I know you can. We will only be a few minutes behind you."

Voices reverberated against the cool stone, streaming from the dimly lit hall opposite the steps.

"Go!" I hissed under my breath, fear tightening my throat. But Will was already moving, his gangly form retreating for the steps. The tight band squeezing my chest loosened, but instead of racing up them, Will ducked beneath, hiding in the small alcove in the shadows.

My stomach clenched as I frantically shook my head, but Will only shot me a self-assured nod, his face a picture of determination, before fading into the darkness.

"Lookie here, fellas." The light fae who'd slapped Greer sneered, earning answering grins from the dozen others with him. "We've got ourselves a live one."

I adjusted my features into a mask of self-control.

"Enough, Bane." The group parted as the voice spoke, exposing a light fae moving toward me with a confident stride. His black boots and dark attire were in stark contrast to the pale tones of his skin.

"Yes, Master," the vile fae name Bane amended.

*Master.* This must be Veles.

A sickly-sweet floral scent filled the air, growing stronger as he approached. His straight, light blond hair was half tied back, the pointed tips of his ears displayed proudly. The strong jaw and firm body gave off the appearance of youthfulness, but his features were warped—dulled—as if a thick film had been cast over his very soul.

The others fell back, sinking closer to the steps—closer

toward Will. It took every ounce of self-control not to glance at his hiding spot.

Veles circled Greer first, kneeling as he inspected her thigh. He reached forward, shredding the remaining fabric to fully expose the brand beneath. Groggily, Greer stirred at his touch, her eyes blinking open and widening in fear.

"Shh," he cooed with the tenderness of a lover. "No need to be frightened, child."

The sharpened tip of his nail sliced through the orange residue on Greer's neck, the pad of his thumb smearing the toxin through the newly opened cut.

Greer's eyes found mine a moment before they fluttered close once more.

"Leave her alone!" I shrieked, thrashing against my chains, and earning snickers from the group of fae. But Veles remained transfixed on Greer's thigh, studying the now fully exposed ink twisted into the shape of a dragon, stark against her light skin.

"Interesting," he mused, a malicious grin in place as he turned toward me, the click of his boot echoing with each step. His finger stroked the curved shape of my ear. "You're not fae," he noted, leaning in and sniffing deeply before facing me once more. "And yet, my brother was correct; you're not quite human either. Perhaps he was correct in proclaiming you as the Dark Phoenix."

Clamping my mouth shut, I glowered at him in disgust.

The crazed tilt of his lips stretched as his eyes darted to Greer, sizing her up before returning to me.

"Interesting, but I'm afraid that I do require answers. Tell me what your role in this war will be." His voice dropped as he drew near, the scent of sweet roses and overly ripe fruit twisting my stomach. His eyes searched mine in earnest. "I wonder, could it be? Are you one of the three opposers? Or do you long for freedom? Will you join us in ridding this world of the weak?"

"If by 'riding this world of the weak' you mean murdering all beings other than yourself, then yes, I am definitely against you. And any other elitist asshole here." The fingers flexed, the power of my limbs returned and eager for an outlet. But I couldn't risk attacking Veles here—not with Will so close.

"Pity. I do hope we can change your mind." He stepped back, the picture of nonchalance as he called, "Bane?"

"Yes, Master?"

"If you would, please. Our guest is in need of a demonstration. Why don't you welcome her into the ways of how humans and human-lovers are treated in our new regime."

Bane's lips twisted into a cruel smile as he stepped toward me, dagger gleaming in the dull flickering torch light. "My pleasure, Master."

Gripping the short length of chains in my hands, I braced for pain. I couldn't take on a dozen fae while trying to rescue a still-unconscious Greer and keep Will safe—let alone face off against Veles. No, I'd have to endure whatever was coming and wait for an opening.

The kiss of the blade was cool against my thigh. Bane slipped the tip beneath the frayed fabric, using the puncture from the earlier arrow, to cut through the length of it and expose the skin beneath.

"No pretty dragon on this one, Master."

Veles's face dropped into a frown. He waved his hand as if already exhausted by this exchange.

"Very well. Proceed."

Jagged, rotting teeth sneered up at me as Bane withdrew a small vial containing a thick orange substance. Tendrils of smoke rose as he removed the lid, allowing the scent of fresh poppies mixed with magic to swirl through the air. He coated the blade before sinking the tip of the metal into my healing wound.

I gasped but managed to hold in the force of my cry, fighting against the renewed burning numbness coursing through body.

"I was told there were fae of great strength fighting along-side you," Veles stated, pacing before us. "Tell me, who were they?"

Clenching my jaw shut, I glared at him.

Veles lifted a brow, holding my gaze a moment before signaling to Bane.

Bane smeared a bright blue substance over my now-bleeding thigh. If offered a coolness to the burning—a comfort.

I was vaguely aware of Veles repeating his question, his words trickling through my sluggish mind. I wanted to answer. I wanted to please him. I wanted...

With a start, I bit my tongue, relishing the pain and the metallic taste of blood that granted a break from the fog long enough to halt my answer.

Veles's amused laugh chimed around me, echoing off the cold stones. "Very good. I see what they meant by immunity to my concoctions. I had thought with the addition of the bell-flower it would weaken your resolve. No matter. Bane, if you would."

A quick jerk, the dagger was back, this time sinking deep into the already tender flesh of my thigh. He twisted, pulling a strangled cry from my lips as a wave of blood flowed down my leg. Bane lathered the blade with both toxins before plunging it deep into my side.

An agonizing howl ripped through me, the sound made all the more jarring by the distorted laughter of the fae surrounding us. My chest heaved as I fought against the pain, fought against the poison flooding my system. I could get through this—I *would* get through this. For my sisters. For Will—

My eyes snagged on the emerging figure by the stairs, terror blaring through my veins.

"No." I gasped, the blade lodged in my gut shaking as I forced the word from my lips. "Don't. Please, don't."

Fae cackled around us, thinking my pleas were a pathetic attempt to stop the torture. Veles's eyes narrowed, always seeing more, but Bane stepped forward once again, eager for my pain. He withdrew the dagger only to plunge it just below my ribs, giving it a vicious twist before yanking it free.

Will stepped out from beneath the shadows, chest heaving and small hands clenched in fury. His wild curls, so similar to Greer's, seemed to rise, as if charged by the electric particles all around us, a moment before he released a fierce roar.

He lunged forward, thrusting his hands out in front of him as a surge of power released from his body in a wide arch, blasting through the fae. They flew through the air, landing with sickening crunches as their lifeless bodies rained down around us. The few nearest him were little more than chunks of flesh, seeping in pools of blood and entrails, Veles among them, his eyes transfixed and vacant. He'd killed them all.

The silence stretched, broken only by Will's ragged breaths. His small form was bowed forward, his eyes transfixed on his hands, now adorned with glowing ancient symbols stretching toward his elbows. The shadow of ebony wings stretched behind him, nothing more than wisps—the hint of what would one day come.

Greer broke the spell, her voice weak and laced with panic. "Will?"

He dashed to her side, reaching for her shackles with tattooed hands. She tried to pull herself up, but could barely manage to lift her head, let alone escape the chains.

"It's okay, Will," she soothed as he nearly lifted her free. "Go get help."

He firmly shook his head. "A good soldier doesn't leave people behind. I can save both of you." Will rushed to my side, eyes swimming in hope. "You should be better now, right? I waited long enough for you to get better?"

He cupped his hands, waiting for me to push off.

The light in his eyes was so typical of Will. Always finding the good in things. Always thinking of the future.

Greer's screams reverberated against the stone, deafening in their agony.

But I didn't understand why she was crying. I didn't understand how she had the strength to crack the stone anchoring the hook or why Will lurched forward. Or how the point of a blade was protruding from his small body.

He looked up at me with pleading eyes. "Ellie?"

Sounds faded and my vision blurred. And all that remained was the growing pool of scarlet surrounding his too still chest.

# 54

# GREER

EL DIDN'T SEE THE LIGHT FAE MATERIALIZE BEHIND WILL, THE tendrils of smoke dissipating nearly as fast as they came. She didn't see the golden dagger gleam in the flickering torch light or the quick jerk of the blade until it was too late. Until our brother collapsed... and our world with him.

I screamed. And screamed. Writhing against the chains anchoring me, thrashing against the poison trapping me in this sluggish body, until the fae grew weary of my noise, ending it with a quick flick of his wrists.

I didn't feel the prick of the dagger as it sank into the soft flesh of my belly. But the scent of poppies hit me. And then I was lost to darkness.

~

Will found me.

"Greer?" his boyish voice called.

I blinked through hazy eyes, but my vision didn't clear. Shadows were all around us, and Will's shimmering form was the only source of light.

"Don't be afraid," he said with a small smile. "The darkness is calm and warm. It feels like an endless hug but not in a suffocating way. It's like I'm being wrapped in quiet happiness."

I shook my head, not bothering to still the tears tracking down my cheeks. "You're dead."

Will's shoulders bowed forward. "Yeah. I tried to save you—Ellie too. I didn't know he could bend light still. He's been gone from this world for so long, but it all makes sense, now. Two of the three are here. They have an army. Draven is strong, but fully in this realm. He's the one to target, the weakest. Olysseus is bound to the other realm. He is the anchor between our world and theirs and cannot leave unless our two realms merge fully. If that happens, Pax will fall."

"I don't understand—"

"I can't stay long. She's waiting for me, but you need to listen. Veles is not defeated. His essence is both a part of this realm and the other. You must seek the Spear of Empyrean. It's his only vulnerability."

"You destroyed him, Will. Veles—his body exploded when you protected El."

His eyes held a vast well of knowledge, aging him beyond his almost-nine years. "His current body was destroyed, but Veles lives. I was the final ward to be broken, the last shield. With my death, the other ward will fall, leaving the realm unprotected."

I shook my head, the salty taste of tears on my lips as I reached for him, but my fingers passed through nothing more than vapor and smoke. "I'm sorry—" My voice broke around a sob, my chest heaving with the force of regret. "We should have kept you safe."

"I don't think you could have," Will said, as if we were debating something as careless as the weather. "She's with me—the goddess. And I don't think this could have been prevented. I think she meant to prepare me as best as she could, though that binding spell Mother performed really didn't help. Our fae affinities should've never been contained. But I'm sure Mother didn't know. I haven't seen her yet, but I can feel her."

My eyes widened. "Mother is with you?"

Will tilted his head, a few unruly curls falling to the side. "Yes and no. She's a part of the darkness. A part of the calm. I don't remember her from life... but something in me recognizes something in her. Father is here, too. And the twins, and so many others."

He smiled then, the freckles stretching across his cheeks. "I'm safe. But you, Ellie, and Lannie still have much to do before we can meet again."

His image flickered.

"Don't go. We'll get your body to Lannie. She'll find a way."

But Will only gave a slow, small shake of his head. "I'm not afraid. Or lonely. Or worried. I'm... happy. Still me but different." His form darkened, the lines of his body blurring, fading into the surrounding blackness. "You need to find the spear. You need to prepare. They're coming."

The shadows swallowed him despite my protests. Despite my pleas. I'd already lost two brothers. She couldn't have another. Not my baby brother—the one I helped raise. The boy with hope and love and light, who enjoyed learning and telling stories, who'd eat endless amounts of chocolate desserts and half-baked cookies, the little boy who had dreams to make this world a better place...

But he was gone.

And at that moment, I couldn't think of a reason not to follow him.

## 55
# ELARA

I WAS VAGUELY AWARE OF GREER'S WAILS AND THE CLATTERING sounds of chains as she fought to break free. Her pain was drowned out by a cold laugh, zeroing my focus on a pair of slick black boots stepping to the side of my brother's broken body.

The fae threw a dagger dipped in orange. The blade sank into Greer's stomach with little effort, forcing her into a deep sleep.

My breathing was jagged, the beating of my heart thundering loudly in my ears as adrenaline coursed through my veins—demanding action. Demanding my stupid, sluggish mind accept what my body already knew to be true.

My little brother was dead.

I tore my eyes away from the expanding pool of scarlet surrounding his small form, forcing my gaze to the one responsible. His skin was gray, the color of ash, and his golden-colored hair had streaks of white. The skin across his hands was spotted, his face marred with lines. If it weren't for the tipped ears, I'd swear the fae before me was human. Every piece of him had aged—all except for his eyes. Silver eyes peered down at me, calculating and cunning in their study. Familiar eyes.

"Veles?" I gasped.

"You recognize me, despite my new form? I'm flattered." His face lit up with a manic grin. "It's one of my many talents, flitting from body to body. Pity about the last one. I prefer the younger, better preserved vessel, but no matter. Now that the raven is dealt with, I can reclaim my true form in this world."

He swept a hand over Will, stepping back to avoid the growing crimson pool from staining his shoes. "This was a sacrifice, I'm afraid. Such a waste of power, but vital for reshaping the realm."

Veles cocked his head, his unbound hair shifting. "There's still time for you to join me. I only wish to rid the world of those unworthy. The northern kingdoms are nothing more than savages, prizing brute strength over intellect. Too long have they abused my people, subjugated us for our lack of physical strength. All because we weren't cruel enough for this world. *Their* world."

He lifted his chin. "I've remedied that. No longer will I stand by and watch my people fall to the north or any that stand with them. No longer will our fae lineage be tempered and tamed by humans. We, the light fae, will rule." Veles stepped closer, raising a weathered hand to my cheek in a caress. "The boy was a necessary loss, but you—you, my phoenix, you are extraordinary."

Bile burned the back of my throat as his rotted breath fanned my lips. His words slithered through my soul, adding fuel to the concealed inferno.

*The boy was a necessary loss.*

Rage swelled within as I stared into Veles's cold silver eyes. There would be time for grieving, but now—now I let myself yield. Yield to every callous thought, every cruel wish, every deathly urge I had. In that moment, I allowed myself to not just accept the darkness, but become it.

I felt something splinter—something release—as the embers

of fury ignited in my veins, searing my soul. Flames licked up my spine, my skin on fire, as a vast well of power opened within.

I yanked against the chains binding me. This time, they split, dropping me to the ground, as the broken ends dangled from my still bound wrists.

His amused smile never faltered, but a hint of uncertainty flashed through Veles's sharp gaze as he took a step back. And then another.

A humming started, growing into a chorus of drums—beats. Heartbeats.

I cocked my head to the side, eyes never leaving Veles's, as the sounds clarified. There were dozens of heartbeats running toward us, the first group of which appeared through the darkened hallway behind Veles.

The light fae fanned out around their leader, their weapons poised and ready for an attack. All of their sights were trained on me. Good. Greer was safe for now, the small red stain across her stomach unable to heal around the dagger, but not growing any worse. And Will... no. I couldn't think about him. Not yet.

"You can't really expect to defeat me." Veles nearly laughed. "Power like yours shouldn't be wasted." His smile waned, his cold eyes narrowing at something he found staring back at him in my gaze. "I will not ask again."

My lips cracked into a crazed smile as I stepped over the form on the floor—shielding him from what was to come.

I lunged, delivering a swift blow to his gut, using the momentum of his cowed body to drive his nose into my knee. A loud crack resonated through the dungeon as Veles flitted away toward the far wall—his lips split into a bloody grin.

"That was beautiful. Pity you have to die." With a sigh, he raised his hand before retreating toward the hall.

"Coward," I sneered, fists clenching. "Face me!"

His silver eyes dropped over my frame, taking inventory

before meeting my gaze. "I only face worthy opponents. Let's see if you're up for the task."

Veles linked his hands behind his back before his chin dipped. The others charged, blocking me from exacting my revenge with a wall of blades.

The first to reach me swiped carelessly with his sword, thinking he could end me easily.

Fool.

I moved into the space behind him, twisting his neck until I felt the crack of bones beneath my hands. Snatching his sword, I inhaled deeply—relishing the tang of fear scenting the air as I met the others with a twisted grin.

The fae rushed forward in a wave. My foot connected with the chest of the first, his bones collapsing inward with a crunch as I deflected a blow to the left. I dodged a third, his swing falling wide in a sloppy attempt that left his neck exposed.

Not one to pass up an opportunity, I sliced through the tender flesh, smiling at the look of horror in his eyes. Spinning, I brought the blade around, sinking it into the belly of another.

More poured from the hall. More fell before me.

I felt the fire along my spine, pushing my body faster— folding me into the shadows. I leaped from one foe to another, hearing the sounds of collapsing corpses thud to the ground behind me as my blade slashed through the next. Until all had fallen.

All except Veles. His face was bright with wonder.

I stalked toward the grinning monster, narrowing my eyes as his hands came together in a slow clap.

"Well done. It would seem you are more fae than either of us realized." His eyes glanced to the tips of my ears. He shifted out of his casual stance, but still did not think to draw a weapon. "It's time for a new vessel, don't you think? This one looks a little... ragged. I must admit, it's not every day one is offered the body of a king. But I'm afraid even kings have their limitations."

My eyes darted to his face, seeing past the film coating his eyes and imagining a bright blue in their place. My mind whirled as the pieces fit together.

"You're the Light King?"

"Tsk. Tsk. I thought you were smart."

I crept closer, assessing my best opportunity to end this. "You are *possessing* the Light King."

He clapped once more, still not bothering to retrieve his blade. "Precisely." He rocked on his heels, thrilled by my deduction. "Now, tell me girl, do you know who it is you've chosen to stand against?"

We circled each other, my sword gripped tight in my hand, while he strolled across the body-lined room with ease.

"It doesn't matter who you are. Your life will end by my hands soon enough."

"You may dispose of a vessel, but you do not have the skill nor the weapons to kill me. I am not of this world, little phoenix. Not anymore. My brothers and I have been shaped into the beasts we now are, forged in the frost of endless night and tempered with soul shattering magic. You are but a speck of dust on our otherwise pristine path—annoying, but easily dealt with."

A pair of footsteps raced toward us—this time coming from the steps. I turned, bracing for what I'd find. A pair of cinnamon eyes glowing with rings of light came into view, followed immediately by a large set of snowy white wings coated in stains of earth and blood. Ryuu was alive, the raw gash along his chest still pink with early healing.

And Zaeth.

Zaeth was here, looking every bit the avenging warrior. His battle leathers were torn, riddled with slits where arrows had once been and streaked with poppy-orange splotches among crimson sprays, but he was alive.

Zaeth stalled as he reached the last step, his eyes darting to the pile of bodies surrounding me, snagging on Will, before locking on Veles. His hand clenched along the hilt of his sword as he came to my side. "Hello, love. Mind if we join?"

But Ryuu was already moving, his body stiff as he joined my other side. His eyes were locked on Greer's still unconscious form curled on the floor—nearly parallel to where Veles stood.. Ryuu's lips pulled back as a deep snarl emanated from his chest.

Veles glanced toward Greer, his lips twitching as he met Ryuu's deadly gaze. "I have no need for half-fae."

Ryuu's jaw clenched, his body coiled like a viper ready to strike.

Veles grinned as he swept his hand toward my sister, stepping to the side with a slight inclination of his head. "Please, help yourself."

Ryuu flitted, snatching Greer and returning within moments. Lying her gently against the stone floor behind us, he took what remained of his cloak and draped it over her. He leaned forward, brushing back a silver-blonde curl before pressing a kiss to her forehead. Greer stirred.

"Ryuu?" Her voice was hoarse, tainted by disbelief and grief. "You're alive."

She pressed onto her forearms, eyes wildly searching. Ryuu shifted in front, trying to prevent her from the gore surrounding her. "You need to lie down—"

"Will." She choked on his name as tears pricked her eyes. "I had a horrible dream. Is he okay—"

Her words were cut short by a strangled cry.

My stomach clenched knowing what she saw—his small form surrounded by an ever-growing pool of scarlet. Sourness seared the back of my throat, but I forced myself not to fall apart. Not to give into the agony of reality. Not yet.

Ryuu murmured words that somehow worked to calm her. Then he stood, his pupils shifting into thin vertical slits and simmering with rage.

Veles stood calmly, hands clasped behind his back. He cocked his head to the side, watching us as a predator would its prey.

"Interesting," he purred. His eyes noted the wide slit along Ryuu's chest before bouncing to the tattered remains of Zaeth's top, the holes from dozens of arrows leaving only scraps of fabric behind. "Very interesting."

He paced along the far wall, keeping his fingers linked along the curve of his spine, his casual tone echoing off the stone walls. "As you can imagine, a being like myself is not surprised often." He stopped and turned to face Zaeth, palms up as a smile played across his lips. "And, yet, here we are. I would like to make you an offer, and perhaps you can sway the others. Join us. This world has been weakened by the blood of the humans, yes, but many of the fae also have short-comings.

"We plan to change that, a culling of sorts. For millennia, my brothers and I have fought to return. And now," he chuckled darkly with a vicious gleam in his cloudy eyes, "now we have an army that cannot be stopped."

"Enough!" I shouted, needing this to end. "We won't join you. We're not murderers."

He furrowed his brows in mock concern. "Oh, but aren't you?" My jaw ticked, the small movement bringing an incredulous gleam to Veles's eyes. "Is that what you fear, little phoenix? That others might tremble from the sheer depth of your darkness?"

I blanched.

Zaeth issued a predatory growl, his fangs bared in warning. But Veles merely held his empty palms in front. "I meant no disrespect. Quite the opposite, really. Power of the body is nothing without the mind to support it. Those lacking in either arena will be dealt with under our rule."

His lip curled as he zeroed in on Zaeth's fangs and Ryuu's

wings. "The northern kingdoms were once mindless beasts. It seems things have changed since my brothers and I left."

Zaeth took a not-so-subtle step in front of me. A curse sounded from Ryuu as he joined him.

Veles cocked his head to the side, calmly watching as Zaeth and Ryuu tensed, ready for an attack. He sighed. "I'll take that as a 'no' for changing your minds, then?" His silver eyes found mine, his smirk widening as Ryuu closed in, blade held high.

Still Veles didn't move, didn't think to defend himself. "Until we meet again, little phoenix."

THE BLADE SLICED CLEANLY THROUGH VELES'S SPINE, SEVERING head from body in a single swing. Elara stepped back to avoid the rolling head, which came to a stop inches from the toes of my muddied boots. I stood, gazing down into lifeless eyes, the silver giving way to a dull blue, as my mind whirled with information I didn't yet understand.

But it didn't matter.

Nothing mattered. Because nothing would return my little brother to me.

I turned away from the still smirking head. Turned away from El's blood-splattered presence, and Ryuu's worried stare, picking my way around the still bleeding bodies until I found Will.

The last of my strength evaporated as I collapsed beside him. Adjusting his cold, too-pale limbs, I gathered him in my arms, desperately trying to warm him. He'd come to me. I'd seen him in my mind—that meant he had to be alive. At least some part of him, right?

Will had come to me, in a dream perhaps. It'd offered a kernel of hope. But now the protection of sleep had lifted, and everything was rushing back in a blaring riot of pain, in shades of red—in shades of blood.

It was too much. My heart raced, lungs heaving as I gripped Will tighter, hating the stillness of his chest.

"Save him," I pleaded, pulling him against my chest, rocking him as I'd done so many times before. "*Please*, Ryuu. You said you'd protect him. You said he'd be safe."

Tears shook free as Ryuu knelt beside me, face twisted in anguish. "He's already gone to the goddess."

Sorrow laced his voice, but it was nothing compared to the mounting panic inside me. "Then bring him back!" I snapped, refusing to listen—to give up. "I don't care what it costs, I'll pay it. Bring him back to me."

El stepped forward, kneeling beside me with a look of sorrow and—*acceptance.*

A whimper escaped me, my shoulders slumped. Because if El thought he was truly beyond saving, my fierce, unyielding sister, if she'd accepted this fate...

"El?"

But she only gave a small shake of her head as her strong arms came around me, imparting warmth and love—holding me as I cradled him.

"If there was any way..." Ryuu's voice cracked, and I felt the last of my sanity splinter.

Wails sounded all around me, consuming in their pain. El gripped me tighter, her own cries adding to mine, as our bodies shook, the both of us spiraling into the agony of this new reality.

# 5 7

# ELARA

SOUNDS OF CLANKING METAL ECHOED AROUND US. I BLINKED, trying to clear my head of the growing numbness. Zaeth and Ryuu were positioned in front of us, facing the steps as they withdrew their swords. I moved Will's head into Greer's lap as I stood, picking up a discarded sword as I stood, forming a wall to hide Greer and Will behind.

"Elara…" Ryuu started, but stopped as I shot cut him off with a glare.

Zaeth shook his head. "She needs this."

I *did* need this. The pain was too much. I couldn't think, couldn't *breathe*. I needed to act, to kill. I needed to destroy every last one of the creatures responsible.

Jarek stepped through the passage, followed closely by Alarik and a handful of others. Alarik's eyes swept the room, glancing over the mounds of corpses before they met my eyes heavy with confusion.

"El?"

No fae. None of the Fractured. It was only our men. I let the sword clatter to the floor as I turned, dropping to my knees beside Greer.

Alarik gasped, his footstep halting. "Is that a brand on your back. El, your ears."

I brought my hand up, gliding over the peaked tips of my once rounded ears, before reaching toward the burning along my spine. The fabric was split and singed, much like the delicate skin beneath.

"It's a phoenix, love," Zaeth breathed, his body lowering next to mine. "A brand, the sister to Greer's dragon. You're a full shifted fae."

*Fully shifted fae.*

I ran my tongue along the length of my teeth, drawing a drop of blood as it pricked the tip of a fang. Dark fae. A dozen emotions passed through me, but none of them stuck. They remained just out of reach, masked beneath a layer of ice and grief.

Alarik inhaled a sharp breath and my chest squeezed. He'd seen Will.

"Jarek! We need you!"

Alarik pushed past me, diving toward Will's small form still cradled in Greer's lap. Jarek flitted to his side, placing his hands over his chest. And for a single moment my heart stalled with the blam of hope. But Jarek withdrew his fingers slowly with sorrow in his eyes as he met Greer's tear-streaked face. "I'm sorry, he's already gone."

Alarik stood, his throat bobbing as he desperately tried to contain the tears welling in his eyes. After a long moment, he found the strength to speak. "The fighting is over. This was our last check. The rest of the men have returned to base—"

"We'll discuss the battle later," Zaeth cut in, his voice low. "We need to leave this place."

"Don't like being surrounded by all the bodies you've killed?" Alarik retorted, grief giving way to anger. I understood that. It was easier.

My gaze strayed... taking in the sheer number of corpses

littering the floor. "I did this." I said, the words a little louder than a whisper, but they heard. The room fell silent except for Greer's subdued cries, as Alarik's attention swung to me.

"What?" He fumbled, shaking his head as if he'd misheard.

"The bodies—the fae. I killed them. Not Zaeth. It was me." The remoteness in my voice was jarring, even to me. Some part of me knew I should care, knew it meant something had irrevocably changed. Just as I knew the look of disgust mingled with fear peering down at me from the man I'd once cared for should hurt. It should touch some piece of my soul... but there was nothing left.

I felt like one of Lannie's patients—the one who had gorged himself on nevernectar and fallen asleep near the fire. His leg had burned nearly down to the bone, and yet he wasn't in pain. Lannie explained it was because the pain receptors were in the skin. They had already been destroyed, and so, even though the wound was horrific, he wouldn't be in pain until the upper layers started to heal.

I felt like that man—like his leg. Like the layers of my soul had seared away, leaving a raw, ravaged chunk behind, too damaged to feel anything but a numbing reprieve.

"Zaeth's right." I said. "We can't stay here."

Greer gave a stiff nod, her fingers stroking the curls back from Will's brow. She looked up, finding Ryuu's side. His wings were bent in a sad slump, but his attention never strayed from her.

"Will you carry him?" Her voice wobbled as another fat droplet tumbled from her eyes, but Ryuu nodded, his wings fanning out as he knelt.

She allowed Ryuu to take him then, tucking him in safe against Ryuu's chest.

Warm tears streamed down my already damp cheeks as I followed them out of the tomb.

~

Last night I'd wept. I'd found the strength to tell Lannie what had happened a moment before Ryuu and Greer entered the infirmary with him.

And then I broke.

I gave into the anguish of knowing I hadn't been strong enough to protect Papa and the twins. I yielded to the pent-up rage of knowing Mother kept our fae affinities from us—affinities that may have saved Will.

Alarik's voice washed over me, words of apologies, of sadness and regret. But nothing felt real. Not the crunch of the forest floor beneath the horses' steady gait, nor the muttered planning of funerals.

Zaeth had once asked me if I'd save my family over the lives of one hundred innocents. I would have given up every beating heart yesterday if I'd meant saving my brother. I would have killed them myself. But Alarik wouldn't. He hadn't. He'd made the right choice. The honorable choice. But Will was still gone.

Evander had come to see me, followed by Vidarr—even Jarek—but I refused to see anyone. Refused to speak.

Alarik's voice washed over me, words of apologies, of sadness and regret. But nothing felt real. Not the crunch of the forest floor beneath the horses' steady gait, nor the muttered planning of funerals. We left Fort Dhara at dawn and the low position of the sun and the familiar setting indicated we'd be back to the base within the hour. But it didn't feel like home. I wasn't sure I'd ever find one now.

We heard it less than a mile from the fort—the shouts of men and the pinging of arrows.

Pausing, I caught Evander's look of dread and Alarik's flash of anger a moment before I dismounted, knowing my fae affinities would carry me quicker than any horse. Sparing one glance, I confirmed my sisters remained safe behind while I rode forward. Ryuu positioned himself in front of Greer, Lannie, and Serephina, offering me a quick nod of confirmation.

My jaw clenched as my eyes lingered a beat too long on the shrouded figure among them. Bile burned the back of my throat, but I pushed it away, welcoming the quiet of my mind as I leaned into my fae abilities. I turned toward the clash of metal and ran.

The promise of revenge flushed through my veins as I willed my legs to pump faster. Jarek, Zaeth, Soter, and I pulled ahead, drawn to the metallic scent of blood carried on a gentle breeze as Alarik and the rest of the humans fell behind.

We broke through the last of the surrounding forest, chests heaving as we noted the scene before us. Shadow wraiths lingered in the tree line as swarms of goblins and the Fractured clustered around the base, hurling battering rams at the brick and mortar. Our warriors were positioned atop the wall, protected by outcroppings of stone that allowed for archers. Bodies of our enemies littered the ground, but a sizable force remained.

The swirling silver light of a portal positioned further back illuminated the length of a figure with glowing runes coating his body—Alderidge. A light fae was positioned beside him, his palms held out as he muttered, sending a ripple of electricity pulsing along the walls.

"He's attempting to break the wards," Jarek said. "I'll take care of him."

"Alderidge, too," I added. That slimy traitor needed to be put down.

I watched as Jarek flitted along the periphery toward his prey, tracking each of his movements without difficulty. I had dipped into my fae affinities before, but now everything was crisp. The dark clouds hovering around the creatures were thick, solidified, just as Jarek's shimmering gold presence shone like a beacon among them—And the emotions. I felt Jarek's anger, his loss, and the overwhelming greed radiating from the shadowed army. Their arrogance, their psychotic desire to cause pain and destruction was so strong I could nearly taste it.

I looked toward Zaeth, finding understanding waiting for me in his eyes. He nodded once, allowing me to take point.

"We'll be right behind you, love."

Returning my attention to the impending slaughter, I withdrew my sword. The weight of the blade was a familiar comfort as I pushed off the balls of my feet, bounding toward the throng of creatures.

The chorus of their polluted heartbeats was a symphony in my mind—drums of war luring me in. The concerto of arterial blood and snapping bones filled my ears as I worked through the crowd—nothing but a ravaging storm of blood and vengeance—delivering death to any and all in my path. There was no thinking, no feeling. Only action. The metallic scent of entrails coated the air, spurring me on, driving me to move quicker, to slice and stab and destroy without mercy. A wild beast set free among monsters.

I felt the give of tissue around my blade, relished the warmth of blood as it misted my face, my body twirling in a deadly dance. The macabre music of pulses quieted as they fell until I ripped my sword free from the last, plunging us into silence.

Cold lifeless eyes stared up at me. They were haunting the way the corpse had fallen, the head tilted to resemble a subtle smile. Just like the one Veles had maintained as he butchered my brother.

My brother. My brother. My brother.

A soul-wrenching scream tore through my chest, devastation reaching deep into the very fabric of my unraveling heart before bursting forth in a wail of unchecked torment.

I raised my blade above my head, plunging it into the Fractured's body with a vicious thrust. I yanked my sword back, only to bring it down again, and again, sending splatters of blood and pieces of entrails flying through the air as I screamed... as I cried. Only when my arms were too tired to lift the blade, only when my voice was nothing more than broken cracked sobs, did I allow my body to collapse, joining the pile of corpses I'd created.

Firm hands lifted me from the carnage. The smell of decaying bodies faded away as hints of fresh rain and cedar-wood surrounded me. Too exhausted to open my eyes, I nuzzled deeper into the firm chest before fading fully into the darkness.

# GREER

I HADN'T SEEN WHAT EL HAD DONE ON THE BATTLEFIELD, BUT I'D heard about it. Alarik had returned less than an hour after he'd left, informing us the battle was over. Alderidge had fled, slipping through his portal as Jarek had taken out a light fae, thwarting his attempts to disband the wards. Zaeth and Soter took out the shadow wraiths, and the humans had managed to pick off a few goblins, but all the rest were slain by my sister.

We'd stepped over disemboweled corpses and beheaded shadow wraiths, picking our way through a field of flesh, until we entered the confines of the base. All around us, men were moving. I was vaguely aware of other shrouds being carried in, of other wails of dread filling the air, but my focus was on Ryuu and the bundle cradled in his arms.

"Thank you," I said, my words hollow, as Ryuu laid Will gently on an infirmary cot. "Will loved you. He would have wanted you here."

Ryuu flinched, startling me enough to pull my gaze from my brother and to his tormented gaze.

"I don't deserve your thanks or his love." His voice cracked as his wings bowed forward. "He was mine to protect and I failed him."

My gut churned with a pang of sorrow, but I forced myself to speak. "No, you didn't. Will came to me after..."

Ryuu looked up, brows knitted together.

"When I was unconscious, he appeared before me and said his fate couldn't have been prevented. He's happy." Tears blurred my vision and I wiped them away before continuing. "Will spoke of the goddess and our brothers and the parents he never knew. He had a sense of peace about him... a maturity. And he gave me a warning."

Ryuu's shoulders pulled back. "A prophecy?"

"No, but he was sure that we needed to find the Spear of Empyrean. Will said it was our only chance of destroying Veles." Ryuu's eyes widened, his tanned face paling. "You know where it is?"

"No, the Spear of Empyrean is lost, but I've been looking into it since he mentioned me holding a spear with a burning tip. The light fae were the last ones to possess it, but that was millennia ago. They feared its power. They were unable to destroy it, but managed to break it into three pieces—or so the legend goes. It'll be nearly impossible to find."

I swallowed around the lump in my throat. "Will chose to spend his last moments telling me to retrieve the Spear. Whatever is required, we'll do it."

Ryuu nodded. "The last body Veles possessed was the current king of the Light Kingdom. We have to assume the other light royals have been corrupted."

"Jarek's light fae. Can't he just return to the capitol undercover?"

"Jarek has spent the better part of this year attempting to infiltrate the walled city. His past complicates things." Ryuu's brows drew together in thought. "But a covert operation may not be such a bad idea. We'll need someone on the inside. Someone who'd pass as a light fae… or as a long-lost royal."

Footsteps sounded a moment before Lannie entered. Her normally sleek hair was knotted, secured in a lopsided tie and the shadows of her eyes were dark from lack of sleep. "I've offered Ser my rooms. She wanted to join us for the funeral, but I insisted she rest."

*The funeral.* Gods, the word sounded foreign—impossible. I teetered between disbelief and utter horror. Between a vacant coldness and an overwhelming crushing weight of grief.

"Vidarr said all the others have been laid to rest, their pyres lit at the first shadows of dusk. We can't wait much longer."

Lannie shared a look with me, the two of us knowing El would never forgive herself if she didn't attend.

Ryuu straightened. "I'll see to the arrangements, and stall as long as I can."

With tender hands, Ryuu lifted our little brother for the last time and swept from the room. Lannie met my eyes with cold determination. It was time to talk to El.

## 5 9
## ELARA

THE STERILE SMELL OF A RECOVERY ROOM SINGED MY NOSTRILS AS my mind stirred. I could feel the lack of grime coating my skin, the fresh clothes draped over it, but I refused to open my eyes. Voices carried from what sounded like a nearby hallway, the echo of their steps across marbled floors growing louder. My stomach twisted. Not wanting to speak yet, I relaxed my features, pretending to sleep.

"She won't want to go with you." Alarik's voice carried through the door, the hinges squeaking as it shut with a click.

"Maybe she will, maybe she won't, but that will be her decision. She's fae, a fact you continue to ignore." My stomach clenched at Zaeth's words.

"What is that supposed to mean?" Alarik hissed in a whisper.

Zaeth's tight control wavered, allowing hints of anger to bleed into his voice. "It *means* I don't like the way you looked at her in that dungeon when she admitted to killing the fae, or the way your face paled when you caught up to us at the perimeter of the base."

"I didn't—"

"Don't lie to me." Zaeth cut him off, the silence stretching for a beat too long. "She's dealing with enough right now. She doesn't need to wrestle with your opinions as well."

The soft padding of footsteps retreating sounded before Alarik's voice came from further back. "I was just... shocked. You have to understand, El was the first person since—" He cleared his throat. "She was the first person I've cared about in years. My entire life has been duty above all else, to the humans of this realm, to the men and their families. But when I found her, I found glimpses of the old me, the carefree me that joked and played. The me that laughed."

"Do you love her?" Zaeth's voice was soft, as if he needed to ask the question but wasn't sure he wanted the answer.

Alarik issued a disgruntled groan, the sound muffled as if he were dragging his hand over his face. "I care for her. Things were going well, but these last few months... it's like I've watched her transform into someone else."

Zaeth scoffed. "She's the same person she always has been, only now she's a fully shifted fae—a dark fae. Perhaps you've chosen to see only the parts of her that meet your approval."

"You think I'm judging her for being powerful or killing those things, but I'm not. I get it. I understand the need for war —for revenge. But I let it grow once, the need to avenge the woman I thought to call my wife. I allowed it to consume me. And my blinded grief nearly got me killed. Worse, it nearly killed those I was entrusted to protect."

Alarik's voice was barely louder than a whisper. "You are right about one thing. I don't understand her. I don't know how the sweet, determined woman I met in the woods could be so fully taken by the lust of killing. When she admitted to killing those fae and what I witnessed of her savagery outside these gates..." Alarik's swallow was audible. "There have been moments of fear, but I care for her anyway. Maybe one day it could have grown into love."

"You cannot love what you fear." Zaeth's low rumble rattled

through me. "When she wakes, I'll offer her a chance to return with me. She'd be able to explore her powers, unencumbered by the misunderstandings of humans."

Zaeth cleared his voice. "May I have a moment alone with her?" I peeked through thick eyelashes, catching a glimpse of Zaeth. His mask of calm was fully in place. "I vow to not disturb her when she's sleeping."

Alarik held his gaze a moment longer before relenting. "I wish we could allow her all the time she needs to recover, but we'll need to wake her soon for the funeral."

The weight of reality crashed down, nearly suffocating me with its impact. I managed to wait for the click of the doors before lurching up.

Zaeth extended a small bucket, completely unfazed as my stomach constricted, yellowish-green bile burning up my throat.

*The funeral.*

The bed dipped with Zaeth's weight as he pulled back my hair, securing it in a loose tie. Another wave of agony tore through me, my tears mixing with the foul liquid contents of my stomach. Zaeth's warm, broad hand moved in soothing circles against my back, until my body calmed enough to stop heaving.

"I was beginning to think you'd feign sleep forever," Zaeth said, offering me a small towel and a glass of water.

I swallowed a gulp, feeling it douse the burning in my throat before settling in my stomach like a cool balm.

"You knew?" My voice was raw.

His sad smile met my question. "Of course, love."

I leaned over, placing the cup and towel on the small table next to the bed. Drawing my legs in, I curled in on myself, resting my head on the tops of my knees as tears trickled along my cheek. "I can't do this."

The pad of his thumb brushed away tears, fresh ones

forming in their wake. "I know it's a lot, love, more than anyone should have to handle, but I need you to keep fighting. Get dressed, make it through the funeral, and then we'll leave this place."

"Leave?"

"I meant what I said about returning to the Dark Kingdom, but it is your choice."

I nodded, too exhausted to think through what that would mean. "My sisters?"

"They were heading to the fields as I entered. I'll inform them you're on your way."

# 60

# GREER

My sisters and I walked across the field, the smoke from a dozen other pyres tinting the dark sky a russet orange, the color quickly fading into a deep purple. Judging by the amount of freshly turned earth, most of the warriors' families had chosen to be wrapped in a sheet of rowan leaves, braided and bound together before sunk below the soil. The earth welcomed her children back, returning their energy to the magic of this world as their spirits were set free.

Those following the old ways chose the sky as their final resting place, and all the freedom it offered. Delivering their bodies to the flames of the pyre, the fire burned away any remaining weaknesses, shedding the last of their mortal confines and allowing them to join the vast expanse above.

Will had always wanted a pyre.

The tears I'd managed to hold in unleashed upon seeing the last patch of undisturbed grass, locking on the small form laid atop the harsh wooden structure. Our footsteps halted at the base of his pyre. His body was too short for the burial shroud adorning it, and my heart twisted as I noted the care someone had taken to tuck the ends in.

Wiping the dampness from my cheeks, I turned to my sisters. As the oldest, it should have been El speaking, should have been her words sending our little brother to his final resting place. But I doubted she'd be able to.

She was little more than a ghost. Her face was ashen, the dark circles beneath her eyes revealing just how exhausted she was, despite the pointed tips of her ears. Fae healed quickly. And that's what she was—what *we* were. But the fatigue—the haunted look in her eyes—wasn't something that would be cured.

My gaze darted to Lannie and her still rounded ears. I expected to see my concern and determination mirrored in her face, but the harsh glint in her eyes made me flinch. Her jaw was clamped tight, her face oscillating between detached control and pent up fury. She was grieving, like we were, but sorrow had yet to replace anger at losing our little brother.

Following her line of sight, I saw Evander carrying a torch toward us, stopping just beside El. He looked to her—everyone did, waiting for her to speak. Her throat bobbed, her mouth opening, but silence permeated the clearing.

Without thinking, I stepped beside her, slipping my hand in hers. Her shoulders sagged as I spoke. "Thank you for joining us."

Red-rimmed eyes peered back at me, clusters of men and families stretching back across the field—all here to pay respect to Will. Very few knew about the prophecy coming to fruition, about Will being the raven, but news traveled fast about his sacrifice to keep my sister and I alive. He'd saved El, allowing her to return to the base in time to destroy our enemy and save the city. Will was known as a hero, just as he'd always wanted to be.

"My brother was a dreamer. He saw the world as a magical, beautiful place filled with love. To everyone else, Will was a

hero, but to my sisters and I, he was a boy. A boy much to innocent for this world and much too young to—"

My throat closed around the word. I swallowed, and tried
again, but my tongue had turned to sand, my mouth running
dry. I couldn't say it. Couldn't think it. Couldn't understand the
weight *that* word carried. Because Will—my charismatic, brave,
always-full-of-questions little brother—was much too young
to *die*.

My chest heaved, my breathing turning to short ragged
gulps of air as my heart squeezed with pain. With loss. El's hand
tightened in mine while Lannie's found my other, but their
sorrow-filled eyes reflected my own mounting panic.

I felt a scream building in my chest, but a moment before it
wrenched free, a soft brush of gentle feathers caressed my
shoulder. Rain and wind and something entirely male scented
the air around me—calming my erratic heart.

Ryuu's wings pulled back a moment later, tucking in tight
behind him as he stepped forward to address the crowd. His
words washed over me as if from afar, until Evander raised the
torch, pausing as he looked to us.

With a dip of El's chin, Evander lowered it.

The fire took hold quickly, licking up the wooden structure
until it was consuming not only branches of pine, but cloth and
flesh and bone—until all that was left was a blazing mountain,
the flames glowing bright against the darkening sky.

Small groups peeled off, returning to their homes for the
evening until it was just us. The moon rose high, the stars
winking into life as my brother's ended and still the three of us
remained.

Lannie pulled away first, stepping nearer to the dwindling
flames.

"Are you leaving for the Dark Kingdom?" Lannie asked,
looking over her shoulder.

El and I shared a glance. "I'm not sure," I answered, tucking a curl behind my now pointed ear.

"There's a lot to consider," El added.

Lannie gave a tight nod, her eyes staring into the heart of the flames. "He never should have been there. I knew he'd try to sneak out. If I hadn't drank the tea, if I'd spent more time with him, maybe…"

Nausea rolled through me. I tried to put my arm around her, but Lannie shrugged me off, pushing past me through the tall grass in the direction of the infirmary. I made to follow but paused when I realized El wasn't behind me.

"You should check on her," El said. "She shouldn't have to be alone tonight."

"You're not coming?"

"Not yet."

I waited a moment. I waited two. El's throat bobbed, swallowing down a fresh wave of tears, desperately trying to hold back the wash of pain and loss. It must have been exhausting. Always trying to shield us.

"I'll stay with her tonight." Familiar words in an unfamiliar circumstance.

El nodded. And I left.

# 61

# ELARA

My eyes stung with the effort of keeping them open. The soot of smoldering embers drifted through the air before me, all that remained of my brother.

Greer retreated, allowing me a temporary reprieve. A moment to breathe—to *stop* breathing and to cry and scream and break. To rage against what this life had become.

Absence.

I had a phoenix brand. Zaeth had been wrong. I should have known. I shouldn't have trusted, shouldn't have let myself believe that I could ever be anything else. It was like a great, gaping chasm had erupted in my chest, stretching and hollowing me out until only a husk of myself remained.

Will *died*.

Will had died and I'd lived and I wanted to destroy this world. Rip it apart and burn the pieces until all that remained were embers and ash—just like the crackling mound before me.

My spine stiffened, the hairs on my arm prickling as the wind shifted. Wiping the tears from my cheeks, I stood, eyes fixed on the glowing oranges of the seared pyre, bright in the darkening night.

"You can come out, now."

Zaeth stepped forward from beneath the trees, the soft light of the moon reaching between the cloud-covered night to glint off the metal of the blade strapped to his back. He was still in battle leathers, the black material coated in swaths of blood. Rich, cinnamon eyes peered into mine, imparting a steadiness I was sorely lacking.

"You were wrong," I gritted out. "You said I was alluring once, but all I bring is death and destruction. Draven knew it the first time we met at Neith. And now Veles knows it, too."

Zaeth stiffened. "You're not the Dark Phoenix."

I shook my head, tears welling in my eyes as my heart beat erratically, grief clawing at my throat. "I am. I'm the reason Will is dead. Veles, Draven, they were after *me*. If I'd only joined him... if I'd just let him kill me—"

"Stop." Zaeth's voice shook, a hundred emotions flashing through his eyes. "Don't think for one moment that your death would bring anything other than more pain to this world."

My body shook with tears, but I managed a small nod. Zaeth held my gaze a moment longer before taking a step back. His shoulders began to tremble, widening as if being weighed down by a heavy force. The shadows moved, swirling and linking together in an intricate pattern that stretched across his back, spanning wide. Zaeth's body grew, the span of his chest thickening, his torso and legs lengthening, as the wisps of darkness solidified, twisting into ebony feathers.

A gasp tore from my lips as his wings flexed.

"You are not the Dark Phoenix, love. I am."

# BONUS CONTENT: ZAETH

MY WINGS UNFURLED, THE HEAVY WEIGHT SETTLING ACROSS MY shoulders as Elara stared. She was coated in gore, her cheeks damp, hazel-blue eyes ringed with red. She thought herself a monster. If only she could see herself through my eyes: an avenging goddess, one beaten and bent, but never broken.

"You are not the Dark Phoenix, love. I am."

The words hung between us, the air heavy with their weight. I hadn't planned on telling her. I hadn't planned on *a lot* of things with El, but like everything else, I was helpless when it came to her. Even when I'd thought her a human, there had been something drawing us together, like the tides shifting with the moon.

We responded to each other, our energy, our heartbeats. I wasn't sure what it meant, wasn't sure why she had a phoenix brand burned along her spine, but I knew we were linked. Against every instinct, I wanted her to see me—to know my secrets. More than anything, I wanted that look of guilt and self-hatred to vanish from her face.

"You're the Dark Phoenix?" El's brows knit together, disbelief ringing through her words.

"I am," I answered clearly. This wasn't her burden to bare. She was dark and deadly, but Elara was good. She was the raw, black diamond in a world of polished jewels. She was whole, true to her form while all others had had their exteriors cut and ground away—mere remnants of what they once were.

"The Reaper of Immortals?" Her eyes searched mine, confusion giving way to something that pricked deeper. "The one responsible for... The end?"

My jaw ticked as I fought the urge to close myself off. Being vulnerable, leaving myself open to her... it would be worth it if it could ease some of the pain in her tear-filled gaze.

"As I said, love, being the Dark Phoenix is not something you need to worry about. There are many monsters in this world, but none to rival me. I am their master. There may come a day when I succumb to the darkness, as the prophecies state, but until that time, I will purge this world of its infestation."

"The brothers," she breathed

I nodded, relieved to see her anguish shift to strategy. Rolling my shoulders, I banished my ebony wings to the darkness. "Among other creatures."

"You're not in league with the brothers?"

El asked the question without faltering, with her eyes locked on mine. It felt like a dagger to the chest. I'd long since grown used to the rest of world hating me, but for Elara to join them... Something searing twisted in my stomach, forcing me to turn away and face the pile of smoldering embers behind her.

"If you have to ask that question," I said, fingers flexing for battle once more, if only to purge this feeling of inadequacy from myself, "then we're done here."

The silence stretched between us, torturing me with each growing second. She thought me a creature delivered from darkness, one bound to serve a life of misery and death... just as the rest of Pax did. It shouldn't have hurt. I couldn't expect her to see anything other than what I was.

Unable to bare the shame, I turned to leave, only to have her small hand grasp my arm before I could flit away.

I stilled, but didn't turn, too afraid she'd recoil if I moved.

"What happens when the darkness wins?" Her voice was little more than a whisper, but I felt the fear as if her emotions were my own.

"What is that delectably devious mind of yours thinking, love?" I dared to ask, and because I was a glutton for punishment, I allowed a glance at her over my shoulder. "Plotting ways to kill me?"

She sucked in a breath, face flashing with shame. She *was* thinking of my death, of what being The Dark Phoenix really meant. Another small sliver of my soul withered, but it was better she keep her distance from me. My fate was sealed, and I wouldn't have this beautiful, powerful goddess before me mourning my death.

Needing her to be okay even when I succumbed to the alluring darkness, I turned to face her fully and spoke:

"Dark Phoenix's vengeance, harsh unbending,
    Torment abounds, unchecked, unending.
    Immense powers merge, blending, pooling.
    Great storms of chaos twisting, spooling.

When wrongs are righted and wounds mend,
    When fear is conquered at battle's end,
    Darkness will spring, devouring all,
    With malicious tendrils, none can stall.

When wicked forces of old arrive,
    Death will reign among the ancient hive."

. . .

She stared at me while I repeated the prophecy, unfazed. My lips quirked, despite myself as seeing her strength. Her ability to face the truth even when it was full of carnage.

"'Torment abounds,'" I repeated, taking a step toward her. I shouldn't, but the gods had already condemned me to a morbid fate. What was a little more torture? "'Unchecked, unending.'"

Her pulse quickened as I neared, her scent sweetening as that glorious, dark ring around her irises flared. She could claim to be unaffected by me, but her body betrayed her every time.

El's gaze dipped to my lips, the flush on her cheeks deepening as her thighs clenched.

"Tell me, love. If my death meant an end to all of this, would you kill me?"

"Yes," she breathed, meeting my gaze. "Without hesitation."

Gods, she was perfect. A twisted, shadowed soul strong enough to clash with creatures beyond our realm, and wicked enough to steal the heart of a forsaken monster like me. "Lucky for me, I remain myself."

"And when you are not?" She licked her lips as she forced the words out, more breath than voice.

I couldn't help but track the way her tongue darted across her full, bottom lip, the color left darker and shinning. She would taste delicious, I was sure of it. Like the sweetest alcohol, burning and soothing all at once.

Swallowing, I forced myself to meet her gaze. "Should the need arise, and I am too far gone to stop myself, Ryuu has already sworn to put an end to it. But you have my permission to take his place."

"I have your permission to kill you?" She asked around an incredulously laugh.

"My time in this world is limited," I shrugged, practiced nonchalance coming easy. "I've known the truth of it for centuries. I've raged against fate, grieved a future denied to me, and have now come to accept it."

I *had* accepted it, but gods if El's presence wasn't proof of the cruelty of the gods, I didn't know what was. I'd had my fair share of lovers and adventure in this life. I'd never felt deprived, cheated of anything.

But El.

She was something else. A beautiful, unrivaled spirit that I wanted to bask in, that I wanted to spend centuries getting to know, because she would never be anything other than captivating.

"I've protected the people of this realm the only way I know how: through death. I've sought out their enemies and made them my own—a feeble attempt to atone for the crimes of my future. But if Fate has her way, if I lose all that I am to the spoken prophecy, I can think of no better demise than to be the object of your fury."

She was close enough that her scent of lavender and citrus engulfed me. Gods, if I could bathe in that smell—if I could bury myself in it. Her sweetness grew, her skin flushing as her pulsed.

Stifling the groan building in the back of my throat, I leaned in, my lips brushing the shell of her ear. It would be so easy to give in... just one kiss.

But one kiss would never be enough. Once I had a taste of her, I'd never be able to stop. I would condemn us both, dragging her soul down into the darkness to stay with mine forever.

Another moment, and I would have done it. I would have let my selfishness win and claimed her as mine. Before I could, El stepped back, meeting my gaze with unflinching clarity.

"If you succumb to the darkness, I will kill you."

# ACKNOWLEDGMENTS

To my husband: Thank you for entertaining our two older children and also helping with baby duty while this book was being finalized. The nights have been long sometimes, but I couldn't imagine this life without you! You are an incredible husband and an even better father. I know our pup agrees and appreciates all the walks you give him! I love you.

Thank you to my phenomenal alpha reader Sarah Trala, my editors at Second Pass Editing, Claire Wright and Darby Cupid, and my fantastic streetteam! Thank you all for enjoying the world of Storm of Chaos and Shadows as much as I do.

To my friends and family. Thank you for supporting me, even though we both know you wish I wrote streamline YA novels.

And to the readers. Thank you for coming along on this journey with me.

# ABOUT THE AUTHOR

C.L. Briar is a graduate of San Diego State University. In her spare time, she likes to participate in impromptu dance parties with her little girls, and to look for "nice bugs" in the backyard, when the weather allows. She lives in Northern Virginia with her husband, three daughters, and hound dog.

Made in the USA
Middletown, DE
09 March 2024